Foreword

Whew! Finally it's finished, after 12 months of actual writing and 4 months of re-writing. I wasn't quite sure how to end it, everytime I planned to finish, it took on more body. The idea of this book initially was to tell a story of nothing but beefing in the streets of Richmond, but in the middle of writing it took on more of a drama feel. People say there's a lot of characters in it, that's because Richmond has 4 sides; Northside, Southside, East End, and West End. Plus the surrounding counties; Henrico, Chesterfield, and Hanover. I want to give a special shout-out to everybody who read this in it's original form and gave me their honest opinions: Carolina aka Donterrio Turner you were the first person other than myself who read this and spread about how good it was. Bear from 22nd St., Pooh Warday from Hillside, Marquell aka Q from Tidewater who I didn't even know when I started this book and then you told me your first name what a coincidence. White boy Rambo who said this was the best street novel you ever read. My nigga Commando from Bad News aka Mr. Keep It Real, Duke from

Hillside, and Drew from Virginia Beach who also said this was the best street novel he'd read and who also stayed on top of me to finish pt.2 which is coming soon. Duke from Creighton who I think actually fell in love with one of the characters. And to anyone else that read this in it's original form that I forgot to mention. I hope you enjoy this, I tried to write a fictional novel with a reality feel. I thank you all for your support.

Marcus A. Campbell Sr. a.k.a. Tony

Acknowledgements and Thank You's

First and foremost I want to thank God, who gave me the talent, skill, and ability to not only be able to write, but also self-publish my own books, for blessing my family and myself thru everything and never forsaking us. Next I want to thank the most important person in my life, my mother Courtney Campbell, for never giving up on your kids no matter how much trouble we got in. If you look the word mother up in the dictionary it would have your picture and name beside it, you are truly and inspiration and my hero. I want to acknowledge my brother Demetrius Campbell a.k.a. Meekie next, do your time and come home, hopefully by the time you get here we be ready to take over the coporate like we did the streets. You know next to mama, your opinion is the only one that I truly trust. Let the alcohol go and let's get this paper.

My kids Lil Tony and Mu-Mu ya'll know daddy loves ya'll. Mu-Mu you gave me the name Fatty Cocino for your cousin Fat Fat, so I decided to give all ya'll different names; you, your brother and your cousins. Even though Lil Tony is the oldest among ya'll and ya'll ages is from 14 to 1, when ya'll grow up you can tell your friends ya'll was featured in a book. To my wifey Tracie, you went from being wifey to wife, 16 years is a long time, whereas everybody else fell off, we still thrive. How many haters have come and went, how many have said we wouldn't last and still we stand. Last time I told you to say "Hi haters, By haters" this time you can say "Look at us now we getting paper."

I wanna thank everybody who bought my first book and supported me. Zach, Frank, Chris, and you too Mervin in Unlimited Performance on Brookland Park Blvd. Zach, Frank ya'll bought my first two books and Chris you bought my fourth. Ms. Veronica Hicks at V and S Unique shop on Brookland Park Blvd. who bought third book and said she didn't approve of the language, but she supported me anyway, I say thank you. To Ghost who bought my first book soon as you heard about it, I say thanks my nigga. K.C. who I was locked up with, thanks for the support. My god mother Ms.Pearl who bought three books, thank you very much.

To my aunt Eleanor in Camden, N.J. who told my mama to make sure they get a book up there and then said they enjoyed it, thanks for the support auntie. My cousin Yarnell who's so used to calling me Tony, that he forgot my first name is Marcus, but never the less, you the only one in the Campbell family down Tappahannock who bought my first book, not once but twice. Not only that you called my mama to check on her and offer help in any way possible, for these reasons you get a double thank you and trust me when I make it you will too, much love cousin. Pimp a.k.a. Kevin a.k.a. K.C., who not only went out with me and tried to help me sell my book, but also helped me get my first interview and photo shoot. A double thank you, you're a true friend and again thank you. To Enel Campbell who came up with the cover design for 'Club S.E.X.' and gave it a true grand opening look, thank you.

To Dannaye Monchel who supported me mentally with your letters on my 6 year bid, and who should have been acknowledged in the first book, sorry bout that, but still here it is now. You're the only person I ever dealt with that I felt didn't have any ulterior motives for dealing with me. Love you baby! To my Sexy Lisa who listens, and debates with me, but most of all encourages me in everything I do. Who's the quiet to my storm, and peace to my havoc, I told you before when I'm around you I feel peaceful and at ease. For this I say thank you and I love you.

To Kenny at River City Seafood on Brookland Park Blvd. To Rachel, who spread the word on Facebook about 'Club S.E.X.' calling it straight "Thug-Fucking." Thanks. To Junie a.k.a. Cuzo who sent me a lil piece of change while I was locked down, one love my nigga and I got you on the back end. To my nigga Todd Hicks who sold more of my first book than I did and would approach anybody asking if they would like to buy a book. You're a walking salesman and promotional man; Head of Sales, as well as a true friend. To you I say thank you for everything and beleive me as I blow, so will you. I never forget my friends.

Last but certainly not least, Sam from Sam's Kitchen on Brookland Park Blvd. who not only bough a book, but convinced some of your girls to buy one also, thanky you. Apple Jack, Mr. B., Jackie, Vivian, and anybody who bought my first book that I might've forgot, thank you and know you're greatly appreciated.

Much Love,

Tony

Dedication

Dedicated to my daddy Felix L. Christain, your boy has done it again dad, I know you sitting up there looking down at me smiling and saying "I knowed Tone could do it, that's my son." It's been 13 years since you went to sit at the side of the lord, but it seems like yesterday. No matter how long its been, we all miss you and will always love you. I know you talking to the lord telling him to look out for your two boys and their mother. To all my family members who passed away, this is to ya'll, yeah Tony did something positive again. I hope you're all proud of me as I am of you.

Shout-outs

First let me start off by shouting out everybody in 'Da R.' Next let me shout out everybody on the North: my niggas from Washington park. Jerry G., Steve S., Nay-Nay, Lil Chris, Derwin, Cheesy, and of course Shaun C.. My niggas from Providence and Delmont. My niggas from the Blvd., Shaun aka Dream, Trinity, Boogie, Curtis, Rico, Hack, K. Stokes, Big Wayne hold your head up; and everybody else from the Bull who I might've forgot to name. To my whole Highland Park family; the Milton and Maryland niggas. My cuzn Short Stuff we been riding for a minute, but we here now my nigga, Russ, Mal, Mervin, Melvin and the rest of ya'll niggas from up there. 4th Avenue niggas; my nigga Rel from the streets to the pen and back to the streets again, they can't stop us or hold us back my nigga. My First, Second, Third, and Fifth Avenue niggas; rep that Park to the end.

To my Meadowbridge family; Chinese Rob, Carlos

aka Julio, Cliff, Black Bobby, Jesse T., G. White, Baby Charles, Lil Worm, Rambo, Shaun M., Cecil, Pooh, Al B., Stinka, Red, Boo-Boo, Mal and Ray-Ray. To all my niggas I been locked down with over the years from the jails to Deep Meadows twice, Powahatan recieving twice, Dillwyn and Sussex II. Dowdell from Whitcomb Ct., Nard M., from Church Hill, Jeff W. from Central Gardens, Ty W., Unique aka Ricky Dyett-yeah peanut from Da R wrote a book. Ray-Ray Minor from Norfolk, Big Chic from Norfolk, Monte from Norfolk, Philly up Sussex II, Fontaine aka Fon Gotti, Lynn, and Lo Jr. from Portsmouth. Hot Dog from Jackson Ward, Chuck from Southhampton County, Do-Dirty, Pep, Ty, Willie Finney from Petersburg, Clint W. from Petersburg. Blah and Rambo from Newport News, Jaime from Whitcomb Ct., Gator from Highland Park, my nigga Truck Jones from da Deuce in Killa Hill. Tae from Fairfield, J- Rock from Prtsmouth, Tink from Creighton, Lil Fred from Mosby, Q. Wright from D.C.- yeah Tone done did it Champ. Nasa and Ant from D.C. and my nigga Blizz Nizzle from B-More, Philly at least we both like the Eagles. Trick Jefferies and Mane-Mane from Raven St.

Introduction

Welcome to my city Richmond, VA. When out-of-towners and society think of Richmond, they tend to think of us as the Capital of the Confederacy or the Capital of the South. The Mayor, City Council and overall city government wants to portray our city as some goody two shoes city, but to me and my people there's another kind of Richmond. To us Cap City has a different meaning, Murder Capital of VA, where niggas won't hesitate to pop a cap in your ass. We take pride in being the Murder Capital, where street people survive by any means necessary.

We relish in being known as 'Rich Town,' 'Rich City,' 'Da R,' or 'Da Big R,' wherever we go whether in the penitentiary or in the street, when you say you're from Richmond respect is instantly given. Ain't no flagging for no colors, it's where you from, what hood claim you. This is our story, so sit back and enjoy. But be careful, cause if you ain't from here or don't have family here, you better handle your business and be out. We don't like out-of-towners, especially if it's not beneficial to us. Richmond, home of the flyest hustlers, drug dealers, and cap peelers you'll ever see.

Dedicated to all the soldiers and money getters who've lived to survive in the streets of 'Da Big R;' The real Middle East.

Rich City Thug-Life

Chapter 1--Northside:

Sitting on the front of his Barton Ave. home talking to his mother Ms. Fox, sister Sassy and one of his middle brothers Cheeks. Fatty Cocino saw the slate gray pick-up truck turn the corner off Brookland Park Blvd. onto Barton Ave. The block was packed on both sides with hustlas getting money, nothing seemed out of the ordinary, until the sound of gunfire pierced the air. 'Cccclllaaak cccclllaak ccccclaak' Catching everybody off guard, the truck had slowed down to a crawl looking as though they were trying to score a piece of crack, dope, weed, or something.

Instead of buying drugs, two people had sat up on the back and unleashed a barrage of bullets on the unsuspecting hustlas. One person shooting on each side of the street, the gunman on the left had a SKS assault rifle and the gunman on the right had a Tec-9 sub-machine gun. Lil Q got caught in the leg and Mel-Mel in the side, Smoke was in the process of serving junkie James when he was barely missed. But Fat Dom got hit sitting on the bench behind them.

Seeing what was happening, both Fatty and Cheeks went to take off when Ms. Fox hollered at them, "Fatty, Cheeks where the hell ya'll think you're going?" "Ma" Fatty said "them our niggas down there." "So what? What can ya'll do for them? But get yourself hit or make the police come question you. Both of you better sit your black asses down, before I knock you down." "Aw Ma" was their reply as they sat back down. "Aw Ma hell" was Ms. Fox response.

Eastend:

Sitting in an apartment on Seldon St., in Fairfield Ct. Black Pete, Lil Rayshaun and Simmy were in Black Pete's baby mama's house counting the take for the robbery they had just pulled over the West End on Rosewood Ave. "2,700" Lil Rayshaun said, "I told ya'll niggas that nigga Gamal be holding, ya'll think cause that nigga walk around looking like a bum he broke. Shawty this nigga flat a half-a-big a day, that's two and a quarter nigga, what the fuck? Nigga probly sell more than that I'm just going off what I saw." "I sho ain't know them niggas was getting it like that," Simmy said....

While this was going on P.J. and Do-Do were up on 23rd St. catching all the dope sales that came thru. "Man if it keep jumping like this, I'm hitting the Sattelite and fucking somebody's daughter tonight," Do-Do said. "I'mma fuck Mesha tonight, shid I want some of that bum ass head she got waiting for me," P.J. said.

Southside:

Over on Chicago Ave. Lil Goo, Slick, Corey Dillard, and Dan Johnson were all standing around shooting the breeze when Corey said to Slick "shoot one bitch." Slick replied "shoot one then, where the dice at?" "Shit nigga you normally have'em with you," Lil Goo interjected. "Only ones I got is open and I know ya'll niggas don't want to play with them," Corey stated. 'I got three packs of min-poos in the car if ya'll want to use'em," Dan said. "Why da fuck you ain't went and got'em then?" Slick asked. "Fuck you nigga, I ain't the one shooting, I ain't got time to be playing with ya'll none shooting asses today."

"I'm bout to hit the Red Roof Inn with Michelle," Dan said. "You pussy whipped ass nigga, that's why you always saying you ain't got no money, cause you keep going to the fucking motel," Corey said. "Don't hate on me cause I got a good pussy bitch that gives me p.o.d.-that's pussy on demand, in case ya'll dumb ass mafuckas ain't know."

Westend:

Dre Jr., Chris Stevenson, Gamal, Danielle, and Stephanie Ellison were sitting in Tiffany's (Danielle's sister) apartment in Randolph Village. "So you telling me, you don't know who the fuck it was that robbed you?" Danielle asked. She was Poppi's girl, but she was also one of the most thoroughest street bitches a nigga would want to meet. Her and her right hand girl Stephanie had no problem picking up a pistol and handling their business. Danielle preferred a 9mm, while Stephanie preferred a .380. However they both knew their way around guns pretty well, add her cousin Sassy to the mix and you had three sexy, dangerous, and volatile females.

"Hell naw I'ont know who it was, but the way I figure it, it had to be somebody that knew me, considering the fact they got me on my block," Gamal answered. "Fo'sho fo'sho," Dre stated "Niggas round here know not to fuck with you, they already know what it is." "Fuck that shit nigga, da streets talk, one way or another we'll find out who did it and when we do, we go handle our business," Chris Stevenson added. "Bet that," Poppi said. "And you know this," Gamal stated firmly.

1701 Fairfield Way- Richmond City Jail: Tier F3

Marty and Spaszo from Creighton Ct. were plotting on stealing Biko from Jackson Ward's commissary bag. "I'm telling you" Spaszo said "when everybody go to chow, we can hang back and snatch the bag before the gate lock. When we get back, we split the shit up real fast before he realize what happened, shit what he go do he a pussy anyway." When chow was called 45 minutes later that's just what they did. They both played the toilet stalls, then went to the back acting as though they were getting themselves together.

Marty snatched the bag carried it to Spaszo's bed, where they pulled the blanket and sheets up over it. Unbeknownst to them Deputy Kirkland who also happened to be Biko's second cousin peeped their move. Knowing that was the area where his cousin slept, he said nothing as the two exited the tier. Nobody on the tier knew Kirkland and Biko were cousins, that was Biko's idea, he knew one day the secrecy would come in handy. To keep things off balance Biko would sometimes curse Kirkland out to give the impression they couldn't stand each.

When Kirkland got in the chow hall and spotted Biko, he gave him the silent hand sweep motion of the pants leg to indicate they needed to talk. After eating Biko started talking really loud to JerMichael two rows behind him, this allowed Kirkland to tell Biko to see him in the hallway when his tier exited the chow hall. As their tier exited, Biko went to Kirkland who told him what he saw and who it was, Biko thanked his cousin and went to see who shit got stolen. Not thinking it was his.

Arriving back on the tier Biko went straight to his bunk in the back, noticing nobody seemed to be upset or angry he decided to look under his bunk. When he did, he discovered it was his bag that had been stolen. Not saying a word to anyone, he put his orange sherbs on and walked up front. Maybe Spaszo forgot what they did, or maybe he figured Biko wouldn't know who got him, whatever the case he went to the toilet stall. He had just sat down, when Biko kicked the door in and started throwing haymakers catching him square in the jaw, blackening one eye immediately and splitting the other. When he finished, Spaszo was sitting beside the toilet and the wall with shit running out his ass.

Marty hearing the commotion, but not knowing who was involved went about his business separating the commissary, when he looked up Biko was coming towards him. That's when he realized he was going to have to fight. Seeing Biko beat Spaszo, the Jackson Ward mob went into action attacking everybody from Creighton Ct. When Biko got to Marty he could see in Marty's face he was scared, what was even worse he knew Marty couldn't fight.

His first right caught Marty in the jaw, the next a left uppercut backed him into the bars and a looping over hand right knocked Marty completely out. When Marty hit the floor, just for good measure Biko kicked him in the face, then dragged him up front to the bars where Kirkland and Officer Smith took him and Spaszo to the hole. Afterwards Biko told the Jackson Ward niggas about his shit being stolen and knowing who did it, but he didn't tell them how he found out.

Chapter 2: Northside

Fatty, Te-Mundre, and Shaun were standing out on Meadowbridge and 1st Ave talking to Marquell, Tom-Tom, Big C and Davon. "Man, I heard it's hot as hell down ya'll end," Marquell said. "Yeah" Te-Mundre said "ever since them niggas came thru and sprayed last week, them people been everywhere." "Shiit you know they jumped out on us the other day, talking bout they heard we was beefing with ya'll," Shaun said. "How the fuck they figure that?" Big C asked.

"Who the fuck knows" Te-Mundre said "them

motherfuckers know damn well we ain't beefing with ya'll, they know Fatty and Marquell is family and they know that Cheeks and Shaun hang down here much as they run their damn names. They was just fishing trying to see if ya'll was go give'em anything." Fatty was rolling a blunt, after he finished he said "I still don't know what the fuck going on." Davon spoke up "I heard it was some niggas from Poe St."

"Why?" asked Fatty "Cause you supposed to have fucked the nigga Mitch's girl while he was locked up." "You saying they was looking for me?" Fatty asked surprised. "Yeah" Davon said. "Nigga why the fuck you just saying something?" Te-Mundre asked. "I told Cheeks, he said he was go tell ya'll." "How you find out?" Shaun asked.

"Cause I fuck with Lil Scoe from down there and he told me, you know he be buying wholesale from me and he ain't tryna to fuck that up. Not with the way I be looking out for him and the quality of flav we got." "You trust this nigga?" Fatty asked as he passed the blunt to Big C. "Yeah" "Don't worry bout it, we'll take care of it, you know them people waiting for ya'll to retaliate," Marquell said. "Aight you got that nigga, but in the meantime is you ready to go holla at DoLo?" Fatty asked. "Yeah nigga, I'm down to one quarter ounce and I'ma flatfoot that," Marquell answered. "Nigga I'm ain't got that, I think I got bout a 16th to 2 grams left," Fatty said.

Eastend:

Sassy was over Hilltop with Danielle and Stephanie picking up Stephanie's lil brother JerMarcus from her aunt Tiny's house. "So" Sassy said, "Stephanie you still fucking with Quinton from Washington Park?" "Shit, him and this nigga Rel from over here too," Danielle stated. "Fuck you bitch, who asked you anything,"

Stephanie replied. "Wait a minute Lil Rel, you talking bout that lil fly ass young nigga Chavon used to fuck with?" Sassy asked. "That's the one," Stephanie said. "Girl you know my youngest brother Shaun beat his ass in da afta hours spot on Hull St. a couple weeks ago," Sassy said.

"For what?" Danielle asked. "Cause when they played 'put you hoods up' Rel said 'Fuck Highland Park'. You know Shaun's young wild ass, he already didn't like the nigga cause he used to fuck with Chavon, so Shaun hauled off and smacked the shit out him. When he tried to fight back, Shaun hit him so fast and so many times it wasn't funny. If I hadn't been there ain't no telling what Shaun would've done to him," Sassy said.

"Yeah, well that ain't got shit to do with me," Stephanie stated emphatically. "Why the hell it don't? You roll with me don't you? You dumb bitch, so you know whoever my cousins got beef with, I got beef with too and that means you do too," Danielle said. "So what ya'll saying is I need to cut this nigga off because Shaun got beef with him?" Stephanie asked. "Nah bitch, what you think?" Sassy asked. "In that case Shaun need to be giving me either some of that dick or money, shit preferably both," Stephanie said.

Southside:

Standing in the corner store at Hull and 34th Lil Goo and Slick were getting ready to buy a box of Dutch Masters cigarillos, Newports, and a couple of Mystics. While they were standing in line Tyshon, Keon, and Blip from Afton came in the store; Keon being high off dope was going into a nod when he bumped into Lil Goo and caused him to drop his bottle of Mystic. Lil Goo turned around and said "What da fuck?" to which Tyshon and Blip both stepped up and said "What da fuck, what?" Slick turned around, noticing the bulge in Blip's shirt told Lil Goo to "let it go," Lil Goo not caring and not listening asked "Nigga you go say excuse me?"

The man working behind the counter sensing trouble, told Lil Goo to "get another Mystic at half price." Lil Goo feeling disrespected, did as the man said and proceeded to walk out the store, but not before Keon called him a "pussy bitch." Hearing this Lil Goo left out saying "yeah aight." Once outside Slick told Lil Goo that he recognized them from being down Afton in Greystone apts and not to worry cause they were going to get theirs."

Leaving out the store and heading towards Afton in Tyshon's blue Delta'88,' Tyshon, Blip, nor Keon saw Lil Goo and Slick parked off to the side of the store. After watching the three of them pull out the parking lot and making sure they were headed towards Afton, Slick put his pale Buick Roadmaster in drive and headed towards Chicago Ave. to get their guns. After Slick got his gray .45 and Lil Goo got his .40 cal they went up the block and told Corey and Dan what just happened, and what was about to go down. "Aight, ya'll niggas got 10 minutes tops to do what you gotta do and get back, it don't take but 2 minutes for real." "Fo sho both replied as they proceeded to the car.

Crossing Columbia and driving down Afton Ave. and coming up to Greystone apts, which were one way in and one way out; they spotted Tyshon, Keon, and Blip standing around or sitting on top of Tyshon's car. Making a U-turn they pulled down and parked on Lynhaven Ave. After checking to make sure both guns were loaded and had one in the chamber, they make a pact; since Slick was driving, he would walk straight back up and turn in the apts, Lil Goo would circle around the apts and come from behind them.

Slick was to wait until he saw Lil Goo, then he was to approach them, at which time Lil Goo was to start dumping and so would Slick. But as with most plans, something fucked up, mainly Slick. He was couldn't wait and when he walked up he just started dumping, hitting Blip in the stomach and sending Tyshon and Keon running right into Lil Goo. Neither Tyshon nor Keon saw Lil Goo rounding the apts, by the time the bullets finished flying both Slick and Lil Goo had emptied their clips.

Tyshon had gotten hit in the back of the head and his torso had five bullets holes in it, Keon got hit in the right arm, back and caught two in his back legs, the one in his back actually hit his spleen. When all was said and done; Keon was paralyzed, Blip was hospitalized and Tyshon was dead. The whole ordeal lasted less than four minutes, Lil Goo and Slick were back on Chicago Ave. within 11 minutes tops.

Westend:

"Okay gentlemen we must remain calm and relaxed, be alert and on point, we want to catch these guys slipping, we're ready to go on my command," Det. Jamess Smithers said into the radio. He was the head of a newly developed street task force aimed at street level drug dealers in the city, he also worked homicides that were considered drug related. Today he was leading a task force of eight officers: 4 detectives and 4 uniformed in raiding a house on Grayland Ave. He and his partner Det. Donald Long had received a report about a house with a lot of drug activity going on.

Riding four deep to a car, they turned onto Grayland off of Meadow and drove past the yellow stucco house they were looking for, they saw three people going inside the same house. Turning on Island Ave. they rode thru the alley behind the house where they dropped off officers King and Taylor, whose assignments were to watch the back door and make sure no one came out. Turning back onto Meadow they turned around again to Grayland, this time they stopped on the corner to check their equipment and make sure everything was in proper order. Outside the cars, Det. Smithers gave his final instructions, "Okay, remember these guys are supposed to be armed and dangerous, not only that, but this is supposed to be the coke factory of the West End."

"So we're looking for anything from drugs to guns to paraphernalia and anything in between. There should be at least seven people inside counting the three we saw going in when we circled the block." While the police were making their way up to the house to take up their positions, the people inside the house were unaware of what was going on outside and actually there were eight occupants inside.

There was Dre Jr. and Gamal playing Madden 2013 for $100 dollars a game, Chris Stevenson, Chantel, Stephanie and Mo Mo in the kitchen trying to figure out which side of town they were going to get some weed from, cause that on their side was straight garbage. And there was Poppi and Danielle upstairs getting their freak on. Poppi had Danielle bent over the bed black ass spread wide and standing on the floor slamming eight inches of hard dick up into her gut from the back.

When the front door came crashing in and the police ran inside hollering "Police get down" everybody inside was caught off guard. Dre and Gamal being the closest to the door, immediately jumped up and were slammed to the floor. Chris, Chantel, Stephanie, and Mo Mo came running out the kitchen and were thrown to the floor one by one. Hearing the music coming from upstairs, Det. Smithers asked how many people were upstairs, since it was Chantel's house she answered "two." Det. Smithers pointed to Det.Long who in turn motioned for a uniformed officer to follow him upstairs.

Coming to the top of the stairs, they followed the music to the back bedroom. Turning the doorknob and entering, they caught site of Danielle's big black ass turned up to the door, pink pussy spread open, kneeling over sucking Poppi's dick. Det. Long couldn't believe what he was seeing, his dick got instantly hard; he had to clear his throat and his mind as he called out "Police!" Poppi wasn't sure he heard right, but he knew he wasn't going to stop until he busted a nut in Danielle's hot ass mouth. Danielle heard them, but thought it was somebody from downstairs playing, won't no shame in her game, she knew her man was ready to bust and she wasn't planning on stopping for nothing or nobody.

But Det. Long quickly ended that by cutting the music off, telling them to stop what they were doing and get dressed. Both Poppi and Danielle looked over to see Det. Long and the uniform officer standing there watching them. Danielle let Poppi's dick slide out her mouth to ask "what the fuck was going on?" Det. Long informed them that this was a raid, they needed to get dressed and head downstairs with him. After getting downstairs Smithers asked "what took so long?" Det. Long answered "she was trying to swallow his salami whole."

The uniforms had already started searching the house, but hadn't discovered anything so far, so Smithers and Long went upstairs and started looking, they searched each and every room, but found nothing. Getting frustrated at their luck they decided to go back downstairs and question everybody in the house. After separating and questioning everybody individually, they finally had to come to the conclusion that there was nothing in the house, which meant they were on a wild goose chase. Which also meant they couldn't arrest no one, because nobody even had so much as a warrant out for their arrest.

After taking the cuffs off and apologizing they were preparing to leave when Chantel asked for the detectives badge numbers. "What for?" Det. Long asked her. "Cause I'm filing harassment charges." Det. Smithers informed her "that they had a complaint and a confidential informant had reported on drugs being sold there. So the complaint and informant's information had to be checked out, in other words filing a harassment charge wouldn't do no good." With that the police left.

Chapter 3: RCJ Chow Hall

As tier G1 enters the chow hall Lt. Wisnewski and Sgt. Beck are standing by the door, Sgt. Maynor is at the window watching the trays come out. Malik from Creighton Ct. is stepping up to get his tray, grabbing the tray he notices his food is short. When he turns around to say something Sgt. Maynor says "either take it or leave the chow hall." "Fuck you," Malik says and Sgt Maynor knocks the tray out his hand, at which time Malik swings around and gives him a two piece which immediately drops the Sgt.

Seeing this, Lt. Wisnewski and Sgt. Beck take off after Malik as Wisnewski tells Jennings at the podium in the hall to call for backup. Running up on Malik they yell for him to "get down on the floor," Malik backs up on the wall and tells them to "come get me." As about 12 more officers come running in, Sgt. Beck reaches for Malik who throws a quick left and cuts Beck's eye. The officers didn't notice Jo-Jo, Meanie, Mont and Claw Head from Creighton duck under the railing to come help their homeboy. Jake, Sonny Boy, and Andrew Turner three old heads who had done time at Spring St. State Prison and who were on tier F1, which also happened to be in the chow hall also came to help Malik out.

Before long it was a full fledge riot going on, with the deputies on the losing end. Eventually more officers arrived; some went in the gun ports and started shooting pepper spray and rubber balls down into the crowd. Hitting some and missing others. The pepper spray eventually had everybody coughing, even the police, within minutes of the arrival of the backups order was restored, with Malik and all the inmates being dragged to the hole. At least four officers had to go to the hospital; Sgt. Maynor had his jaw broken, Sgt. Beck ended up with a split eye and a black eye and Lt. Wisnewski ended up with two black eyes and a broken nose.

Malik ended up with a cracked rib, two teeth knocked out and a broken ring finger. With the jail being in the uproar that it was in, Sheriff Andrew Bilkins declared the whole jail on full restriction; meaning no television, telephones, or visits for at least week.

East End:

Sitting in Ayanna's house in Seven Gables, her cousins from New York; Tre, Ski, Cap, and Turk had brung down 9 oz's of coke, a q.p. of weed and 350 Ecstasy pills. Their plan was to set up shop at Ayanna's sister's Cassidy house in Whitcomb Ct. Though they had been coming down to Richmond for years they had never hung in Whitcomb Ct., therefore they knew no one over there other than Cassidy, who told them it would be cool because everybody fucked with her baby daddy and he wasn't from over there. What she didn't know was her baby daddy Stan, grew up there, but moved when he was twelve years old.

"Man," Cap said "Cassidy says it's a gold mine over there and you know since we been coming down here that's all we been hearing; is how they get major money over there in Whitcomb Ct." "Yeah, but check it son, we need to be cool cause don't forget we don't know these niggas and we'll be on their turf," Tre said. He was the unquestioned leader or O.G. of this four man group of Bloods, who also happened to be all brothers that came down to get a toehold in VA. "Man fuck these slow ass VA niggas, what the fuck they go do yo? It's NY all day son. These country ass niggas don't get gully like the city," Turk said. He was the youngest, but also the most trigger happy of the crew. "Yeah aight, just don't get it twisted nigga, these niggas don't have no trouble shooting a nigga and we go be in their projects, so don't sleep nigga," Tre emphasized....

Over in Fairfield Black Pete and Lil Rayshaun were getting ready to ride over Highland Park to go see Tierra a girl Lil Rayshaun was fucking. "Nigga I told you that nigga Gamal ain't know who stuck him up, the streets say they know he got jacked, but not by who," Lil Rayshaun said. "Even if he find out who did it, what da fuck we care, be like Beans in this bitch "Get down or lay down," Black Pete said.

Northside:

Sassy and Simmy were at Leonardi's having just left VA Center Commons Mall, where Simmy had just bought Sassy a Juicy Coture outfit and some Manola Blahniks. "Boy where the hell you get all this new finagled money from, acting like you Tone-Tone or Meek-Meek or somebody." She was referring to her God uncles two old head gangsta's from around her way. Simmy looked at her, he couldn't help from bragging, he really wanted Sassy to be his girl, so he was trying to impress her when he said "him, Black Pete, and Lil Rayshaun caught a lick in the West End."

Had he been paying close attention he would've noticed Sassy's reaction, but being young he was full of himself and thought he was the man in her eyes. Sassy remembering what Danielle said about Gamal getting stuck up said "Boy stop playing you know ya'll ain't stick nobody up, cause if ya'll had I would've heard about it."That's when Simmy told her "they got some nigga over on Rosewood that Lil Rayshaun knew." Sassy knew right away it was Gamal, but she played her hand smooth and finished her meal after which Simmy took her home and said he would call her later.... Te-Mundre, Cheeks, and Shaun were walking out of McDonald's on Mechanicsville Tnpk and Magnolia Ave when a green Chevy Cavalier turned in and unleashed a barrage of bullets. Inside the car were Y.K., Jigaloo, and Rel from Hilltop. They had been driving down Mechanicsville heading to KFC when Rel spotted Shaun going in McDonald's. Being the opportunistic snake he was, he told Y.K. to turn the car around.

It just so happened that he and Y.K. both had their guns on them; Y.K. had his .38 revolver which he handed to Jigaloo and Rel had a .44 snub-nose revolver. They both preferred revolvers because that way they dropped no shells, which meant no fingerprints for the police to recover. As luck would have it, when they turned into the parking lot Te-Mundre, Cheeks, and Shaun were in between McDonald's and their car. Soon as the shots were fired they had to duck and run for cover.

Te-Mundre tried to make it to their car but had to duck and hide behind a white jeep Cherokee; Cheeks scrambled behind a orange Granada which got hit twice, once in the door and the passenger side window. And Shaun who Rel was really trying to hit, ran and jumped in a red four door Acura TL with two females inside sitting in the drive-thru. Almost as soon as the shooting started, it stopped and Y.K. sped off squealing wheels heading back towards Hilltop.

After realizing the shooting had stopped and the car was gone Te-Mundre and Cheeks came out from where they were hiding. Shaun apologized to the females, gave them both $50 and walked over to where his brothers were, "Ya'll niggas alright? Ain't nobody hit is it?" he asked. "Yeah nigga we aight and nah ain't nobody get hit, but who the fuck was those niggas?" Cheeks asked. "I think it was that nigga Rel from Hilltop, at least that's who I think it was, but I don't know the car," Shaun said. "It looked like Y.K. from Hilltop car," Te-Mundre responded. They decided to find out if it was Y.K. and Rel and if so they would handle it.

Southside:

Sonya hung up the phone and told Crystal "Come ride with me, I got some shit to handle." Crystal seeing her sister put a razor blade in her mouth knew her sister was going to fight and more than likely it was behind her no good man Dan Johnson and some funky ass bitch he was fucking. Crystal had told Sonya about keep fucking with that nigga, one day somebody was going to get seriously hurt. When they got in Sonya's red Acura TL, Crystal asked Sonya "So are you going to tell me what the fuck is going on and where the fuck we going?"

"That was Charmaine she just saw Dan over Village South standing outside all hugged with a bitch." "So what? You go beat her ass because you know you can't beat Dan,"Crystal asked. "Shit I'ma beat her ass and his ass too, but I ain't talking bout it I'm just going to handle my business," Sonya said. It normally takes between 12-15 minutes from Ruffin Rd to Village South (the old Southgate) but Sonya made it there in less than six minutes.

Turning into the apts she immediately spots Dan's black Lincoln and Dan with some short bitch that looked like Michelle standing there kissing. This pissed her off even more, because even though she and Michelle didn't hang out like they used to, they still were supposed to be friends and Michelle knew that Dan was her man. Sonya pulled up and jumped out "I'ma fuck both ya'll mafuckin ass up." Dan hearing Sonya's voice turned his head just in time to see her swinging a wide hook at his head. As he released Michelle and turned to face a fuming Sonya, he made the mistake of stepping too far to the left side, leaving Michelle wide open and vulnerable to Sonya's right hand which connected squarely to Michelle's right eye.

Dan seeing Crystal coming didn't know whether to grab Sonya or watch Crystal, because he knew that Crystal was the one he needed to keep an eye on. She would be the one with either, the gun, razor or some type of weapon and wouldn't hesitate to use it on him or Michelle. This slight hesitation gave Sonya time to follow up with a kick to Michelle's stomach. Michelle doubled over and that's when Sonya caught her with a quick left, then came a loud scream.

Sonya had come around the right and buck-fiftied (cut) Michelle on her right cheek. Dan hearing the scream immediately looked to his right, reached out to grab Sonya who spun around, came down with a swinging slice and caught Dan high up on his right shoulder. Dan feeling the slice still was reaching out to grab Sonya when he felt something crash into his head. It was Crystal, who thinking Dan was trying to defend Michelle, had picked up a Miller (MGD) 32 oz. bottle and smashed it over his head.

Dan fell to his knees; he was actually trying not to hit Sonya but after Crystal hit him he had no other choice. As Sonya moved in to kick him in the face, he grabbed her leg, pulled her down slapping her at the same time, then he turned around and backhanded Crystal knocking her to the ground. "Looking down at Sonya he yelled "YOU CUT ME, WHAT DA FUCK? Being mad is one thing but you fucking cut me, then your sister hits me with a bottle ya'll lucky I don't fucking kill both of ya'll.

Michelle had gotten up and was trying to get in the house when Sonya yelled "I ain't finished with you yet bitch, wait til I catch your motherfucking ass. How da fuck you go fuck my man? We supposed to be better than that." Then turning to Dan she said "Nigga I'm tired of this shit, I ain't fucking wit your ass no more, but then again two can play this game you just watch."

Dan not realizing Sonya saw him and Michelle kissing said "Sonya it won't even like that, I came over this way to get some smoke from her brother, we smoked a blunt together then we got to joking about who was the highest." "Fuck you bitch," Sonya said getting in the car.

Chapter 4: West End

Sitting on her sister's front porch Danielle was smoking a blunt when her cell phone rang, "Hey girl what's happening?" It was her cousin Sassy. "Ain't shit, sitting here puffing on a blunt, why? What's happening with you?" Danielle replied. "Nothing just got back from the club, paying nem mafuckas for mama's party coming up." "So ya'll still having it?"

"Yeah Fatty and the boys said they wanted to do something different for mama this year." "I know that's right, how old is

Aunt Fox going to be anyway?" "Shit sixty-eight going on 18."
"Whaat I don't believe it, I ain't know she was older than 62. My
auntie look good and she still got it going on." "I know right,
talking bout she want some Dereon Jeans to show off her butt,"
Sassy said laughing. "What? No she didn't, get it auntie,"
Danielle said laughing also.

"Yes she did, but the real reason I called, is I got some info
for Gamal." "What kind of info?" "Girl you know I ain't go talk
on this phone, but how bout ya'll meet me and Fatty at Byrd
Park in a hour." "Aight let me contact Gamal...."

At the police station on Meadow, Det. Smithers and Det.
Long were talking to their CI Filmore Dean. "Now tell us again
how you figure they sell drugs out this house, cause when we
went in there won't no drugs nowhere," Det. Long stated. "Man,
what the fuck? I told ya'll I go there every day to buy at least
$20 dollars worth of crack, sometimes more," Filmore answered.
"What you mean sometimes more?" Det. Smithers asked. "Man
they sell everything from $10 rocks to 16ths, but they won't sell
more than that."

"Why is that?" Smithers inquired. "I'ont know, but I heard
cause they don't think nobody smokes more than a 16th at a time
and they don't have enough weight to sell to the hustlas,"
Filmore said. "So how much you think they buying altogether?"
Det. Long asked. "I'ont know altogether maybe a ounce and a
half if that, ya'll gotta remember they is small time. It's just so
many of them be together, it's hard to say who's really selling
and who ain't. Cause all of'em don't grind."

'Well I'm beginning to think don't none of them sell, we
ain't even find no paraphernaliaia lying around," Det. Long said
emphatically. "I'ont know what to say other than maybe they
hadn't re'dup yet." "You willing to wear a wire?" Det. Smithers

asked. Filmore got uncomfortable at that question; being a confidential informant was one thing, but wearing a wire was another thing.

"Nah man I can't wear no wire." "Well if you don't we have no case and that means you go to jail for three years," Det. Long said. Filmore blew out some air "can I at least think about it man, that's putting my life on the line." "Yeah you got one week, after that deals off, Det. Smithers said.

Northside:

Fatty was walking out the Mexican store on Brookland Park Blvd., when he heard somebody say "hey my friend come here." Turning around he saw 'Curser' the Mexican guy from the store he had just left out of. "You talking to me?" Fatty asked him. "Naw I'm talking to myself, who the hell else you think I'm talking to?" "First off my name is Remy not Curser, but I'll let you continue to call me Curser because I like you."

"Anyway what the fuck you want?" "I see you and your brothers come in here all the time and ya'll always buy the same things; plastic bags and razor blades. I'm not dumb. I know what you doing, plus I see ya'll outside all the time." "So the fuck what, nigga? That don't mean a damn thing, you the police or something?" Remy smiled "Nah my friend I'm far from the police, as a matter of fact why don't you come take a ride with me so we can talk and I'll show you a couple of things."

Fatty wasn't stupid, he had a feeling Remy wanted to do business with him, he just didn't know on what level, whether Remy wanted to buy from him or sell weight to him. While thinking of this his cell phone rang, glancing at the number he saw it was his house, he told Remy to hold on a minute as he answered. "Hello" "Hey big bro where you at?" Sassy asked.

"Up the street, why?" "Cause I need you to ride with me over Byrd Park to meet up with Danielle and Gamal."

"Well I'm talking important business right now, can't it wait?" "Not really, I got something I need to tell them, but I want to run it by you first," Sassy said. "Aight, I be there in ten minutes." "Okay" Fatty told Remy "his sister needed to see him fast, it was an emergency." Remy said he "understood" and told Fatty to meet him there Friday evening around 5:30. Fatty agreed and headed home.

Walking up to the house Fatty saw his brother Te-Mundre up the street on the other side of Barton with the rest of their niggas trying to dump the rest of his pack. Walking in the house he went straight to the kitchen where his mother was cooking. "What's for dinner Ma?" "What the hell you mean? What's for dinner? It don't make no damn difference, you go eat it anyway," Ms. Fox said. "I know Ma, but I still wanna know what you cooking."

"What the hell it look like? Meat loaf, mashed potatoes and string beans, it ain't ready so while you wait you can take the trash out. Make yourself useful for a change. Damn!" "I love you too, Ma," Fatty said kissing her on the cheek. Hearing her brother's voice Sassy came into the dining room and asked if he was ready, Fatty wanted to know "what the rush was." Sassy told him she'd told Danielle to meet her in a hour." "Lemme take this trash out and I'll meet you round front."

East End:

Over in Whitcomb Ct. Tre, Ski, Cap, and Turk had it jumping using Cassidy's house as their main base. They had already sold out of everything, made a return trip to New York and came back with double what they had at first. They'd been back for three days now and already were down to 12 ounces of coc, a little over a q.p. of weed and about 500 x-pills. With their product taking off, the other hustlas in Whitcomb noticed sales were down, eventually word got out about the New York Boyz on Bethel taking over.

Kalil, Maurice, Matt, and Stan were over on Ambrose St. trying to catch some money when they saw crackhead Diane walking their way. "What's up Diane?" Matt said. "Hey baby," she responded as she continued pass them. "Where da hell you going?" Matt asked since she was one of his regular customers. Without thinking she replied "over on Bethel."

"On Bethel, for what? I'm right here." "Yeah, but them New York niggas got better product and better quantity than anybody around here. Shit Stan know, they grinding out his girl's house," Diane said. "Shawd you better not bring yo muthafucking ass round here no more, if you do I'ma spit in yo face," Maurice said. Diane knew she was wrong, but shit compared to the New York niggas these niggas shit was straight garbage.

'Shawd what da fuck Stan? Them niggas post up in Cassidy's house, what da fuck going on?" Kalil asked. "Man, look they her cousins and they supposed to be Blood, the nigga Tre supposed to be the O.G. he's the coolest one. But dem two niggas Cap and Turk they the wild ones, talking bout they go turn Whitcomb into a Blood project," Stan said.

"Say what? Who da fuck they think they is and why the fuck you ain't said something before now nigga?" Maurice snapped. "First off nigga, I told Cassidy she was dead wrong for letting them niggas post up shop in her house. Then I told them niggas this Richmond, VA not Richmond, CA or New York, we turf bang not gang bang and we don't respect that color shit."

"Plus when dem niggas first came down they bought 9 oz.s, next time they bought 18 not to mention the weed and 'X' they had. I was waiting for them to reach a brick before I said anything cause I knew ya'll niggas was gonna want to get'em," Stan said. "And you know this nigga, now besides that what was Cassidy's response?" Matt asked. "That it was her house, they were her cousins and won't nobody go tell her who could and could not grind out her house. Much less who she could have over there," Stan replied. "We go do like you said, let'em reach a brick, then we go decide how to get'em wit out Cassidy knowing." Kalil said.

HCJ-Henrico County Jail West: Dayroom 28

Darrell who's been down for 8 1/2 months and has another month and a half to go on a simple poss. of cocaine charge is on the phone calling his wifey boo Angie Jackson. Angie's laying across her bed looking her long black snake 'Jumbo' in the eye, petting him and asking him if he "was going to be a good boy for her tonight." When the phone rings 'Jumbo' jumps in her hand, she smacks him playfully and tells him to behave cause it was Darrell on the phone.

Answering the phone Angie says "Hello." "Hey baby wha'chu doing?" Darrell asks. "Nothing just laying here looking at T.V." "Wha'chu watching?" "South Central." "I still don't think that's betta than 'Menace to Society,' Darrell says."Me either," Angie says in a dry tone.

"Damn baby another month and a half and I'll be home blowing your back out, I can't wait. But Angie didn't reply because as she made her last statement, her head was being forcefully pushed down towards 'Jumbo' by a black hand. As Darrell talked she began kissing all over Jumbo's head, which made him jump in anticipation. After Angie didn't respond to him immediately, Darrell called her name "Angie Angie" "Hmm" "What the fuck you doing?" "Smack smack" "Angie."

"What?" she answered. "What the fuck you doing, you couldn't answer me?" Darrell wondered out loud. "Nothing boy just eating a sucker I got from the bank today." "Yeah well that ain't what it sound like." "Look did you call here to talk or accuse me of something cause if you ain't got nothing to say I can get off the phone," Angie replied while massaging 'Jumbo.'

"Damn all I did was ask what you was doing?" As he was saying this Angie was engulfing 'Jumbo,' sliding him more and more into her mouth. She had a good 6" inches in when she heard Darrell say something about Big Ed. The only answer she could give was "ump ump." "What da hell you mean um um, fucks going on Angie? Where Lil Darrell at?"

By this time Angie had a long black finger working in and out her hot pussy so well that she didn't try nor could she hide what she was doing. "Sluurp slurrp slurp, ugh ungh unngh," was the sound she made as she slurped and deep throated 'Jumbo' at the sametime. "Angie, what the hell you doing?" Darrell yelled, but Angie couldn't answer because her head was being held down. Finally her head was allowed to come up for air.

She was gagging and coughing as she heard Darrell call her name again. She couldn't believe she had just done that with him on the phone, "What Darrell? Damn, I was choking on the sucker, you want me to answer while I'm choking." "Don't fucking play with me Angie, I swear to God, don't play with me."

Abruptly the phone was snatched out of Angie's hand, "Hey yo playboy, check this out, me and shawdy tryna have some fun aight, you really wanna know what she was doing? She was sucking my dick and I couldn't cum cause you on the phone keep asking her questions, what you need to do is get the fuck off the phone, let us handle our business and when you come home she'll be here waiting for you." Angie couldn't believe what just happened, now she was really afraid for both of their lives.

This nigga thought he was a gangsta, he just didn't know or realize who Darrell was and what he was capable of doing? Darrell himself was speechless, he couldn't believe Angie had played him like that nor could he believe she would let a nigga talk to him that way. "Okay play-boy you got that, go on ahead continue to have fun with that slut, just lemme holla at her right fast," Darrell said trying to control his temper. "Here Angie" Angie was so petrified she couldn't even answer straight, "Hel-Hello," "Two things, first where Lil Darrell at?" "In-in his room, sleep." "And number two, I get out in a month and a half seven o'clock sharp, don't be late." With that Darrell hung up.

Chapter 5-Southside:

Standing on the corner of Lynhaven and Afton Aves., three members of the treacherous (LBC) were discussing the shootings of Tyshon, Keon, and Blip. "Ya'll niggas hear who they say supposed to shot Blip and nem," Lil Ron-Ron asked Lil James and Lil Big Head. "I heard it was some niggas from off Bainbridge," Lil Big Head stated. "Nah yo I heard it was some niggas from Chicago Ave," Lil James said.

"Whatever nigga, we go ride on both they strips this week, I want the whole LBC down with this. We go let niggas know ain't shit sweet round Afton, fo real, we go take it back to the late 80's, early 90's. Even if Keon nem was dopefiends, they still was from Greystone you feel me," Lil Ron-Ron said....

Over in Ruffin Rd. apts Juice and Monopoly were sitting around talking about how broke and fucked up in the game they were. "Man," Juice said "This shit don't make no sense how broke we is now, damn we just had bout $7,500 and done ran thru that already. I ain't really tryna to get a nigga this week, but I need some money like yesterday." "I told you nigga, its some cracka mufuckas that's supposed to be holding weight like that in Brandermill," Monopoly said."

"How da fuck do you know bout some niggas out in Brandermill nigga?" "I told you I was over my cousin Dizzy house bout two months ago and he took me over some nigga's house to buy some weed. It was two cracka boys,one black ass nigga and a skinny ass cracka bitch out there. It was the two white boys and their sister's house, I think the nigga is the sister's boyfriend. But from my understanding its the cracka boys weed, the nigga is supposed to be their muscle or security or some shit. You can see in his face he a bigger pussy than his bitch is," Monopoly said.

"You remember how to get to their house?" Juice asked. "Hell yeah nigga, much as I go hang out at my cousins house." "So when you want to do this and bout how much you think they holding?" "We can do it late Saturday night, early Sunday morning that's the best time if we want to get some money or weed. But if we want a lot of weed, I guess we should hit it moreso during the middle of the week." "I think Saturday night early Sunday morning, catch'em when they real decent and least on point," Juice said. "Yeah bout 12:30 to 1:30 in the morning be bout the best time."

Westend:

Fatty, Sassy, Danielle, and Gamal were standing by the

lake in Byrd Park. Sassy had already filled Fatty in on what she knew about Gamal being robbed, who told her and who was with him. Sassy was wondering if she should just tell Danielle or both Danielle and Gamal. Even though Danielle was their cousin, Fatty had taught her to confide street business to nobody other than her mother and brothers. That was because he knew they wasn't going to tell on each other, but Fatty knew Danielle was as thorough as they came. She'd been schooled by their Uncle Black from an early age.

Gamal he knew from school and from hanging with Danielle, how thorough he was, he wasn't quite sure. He knew he had to be cool if his cousin fucked with him. Fatty had told Sassy not to say anything about what she knew until he told her to. "Ay yo cuz, lemme holla at you alone for a minute," Fatty said to Danielle.

They stepped off from Sassy and Gamal who commenced to making small talk. "Ay cuz how well you trust this nigga?" "That's my baby, I love him to death, like the brother I don't have; as far as trust what kind of trust you talking bout?" Sass said something bout him getting robbed, she may have some info for ya'll but before I let her tell ya'll, I gotta know this shit ain't coming back to her."

"Cuz fore I let anything or anybody find out Sassy told us anything I'll be dead first. As for Gamal, you know I don't deal with no suckas and this nigga is the closest person that I know who reminds me of you. His morals and principles are all like yours, he believes all snitches should be killed. Is that enough trust for you cuz?" Danielle asked him. 'Yeah aight come on."

Sassy and Gamal were talking about which clubs were the most jumpinest in the city, when Fatty and Danielle walked back up."Gamal we heard about you getting robbed and Sassy's got some info for you, but before she says anything, let me first say I don't want my sister's name coming up in no kind of way behind this shit. If you need somebody to ride with you to handle your business all you gotta do is give the word and you got it," Fatty said. "Go head sis tell'em what you told me."

"Well" Sassy began "Yesterday this nigga name Simmy took me to the mall, then to Leonardi's to eat, anyway he had all this money he was blowing. When I asked him about it, he started bragging trying to impress me. Talking bout how him and his boys Black Pete and Rayshaun or something caught this sweet lick over the Westend. When he said it, I remembered Danielle said something about you getting robbed. I waited a day before I called cuz and asked her to meet here where nobody could hear us talk, plus I had to talk it over with my big brother and see what he had to say."

"You say his name was Simmy?" Gamal asked. "Yeah" Sassy replied. "And who else?" "Black Pet and Rayshaun or something, he said the nigga Rayshaun knew you." "Rayshaun, I don't know no damn Rayshaun," Gamal said thinking out loud as he walked off to sit on a bench and think to himself while everyone else just stood there looking. Sassy and Danielle looked at Fatty as to what should they do, he told them to "just stay where they were and give Gamal time to think.

All of a sudden Gamal stood up and said "I know he ain't talking bout Ms. Emerson's grandson Lil Ray-Ray from Fairfield. But that's who its gotta be, cause that's the only Ray anything I know that would know I hustle around my house. Thanks for the info Sassy, don't worry your name won't ever be mentioned after this, I 'ma always be indebted to you and your brother. Fatty I got my niggaz to roll with me, I appreciate the offer and if I need you I'll holla at you, but before I get them niggas I gotta make sure it was Ray-Ray." "That's what's up nigga, handle yo bizness and let me know what's what, cause you know I still gotta look out for my sista and cousin's safety," Fatty said to Gamal.

"Aight you got that," Gamal said as they gave each other dap and parted ways.

Northside:

Marquell was sitting on junkie Deborah's porch on Arnold Ave. in Highland Park talking to Big C., Tom-Tom- and Davon. "Ya'll niggas ready to put in work on them Poe St. niggas tonight?" "No question" Davon answered, "You want me to call Lil Scoe and give him a heads up on what's go happen tonight.?" Despite what everyone else thought of the Poe St. niggas, Davon fucked with Lil Scoe, he thought Lil Scoe was one of the realest young niggas coming up. Plus it was Lil Scoe that told him who hit Barton and why, so for that reason alone he felt that Lil Scoe should know what was going down.

"Nah," Marquell said "Even though he told you everything, the fact remains he still from down there and who knows if he's trying to play both sides of the fence. All I can say if he's out there don't shoot in the area where he's at?" "We doing a drive-by, or what?" Big C. asked. "That's what we should do," Tom-Tom said "but I think we should use two cars and hit them at the same time from opposite directions like one car coming up Poe and one car coming down." "Who cars we go use, you know we can't use our own cars?" Big C said.

"I'm going to my rental house up on Pollack and get two cars for us, that way they can't trace the cars back to us, and I'm go call Fatty to let'im know it's going down tonight," Marquell said. Fatty was just sitting down at the table with Ms. Fox when his cell phone rang, looking at the phone he saw it was Marquell. "Yeah" In the background he heard his mother say "that damn phone I hate it, you can't even sit down and have dinner with your mother without it ringing. I'm go take it and throw it in the trash myself."

Fatty shook his head smiling as he heard Marquell say "What's up my nigga?" "Nuttin shawd just sitting down wit Ma Dukes to eat dinner, why what's up?" Fatty responded. "Shit just calling to say tonight bout 8:30." "Aight" Fatty said, he and Marquell had been boys since nursery school when they were 4 years old. They were brothers without being blood brothers. So he knew if Marquell said 8:30 he really meant 9:30, his plan was to make sure he and his brothers were somewhere public or where they could be seen so nothing could come back on them.

After hanging with Marquell, Fatty asked his mother "where his brothers were?" "Why?" Ms. Fox wanted to know. "Cause that was Marquell and he said there was a summer league basketball game at the Ashe Center tonight." Ms. Fox said "Cheeks and Shaun were gone to help their godmother Ms. King and Te-Mundre had called and said he and his girlfriend Te-Te were going to the movies." "Good" Fatty said "I'm going to the basketball game."

"What have you heard about the shooting up the street?" Ms. Fox asked, and Fatty told her what Davon had told him. "Wha'chu doing messing with a girl from Poe St., and you still messing with Sherry anyway." "Come on Ma" Fatty said, "You know daddy and my uncles on both ya'll sides were playas, so its only natural your kids go be playas too." "Yeah but they won' t my kids and I'm telling my oldest boy he better watch where he stick his lil thing before he gets hurt." "I ain't even go say nothing, just know all the girls love Fatty Cocino." " Whatever boy, you heard what I said, now help me clean this table off...."

At 8:56 Marquell and Big C were at crackhead Bubba's house on Pollack St. talking to everybody that got high; Raymond, Dennis, Shirley, Skitzo, and Carol trying to decide whose cars they were going to use. "I'm saying Dennis lemme get your car for bout two hours and Carol let my cousin get your car for bout an hour, hour and half tops," Marquell said. Dennis had a off brown four door 96' Bonneville and Carol had a dark blue four door Mercury Sable. "What ya'll want these cars for Marquell?" Carol asked, secretly she had a crush on Marquell and would do anything he asked her to do.

"I'm going to Azeala Apts," Big C said. "And I'm going to the summer league basketball championship game at the Ashe Center," Marquell said. "Yall niggas betta look out then and not no small shit either, cause I know you Marquell you subject not to show up for 4 hours instead of 2," Dennis said. "Aight you got that," Marquell said.

Chapter 6-Northside:

Pulling up on Arnold Ave. Marquell and Big C picked up Tom-Tom and Davon then drove to Tom-Tom's house on Forquean Lane to get their guns. Inside the house they went down to the basement where Tom-Tom reached behind the old washing machine and pulled out a blue Velcro gun sleeve that held seven guns. He then pulled out a black gun sleeve identical to the first one, this one held another seven guns. They kept their artillery here because no one knew where Tom-Tom lived and they did no dirt around his house, plus his mother was always at work or one of her church functions.

The blue sleeve held two P-89 9 mm's, a gray Glokk 17, two .380's one chrome the other black, and two10 mm's. the black sleeve had two Tec-22's, a Tec-9, a Sig Saur 9 mm, two Desert Eagles one a .44 and the other a .50 cal and a Glokk 40. Marquell instantly grabbed the Glokk .40, everybody knew that was his baby. Tom-Tom grabbed the twin P-89 9 mm's, Big C. picked up one of the Tec-22's and Davon chose to pick up the Glokk 17. After each person checked their guns and loaded their clips with plastic gloves on; Marquell gave the instructions. He would drive the Bonneville, Tom-Tom would ride with him sitting in the backseat, Big C and Davon would ride together.

They would all go through Richmond Henrico Turnpike; Marquell and Tom-Tom would turn on Lamb Ave., pull down and wait while Big C and Davon would go up to North Ave and turn down Poe St., Davon would drive while Big C rode in the back. At 9:25 they loaded up and pulled off. It just so happened that Romell from Poe St was having his 22nd birthday party that night, everybody who was anybody from that area was out in full force. The party was in the back of the Poe St. apts., but there were about 10 or 12 people standing in front of the apts.

When Marquell saw Davon and Big C turn the corner off North Ave he told Tom-Tom "showtime," he gave them about 40 seconds before he made a right onto Poe. He saw Davon slow down, then he heard Big C letting the Tec-22 go 'Tat-tat-tat tat tat.' He saw niggas and bitches scrambling for cover, he also saw at least one person hit the ground. As Davon passed them Marquell held the .40 cal out the window across his left arm as he was driving and let go at the sametime Tom-Tom let loose a barrage with the twin P-89 9 mm's. Marquell saw at least another three people drop as he sped off turned right onto North Ave. then made another right onto Roberts St heading to Davon's house on Harold Ave.

Davon had a bucket of battery acid in his garage, they

broke the guns down, dropped them in the acid and watched them burn and dissolve.

Southside:

At the same time that was going on five members of the LBC were sitting inside Lil Ron-Ron's apartment in Afton getting ready to ride on the Bainbridge niggas; there was Lil Ron-Ron, Lil James, Lil Bighead, Lil K.O. and Lil Dread. "Aight yo this the plan, we go do a drive-by and a walk-by on these niggas; Dread, Big Head and James go ride in the car that do the drive-by. Me and K.O. go do the walk-by. When ya'll come down Hart St and hit them niggas in Clopton Terrace, we go walk down 27th and hit'em as they try to run. We'll meet back here," Lil Ron-Ron instructed. "Err'body strapped?" Lil Big head asked.

"Yeah" they all answered. "James since you go be driving, you should leave your gun in case we have to run from the police. That way they can't connect you to us once we jump out and run," Lil Dread said. "Shid, I need to be strapped too, just in case sumthing goes wrong," Lil James said. "Nah nigga, Dread's right we ain't trying for nobody to get caught up, the only reason I'ma be strapped is because me and K.O. go do the walk-by and won't nobody know what we riding in," Lil Ron-Ron said.

As they loaded up in the cars, each person checked his gun. Lil Dread had a 9 mm Beretta, Big Head had a .44 snub nose, K.O. had a S &W .45 and Ron-Ron had a gray Glokk 17; everybody had hollow point bullets that Dread's older brother Cecil had given them. Lil James, Big Head, and Lil Dread were riding in Big Head's uncle Joe's baby mama Joyce four door green Chevy Cavalier. Lil Ron-Ron and Lil K.O. were riding in K.O's godsister Mya's red Honda Accord. Riding down Hart St.

the cars were following each other when Ron-Ron made a left, then made a right on 27th and parked. Once they were out and walking Ron-Ron called Big Head and hung up.

Then he heard the sound of Big Head's .44 barking 'booom booom booom' and Dread's 9 'bok bok bok,' then they saw niggas and bitches running. That's when he and K.O. walking side by side let loose with their guns 'bok bok bok, bark bark bark bark.' They saw one person fall and another one stumble as he ran. What surprised them was the short bitch in the dark colored tights who instead of running around back of the apts, ran to a shrubbery bush reached down on the ground and came up firing; 'Clack clack clack clack.'

Now it was Ron-Ron and K.O. who had to duck and run cause them bullets were getting mighty close to them. As they turned and ran Lil K.O. continued to fire over his shoulder sending a bullet in a window smashing into old Mrs. Crayton's sofa. Luckily she was in the kitchen when it happened, she heard it though and called the police. Lil Ron-Ron and K.O. made it back to the car out of breath not believing what had just happened.

Channel 6 11 at 11 News:

"Good evening we begin tonight's news with some breaking news, Richmond police have responded to two separate shootings in the city, one in Northside and one in Southside," Lisa Sommerville the news anchor said. "Our Janice Avant is on site in the Northside and Kirk Wallace is on site over the Southside. At this moment we send it out to Janice Avant."
"Thank you Lisa, according to Richmond police there was a drive-by shooting here in the 100 block of Poe St. at the Poe St. apts. According to reports there was a party here on Poe St.,

several people were standing in front of the apts when a dark colored car made a left off North Ave onto Poe St.

At about the same time, another car made a turn onto Poe off of Lamb Ave and that's where the confusion comes in. Some people say the car coming off North Ave started shooting and some say the car coming off Lamb Ave started shooting, no one is quite clear which car did the shooting. What is clear is that one or probaly both of the cars started shooting and at least 4 people were shot. According to police one female and three males were hit, at least one person is believed to be dead. That's all we know at this time, back to you Lisa."

"Janice, do police know what kind of cars they were?" "No Lisa, all they know is that they were two dark colored four door cars traveling in opposite directions." "Thanks Janice and now to our other late breaking news, Kirk Wallace is on site at the shooting over the city's Southside. We now send it over to Kirk." "Thanks Lisa, Richmond Police responded to a shooting here in the Clopton Terrace apts on Midlothian Tnpk.

According to reports, sometime between 9:15 and 9:30 tonight gunfire erupted as a four door dark colored vehicle sped by shooting out of the window. As this was happening people started running for cover when two or more people walking from the direction of 27th St also started firing. During this time a bullet went thru the window of an elderly woman here and lodged itself inside her sofa, luckily for her she wasn't on the sofa though. It is not known whether the people firing the guns were shooting at each other or shooting at the group of people standing around. At least two people possibly more were hit, although it's not known whether their injuries were life threatening or not.

Once again gunfire erupted here at the Clopton Terrace apts

on Midlothian Tnpk at least two people were hit and a stray bullet went thru the apt of an elderly lady who thankfully, wasn't hurt. At this point all the police are saying is that they're looking for a dark colored four door car and two people seen walking down the street at the time of the shooting. Now back to you Lisa." "Kirk do the police know if the shooting over Northside, and the one over Southside are related?" "At this time Lisa I'm not sure, they're not saying, but we'll try to find out."

"Thanks Kirk, once again there were two shootings in the city of Richmond tonight. One in the Northside where at least four people got hit, and one in Southside where at least two people were shot. At this time it's not known whether these incidents were related or not. In other news."

Chapter 7- West End:

Gamal, Dre Jr., Poppi, Chris Stevenson and Danielle were at Gamal's house sitting on the front porch discussing what Sassy had told Gamal and Danielle. "Lemme ask ya;ll niggas something," Gamal said. "Besides Ms. Emerson's grandson, do any of ya'll know anybody by the name of Rayshaun?" Everybody looked around at each other trying to think, but nobody came up with anything. "Well do any of ya'll remember seeing Ray-Ray around here about the time I got robbed?"

Again everybody got to thinking when Poppi spoke up, "Shit that's hard to say since that lil nigga be round here so much, it's hard to say when he was round but I know I ain't seen'im since you got robbed. Why?" "I think he had something to do with me getting robbed." "How you figure that?" Dre asked. "Let's just say I got some reliable info. Do ya'll know if he hang with anybody name Black something and Sim or Simmy?" Gamal asked.

"Yeah I think his right hand man name is Black Pete," Dre replied. "And don't them niggas live in Fairfield?" "Yeah," Dre said again. "Why da fuck this lil nigga wanna rob me? All he had to do was come holla at a nigga, I would've done what I could for'im." "So what you go do nigga?" Chris spoke up and asked "I mean now you know who it was, how we go get them lil niggas back?"

"I don't know yet, but all three of they asses go pay, they wanna rob me in front my house, fuck that somebody's ass gotta pay," Gamal stated. "I feel that," Poppi said "but what about dem people coming up in Chantel's house the other day saying they had a complaint, but most importantly a confidential informant?" "Do ya'll really believe there was a confidential informant?" Danielle asked. "Hell yeah I do" Gamal said "cause if not, they would've tried to do a stake out first, but they acted like they knew what they were looking for."

"So that means it's two snitches we have to worry about?" Chris asked. "Nah, I don't think so," Dre said "I think the part about a complaint was a lie they told to try and throw us off, to make us think somebody was complaining against us. But I do believe they got a snitch, how else would they know to hit Chantel's house? We don't really do nothing out of there." "That's the truth," Poppi said "So who the hell we been dealing with from there?" "There's Sharon that always spends at least $50, Danny that comes every Tuesday and Thursday, Sarah with the El Dog, and Filmore Dean," they all put in.

"So out of all them, who ya'll think it could be?" Gamal asked. Nobody said anything. "Well I know what we go do, we go change up the way we do things until we find out who it is," Gamal asserted.

Northside:

Fatty walked in his house and went upstairs, as he was closing his room door Ms. Fox came out the bathroom, "Fatty I want to talk to you." "Aight," Fatty responded. "Ain't no aight boy, I want to talk now, so bring your ass out that room and meet me downstairs ." "Okay Ma." Ms. Fox then went in Sassy's room and told her to get her ass downstairs asap; Cheeks, Shaun, and Te-Mundre were already downstairs Ms. Fox had sent them to the store earlier and they were just getting back. Ms. Fox then made her way downstairs to where all her kids were, she called them all into the living room and made them all sit down.

She stood and looked at them, her kids, her babies. She wasn't stupid she knew what her kids did, but she also understood that times were hard and in their own way they all helped out with the bills and with each other. Although she knew what they did, that didn't mean she approved of it, there was her oldest Fatty 25, Te-Mundre 22, Cheeks 21 Shaun 19 and her baby girl Sassy 17. She knew that her boys wouldn't let their sister do anything illegal especially Fatty, but she also knew Sassy had just as much going on in the street as her brothers.

"Let me start by saying I know Cheeks and Shaun you were with Laverne last night, so right now I'm not talking to you. But Fatty and Te-Mundre I want to know where ya'll were last night." "For what Ma?" Fatty asked. "Boy I'm asking the questions here but I'ma tell you anyway. After our talk yesterday I saw the 11'O clock news and saw about the shootings down on Poe St. and over Southside.

I ain't stupid, I know what you told me Fatty and I also know Marquell called you yesterday. Then you got off the phone asking bout your brothers, so I want to know straight up if ya'll had anything to do with it? And if not where were you at?"

"Ma" Te-Mundre began "you know where I was at, I called and told you, me and Te-Te went to the movies then I stayed over there. I just happen to wake up early and decided to come home."

"You right baby I just had to check and make sure, now Mr. Fatty where were you and I want the truth." "Ma here go the ticket stubs to the game I told you I was going to, then after that I went over Sherry's house. I swear Ma I had nothing to do with those shootings." "Uh Huh, if you didn't, then you know something about it. What was that phone call from Marquell about?" "I told you he called to see if we were going to the game," Fatty said.

"I dun told ya'll asses bout them streets, Fatty if you had been with Sherry in the first place them boys down that street wouldn't have gotten shot. So what now? I suppose the police and the Poe St. niggas go think ya'll had something to do with what happened last night." "Naw Ma I got proof where I was, plus Coach Arskins can vouch for that, I talked to him last night. As for the Poe St. niggas they'll find out it wasn't us, you know the streets talk and even if they do think it was us, they can get it any time they want it," Fatty said with emphasis.

"Boy shut your damn mouth you want to go to jail or worse, I'ont know why ya'll don't go somewhere and get a damn job anyway." "Aw Ma" they all said in unison. "Aw Ma nothing, I ain't raising no damn crime family who the hell ya'll think ya'll is. All of you going to get yourselves together I mean that, Sassy that goes for your ass too, now get your ass in there and cook us some breakfast. The rest of ya'll get the hell out my face until breakfast is ready.

All four boys stood and went on the front porch. Fatty nodded for Shaun to go see where their mother was, since they were kids this had been a signal they used to communicate without talking. Shaun came back and said that Ms. Fox went upstairs and was ironing clothes. "Good" Fatty said. Then he got down to business.

"That was Marquell and nem that hit Poe St. last night and Cheeks how come you ain't tell nobody what Davon told you?" "Man with everything going on I thought I had, damn my bad bros," Cheeks said to his brothers. "That sound good, but ya'll niggas gotta start being more on point," Fatty stated. "Now what's this I hear bout ya'll getting shot at on Mechanicsville?" "Damn nigga you find out everything don't you?" Cheeks asked. " What da fuck you think, ya'll my brothers I'm supposed to know, now start talking."

"We was at McDonald's bruh," Te-Mundre started and he proceeded to tell Fatty everything that happened. "So ya'll know who it was?" Fatty asked. "We think it was Y.K. and Rel from Hilltop," Cheeks said. "Why is that?" "Cause you know I beat the hell out Rel in da afta hours spot over da south," Shaun said. "So how ya'll planning on handling it?" Fatty wanted to know.

"We go bust they ass," Cheeks said. "When?" Fatty asked, he wanted to see what they had learned. " "Soon's we see'em," Te-Mundre said. "Nah uh," Fatty said "Ya'll go wait at least til we hear they beefing again, then we go hit'em, that way they'll think it was whoever they was beefing with and not us. Now check this, ya'll know Curser up there in the Mexican store?" Everybody nodded their heads, "Well I'm supposed to meet him today at the store bout 5:30."

"For what?" Shaun asked. "Business, I know he wants to do some, I just don't know on what level yet." "You want one of us to go with you?" Cheeks asked. "Nah, I be aight." "We all go be here waiting on you just in case shit don't go right," Te-Mundre

said.

Southside:

Over in Clopton Terrace Snooky Boo, Twist, Jaman, Rowland, and Davey D., were sitting in Twist's grandma's Mrs. Erma house discussing the events from the night before. "This shit is unfucking believable, who da fuck was dem niggas last night?" Snooky Boo asked. At 20 years old, standing 5'2" she went just as hard as any nigga, her oldest brother Toine B who had 10 years in the Feds made sure of that. Roland her older brother by a year spoke up.

"I'ont know, but that shit look funny as hell, ain't nobody from round here get to beefing with nobody did it?" Everybody shook their heads 'no' as they all looked at each other. 'So who we know that's beefing round this way?" Snooky Boo asked. "Ya'll know Tyshon from Afton got killed the other week and Blip and Keon nem got hit too," Jaman said. "Yeah, but by who?" Davey D. asked.

"From what I hear it was supposed to be some niggas from Chicago Ave., but then word in the street was we supposed to had something to do with it," Twist said. "And where you hear this at?" Snooky Boo asked. "From my cousin Sonya, you know she fuck with that nigga Dan Johnson from Chicago Ave. He told her to stay away from Afton awhile cause they was beefing with'em and this was after Blip and nem got shot," Twist said. "Well who put the word out that it was somebody from here?" Roland wondered.

"Who knows, but if that's what's floating around then it more than likely was them LBC niggas, ain't they from Afton?" Jaman said. "Who da fuck cares? They came shooting at us, plus a bullet went inside Mrs. Crayton's house. We go handle this shit tonight," Snooky stated and everybody knew she meant it....

Over in Afton Lil Ron-Ron , Lil James, Lil Big Head, Lil K.O. and Lil Dread were sitting in Lil Dread's house. "Cuz, I can't believe a bitch came up and started shooting," Lil K.O. said. "Ya'll sure it was a bitch that started shooting back?" Big Head asked. "Yeah nigga and that bitch knew how to handle a gun," Lil Ron-Ron said "Shit I told you we had to run cause the bitch was getting close to hitting one of us." 'Yall know a bullet went in a old lady house, it ain't hit nobody though, but the police and the community mad as hell, therefore we should wait at least a week before we hit dem niggas on Chicago Ave," Ron-Ron said.

Chapter-8 East End:

P.J. and Do-Do were at Fairfield Commons Mall looking for a birthday gift for P.J."s seven year old niece Lil Mama; Do-Do spotted a Baby Phat outfit and called P.J. over to look at it. "Nigga that shit look to grown for Lil Mama." "How you figure that?" Do-Do asked. "Look at it, it look like something my sister would wear just smaller," P.J. said.

"Let's ask shawdy behind the counter," Do-Do said. "Aight" "S'cuse me S'cuse me" "Yes" "Could you step over here and help us decide on something please?" Do-Do asked. "I'll be there in a minute," the clerk replied. Do-Do and P.J. continued to go back and forth over the outfit as the clerk walked up; when they turned around they both stopped talking and was like 'Damn!" Simply put shawdy was 'BAD' with a capital B; she stood about 5'4" 135 lbs. ass for days, caramel complexion with long silky wavy black hair and perfect even white teeth.

"Damn, do I look that bad?" she joked. "Huh" "Oh nah nah," they both answered. "Don't take this the wrong way, but if

I knew you looked that good I would've came over to you and asked for your number cause I want you and I mean I want'chu all to myself," P.J. said. All she could do was giggle and say "Oh really." "Yeah really," P.J. said. "So what's your name?"

"Shantrice but everybody calls me Tricey," she stated while looking at P.J. "Aight Tricey, we tryna find something for his seven year old niece's birthday. I picked out this Baby Phat outfit but he says it's too grown, wha'chu think?" Do-Do asked. "I don't think it's too grown, I think it says I'm a fly lil lady," Tricey said. Right then P.J. knew he had to have her. "That's the problem now," P.J. says "she thinks she's too fly and too damn grown."

"Awww gotta protect your baby girl ain't that sweet, I wish I had somebody to protect me," Tricey said. "Shit damn right I'ma protect my Lil Mama and you too, but who's gonna protect you from me?" P.J. asked. "Who said I need protection from you?" "I did, tell you what, we go look around some more that'll give you time to think about it and write your number down, I'll get it when I pay for this," P.J. said. "Aight," she said.

Unbeknownst to either one of them, Tricey's boyfriend Teco was standing in the mall with three of his boys watching what was going on. Tricey got back to the counter and went to write her number down, when she turned around there was Teco and his nigga Delwin standing there. "What the fuck you doing Tricey?" Teco asked. "What the fuck it look like, I'm working." "Naw I saw how you and that lame ass nigga was looking at each other and what's that you wrote down?"

"If you must know, it's his niece's size so we can order her a Rocawear outfit for her birthday." "Lemme see it." "No" "Lemme see it Tricey, I'm not playing," Teco threatened. "Why do I have to show it to you, it's for his seven year old niece, you don't need to see it." Soon as Teco said "I don't give a fuck if its his mama's bra size, I want to see it now." P.J. said, "whose mama's bra size" from behind them.

He and Do-Do had already peeped the scene and guessed correctly that the other two niggas in the hallway were with Teco and Delwin. Not that they cared, they both were strapped although the guns were in the car. "Nigga I ain't talking to you, I'm talking to my woman," Teco sneered feeling bold because he figured they had P.J. and Do-Do out numbered. "Yeah but you talking about me, so I ask you again whose mama bra size you talking bout?"

"Nigga fuck you how bout that," Teco said. "Yeah what the fuck ever, Ms. Tricey can you ring this up and I'll be taking that paper, ain't no need for this nigga to be looking at it," P.J. said. "Aight," Tricey said laughing to herself. As they walked away from the counter Do-Do told Teco "you just got fucked decent." "What da fuck he mean by that?" Delwin asked Teco.

"Yeah what he mean Tricey?" Teco asked her. "How the hell I know, if you want to know why don't you ask him what he meant." Teco always trying to show off said "come on Delwin," and Delwin always looking for a fight, was down. Although they were from Newbridge they weren't used to fighting everyday unlike P.J. and Do-Do who were from the city. Walking thru the mall Do-Do looked behind them to find Teco and all three of his boys following them, "Man I'ma knock one of these soft ass county niggas out if they start talking shit," he said.

"You take two and I take two," P.J. said. "Aight" "Ey yo fuck you mean I just got fucked?" Teco asked "Nigga I know you hear me talking to you." P.J. and Do-Do kept walking. "Oh now ya'll wanna act like some pussies cause ain't no bitch here to impress," Teco continued feeling bold. Bronco the biggest of the four man crew said "fuck that I bet I can beat both they asses by myself." Getting to his Cutlass P.J. opened the door and put his niece's outfit inside, Do-Do had already turned to face the group.

"Now, who you calling a pussy nigga?" Do-Do asked. "I'm talki-bop-P.J. hit Teco in the mouth 'bop bop bop,' he hit'em with a three piece and Teco was down. 'Smack'- Do-Do opened hand smacked Bronco 'buup buup crack- two to the body and a uppercut to his nose and Bronco was down. Delwin and Zigi seeing their boys get their asses whipped so thoroughly wanted no parts of P.J. and Do-Do, they started backing up at the same time. "Who da pussy now?" P.J. asked Teco who had blood running out his mouth and couldn't answer.

'Smack' P.J. smacked the shit out him and asked again "who da pussy now?" "I'm the pussy." "Like I said you just got fucked," Do-Do said as he and P.J. got in the car and pulled off....

Over in Whitcomb Ct. Stan and Tre were talking "Yo son, I know you and your homies been missing money lately," Tre said to Stan. "How you come to that conclusion?" "Easy nigga, you figure we flattin a onion to two onions a day, plus damn near a q.p. of weed a day, can't nobody be making no serious money on the flat foot tip. Maybe selling weight, but not flat footin, not to mention the 'x' pills got these young niggas going crazy son." "We still eating nigga, ya'll up top niggas ain't go stop our cash flow," Stan replied.

"I hear ya, but yo check it nigga why don't you and your crew come get down with us, the prices'll be cheaper than what ya'll paying already." "How you figure that?" "Yall paying what 11-1,200 a onion, which mean 275-300 a quarter, we'll give it ya'll for a 'g', which is 250 a quarter," Tre stated. "Nigga that ain't no muthafucking deal, shit we already paying 250, you betta come betta than that." "Yo son I told what I could do, now I may be able to swing 975 or 950 at best."

"Naw shawty you go head and keep yo shit we be aight, I might holla for some smoke though, what I get for a dub?" "For you fam 6 grams." "Aight that's a bet." "One more thing son, what's up wit you and your niggas joining the set?" Tre asked. "What set you talking bout?" Stan asked although he already knew what Tre was talking about. "You know what set I'm talking bout, I'm talking bout that blood blood nigga."

"I told you before we don't do that color shit here in Da 'R'," Stan said. "We already got a few of your homies go join up." "Them niggas know they go have to get the fuck outta Whitcomb, cause that means they turned their back on Whitcomb," Stan said calmly. "You do know that means ya'll will be starting a war with us once they join don't you," Tre stated. "It is what it is shawty?" Stan responded.

"So that's how you feel?" Tre wanted to know. "I mean them da rules of my city and real niggas from the streets know that, now give me my weed so I can bounce."

RCJ-Tier F2:

Belvin from Q St. was on the phone talking to his mother telling her to call his lawyer and make sure an appeal had been filed for his five year sentence for robbery. "Hold on Ma I thought I had the lawyers card, let me run to the bunk and get it." While Belvin was at his bunk, Deshaun from Woodcroft walked up and hung the phone up,then started dialing. Walking back up Belvin asked Deshaun "why he hung up on his mother?" Deshaun said " he didn't know anybody was on the phone and handed Belvin back the phone.

Belvin mad because Deshaun hung up in his mother's face took the phone and 'plap' smashed Deshaun across the bridge of his nose. He then proceeded to pummel him to the ground with the phone. Officer Jackson was coming up the stairs from F1when he saw what was going on and called for immediate backup. When Capt. Olson, Lt. Parham, Sgt. Maynor, Officer Dickens, and Officer Bailey arrived they found Deshaun on the floor in a crumpled mess bleeding from his eyes, nose, and mouth where he had two teeth knocked out.

Capt. Olson asked Jackson who did it and Jackson pointed to Belvin, the other officers grabbed him and escorted him off the tier to C building which was the hole. As for Deshaun, they had to call medical to come see about him and take him out on a stretcher. "Next fight in here, ya'll going on full restriction I mean that" Capt. Olson said "only reason ya'll not going now is because we got the ones who were fighting." Then all the officers walked out.

HCJ-Dayroom 28:

"Darrell Jenkins Darrell Jenkins," Officer Snell called out. "Yeah" Darrell answered. "You gotta go to classification." "Aight" Darrell put his jail uniform on and headed to classification, on his way down he saw Chazz from Delmont going to visit.

"What's happening Chazz?" "Shit going to visit, da girl came to see a nigga. What's up wit'chu?" "Going to classification." "You going home today?" "Naw I got another month." "Shit I got 12 months for driving," Chazz said. "What dayroom you in?" Chazz asked him. "28" Darrell replied.

"I'ma see if I can get moved over there today." "Do that," Darrell said. "Jenkins where you going?" Officer Felton asked.

"Classification" "Well let's get there then."

Once in classification, Mrs. Jasper who was a tall thick Puerto Rican mixed with Italian, with an hourglass figure, an ass that would put Trina and Lisa Raye to shame and who could've easily been voted one of the ten most beautiful people in the world. Called him in to her office. "Mr. Jenkins have a seat, you go home when Mr. Jenkins?" "In a month" "Well today may be your lucky day," Ms. Jasper replied. "What make you say that?"

She turned around to face him and said "you go home Monday so we doing your release plan today." Darrell thinking she was joking, said "yeah right" " You don't believe me? Come here and look." Darrell stood up and went to her desk, she pulled his name up in the computer and turned back to face him. When she turned around she was staring directly at his dick print, becoming startled she jumped and said "Oh my" chuckling to herself.

Turning back to the computer she pointed to the screen, "That's your old release date and here's your new one after DOC calculated your time." Knowing everyone in classification was gone to lunch Ms. Jasper couldn't help thinking about Darrell's dick print,which made her juices start flowing and made her nipples hard. When she turned back to face him her face was flustered, he could see it as well as how hard her nipples were. She looked around, cleared her throat and asked "is that really all you?"

Darrell not believing he heard her right, asked her what she said and she repeated it again. Darrell answered "Wha'chu think?" "Let me see," she countered. Darrell not wanting to get tricked up said "Naw shawd, if you wanna see it, you gotta pull it out yourself." Mrs. Jasper quickly reached up grabbed his waistband reached inside his uniform pants and boxers, grabbed his dick and released it.

As soon as she saw it her eyes grew wide, she couldn't believe its thickness and girth. She quickly ran her hand up and down its length before inserting it in her mouth, she had problems at first because she'd never had a dick that big in her mouth before. Darrell couldn't believe his luck, he hadn't beat his dick in three months so he knew it was only a matter of time before he bust off. Mrs. Jasper pulled his dick out her mouth and said "hurry up." When she reinserted it back in her mouth she applied a little more pressure with her sucking and before Darrell knew what was happening he was gushing down her throat.

To his disbelief she swallowed it all, he could hardly keep his balance, he grabbed her head and held onto the edge of her desk. He was so weak all he could do was tuck himself back in and sit down. Mrs. Jasper went rinsed her mouth out, came back and acted as if nothing had happened, "Ok Mr. Jenkins, it says here you'll be released to your mother's house in Richmond, is that true?" "Yeah" "Ok you're to report to District 1 probation and parole office on 17th St within 72 hours of your release, I just need your signature right here," she said handing him some papers.

After he signed the papers, Mrs. Jasper also signed them, then she wrote something on a separate sheet of paper and handed him everything, wished him good luck and told him to make sure he put the papers somewhere safe. As Darrell left out he looked at the papers and saw that she had wrote her phone number and address on the paper along with two words 'call me.' Because of the time he had to go thru the visitation room. As he was going thru, he passed Chazz sitting at a booth talking to his girl, 'hold up' he backed up, that was Jakeela his main man Jeff's baby mama. What the fuck was she doing down here and not seeing Jeff, wait a minute Chazz did say his girl was coming down.

'Oh shit wait til I get back and tell Jeff, Darrell thought to himself; Chazz knew that Jakeela was Jeff's girl, so he essentially was violating. Arriving back in the dayroom he told Jeff about his release date and about seeing Chazz going to visit. Then he told him who came to visit Chazz. At first Jeff thought he was joking, "Man go head with that shit, stop playing with me nigga." "Shawdy I wouldn't play like that cuz, I know how crazy your dumb ass is over that girl, hell you would shoot me behind her and me-n-you is closer than brothers," Darrell said. "Did they see you?" "Nah they was too busy being into each other to notice me."

"You said Chazz trying to come over here." "Yep" "That's what's up, I ain't go say nothing bout Chazz when I call her, I'ma wait to see what he got to say first, nigga musta forgot me and you like brothers," Jeff said. " I guess he figured I wouldn't see them, but didn't she come visit you this week already?" Darrell asked. "Yeah" Jeff answered. "So they both figured you wouldn't find out." "Well they was wrong, now won't they," Jeff said. "That they was my nigga, that they was."

Chapter 9- West End:

Dets. James Smithers and Donald Long were sitting in Capt. Spurlock's office, "So gentlemen what do we have so far on this supposedly drug house you told me about." "Well Cap as you know this info we received turned out to be bogus, so we gave our CI until today to have something for us,"

Det. Long said. "And do you really think he'll have something for you?" "Not really but he has been reliable in the past," Det. Smithers answered. "Let's say for the sake of saying he don't bring you nothing, do we have anything we can use for leverage against him?"

"Actually Captn we told him if he didn't have some useful information for us that he would have to wear a wire while making a controlled buy," Smithers stated. "And what was his response?" "You could see this made him uncomfortable, in fact his words were 'Snitching I don't mind, but I'm not wearing a wire," Det. Long said. "Well ya'll need to come up with something and fast, Chief Morrison is on all the Captains backs to come up with some answers to the recent shootings that've been taking place in the city," Capt. Spurlock stated. "Aight Captn we'll get on it and go look for Filmore later this evening or sometime tomorrow," Smithers said.

With that the two detectives left out. "So genius what's our next move?" Det. Long asked his partner. "The way I see it, today's Friday and Friday typically is the busiest day of the week for most street corner hustlas. We can either (a) wait til tomorrow and see what Filmore has for us or (b) we can ride out later tonight and see what's going on for ourselves while also looking for Filmore," Det Smithers said.

North Side:

Never one to meet anybody at the time he's supposed to; Fatty showed up at the Mexican store at 5:47 and found Curser outside smoking a cigarette. "What's happening Curser?" "You late that's not what's happening," Curser responded. "Man, look I was doing something for Ma Dukes, so now what? I guess you don't wanna talk." "Lemme say this I don't like to wait for nobody unnerstand, that's the first rule of doing business with me, unnerstood."

Áight man damn, you got your ways and I got mine, now you still wanna talk business or what?" Fatty asked. "Hold on a minute," Curser said. He then walked inside the store to let his sister know he would be back in a few, when he came back out he told Fatty to "come take a ride with me." They walked around to the back of the store to a burgundy and gold Infinity Qx 56 truck, Fatty was impressed although he didn't let on that he was.

Once in the truck and on their way Curser started talking again "I see you and your brothers come in the store and buy the same thing most of the time." "What would that be?" "Sandwich bags and razor blades." "So" "So nothing, I know what ya'll up to , I just don't know what you selling." "Look shawdy I don't know what da hell you talking about, we ain't selling shit, my mother makes us sandwiches and we use razor blades to shave our faces.

"I like that answer I really do, at least I know you ain't no snitch," Curser said. "Hell nah I ain't no goddamn snitch, all snitches should have their heads blown off with their tongues cut out," Fatty stated emphatically. He said it with so much conviction that Curser knew he meant it and respected him even more for it. "Check this amigo, open that console hit play for the CD player, then reach down grab the CD case and hand it to me," Curser said. Fatty did as he was told, when he came out with the CD case Curser told him to open it and hand him 'Yo Gotti's Cocaine Music 4' CD.

When Fatty opened the case all he saw was something white wrapped in plastic, he wasn't sure but he thought he was looking at a whole brick (kilo) of cocaine. Not knowing what Curser was up to Fatty said "Maan what da fuck?" To which Curser asked "you alright? I mean you do know what that shit is don't you?" "Yeah nigga I'm cool, but what da fuck kind of games you playing? Showing me a whole key and shit."

"Listen man, wasn't no sense in beating around the bush asking too many questions, I just decided to let you know what kinda business I'm talking and what level playing field I'm on. That alright with you? Damn. I mean ya'll do be slinging coke right or wrong?" Curser stated. "Yeah we sling flav but not this much flav," Fatty replied looking at the brick in his lap. "I know ya'll not on this level, I just wanted you to see what level I'm on, now are you trying to get down or what?"

"Hell yeah I'm tryna get down, but I don't take no fronts from nobody, I pay my way that's the only way I'll do business with you or anybody else for that matter," Fatty said. "Okay Amigo I respect that, now tell me what you paying for an ounce." "We pay bout a 'g' a ounce." "And how much ya'll copping?" "Bout two and a quarter." "What ya'll paying for that?" "Bout two g's." "How bout I give it to you for 750 an ounce and four and half for 2,800,?" Curser asked. "Man that would be the move," Fatty replied."

"So when you want to start doing business?" Curser asked. Fatty had to think about that cause he and his brothers still had some work to get rid of, plus they had that problem over Hilltop to take care of. Not to mention talking to Marquell. "Lemme get rid of what I got left, talk to my brothers and I'll get back to you on Sunday," Fatty said

"Aight Amigo, now let me ask you this, you smoke weed?" "Nigga as many Dutch's I buy out your store, you go ask me some shit like that." "Open the glove compartment hit the red button, grab that bag of real Jamaican ganja, dem Dutch's and roll up," Curser said. "Damn you got buttons and compartments all thru this bitch don't you?" Fatty asked him.

"Never can be too careful Amigo, lemme ask you one more question." "Go head." "How many brothers you got?" "Five and one sister," stated Fatty including Marquell in his count. "Damn a whole starting five, plus one off the bench," Curser stated. "That's fo damn sho...."

Shaun, Te- Mundre, and Sassy were at Sam's Kitchen on Brookland Park Blvd. Sassy was standing at the window talking to Sam while Shaun and Te-Mundre were trying to figure out what to order, when Sonya and Charmaine walked in. Charmaine who worked in Sam's husband Jock beauty salon spoke to Sam, Sonya not knowing anybody spoke to no one in particular and stepped up to look the menu over. While Sonya was looking the menu over Shaun and Te-Mundre were looking her over.

"Bruh its sumpin real familiar about shawdy right there," Shaun said. "Nigga get da fuck outta here, er'body look familiar to you," Te-Mundre said. "Watch this nigga," Shaun said as he stepped to Sonya. "What's up Ms. Lady?" Sonya turned to look at him and spoke back, "Hey how you doing?" "Actually not too well."

"Why is that?" Sonya inquired although she could care less. "Cause I was telling my brother you look familiar I just don't know where from." "Naw boo I think you got me confused with somebody cause I ain't even from this side of town," Sonya said with attitude. Sassy who had stepped to the window to speak with Charmaine about Charmaine doing her hair turned around to see who this bitch was that was coming off on her brother. Just then Charmaine said "Oh shit Sonya they gettin' ready tow your car," this made everybody go to the window and look.

Sonya and Charmaine stepped outside to see what was going on. "I told you dat bitch looked familiar, dat's the bitch that was driving that AC that day them niggas shot at us at Micky D's," Shaun said. "You sho bout that bruh?" Te-Mundre asked. "Yea mafucka I wouldn't forget nut'in bout that day, especially potential witnesses, but since it ain't been no cops sniffing us out I guess her and that other bitch kept their mouths shut."

After Sonya paid the tow truck driver not to tow her car, went and parked it around the corner, her and Charmaine re-entered the restaurant with Sonya cursing up a storm. Sonya placed her order and Shaun made his move again, "Check this Miss Lady, I told you you looked familiar." "And just how do you figure that?" "Cause didn't I give you fifty dollars?" "Nigga you got me fucked up, you ain't neva give me no fifty dollars sorry wrong bitch," Sonya snapped.

"Oh really" Shaun said smiling "So you saying that won't you at McDonald's on Mechanicsville that day them niggas got to shooting at us." Soon as he said that recognition jumped in Sonya's eyes, "Oh my god that was you that jumped in my car wasn't it?" "And you know this," Shaun said beaming. "You gotta excuse me for not recognizing you, but under the circumstances I'm sure you understand," Sonya replied. "That's aight, but you always gotta be aware of your surroundings and the people in them, now since we didn't get a chance to formally meet, my name's Shaun."

"Sonya" "Now that's better, I hope we didn't scare ya'll too much at Micky D's," Shaun said. "Naw, but me and my sister was wondering if ya'll were alright," Sonya answered. "Yeah we all good, but I'll be even better if we exchanged numbers." "You didn't even ask if I had a man." "That's because the first time I saw you, you were with your girl and this time you're with Charmaine plus you giving a nigga some conversation. So I figured you either ain't got no man or he fucking up big time, either way good for me."

"Actually I do have a man, no let me rephrase that, I have a little boy that's wants to be a man, so yeah we can exchange numbers and what about your girl?" "Again when we met, I was with my two brothers, this time I'm with one of my brothers and my sister." "Here Sassy ya'lls food ready," Sam said "and take your brothers up out here, keep trying to pick up my customers."

East End:

Y.K. and Jigaloo were sitting downstairs in Rel's sister Jewel's who Jigaloo happened to be fucking apartment cutting and bagging up coke. Rel had Stephanie upstairs with her legs in the air trying his best to kill her pussy, he knew Stephanie thought she was playing him, but he didn't care she wasn't his main girl. Truth was she had some bum ass head and was a certified freak, last time they had fucked she'd taken his dick straight out her pussy and let him cum all in her mouth. He hit her off real decent with $500 so she could pay her light bill and still have money left over for herself.

After pulling out and cumming all over her titties he got up went to the bathroom and washed up, when he came out he told her he was going downstairs to smoke a blunt and she could come down after washing up. "Got damn nigga you was moving furniture up there won't you?" Jigaloo said to Rel as he came into the kitchen. "Fuck you mafucka, ya'll niggas ain't done yet, damn it don't take nobody 45 minutes to cut up a quarter ounce a piece, shit a nigga tryna smoke a blunt," Rel said. "Nigga the blunt rolled all's you gotta do is spark it," Y.K. answered.

After sparking the blunt Rel asked "Ya'll niggas still ain't heard nothing bout da other day at McDonald's?" "Fuck wrong wit'chu nigga, you know betta than to be talking bout that shit wit that bitch in da house," Jigaloo snapped. "Fuck her, she upstairs in the bathroom, besides shawdy from da West End she don't know that pussy ass nigga Shaun from Northside and even if she do know him, she don't know it was us that shot at him that day," Rel said. In actuality Stephanie was coming down the steps and heard everything that was said. She went back upstairs in the bathroom, made some noise like she was just finishing up, went back in the room, then came downstairs making noise so they could hear her.

"Rel I'm ready to leave now, I'll hit you up a lil later, you got a lil sumpn sumpn for me?" "You know it," Rel responded handing her $200. Soon as she got outside in her car and pulled off she called Danielle "What's up bitch?" Danielle answered. "I know who shot at your cousins a couple of weeks ago, that's what's up," Stephanie countered. "You what?"

"You heard me, I know who shot at your cousins," Stephanie said again. "Who?" "That nigga Rel and his boys Y.K. and Jigaloo." "How you know?" asked Danielle not sure if she should believe Stephanie. "Cause I just left from over Rel's sister house getting my fuck on, and over heard them downstairs talking about it. Rel asked' em if they heard anything about what happened at McDonald's and one of them cursed him out saying not to be talking bout that while I was there."

"Rel said I was from the West End and that I didn't know Shaun and nem from the Northside. Ha! Little did he know," Stephanie said. "Thanks girl I'ma make sure my cousins know about this, but make sure Rel don't know you heard them talking," Danielle told Stephanie. "Never that," Stephanie replied "I'll see you when I get to that side of town." "Aight...."

Over in Whitcomb Ct. Stan was relating his conversation with Tre to Kalil, Reece, and Matt. "So you tryna tell me they got some niggas from round here buying weight from them and ready to rep that color shit?" asked Kalil. "That's what I'm telling you nigga," Stan replied. "Fuck that we gotta do sumpin bout dem niggas, fuck they think they is," Matt said. While discussing the problems with the New York Boys they walked thru the cut to Bethel St. where they saw Bayshon get out the car with Ski and Turk.

"Aight son, hit us up when that's all gone and tell that bitch Nicole I said what's up, holla at a nigga," Ski said. "No doubt," Bayshon replied. As both Ski and Turk let off the Blood call "Blllack blllack," Bayshon heading towards the cut never saw Stan and the crew until he was right up on them. "What's up nigga?" Reece asked catching Bayshon off guard. "Shit my nigga, what's up?" answered Bayshon.

"You tell me, I see you kicking it with the New York Boys got them asking bout Nicole and shit, plus you buying weight from them too," said Reece. "What? You thinking bout banging that color shit, cause if you is, you know you gotta get the fuck from around here," Matt spoke up. "Says who?" challenged Bayshon. "Says this mafucka," replied Kalil pulling out his black 9 mm and smacking Bayshon cross the face, then he stuck the gun up in Bayshon's eye and told him to "give up what he got from the New York Boyz." "Man, I owe them $175 for this," Bayshon said.

"You let them niggas charge you 175 for a pool ball, you stupid mafucka I should shoot you just for G.P. letting them out of town niggas pimp you like that," Kalil snapped. "Who else supposed to be getting down with them niggas?" asked Stan. "I'ont know but they say it's bout five more people round here," replied Bayshon. "Nigga I'ma let you keep the pack but you betta not pay them niggas shit, you hear me, matter fact stop fucking with'em altogether. Next time you might not live to talk about it, you got that."

"Yeah Kalil" "And you betta not tell'em niggas what we

talked about, got that." "I said yeah Kalil I understand man, damn." "Good now get the fuck away from here," Reece told him. "Fuck waiting around I say we run up in Cassidy's now and hit them niggas for whatevea they got," Reece said. "With no masks or gloves? Nigga you crazy, plus they know Stan, how da fuck we supposed to pull that off?" Matt said.

"For one, Stan not go be with us and since they grinding out Cassidy's that means they answer the door for anybody, we either knock on the door and when they answer, run up in there. Or we can catch one of'em outside and run up on'em," Reece said. "I say we lay on'em and when one come out we run down on'em, walk'em back in da house, jack'em and leave'em duct taped. But it's gotta be done when Cassidy's at work," Reece said.

"Nah fuck that, let's go knock on the door and run up in there. Matt you go to the door, when they open it, stick your gun in they face, we go be right behind you. Stan go stay on the outside and keep watch out," Kalil said. "That's a bet, but we gotta go get the duct tape from my house," Matt said. After retrieving the duct tape and checking their guns, the four man crew made their way back over to Bethel St.

Kalil and Reece posted up beside the building while Matt went to the door and knocked. Cap came to the door, opened it and asked Matt what he wanted. Matt said that Junkie Stacie told him he could get a gram for $45 over there." "Who you say told you that?" "Stacie, you know short phat ass brown skin Stacie," Matt lied. Cap being greedy fell right into the trap and opened the screen door at which time Matt pulled his .40 cal from his back pocket and stuck it in Cap's face.

Reece and Kalil were right behind him as he pushed Cap back up in the apt., Reece covered Cap's mouth with his hand

and allowed Matt to tie a blue bandanna similar to the ones they were wearing around his face. They turned Cap around and walked him up the stairs into the living room where they caught Tre, Ski, and Turk all off guard. "What's up my niggas?" Matt said. "Yo what the fuck son?" Turk said. "Ain't no what the fuck, what it look like nigga?" Reece said.

"Fuck ya'll niggas thought, ya'll was just go set up shop and recruit in our hood, this Whitcomb Court not Blood Court mafuckas. Now I want everybody hands up where we can see'em, first wrong move and your homeboy here catches one," Matt said. The three N.Y. Boyz did as they were told, none of them wanted to jeopardize their brother's life. "Now I'ma say this one time and one time only, first I want to know which one of ya'll is strapped cause I know ya'll not sitting up in this bitch and not strapped," Reece said. "Yo son I got my gat on me," Ski said.

"Aight, who else?" Reece asked. Tre knowing Turk never took his gun off him looked his way which made Kalil say "Nigga if you strapped you betta come up off it, if not I swear to god I'll cap yo mafuckin ass." Ski pulled his gun out and handed it to Matt who was standing the closest to him. Turk kind of hesitated which made Kalil point his .45 at him as he said "Nigga don't matter to me whether you live or die today." Looking in his eyes over top the bandanna Turk knew he had no other choice, so he handed Kalil his gray .45. Reece then turned his attention back to Tre "Where yo gun at?"

"Yo blood do I look like some kind of fool, if I had one on me I would've gave it to you already," Tre said. "Nigga ain't no muthafuckin Blood here, this Dub-C (W.C.) all day err'day," Reece said. "Now I want ya'll niggas to empty yo pockets, turn dem bitches inside out one person at a time starting with you over by da stereo." "Aight you got it Duke," Tre said, pulling out a knot of money and a bag of weed. Matt stepped up and took everything from him then it was Ski's turn, he too had a knot of money, some weed, and what looked to be a couple of 'x' pills.

Again Matt stepped up and took everything. Now it was Turk's turn "Ay playboy don't try nothing stupid, I can see you thinking bout it but don't do it," Reece said. Turk was actually thinking bout bucking, but there was still a gun to Cap's back, so he did as he was told and emptied out his pockets as well. He too had a knot of money, but that was all. After Matt took Turk's money Reece told Cap it was his turn now and to move real slow.

Cap did as he was told and handed Reece everything in his pockets. "This what we go do ya'll follow directions, don't try no funny shit, we'll let ya'll live, but anything funny and we shoot everybody. That I give my word on," Reece said. "We go start by duct taping all ya'll hands together behind your backs."

"Fuck that Duke, ain't nobody duct taping me," Turk said. "Jump then nigga," Kalil said as he turned the .45 on him 'you go be the first one we tape up." Matt pulled out the duct tape walked behind Turk, pulled his arms behind his back and taped his wrists together like they were handcuffed. He then did the same to Cap, Tre, and Ski in that order. "Now one last thing and we'll be on our way, where the work at and don't tell me you don't know what I'm talking bout," Reece said.

"Naw son, ain't no more," Tre said frustrated at what these niggas were doing. "Really, well how bout this," 'fop fop' Reece went upside his head with the gun. Seeing what Reece did Kalil hauled off and 'blop' hit Turk across the jaw with the handle of his gun. Seeing his brothers get hit, Tre spoke up "Aight nigga" "Aight what?" Reece asked. "Look in da kitchen in da last cabinet on the bottom, it's in that last gym bag," Tre said.

Matt went in the kitchen to look, he came back out and said "We hit the jackpot nigga." "What we got?" asked Kalil. "We got some coke, weed, and look like some 'x," Matt said. "Leave the 'x,' "What?" "Nigga I said leave the 'x' we don't need it, we don't sling it and none of us use it, so just leave it, but keep everything else," Kalil said.

"Now put tape on their mouths, take'em in the bedroom and tape their ankles together," Reece said. Tre spoke up "I thought you gave your word." "I did nigga, I ain't say do nothing to ya'll but let this be a lesson don't come in our hood tryna sell nothing and don't be trying to recruit nobody from here to join that color shit. We rep Whitcomb and nothing else. Now in the bedroom, oh and tell that pussy ass nigga Stan since he let ya'll grind out here, his ass gotta pay too, so I hope ya'll been paying his punk ass nice," Reece said. "Let's roll fellas," he said to the others.

Chapter 10-West End:

Filmore Dean was caught between a rock and hard place, he knew he couldn't wear a wire but he also knew he had to have some kind of information for the detectives. They had given him until the end of the week to have something for them. But so far the only thing of significance he had was that Gamal and his crew had switched up the way they handled business. They no longer dealt with anybody at Chantel's house, you had to catch them on the outside and then wait for them to come back with your product. He did hear however, that Gamal had been robbed in front his house some weeks ago and that he didn't know who got him. As Filmore was walking down Lakeview Ave he ran across Duke one of his get high buddies who he'd been running with for years.

"Duke where you headed to nigga?" "Shid tryna find somebody to help me move this air conditioner," Duke answered. "You can't move it by yourself." "Nah mafucka its one of them industrial air conditioners, they getting up at that new grocery store on Meadow." "Where you taking it to?" "I got a nigga live up on Powhatan that buys all that kind of stuff, I just need some help moving it."

"Bet. You know I'll help long as it's a even split," Filmore said. "Nah nigga, being that it's my deal and connect, its go be 60/40. He pay me $150, so that's 90 for me and 60 for you. We go get this straight before we ever get the money, I know your money hungry ass," Duke said. "Aight nigga, 90 for you and 60 for me that beats nothing," Filmore replied.

They went thru the alley where Duke stashed the push cart they were going to use. "How we supposed to get inside the store this time of night?" Filmore wanted to know. "It ain't in the store, it's in the back on a trailer under a tarp, they think cause its pushed so far back won't nobody notice it. But I saw it when I was cutting thru there."

When they got to the back of the store Duke hopped up on the trailer pulled the tarp off and started trying to move the A.C. by hisself. "Nigga you just go stand there or you go help me?" Duke asked Filmore. "I thought you had it dawg, I got you though." With that Filmore jumped on the trailer and began helping Duke, finally they got it on to the trailer.

"Nigga I hope your man's got that guap cause this bitch heavier than a mafucka," Filmore said. "Yeah nigga he got it, I talked to him before I ran into your ass," Duke responded. They were moving thru the alley when they spotted a police car ride by. "How far we gotta go? You see them people just now?" Filmore asked. "Naw I'm blind, shut the fuck up, we go cross the street, go down bout four houses cut thru the abandoned house yard and from there it's bout a three minute walk."

But unbeknownst to the two thieves they had been spotted by the police; "What the hell?" Det. Long asked. "What the fuck you talking bout now?" asked Det. Smithers. "I just saw what looked like somebody pushing a cart down that alley." "Yeah right and what was they pushing a grocery cart?" "I don't know but it was a cart of some kind, turn the car around and let's see," Det. Long answered.

After making a U-turn the detectives saw Filmore and Duke come out the alley. Filmore and Duke couldn't see the oncoming car because of the headlights, so they had no idea it was the police until they were right in their face. "Ain't this a bitch Long, I guess you were right and look who it is Filmore Dean, we was just talking about you." Det. Smithers said. "Who that you got with you Filmore and what ya'll pushing that cart for this time of night," Det. Long asked getting out of the car.

Duke looked from Filmore to the police trying to figure out how they knew Filmore's name and whether or not he should take off and run. Det. Smithers figuring what Duke was thinking told him "don't even think about it, you won't get nowhere and you'll end up down 9th St. with a charge, Filmore here is our friend. Right Filmore? Tell'em. "Now what do we have here?" Det. Long asked as he pulled back the tarp and whistled "whew, well I'll be damned an industrial air conditioner.

Now I wonder where ya'll got this from and furthermore where you taking it to now?" "What's your name?" Det. Smithers asked Duke for he too was now standing outside the car. Before Duke could answer, Det. Long said "I'ma tell you right now we want both your real name and your street name, don't try to lie to us that'll only make matters worse." Duke looked at the two detectives then at Filmore who just dropped his head, with that he answered "O'shea Wright but everybody calls me Duke."

"And how come they call you Duke?" Smithers asked. "Cause growing up I liked the Dukes of Hazzard, I used to always holla like I was one of the Duke Boys, so everybody started calling me Duke." "Ok Duke, well my name is Det. Long and this is my partner Det. Smithers, since we caught ya'll red-handed with this air conditioner that I'm guessing came from that new store on Meadow. I'm hoping you got a good enough excuse for me not to lock yo is record.

Filmore spoke up, "Man we was just moving it down the street that's all, damn." "Moving it where Filmore?" Det. Smithers asked. "We was just taking it to my house," Duke said. "Oh really, here's what I think, I think you were going to sell it for drugs or money, now I'ma give you one more chance to tell the truth," Det. Smithers said. This time when Duke spoke he said "Okay yeah man I had somebody lined up to buy it, damn can't a nigga get his hustle on?"

"Sure" said Det. Long "And since I'm feeling generous tonight I'm thinking bout letting you get your hustle on, but on one condition. I want you and Filmore at the station Monday morning by 11:00 a.m. and you better have some useful information for us or your black asses going straight to lockup looking at ten years or better, understand?" "Yeah we got it," Filmore said but Duke didn't answer all he kept thinking was he wasn't no snitch. Det. Smithers said "You ain't gotta think abut it. Fuck it Long let's lock his ass up now." "Naw hell naw, aight ya'll got a deal," Duke said. "That's good," Det. Long said "and don't forget be at the station by 11:00 a.m. or we coming for you, no questions asked. Duke didn't know what to say, he wasn't a snitch but he also knew he had 17 years over his head. Plus this would be a grand larceny charge, another felony and he already had four felonies on his record.

Southside:

Riding thru Hillside Court just leaving Jaman's aunt Selma's house getting some 512 Diddy's (percocets) to sell. Snooky Boo, Twist and Jaman were on their way back to Clopton Terrace when Snooky said "Ya'll know we go take that ride tonight?" Jaman who was driving asked "You think that's a good idea? To hit so fast when da police is still coming around asking questions." "Shit dat's the bes-oh shit! Lookee what the fuck I see," Snooky Boo said. Coming up in the curve of Rosecrest Ave they saw Lil Dread standing beside a gold Honda Accord and Lil K.O. walking up towards the apartments where some females were standing.

Snooky who was riding in the passenger seat told Jaman "to go round the block," then she looked back at Twist in the backseat and said "you ready to put a cap in these mafuckas?" "That ain't but two of'em, I thought we was go get'em all at the same time," Twist said. She wasn't scared, she just wanted to make sure Snooky knew what the hell she was doing. "So da fuck what? This the best time to hit'em they'll think it's somebody from Hillside," Snooky answered.

"Hold up I know ya'll ain't planning on shooting out my car? Jaman said. "Why not?" countered Snooky "Ain't nobody go notice your car, all they asses go be ducking and running from these baby missles we go be firing at them. Now let's hurry da fuck up before they leave." With that said Snooky cocked her nine and asked Twist "You ready bitch?" as an answer Twist cocked her .380. Coming to the curve again Lil K.O. was walking back to the car that Lil Dread was leaning against.

Next thing anyone hears is 'Blaka blaka Blaka Clak clak clak, gunfire erupting. As Dread was turning around he caught one in the left shoulder and one in his left forearm as he was falling. Lil K.O. saw the two bitches hanging out the car window as he ducked and pulled his 10 mm out his waist and started firing back while running back towards the apartments. But before he could reach the porch he was hit in the right calf muscle, seeing that Jaman hit the gas.

Northside:

Smoke and Lil Q were standing on the corner of Lamb and Crawford Aves talking, "Fuck that shit, I feel what Cheeks said bout da Bridge hitting Poe St. up, but it was us they hit. I'm the one got shot; me, Mel-Mel, and Fat Dom so I figure it should at least be one of us that get back at them," Lil Q. said. "I feel yo pain my nigga, but like Cheeks said the police go be watching us for a while, anything happen round this way and what strip you think go be da hottest. The good thing bout the other night is all us was either at the hospital or da basketball game, so we were accounted for. Shit they was afta Fatty anyway and he handled that shit like a true mobsta nigga, Al Capone, Lucky Luciano, Bumpy Johnson style nigga," Smoke said.

"Mel-Mel go have to wear a shit bag for a while at least shawdy, and they saying Fat Dom may have a bullet lodged inside him for life. Fuck that I gotta get somebody's ass back," Lil Q said. Neither Lil Q nor Smoke saw or heard Cheeks come out the house and stand on the porch two houses from the corner. When he spoke they both jumped and reached for their guns, "Naw nigga wha'chu go do is stand down like I said. I feel your pain too, but my brother working on sumthing big for all us, what you need to do is chill before you fuck up his plans." "Whatever shawdy, again ya'll ain't the ones got shot, I am," Lil Q said angrily.

"Naw but we the ones backing ya'll in beefs and we the ones go be hitting ya'll with that weight soon, so again you need to do like I said and chill," Cheeks said. Lil Q could see that Cheeks was getting mad and everybody knew how that family got when they got mad, so all he said was "Aight nigga, I'ma leave that shit alone for now. But tell Fatty I still wanna strike back at them niggas somehow." "That's a bet," Cheeks said as he walked off....

Fatty and Marquell were standing in front of Ms. Fox's house by Fatty's Cadillac Deville talking bout Poe St. and everything else. "Shawdy thanks for handling that bizness for us, you know I owe you one," Fatty said. "Nigga you don't owe me nothing we's brothers and that's what brothers do, now fuck dem niggas on Poe, what's this bout a connect you was talking bout?" Marquell stated. "That nigga Curser from the Mexican store up on the Blvd., took me on a ride earlier today, he got that shit we been looking for nigga and its cheap," Fatty said.

"How cheap bruh and is it soft or hard?" "I'ont know if it's soft or hard, but I'd assume hard for the prices he talking 750 a ounce and 2800 for a big," Fatty said. "How da fuck you know he got it like that?" asked Marquell. "Cause that nigga told me to open the armrest console, reach inside, hit a button and grab a CD book. When I opened it there was a whole brick inside nigga." "Get da fuck outta here, you for real?"

"C'mon nigga you know I ain't go joke bout nothing like this," Fatty said. "When we go holla at him." "I told'im I had to talk to my brothers and take care of some other business, then I'd be in touch." "What kinda business?" "You know some niggas from Hilltop shot at my brothers at McDonald's on Mechanicsville da other day. I wanna handle that first, but I told him I'd contact him Sunday and let him know when we can start doing business.

As for how much, I say we get a onion first just to see what it's like, I take half and you take half, see if the fiends like it. Then we know whether or not to get a whole big." I'm feeling that, but what's this bout your brothers getting shot at, ya'll niggas beefing with da whole city ain't it." "Naw mafucka we ain't beefing with the whole city, this behind some bullshit too, Shaun beat Rel from Hilltop's ass in da afta hours spot. So dem niggas caught my brothers slipping and dumped on'em, but don't worry my nigga we got this one trust and believe that.

This personal, they shot at my brothers plus you just dumped on them Poe St niggas, you need to chill; But I love you man, you right we is brothers and like I said I owe you." Fatty said. "Aight nigga with that sympathetic shit, I hear you, just take care of business so we can start handling this other business," Marquell said.

Chapter 11-HCJ Dayroom 28:

Chazz walked in the dayroom and looked around because it was Saturday and so early in the morning he didn't think too many people would be up. He was partially right, there were nine people up but one of them was Darrell who was on the phone. "What's up nigga?" Darrell said. Chazz dropped his things and went to dap Darrell up, after they did the handshake backslap Chazz answered "Shit my nigga what cell you in?"

"Eleven, what cell you in?" "Cell 3" Chazz answered. "You in the cell with Maytag and Leon," Darrell said "lemme finish this phone call and I'ma get back to you." "Aight nigga." "Aight baby I'ma see you first thing Monday morning," Darrell said into the phone. "Yeah yeah, like I said I'ma turn shit around on your ass nigga, you know how niggas say feed'em then fuck'em. Well I'ma fuck ya then feed you, naw check that I'ma feed ya while I fuck you."

"So you say," Darrell replied. "Aight boo see you Monday morning and like I said leave that dick alone this weekend so I can drain it first thing Monday morning." "You got it sexy, talk to you later." "Darrell" "Yeah," Darrell answered. "Love you baby." "I love you too my love," Darrell said.

Darrell hung up the phone and walked over to Chazz who was sitting on the table. "How da hell you manage to switch dayrooms shawd?" "Shid I tol'em I was beefing wit one of da ole heads in there and if they didn't move me they couldn't give me a charge if I beat da ole head's ass," Chazz said. "Was you beefing for real?" "Hell naw" Chazz replied "ole head the one told me what to say."

"I'ma knock on your cell door so one of 'em can open the door and I'ma introduce ya'll while you put your things down," Darrell said. Knowing that Jeff said he was going to take a shit then going to sleep, Darrell was hoping Jeff would hear him and Chazz talking and come out the cell. After introducing Chazz to Maytag and Leon, Darrel went and sat on the table when he heard a door buzzing open, looking up he saw Jeff looking down over the railing. "You need to get in the cell?" Jeff hollered down and asked him. "Naw," Darrell replied and gave a slight head movement to indicate for Jeff to come downstairs.

Jeff kinda knowing what was up, came down and asked Darrell "what he wanted?" Just as he got to Darrell, Chazz picked that moment to walk out the cell. "What up nigga?" Jeff spoke. Chazz not knowing Jeff was in that jail was caught off guard, "Oh shit! What up nigga? I ain't know you was locked up." Chazz walked up and he and Jeff dapped each other up.

Darrell jumped right to the subject, "Chazz didn't you tell me your girl was coming to see you yesterday?" "Yeah," Chazz answered not knowing Darrell saw him and Jakeela together. "What yo girl name is?" Darrell asked. "Lanay" "So that's who came up here?" asked Darrell. "Yeah," Chazz lied.

"So you saying that won't Jakeela I saw you talking to?" Chazz was stuck he ain't know what to say, finally he said "Yeah that was her." "So where was Lanay?" Jeff asked. "She had went to the bathroom," Chazz lied again. "So you saying Lanay and Jakeela know each other, they cool like that?"

"Yeah nigga, that's her godsister, fuck you questioning me so much bout my girl for?" Chazz said angrily. "Nigga first off you wailing, Jakeela's godsista name is Marie, second Jakeela's my girl and you know it, that's why you standing here lying in my face. But I'ma give you a chance to explain yourself," Jeff stated. "I ain't gotta explain myself shit, but since you want to know I'ma tell you.

Shawdy pulled up on me at Chicken Box and asked me if I was going to buy her a 'Big Chic' and I was like if I buy you a 'Big Chic' what you go buy me? She said 'First you gotta buy me a 'Big Chic' with a Cherry Coke, then you gotta call me.' I'm like damn I ain't even got your number, so she asked to see my cell phone and when I gave it to her she programed her number in it saying 'now you do.' I walked her to her car and was like ain't this Jeff's car? She said 'naw it was her car and she just let Jeff use it sometimes.'

I'm like ain't that your man and she said you were her baby's daddy and that's it, ya'll ain't have no relationship other than the kids. Long story short, I called shawdy that night, she came thru Providence scooped me up, I fucked her that night at the Super 8 and been fuckin'er ever since. We went to Potomac Mills in the car and she bought me two pairs of Jordans. When I asked when do you come see the kids, she said you was down the city with ten years for a coke and dope case. She told me yesterday she was thinking bout getting my name tatooed across the bottom part of her back, above the crack of her ass."

With that last statement Jeff punched Chazz with a two-piece catching him in the eye and the jaw, Chazz stumbled backwards landed on one knee then charged Jeff who backed up and two-pieced him again. This time when Chazz went down to one knee Darrell stood up and kicked him square in the face, Jeff said "Yeah nigga that's my baby mama and my bitch you knew that, so stop acting like you didn't know and just to let yo dumb ass know she come down here and see me every week, sometimes twice a week you dumb bitch," Jeff said all this while kicking and stomping Chazz on the floor. Finally he stopped went in Chazz's cell asked Maytag and Leon which bags were Chazz's, grabbed the two bags walked back out and said "consider this a down payment for fucking my ho. Jeff and Darrell then walked off and went upstairs to their cell with Darrell saying "Ole hoe ass nigga."

East End:

Sitting in Ayanna's house Tre, Cap, Ski, Turk, Ayanna, Cassidy, and Stan were discussing what happened in Cassidy's house. "Fuck what ya'll talking bout somebody's head go roll and I mean soon," Turk stated. "Turk I feel you son, but first we gotta find out who it was," Tre said "One thing we know for sure they was from Whitcomb." "What I don't understand is, who would've done that shit knowing ya'll was in my house and I was

Stan's girl?" Cassidy said.

"I tried to tell ya'll Cassidy's name won't shit when it came to the drug game over there, yeah she know a lot of people but still she not into that scene. Plus she not from around there originally so how she go bring some outsiders especially New York niggas over there and let'em set up shop thinking they go take everybody's business," Ayanna said. "Don't forget recruiting the young niggaz talking bout they go be Bloods and this go be a Blood hood, I told ya'll that shit won't go fly. Maybe getting money niggas would've let ya'll slide, but now you talking that color shit and niggas ain't playing that shit," Stan said.

"Fuck that shit son, dem niggas shoved a burner under my nose, them projects go run that red my nigga that's my word," replied Cap. "Not to mention they came in here wearing some motherfucking slob ass crab flags," Turk said. Thru all the discussion Ski hadn't said nothing, he was thinking bout what the robbers said about Stan letting them grind in Whitcomb in the first place. "Whoever they was, Stan'll know soon enough."

When Ski said this everybody turned to look at Stan who spoke up "Da hell that's supposed to mean?" "Hold up nigga I ain't saying you know who did it, I'm saying before they left out the spot, they said 'tell Stan's pussy ass since he let ya'll grind out here, his pussy ass gotta pay too.' So I figure they'll be coming for you soon," Ski said. "You damn sho right Ski, so if they know your name that means even if they wear masks you should at least be able to tell who one of'em is," Tre said.

"How da fuck they figure I let ya'll grind out here, them niggas crazy, but one thing for sure two things for certain. I'ma keep my strap on me at all times shawd. And since those punks ass niggas wanna throw my name up in it, somebody's ass gotta drop and it damn sho ain't go be me," Stan said. "Alls I know is somebody betta pay coming up in my shit, robbing my fam and threatening my man, nah these niggas must don't know who the fuck we is," Cassidy said. "Cassidy shut da fuck up, you ain't go do shit and don't go out here running your damn mouth bout nothing, just give it time it'll eventually come out," Ayanna said.

"In da meantime we go switch things up a lil bit, instead of everybody being in the house at the sametime, at least two people go be outside and whoever's in the house go keep watch on them. We go do this for a couple of weeks just to show these niggas they can't stop us and they ain't running shit over here. But first Cap and Turk ya'll go catch the bus up top to re-up and when ya'll get back we go flat the whole thing , then we go switch gears and set up shop somewhere else. But we also go keep our eyes and ears open too, cause we go pay these niggas back before it's all over and done with," Tre said.

Northside:

Cheeks and Te-Mundre were riding down Old Brook Rd. going to check on their cousin Skeeta when they spotted what looked like Y.K.'s green Chevrolet Cavalier coming down getting ready to turn out of Pine Camp. "Shawd I know damn well we ain't catch them niggas over here slipping," Cheeks said. "You got your tone on you Mundre?" "You know it, slow down so we can give'em time to get to the stop sign and make sure it's them," Te-Mundre said to his brother. Just as Y.K. and Rel got to the stop sign Y.K. looked over, he and Te-Mundre locked eyes as recognition hit them both.

Te-Mundre came up with his .40 cal, Y.K. hit the gas and turned out just as the first shots rang out. Ping ping ping ping, you could hear the bullets slamming up against the car as Y.K.

turned out swerving back and forth across the street. Skeeta and her brother Brent were standing on the porch and saw what was happening. As Y.K. continued to swerve back and forth Cheeks hit the gas behind them while Te-Mundre continued shooting out the window. Ping ping splat whizzz whizzz.

You could hear the bullets smacking the car and whizzing by as Te-Mundre missed some. Y.K. wound up hitting two parked cars before coming to a complete stop on the right side of the street, Cheeks pulled up beside them, reached between the seats pulled out his all black 9 mm Beretta and jumped out the car. Cheeks stood on the driver's side as Te-Mundre stood on the passenger's side and they both let loose on Y.K.'s Cavalier. Bop bop ping ping ping; "Let's go nigga," Cheeks yelled, then they jumped back in the car and took off.

Skeeta and Brent continued to stand outside watching the other car, they saw Rel crawl out the passenger's side and collapse to the ground. From somewhere in the distance they heard police sirens, as the sirens grew closer Skeeta told Brent "Come on let's go in the house before the police get here." Once in the house Brent said "Skeeta that was Cheeks and Mundre, you think they killed them dudes?" "I'ont know but I know we can't tell nobody what we saw, you hear me?" "Yeah" "I mean it Brent, if we tell anybody then Cheeks and Mundre could wind up going to jail and we don't want that, now do we?" "No, but that was real gangsta sis, our cousins some gangstas huh?" "I'ont know what they is, all I know is they my cousins and I love'em to death," Skeeta said. Looking out the window at the police and paramedics putting Rel in the ambulance, then taking Y.K. out the car laying him on the ground and placing a sheet over him signaling death. Skeeta saw the police talking to some people who were in Pine Camp playing basketball, she saw the police writing something down. This told her these people were snitching on her cousins.

Skeeta picked up the phone and called Sassy "What's up lil cuz?" Sassy said answering the phone. "That's why I'm calling, to tell you what's up. Tell Cheeks and Mundre I said to lay low cause the police were just talking to some potential witnesses that were in the park," Skeeta said. "What da hell you talking bout girl?" "Look cuz, just tell'em what I said, if they want you to know they'll tell you. "Aight Skeet lemme call'em now." "Love you big cuz." "Yeah yeah lemme call my brothers, but I love you too and thanks lil cuz, I'ont know what for but thanks anyway," Sassy said as she hung up.

East End:

Do-Do was sitting on the sofa smoking a blunt watching Webbie's and Boosie's movie Ghetto Stories in Newbridge Apts when hears a key in the front door. Knowing P.J. was in the back fucking Tricey he didn't think anybody should've been coming in the apt but when the doorknob turned he knew better. He grabbed his .44 revolver off the table and placed it in his lap, when the door opened there stood Teco, Tricey's boyfriend. "What da fuck? Fuck you doing in my house nigga?" Teco asked rushing inside. "Slow down shawdy," Do-Do said holding up the gun, "first lock that door then sit yo ass down."

Teco glared at Do-Do "What nigga, buck if you want to," Do-Do said. After Teco did as he was told, Do-Do said "I'ont know bout this being your house, but shawdy opened the door and let us in." "Fuck you mean us?" asked Teco. "Us nigga just like I said, me and my nigga from da other day at the mall." At that moment Teco heard ,"unh unh unnh shit unh" "Da fuck is that?" he asked.

"I guess that's yo bitch getting her back blowed out by my nigga," Do-Do said laughing. "Da fuck" Teco said as he was getting ready to run in the bedroom. "Hold up nigga" Do-Do said standing up with the gun in his hand. "Fuck you think you going? Sit yo ass back down in that chair and wait til my nigga get finished. "What?" "You heard me shawdy unless you wanna talk to my other nigga right here," Do-Do said waving his gun.

Looking from Do-Do and the gun to the bedroom Teco said "Nigga fuck you" and went to take off again. This time Do-Do pointed the gun at him and said "Go head nigga don't make no difference to me, I ain't got no problem shooting yo punk ass." Teco looked in Do-Do's eyes and knew he won't to be fucked with, he went back and sat down in the chair while Do-Do sat back on the sofa watching the movie. All of a sudden they could hear the bed squeaking 'ehw ehw ehw' and the head board smacking the wall 'bump bump bump bump. Then it seemed like Tricey just got loud with it 'unh unh unnh unnnh shit ooh alll shit I'm cumming damn ungh ungh.'

Then they heard 'smack' and "aargh yes do that again" 'smack.' "Who pussy is dis?" "It's yo's, it's yo's, damn I swear it's yo's." "It better be you hear me?" 'blop blop blop.' "All shiit I'm cumming again." then P.J. said "damn I'm getting ready to cum," then movement, then quietness and all of a sudden "ahhhh shit ahhh shit, girl what da fuck." All of a sudden silence.

Do- Do had been watching Teco the whole time, he was mad as hell you could see it in his eyes that he had tears coming out. His jaws were enflamed, he kept cracking his knuckles and saying over and over "I'ma kill this bitch, I'ma kill this bitch." "Finally Do-Do told him he could "go in the bedroom but he betta not try nothing funny cause he was go be right behind him with the gun." \Teco went to take off and Do-Do told him to "slow down." When they walked in the bedroom they saw Tricey sitting on side the bed with P.J.'s dick in her mouth.

She was just finishing up with a 'ssluurp pop' when P.J. looked up and asked "da fuck's this?" "It's cool cuz, this nigga came in while ya'll was doing ya'll thing so I made his ass sit there and listen," Do-Do said "Nigga said it's his house." "This is my house nigga, Tricey you's a nasty ass trifling bitch, my niggas told me you was a ho but nah I didn't believe'em now I see for myself they was right. You must be leaving when they leave cause yo ass sho ain't staying here no more," Teco said angrily. "Nah shawdy she ain't leaving wit us, this yo bitch you keep'er, we out," P.J. said as he and Do-Do walked out.

Soon as the front door closed Teco slapped the fuck outta Tricey 'spow' "fuck wrong wit'chu 'slap smack' fucking a nigga in my house, bitch is you crazy?" "Teec I'm s-s-sorry," Tricey pleaded. "Oh I now you sorry, you's a sorry bitch, you assed out now." 'Spop smack smak' he smacked her again and again "aiiiiii" Tricey cried out. Teco punched her in the face and kicked her in the stomach.

"Your ass gone tonite bitch, I mean that and don't come back, get the shit you came here with and no more. When you see another bitch sporting yo shit don't get mad." he smacked her one more time, left her on the floor crying, hurting and wishing she had never set eyes on P.J. She knew she didn't have nowhere to go and P.J. had said she couldn't go with them, she felt that was real fucked up. "Hurry da fuck up and get out my mafuckin house before I kill yo trifling ass," Teco yelled.

Meanwhile P.J. and Do-Do were laughing bout what happened on their way back to Fairfield, "Nigga yo ass crazy," P.J. said "How da hell you go make dude sit there and listen to his girl get fucked." "Fuck dat pussy ass nigga, serve his dumb ass right, that's what he get for having a slut for his main girl," Do-Do replied. "I know right, shawdy did have some bum tho and her head game was on point specially afta a nigga dun bust off and she sucked him off right afta," P.J. said reliving what just happened between him and Tricey. "Damn nigga she did have a banging body tho, I was hoping you was go let her come with us so I could get me some," Do-Do said. "I would've but that nigga woulda been more problems than it was worth, don't worry with the fucking she got tonight she'll call again, I guarantee it," P.J. "Yeah if that nigga don't kill her first," Do-Do replied "I know right," said P.J.

Chapter 12-West End:

Ray-Ray was sitting on Ms. Emerson's front porch smoking a blunt and looking down the street at Gamal's house thinking bout how they had come off without a glitch. Just as this thought crossed thru his mind he felt something touch the back of his head, "Yeah nigga, don't try to move, what you thought you was go get away with that shit? Now what you go do is stand up and walk around the back nice and slow, if you make any and I do

mean any noise I'ma bust yo ass here and now. Now move."
Ray-Ray contemplated what he should do, he had no doubt that
whoever was on the other end of that gun would use it if he tried
something stupid.

But at the sametime he figured they didn't want to shoot him
cause if they did, they would've done it by now, he decided to
get up and walk around back to see what they had in mind.

Chris Stevenson wouldn't let him see his face as they
walked, once in back of the house Ray-Ray saw Poppi standing
on the other side of the house and Dre Jr. was standing beside a
car parked back there. "Walk over to the car nigga, you go be
alright," Chris said. "Get in" Dre said, Ray-Ray hesitated "
Nigga you ain't go die tonite unless you don't cooperate, now get
in before I change my mind." Ray-Ray got in the backseat with
Dre beside him, Poppi driving and Chris in the passenger's seat.

"How da fuck you go rob a nigga that live on the same
block as your grandma, you's bout a dumb ass nigga. What you
thought we wasn't go find out it was you," Poppi asked as he
drove thru the alley and stopped behind the abandoned house on
the corner. Ray-Ray looking out the window saw Gamal coming
out the backyard heading towards the car and tensed up "Nigga
didn't I tell you yo punk ass go live tonite? Relax we just wanna
talk that's it," Dre said. Gamal slid in the car, first thing he did
was punch Ray-Ray square in the face.

"Nigga how da fuck you go rob me then come back round
here and don't watch your back. You gots to be either a stupid
mafucka or a brave ass nigga, or maybe you just thought shit
was that sweet round here. First thing you go do is tell us who
was with you then we'll go from there." "Man I ain't have shit to
do with you getting robbed," Ray-Ray said. Gamal pulled his
gun from his waist and after ejecting the clip and taking the

bullet out the chamber, turned the gun around in his hand and 'whop whop' hit Ray-Ray across the jaw and face splitting his lip in the process.

"Nigga didn't we tell you if you cooperate you live, now I want those names and before you start lying lemme tell you we already know who was with you, one of your dumb ass niggas can't keep his mouth shut. He had to go bragging bout what ya'll did and told everything, now I'm not go say who it was, I want to see how you go carry it,' Gamal said. "And I told you I ain't rob yo mafuckin ass, so fuck you," replied Ray-Ray. "Fuck that Gamal I say we go head and cap his dumb ass, we already know who the other two was anyway, he wanna keep acting like he supaman and shit," Chris Stevenson said.

"Ya'll know what da bad part is, I fuck wit da lil nigga all he had to do was come ask me for something and I woulda did what I could for'im. But naw fuck that," Gamal said as he reloaded his gun and cocked it. "Poppi let's head out to Louisa and find a spot in da woods to get rid of this nigga, I'm tired of pussyfooting around with'im." Ray-Ray still didn't think they were going to hurt him, but when Poppi hit the highway and he saw that they were indeed headed towards Louisa he changed his mind. "Aight you proved your point," Ray-Ray said.

"Naw nigga I ain't proved shit cause you still ain't start talking yet," replied Gamal. Dre who had been quiet since Gamal got in the car hauled off and just started punching Ray-Ray "Nigga you go talk or you go suffer before you die." "Aight aight man aight it was Black Pete and Simmy that was with me." "Hold up Dre, you said it was who?" asked Chris from the front seat. "It was Black Pete and Simmy," Ray-Ray said again.

"Them niggas from Fairfield too?" asked Gamal. "Yeah man." "That's good, that's real good, now you go show us where both of'em live and hang out at," Gamal said. "Turn this mafucka around Poppi, let's head over to Fairfield, these punk ass niggas wanna rob me and brag about it, shiit somebody's ass in trouble." "What I want to know is why you do it, why da fuck you go rob a nigga that live on the same block as your grandma. Don't you realize you jeopardized your grandma's life, you lucky Gamal respects her, I know niggas that would've went afta her just to draw you in a beef," Dre said. "Fo real or either they woulda just shot you on the front porch and nine times outta ten they woulda missed you but woulda hit yo grandma.

"What da fuck you woulda did then? Snitched to da police and tell on yo self in the process or get back at'em and still be caught up in a beef," Poppi stated. "Lil shawdy why you ain't just holla at a nigga to see if I could put you on?" Gamal asked. "Cause man, I figured you wouldn't do it for two reasons, one you know my grandma and two you was go say I ain't need to be doing that I was too young," answered Ray-Ray. "You probly right, but I would've done something for ya, now look; you and yo homies gotta get fucked up, but the one I really want is the one that was bragging bout what ya'll did. I ain't go tell you which one it is but I know the name," Gamal said.

Driving past Armstrong-Kennedy high school Poppi asked "Where to?" "Make a right on Seldon," Ray-Ray said "Stop right here," he said stopping them in the middle of the block, nodding his head he said. "That's Black Pete's girl slash baby mama's house, now go up make a left then make another left on Rosetta." As they rode on Rosetta Ray-Ray said "That's Simmy's mama's house" pointing to an apartment near the corner "now make a right and go up to Phaup St." Poppi did as Ray-Ray told him.

"Stop right here, third door from the corner that's Simmy's

cousin Sheila house, Gamal please don't kill my friends we ain't mean no harm just trying to get some paper that's all." "We not go kill'em based on the strength of your grandma, but their ass go pay, just like yo ass go pay and you betta not tell'em we coming for'em cause if you do then your ass will die. Unnerstand me?" Gamal asked. Ray-Ray nodded his head and Dre smacked him upside the head " Nigga when somebody ask you a question you answer with ya mouth, now answer the question." "Yeah man I understand you," Ray-Ray answered. "Now let's get back round da way and do what we gotta do," Gamal said.

Southside:

Having just left MCV Hospital the remaining members of the LBC: Lil Ron-Ron, Lil James and Lil Big Head were inside Lil Big Head's older brother Slinky's apt. "Yo fuck that my niggas laid up in da hospital cause niggas wanna shoot at'em, oh it's on tonight, we getting ready to ride on Chicago Ave. in a very few minutes," Lil Ron-Ron said. "But we don't know if it was them or not, it coulda been some niggas from Clopton Terrace or even some niggas from Hillside you know most of dem niggas don't fuck with us anyway," Lil James said. "Plus that broad Debbie said it was some females hanging out the car shooting," Lil Big Head said, "And da only place we know that got females busting is dem mafuckas over Clopton from da other night."

"True dat, but we still gotta hit dem Chicago Ave niggas from that shit wit Blip and nem, even if it won't dem the streets say it was. We already hit Clopton Terrce and might've started a war for nothing, so we go hit Chicago tonight and go back at Clopton in a day or two afta K.O. and Dread get out of the hospital," Ron-Ron said. "Ron you know the police go be all over K.O. and Dread specially wit dem being from Afton and what happened to Keon and nem. They go think we inna beef and gonna wanna talk to both of'em and everybody they hang with," Lil Big Head said. "No shit you ain't see the way the police was watching us at da hospital, I bet they was asking their families bout us," Lil James said. "Ya'll niggas do have a point, but we still go ride on Chicago tonight I don't care what ya'll say," Lil Ron-Ron said vehemently....

Meanwhile Juice and Monopoly were preparing to rob the white boys out in Brandermill. They rode out there earlier than planned because Juice wanted to make sure Monopoly knew exactly where he was going, plus they wanted to get a lay of the land and see if the house was jumping that night. They were riding in Juice's girl Tabitha's car so if they ran into Monopoly's cousins they wouldn't recognize the car. "We gotta ride by Dizzy and Hakeem's house first, that way I can make sure I can find the house from there," Monopoly said. They rode for another 10 minutes when Monopoly said "turn right there" they made a left "now make a right, that's Dizzy and Hakeem's house right there."

"Nigga I know where da fuck they live," Juice said "or did you forget." "Naw mafucka I was just saying, aight make a right, then make another right, that's it there the one on the corner," Monopoly said. "We go ride by make a u-turn and come back up, don't look like they got no alarm system sign out front," Juice said. "I ain't never see no alarm when I went over there, now that you mention it, I ain't never seen'em go to no alarm," Monopoly said. "They pro'ly don't got one considering the fact they young, they pro'ly think people out here scared to try them. We not from out here and we not go try, we is go get'em," Juice

said.

They made a u-turn and were driving back past the house when they saw a black BMW sitting in the yard with lights on and the doors open. Riding pass they also saw a small petite white girl about 21 or 22 and a black guy bout 6'0 200 lbs., they were taking what looked like gym bags in the house. "At least we know two of'ems in da house now," said Juice. "Yeah but the question is how many in there?" asked Monopoly. "We go make one more round before we decide what to do," Juice said.

After making the u-turn as they were coming back past the house they saw one of the white boys come out the house get in the BMW, back up and pull off. "Aight nigga we know that's at least one less person that's in there, you wanna go head and do this shit now? asked Juice. "Shit don't make a difference, first we gottta find somewhere to park," Monopoly replied. "What betta place to park than the front yard, they slingin weed from there so the neighbors used to seeing different cars in the yard, besides it's dark and it's late. I bet they ain't even go look at the car, they'll think it's a customer," Juice said. "Aight let's do it but first pull over right here so we can check the guns, the good thing is they ain't got no screen door, so when we knock they pro'ly go just open up like they do when me and my cousins come over here," Monopoly said.

After checking to make sure their guns were loaded; Monopoly's Desert Eagle .44 and Juice's Glokk-21 .45 cal and tying their bandannas around their heads, Juice put the car in drive and pulled into the driveway, both tucked their guns and walked to the house. Monopoly stood off to the side while Juice knocked, when they heard the locks turning to open the door the masks came up and the guns came out. Just as the door was being opened Juice kicked it in, clubbed the white bald-headed guy across the face with the butt of his gun knocking him into the wall and down on the floor. "Shut up mafucka and answer me, how many mo people in here?" Juice asked. "Two," replied the terrified white guy.

"Get yo punk ass up," Juice said as he pulled him to his feet. They made their way thru the hallway, Monopoly had taken the lead and as they came to the bottom of the steps the black guy stepped out from the living room on the left hand side. "What th-" his words got cut off as Monopoly hit him across the bridge of his nose and eyes sending blood up on the walls. Monopoly hit him two more times when the white girl came out the kitchen rolling a blunt to see what all the commotion was. When she saw her boyfriend getting hit she started screaming.

Monopoly turned the gun on her and said "shut da fuck up bitch before yo ass die in dis mafucka." The white girl tried to calm down but was still making noise so Monopoly went to her and smacked her across the jaw with the butt of his pistol knocking her to the ground and effectively shutting her up. The white boy seeing his sister get hit went to jump and Juice hit him in the back of the head, thus ending any fight he had left in him. Picking the white girl up by her hair Juice said "Now I want both of ya'll pussy mafuckas to come in here and take a seat fore I kill this bitch and ya'll too." Both guys staggered to their feet and made their way into the living room where Juice told them to "sit on the sofa."

"When I release your hair I want you to put yo arms behind your back, you hear me?" Monopoly asked the white girl. She nodded her head 'yes,' Monopoly released her pulled out a roll of duct tape and taped her hands together. " Now I want you to lay face down on the floor, don't look at me like that bitch ain't nobody go rape yo skeleton ass, now do what I said before I do kill yo ass," Monopoly said. The white girl crying hysterically did as she was told, then Monopoly stepped up grabbed her feet pulled them up as close as he could get them to her hands and duct taped her wrists and feet together in a hogtie style. Then he stepped around and taped her mouth shut.

Next he called the black guy over "Man please don't kill us," he pleaded. "Shut da fuck up nigga, you's a bigger pussy than the one yo girl's got between her legs, now get down on the floor and put yo arms behind yo back and bring yo legs up like yo bitch," Monopoly said. After the black guy was restrained and his mouth taped up, Juice said to the white guy "I'm guessing that's yo sister and her boyfriend right there." "The white guy nodded his head 'yeah,' "Well it's like this, if you want them to live you're going to give us all the money and drugs you have in da house, don't try to hold back cause we'll search this whole muthafuckn place and if we find more than what you give us, we shoot somebody unnerstand?"

"Yeah man" "Good then let's go," Juice said. Juice and the white guy walked thru the house and went into the kitchen to a back room that had some steps that led down into a basement. The white guy went to a workbench moved it out the way then moved some wooden boards, reached down and started turning a dial. "Damn ya'll got a safe in da floor? Ya'll getting major paper huh?" Juice asked. The white guy didn't comment he was both mad and scared, Walt was supposed to be their security but he was tied up upstairs. He believed what the stick-up guy said about Walt being a big pussy, he could see it in his eyes and hear it in his voice that Walt was really scared.

Once the safe was open he reached in and pulled out four big camouflage military duffel bags and threw them at Juice's feet. Juice looked in each one and all he could see was money

"Damn! Now where the drugs at?" The white guy got up off the floor went to the clothes dryer sitting in the corner, opened the door reached in and pulled out three smaller all black duffel bags. "Damn mafucka, ya'll was cakin it fo real. Why da fuck ya'll ain't got no real security cause I know dat punk ass scared ass nigga upstairs ain't yo security. Ya'll gots to be da dumbest hustlas I ever met," Juice said.

"Aight just leave all that right there, I hope that's all of it I would hate to have to kill ya'll up in dis mafucka." The white guy followed by Juice made their way back upstairs where Juice told him to "take his place on the floor next to everybody else." After hogtaping the white guy Juice motioned Monopoly to come on and follow him, once down in the basement Monopoly noticing all the duffel bags on the floor whistled "whewww, damn I know all those ain't for us." "Why they ain't?" asked Juice. "Now hurry up nigga and grab what you can, I'ma come back and get what we can't carry up now."

They both hauled two of the camouflage duffel bags onto a shoulder then they picked up a smaller duffel bag apiece in each hand and carried them upstairs outside to the car. When they went back in the house Monopoly stayed upstairs while Juice went back and got the rest of the bags. he checked the deep freezer and the dryer and found they were both empty, satisfied he grabbed the three remaining bags and went back upstairs. "We leaving now, but before we do, once ya'll hear the front door close I want ya'll to start counting backwards from 100 and don't stop until you get to zero before you even think about trying to get loose. You got me?" asked Juice.

Everybody nodded their heads yes, but just as they were turning the corner to go out the door Monopoly looked back and saw the girl was trying to roll over. Going back in the room he said "Bitch didn't you hear what da fuck he said." He walked over to her put the gun next to her head and pulled the trigger 'Blaow.' The girl jumped and tried to scream "now do what da fuck we told yo dumb ass to do." Monopoly stood up walked out the front door and got in the car "Man I know you ain't shoot nobody?" Juice said. "Hell naw nigga, but the bitch had already started trying to get loose before we even made it out the front door. So I had to go back and put da fear of dying in that bitch, I shot right beside her ear," answered Monopoly.

Chapter 13- Southside:

Lil Ron-Ron, Lil James and Lil Big Head had decided that tonight Chicago Ave was go feel the full brunt of power from Afton, they had given dope fiend Maze two eggs of dope to rent his Jeep Cherokee. Lil James was in the passenger seat, Lil Big head was driving and Lil Ron-Ron was in the backseat with his choppa he had been dying to use on niggas since he got it and Lil James had the SKS with the foldout stock. Lil Big Head drove up Chicago Ave first to see who was out there, they saw Lil Goo on the side of a house making a sale; Slick, Corey Dillard, and Dan Johnson were standing in front the same house. Three houses down they saw Conan, Arthur Gantz, and Jamel all sitting on the porch of another house. "This what we gon do" Lil Ron-Ron said to his crew.

"James you get out once we turn the corner, Big Head going round the block and drop me off by da alley, I'ma walk thru the cut come out to the second house cut thru the yard walk up on dem first niggas and dump. Big Head go make a u-turn, come back pick me up in da alley once I start dumping, you woulda had time to walk up on dem other niggas and started dumping. We'll pick you up in da same place we drop you off, then we go keep on thru da alley to the next block, come out on da street and head back to Afton." So as Big Head came back down the street and made the turn they let Lil James out, luckily for him he was tall with long arms that way he could tuck the SKS under his armpit. He stepped into the alley took a minute to get hisself together and proceeded on his way.

As he was turning onto Chicago, Lil Ron-Ron was coming thru the ally on the opposite end. Walking between the second and third house from the corner Ron-Ron saw the crack head that Lil Goo was just serving walking down the street with his head down never seeing Ron-Ron coming thru the cut. Lil Ron-Ron waited a couple of seconds then he rounded the house holding the choppa nose down and seeing Lil James coming from the other way. Corey Dillard was the one who spotted him "What da fuck dis nigga doing?" Corey asked noticing the way Lil Ron-Ron was walking.

Noticing everybody turn and look his way Ron-Ron tried to walk as normal as possible, he hadn't quite got past the third house when he pulled the 'AK' up and started firing 'chop chop yop yop yop.' All four guys tried to run as Ron-Ron swept the 'yoppa' back and forth; Slick who had come back round the front got hit in the side and went down, Lil Goo got grazed across his lower back and his left elbow as he tried to run. Dan Johnson got hit in the back of the ankle knocking him to the ground instantly where he tried to crawl to safety. And Corey being the first to notice Lil Ron-Ron in the first place made it around the side of the house just as three bullets slammed into the house.

Down the street seeing what was happening the three guys sitting on the porch all tried to get up at the sametime and run in the house. But none of them noticed Lil James until they heard the SKS 'yop yop yop yop yop,' Jamel was the first to holla out "awww" as the 2.23 bullets tore into his back. Not being able to get in the house cause the front door was locked; Conan and Arthur tried to jump off the side of the porch at the sametime to run around the back. While Arthur made it over clean Conan got hit in the right forearm and the right side, he hit the ground with a thud and lay there as Arthur ran around back.

Lil Ron-Ron having finished dumping ran back the way he came, between the houses and thru the alley where Lil Big Head picked him up. Going thru the alley the passed the house where Lil Ron-Ron had just finished dumping and spotted Corey Dillard peeking around the corner; Ron-Ron hopped out the car and unleashed 'yop yop yop yop yop.' Corey hearing the car turned around just in time to see Lil Ron-Ron leveling the gun at him, took off running again. This time he wasn't as lucky as the first time, as one of the rounds slammed into his right shoulder propelling him to the ground. Seeing this Ron-Ron jumped back in the truck and Lil Big Head sped off.

Coming to the end of the alley they picked up Lil James who had just arrived there himself. Unbeknownst to them Arthur who had managed to get away from Lil James was hiding in a garage right there. Looking thru a crack in the door he saw the Cherokee pull up and Lil James get in, he knew it was Lil James and if so that meant the other people involved had to be members of the LBC....

Meanwhile at the Sattelite Club; Sonya, Crystal, and Charmaine had a table by the far wall. All three ladies were sipping on different drinks Sonya had a White Russian, Crystal was drinking Patron' and Charmaine had a Blue Motorcycle. "Girl I can't believe you got your ass out here tonight, Dan's go snap," Charmaine said talking to Sonya. "Number one I'm a grown ass woman, I don't have to ask or tell Dan shit about where the fuck I'm going. Number two fuck Dan, that was the final straw when I caught him with that bitch Michelle. I told his ass then, two can play that game and that's just what the fuck I plan on doing starting tonight, playing the game," replied Sonya.

In truth Sonya was tired of putting up with Dan's bullshit, it just so happened she had talked to Shaun earlier that evening and he mentioned that he and his brothers were thinking about going to the Sattelite. So when Crystal mentioned her and Charmaine were going there tonite, Sonya said she was going also, hoping to run into Shaun. "That shit sound good, but if and when Dan find out I bet yo ass be singing a different tune," Crystal said. "Whatever bitch, you heard what I said, now fuck both of ya'll and Dan too cause right about now I'm going to get my dance on," Sonya said taking a sip of her drink and hitting the dance floor to Yo Gotti's '5 Star Chick.'

Right at that time the 'Family'; Fatty, Te-Mundre, Cheeks, Shaun and Sassy were walking in and thru the club, Sassy got in because Fatty knew one of the security guards. With Fatty in front they drew more than their fair share of attention, from both niggas and bitches. Before they all could get completely seated at their tables on the far side of the club, the waitress Shannon was there taking orders. "What's up Fatty aka Mr. Sexy Man? You want your usual Goose and Juice?" "No question" replied Fatty he and Shannon knew each other from him coming in there all the time, he always tipped her good and she always gave him prompt service.

Of course she secretly was trying to get Fatty to tap that ass, but he wasn't interested in her like that. "And you Mundre?" "Shawd you know I want the samething my brother getting that's the family drink." Cheeks said "Gimme a Henny and Coke," Shaun ordered the same as Fatty and Te-Mundre, and Sassy because she was underage to begin with only ordered a Pepsi.

Crystal noticing how fast Fatty and nem got service said "Damn! Who da fuck them mafuckas is that they got that bitch running to'em like that." Charmaine who had peeped them when they walked in said "I ain't sure, but I think that's the nigga Sonya gave her number to the other day, at least it look like'im." "What nigga? Which one?" asked Crystal not believing what she was hearing. "The one with da green Polo shirt and small Jesus piece hanging round his neck," replied Charmaine. Crystal looking at her sister on the dance floor doing her thing and oblivious to who and what they was talking about, asked "Where she meet him at?"

"The other day when she came to the shop and we walked to get something to eat, sumthin bout McDonald's and a shooting or some shit," answered Charmaine. "Fo real, wait til this bitch get ova here she ain't said nothing bout that," stated Crystal. Fatty was talking to Corn Cob and Bo, while Te-Mundre was telling Shaun "Yo young ass betta not get drunk tonight then go home acting like a fool and have mama cursing er'body out." "You know his young ass can't handle his liquor," Cheeks said. "Fuck both ya'll, ain't nobody gettin drunk and Sassy telling mama, is ya'll niggas crazy," Shaun said.

"Ain't that that bitch you met in Sam's the other day?" Sassy asked. "Where?" asked Shaun. "On da dance floor with the pink and blue Dereon outfit on." "Damn sho is," answered Shaun. "Shawdy looking damn good too, you hit that yet," asked Te-Mundre. "Nah I just really talked to her for the first time on da phone today, she was the one driving the AC at McDonald's that day."

"So that's why you wanted to come to the club tonite, huh?" asked Sassy smartly. "Shut da fuck up Sass, damn! You talk too fuckin much," Shaun stated. "So where her man at? Cause she damn sho said she had one?" Sassy said. "Tell you the truth I'ont know and I'ont care Sass, I just know I'ma holla at her and see what's up," Shaun said. "Who she wit?" asked Cheeks.

Looking around Sassy said "ain't that Charmaine and I don't know who the other broad is, I'm guessing her sister." "Man I been tryna to get with shawdy from da shop for awhile, what's up wit her Shaun?" Cheeks asked. "I'ont know Cheeks, me and shawdy ain't kick it that long, but shit there she go nigga you can holla at'er tonight," replied Shaun. While they were talking their drinks arrived, a few minutes later Sonya came strutting off the dance she ain't even acknowledge you man," Te-Mundre said.

"That's aight nigga she will befo we leave here, specially once her girls tell'er I'm over here, you know they saw us come in," replied Shaun. "That don't mean they know who you is tho nigga," Cheeks said. "Naw but I bet Charmaine recognized him, she was with her the other day, not only that me and Charmaine's cool so I know she reconized me," Sassy said.

"Bitch yo ass think you so fucking slick talking bout you wanted to hang out wit me and Charmaine, you knew that nigga was coming here tonite and why you ain't say nut'in bout running into him?" floor and walked straight to her table. "Damn bruh, Crystal said. "What da fuck you talking bout now Crystal?" Sonya asked her sister. "She talking bout that nigga you met the other day you came to get your hair done," answered Charmaine. "Who Shaun? What about him?" asked Sonya. "What about'im? Oh bitch, like you ain't see'im come in here wit dat broad and dem three other niggas like they run sumthin, act like you ain't know he was coming here tonite," said Crystal.

"He said he might come here he wasn't sure, now you say they in here, where they at?" "You ain't see'em sitting at those tables down towards the bar when you came off the floor?" asked Charmaine. "Nah I won't really paying much attention I was so hot and tired, tell you the truth I ain't think he was coming," Sonya said while looking in the direction for Shaun and the Family. Just as she spotted Shaun out from everybody else; Shaun, Cheeks, Sassy, and Te-Mundre all seemed to be looking in their direction. Almost at once she and Shaun made eye contact, Shaun got up and started towards her table, then Sonya got up and met him halfway.

"Hey you," Sonya said. "S'up Ms. Lady," Shaun responded. "I ain't see you sittin ova there, you saw me come in?" asked Sonya. "Naw we been here bout 15 minutes and you was already on the dance floor." "Damn, I see it's a lot of ya'll, all them yo peoples?" Sonya inquired. "Yeah them other three niggas my brothers and you already met my sister Sassy," he said. "Damn, all ya'll came out tonite, a family affair huh?" she remarked "My sister said ya'll came up in here like ya'll run something or what not."

Shaun laughed "People always say that, if she thought that was bad she should see us when we wit our mama. Her wit her 5'2" ass think she the baddest woman on the planet, think she both the queen and the First Lady. Which to us she is of course." Sonya laughed just as Crystal and Charmaine walked past them "watch the table Sonya while we hit da floor," Charmaine said. With that Charmaine and Crystal hit the dance floor and started doing their thang.

"Shawd, I swear I wanna fuck the shit outta Charmaine, got damn shawdy bad and phat as a bitch," Cheeks said. "Who da o'er shawdy is that's wit'em?" asked Te-Mundre. "I'ont know but she bad as a bitch too, matter fact she might be da flyest out da bunch," responded Cheeks. "My brothers I swear everywhere we go ya'll niggas always tryna fuck something, but I can't even holla at a nigga without ya'll wanting to fuck'im up," Sassy said.

"That's cause most niggas only want one thing, you know that. When the right one comes along you'll know, but who you think you talking to, we all know you ain't no virgin," Te-Mundre said. "Yeah somebody done tapped that ass befo, we just don't wanna hear no niggas out here disrespecting you or your name, calling you a ho cause you done fucked every nigga you talked to," Cheeks said. Fatty had finished talking to Corn Cob and Bo, and was talking to Doreen a broad he had fucked the week before; when he looked around and went to say something "Who dat Shaun talking to? he asked.

"Some broad he met at Sam's the other day, who was at McDonald's or some shit," answered Sassy. "I'm going to the bathroom and bar," Fatty said getting up and walking off. Te-Mundre kept watching Charmaine and Crystal on the dance floor "You right Cheeks all three of'em bad, but I think da other broad might be the baddest of the three," he said. "No doubt bruh, shit you might as well holla and see what's up," stated Cheeks. "You know I'm on top that," replied Te-Mundre.

"Well ya'll sit here and ogle all ya'll want, but I'm go hit da floor and see if I can find me a balla balla tonight," Sassy said laughing. "Yeah for his ass to get fucked up in here," stated Te-Mundre. "Fo sho," replied Cheeks. "Ya'll mafuckas know ya'll ain't right, but I love ya'll anyway," Sassy said jumping up sashaying out on the floor and commencing to taking the floor over. "What's up Sassy? I was wondering if your brothers were going to let you on the floor or if you was too gangsta to dance like them," Charmaine said. "Nah girl you know I had to sit back and observe first," Sassy answered back.

"All four of them niggas your brothers?" asked Crystal. "And you know this." "Damn, I know they be on your back, I bet they don't let you holla at nobody," Crystal said. "Gurrl you don't know the half of it," Sassy answered... "That's your sister from the other day right," Sonya asked Shaun. "Yeah that's my only sister." "And the rest of them guys your brothers?"

"Yeah" "Damn yo mama had a whole starting five, I know your sister catch hell." "True, but we let her do her own thing just don't disrespect herself, plus my mama make sure she carries herself like a lady and not think cause she got four brothers she can go round starting trouble." "That's good." "Yeah, but she still got a smart ass mouth, why you think we call her Sassy" he said laughing, "Now what's up wit your girls?"

"Charmaine you already know she's my cousin and the other one is my sister Crystal she's the oldest of us two, but of the three Charmaine's the oldest." "My brother Cheeks the light skin one wit the braids was talking bout Charmaine, say he's had his eye on her far awhile." "Why he ain't holla at her?" "Hell if I know, but fuck all that what you doing when you leave here?" asked Shaun.

"I'ont know probly hit Waffle House or sumthing as usual." "That's what's up, we definitely go hit the one up on Hull St when we bounce. What ya'll drinking on?" asked Shaun. "I'm drinking a White Russian, I'ont know what they drinking." "Damn, you drink White Russians too that's my drink, tell you what ya'll order ya'lls drinks and send the waitress ova to my table aight."

"You don't have to do that." "Ain't no problem ya'll cool, besides my oldest brother Fatty's cool with the waitress, she think we'ont know she wanna fuck'im, so she always look out for us when we come in here." "How ya'll figure she likes him?" "Shit she don't try to hide it, the way she be falling all over herself to wait on him, flirting and shit." "Oh she really got it bad huh?" "You know it. I'ma head back to my table, send the waitress ova when ya'll ready to order and I'll talk to you again before we leave here or either at Waffle House." "Ok and thank you." "No problem."

As Shaun headed back to the table he spotted Fatty at the bar talking to a female that looked like Milnet a stripper bitch he used to fuck with. "I'm saying what's good for the night tho?" Fatty asked in Milnet's ear. "Don't fucking play wit me Fatty err'time you see me you ask me da same fucking question, then yo black ass wind up leaving out here with another bitch." "Man look, I said what's up for the night, you want me to leave out here with you or some other bitch, damn."

"You still fucking wit that bitch Sherry?" "Maan fuck'er, what I'm saying is do you want me to bust yo ass up tonight or not?" "You know I do, but I got my cousin and nem wit me," Milnet answered demurely. "So what I got my brothers and sister wit me, just meet me at Waffle House on Hull St when we leave here and we'll work sum'in out. We in two cars, so no matter what you leaving there with me."

"Whateva" "Whateva ass, you heard what I said." "Yeah yeah, now buy me a gin and juice," Wilnet said... Crystal and Charmaine had come back to the table with Sonya "damn it's hot up there I'ont know how you and ole girl out there dance so much and not look tired," Crystal said. "What girl?" asked Sonya. "The one that came in with that nigga you met the other day."

"That's his sister Sassy, she's young so she can't drink that's why she don't look tired, as for me I don't dance as hard as I used to specially when it's hot up in here." Sonya replied " And Shaun says for us to order what we want to drink and send the waitress over to their table so he could take care of it. "Damn bitch you caught you one didn't it?" said Charmaine. "Shut up," Sonya retorted. "Talking bout me, shit his brother got his eye on you." "How you figure that and which one?"

"How you think, he told me and it's the light skin one his name is Cheeks I think Shaun said." "Yeah that's his name, he come in the shop all the time, he ain't never said nothing to me other than to speak," Charmaine mused. "I told Shaun he should say something to you and he said he was going to tell'im," Sonya said. "Damn, ya'll got two of the brothers maybe I can get one of'em too, which one I'ont know," Crystal said. "If I had my guess I would say Te-Mundre the brown skin one sitting there watching Sassy, cause I just saw the other one Fatty I think whispering in some bitch's ear," Sonya said before she called the waitress over.

They placed their orders and Sonya pointed over to Shaun telling her what he said. At first Shannon acted like she had an attitude when she thought Sonya was talking bout Fatty, but when she figured out it was Shaun she calmed down and went to the table to confirm what Sonya said. "That bitch act like she fucking that nigga or something," Crystal said. "Nah but she want to according to Shaun, I'm supposed to meet him at Waffle House on Hull St when I leave here."Fo what? Bitch I know you ain't giving up the ass that quick," Charmaine retorted.

"Hell naw bitch, we just go get something to eat, damn." "Yeah right, don't forget I was there when you told Dan two can play that game," Crystal said. "What da fuck eva," Sonya came back with...Over at the Family's table, Sassy had come back and sat down "Can a bitch get a Pepsi or something I'm thirsty as hell." "I guess so the way you was shaking yo ass, look at that nigga you was dancing with, he can't take his eyes off you. He don't know if one of us is your nigga or what, but he looking harder than a mafucka," said Te-Mundre.

"Leave that boy alone Mundre, that's Tajon we go to school together," replied Sassy. "That boy ain't in no damn school Sass," Cheeks said. "Why he ain't, he ain't nothing but 18 and he just turned that this week, his cousins bought him here to celebrate." "How da hell you know so much just from dancing?" Shaun asked. "Cause he live on Cliff Ave. I saw him at the store today and he told me," replied Sassy.

Who dat broad you was talking to?" Fatty asked Shaun as Shannon approached the table. "Which one of ya'll supposed to be paying for their drinks over there," asked Shannon. "Me," Shaun said. "That'll be $21.00, I thought they was talking bout my baby," Shannon said rubbing Fatty on his shoulders. "Nah I'ont even know'em Shannon, besides if anything they would be buying me drinks," Fatty said. "I know that's right sugar," Shannon said as she walked off to get Sonya and her crew drinks.

"That's Sonya she was the one driving the AC I jumped in that day at Mickey D's, the other two are Charmaine and Crystal. Her cousin that work in Unlimited Performance and her sister," Shaun responded to Fatty's question. "I'm supposed to meet up wit her at Waffle House on Hull St when we leave here," Shaun finished. "Word, I'm supposed to meet Milnet there too," replied Fatty. "Wait a minute ya'll two meeting these bitches at Waffle House, what about the rest of us?" asked Sassy.

"I told Sonya what Cheeks said about Charmaine so now he on his own, I'ont know what's go happen with that. As far as what's go happen to ya'll, you know damn well all us going there together. Now if me and Fatty do get some ass, then ya'll will take the other car and go straight home," Shaun said. "How ya'll know I wanna go straight home?" Te-Mundre said. "Somebody gotta go home too make sure Sass gets home safe, now who it'll be we'll decide later at Waffle House," Fatty said.

As Fatty finished that statement Lil Boosie's 'That Pussy Keep Calling Me' came on and as everybody started nodding their heads they saw four women approach Sonya's table. Next thing they knew one of'em had thrown a drink in Sonya's face and all hell was breaking loose. Michelle, her cousin Trina and her girls Daneisha and Leslie had been in the Club for a while when they spotted the Family coming in and then seen Shaun and Sonya talking. "So what'chu go do let that shit slide or what?" Trina had asked. "Naw, I'ma get dat bitch fore we leave here tonight," Michelle replied.

Watching the interaction between Sonya and Shaun, Michelle was even more pissed off cause Dan Johnson had cut back from fucking with her as much after the shit between her and Sonya. Now here this bitch was in here fucking with another nigga. Soon as Michelle threw the drink in Sonya's face Crystal went into action, she grabbed her glass from the table and smashed Daneisha who was standing directly in front of her in the face. Charmaine jumped up and went after Trina who caught her with two wild swings but not before Charmaine landed a solid right to her eye. This left Sonya to go after Michelle and Leslie, which even though it was two on one, really wasn't no fight because neither Michelle nor Leslie could fight.

When Sonya jumped up, Michelle jumped back, this gave Sonya time to catch Leslie with a left to the jaw that dropped her instantly. Then she went after Michelle, who she grabbed by a handful of weave and started giving uppercut after uppercut.

Then she kneed her in the face and hit her with the other hand, Charmaine and Trina were going at it but Trina was no match for Charmaine. Although Trina got in some fairly decent shots, Charmaine had hit her with sharp crisp punches to the point that Trina was sitting on the floor with two black eyes, a bloody nose and a bloody mouth. Daneisha was never really in the fight after Crystal hit her with the glass, then proceeded to punch her on the jaw and side of her face, when she fell Crystal kicked her in the stomach causing her to curl up.

By the time the deputies got thru the crowd, the fight was over. They tried to help Michelle and her crew while Sonya and her fam made their way to the front door. Outside she found Shaun standing by the door, he asked if she was alright "yeah" she said "and I'm still going to Waffle House." "That's what's up," he responded "and for the record, ya'll handled ya'lls business." "Whateva," she answered walking off. "I'ma see you at Waffle House," Shaun called after her. "Aight."

Chapter 14- East End:

Rel and Jigaloo were sitting in Rel's house while his mama Mrs. Klinksdale was gone to church. "Man I can't believe Y.K. gone shawd, dem punk ass niggas gotta go and look at you all shot da fuck up, you lucky to still be here," Jigaloo said. Rel who had been hit in the shoulder, chest and arm looked like a mummy with all the bandages wrapped around his body said, "Yeah they go pay but we go have to wait awhile. The way da police were at me up the hospital, kept asking me over and over did I know what it was behind or who I had a problem with recently. I tole'em me nor Y.K. had any problems that I knew of, the way they was acting made me feel like they knew bout what happened at McDonald's."

"How da fuck could dey know that, Y.K's dead, you ain't

tell'em shit, and I damn sho ain't tell'em shit, you think one of them bitch ass niggas told'em they think it was us?" Jigaloo asked. "Nah, if so why would they shoot at us that day, that would only make da police look at them. I think we should lay low for a few tho, wit da way they was acting I know they go be coming round asking questions and waiting for retaliation," Rel stated. "What about that bitch you had over here the other day, you think she heard us talking and told the police?" Jigaloo asked.

'Stephanie? Hell nah cuz! That bitch's a true hood rat, besides she didn't hear shit anyway," replied Rel. "Wit da money she be getting from you, plus da crime solvers money she'll be sitting real nice." "Man, I told you that bitch ain't hear what da fuck we was talking bout, don'tcha think if she woulda went to the police they woulda been round here before now asking questions?" Rel retorted. "Alls I know is I 'ont give a damn bout da police, I'm go get dem niggas for killing Y.K., if not them somebody anybody from Northside-Highland Park," Jigaloo responded. "I feel that...."

Later on that day Bayshon was talking to J-Qua from Mosby Court at Aamco on Mechanicsville when Tre and Ski pulled up to get some gas. "S'up Bayshon," Ski said getting out the car "S'up Ski." "Ey yo Bayshon lemme holla at you a minute, son," Tre called as he stood by the car. "Aight, hold on a minute Jay I be right back," Bayshon told J-Qua. "S'up Tre," Bayshon said walking up to them.

"Bayshon where da hell you been? We ain't seen you or heard from you?" "Tre I ain't go lie to you shawd, my hood's in a uproar right now cause of ya'll niggas. The old heads blaming the young niggas for letting ya'll come in and make money without permission, word going round if anybody get caught doing business with ya'll they go get fucked up," Bayshon explained. "So what you telling me son, is your hood declared war on us?" Tre asked.

"Pretty much so, I know Herring and Thedo got approached and niggas sent word that they knew I be coming holla at ya'll, say if I keep fucking with ya'll they go fuck around and rob me or worse. I'ont know how true it is but I heard a couple of junkies done got their ass whupped for fucking with ya'll," Bayshon said. "I know I owe ya'll some money and shit, I got ya'll but let this shit die down first, I know I'ma catch hell cause somebody go see us talking but I'll be aight," he finished. "Ay yo son, check this I appreciate your honesty and realness but lemme ask you this, you hear anything but us getting jacked?" Tre asked. "Nah I ain't heard nothing like that, although I wouldn't put it past these niggas round here," Bayshon replied.

"Yo keep your ears open aight, don't worry bout these niggas, if you need some back we got you and don't sweat that lil bitty ass money. You just gave me more than money and that was loyalty and honesty. I respect that son, word to my mother I respect the hell out of you for that," Tre stated sincerely. "Thanks Tre and I'll keep my ears to the street, I be back round there soon's this shit die down." "Aight nigga stay up," Tre and Ski gave Bayshon dap as they got in the car and pulled off.

John Beechnut and Jerry Tinsley from Tiffany Meadows and Alan Noble from Country Place all out Highland Springs were at Luck's Field in Church Hill playing basketball. "Nigga didn't I tell you to stop smacking me in my mafuckin face," Lil Go-Hard from Mosby Court said to Jerry Tinsley who had just hit him in the face for about the fourth time as Lil Go -Hard drove to the basket. "Man it's just basketball you act like he mean to do it or something?" Alan Noble said. "Fuck that he betta not do it again," Lil Go-Hard said.

Ike and Artez; Lil Go-Hard's uncles had walked up to Luck's field then when on to Bennie J's to get some dope, which is where they are now. "Ya'll mafuckas always tryna come short just cause we grew up together, but not today. Today ya'll need straight money or no can do," Bennie said. "Come on Bennie you know if we had it we'd give it to you damn," Ike said. "Yeah right, like day fo yesterday or the two days last week when ya'll was shot, but that ain't even the point. Dude upped da prices on me, so I gotta at least see some of my money back befo I can start looking out."

"Aight, but don't get rid of everything cause we be back in a short," Artez said. "I ain't making no promises but I'll see what I can do," Bennie said. "Aight fam, we be back later," said Ike.... "Nigga ya'll must take me for a motherfucking joke or something, fuck ya'll niggas keep hitting me in my fucking face for," Lil Go-Hard said. "Man goddamn, ever since you been out here you been crying like a lil bitch, man up mafucka," Alan Noble said.

If he had known who he was talking to, he wouldn't have made that statement. Lil Go-Hard won't but 16 years old, but he had been fighting with grown men since the age of 13 hanging with his uncles, he was known throughout the city as a knockout artist. Alan Noble made his statement at the bottom of the court, as they ran back up the court Lil Go-Hard caught him with a right cross that dropped him. John and Jerry seeing this ran up on Lil Go-Hard who squared himself up and started letting go with sharp crisp left-right combinations. The rest of the players just stood around and watched, most of them knew who Lil Go-Hard was and had seen him in action, it was a known fact he would fight any and everybody.

Ike and Artez walking back saw what was going on and still took their time getting back to the court. They knew their nephew and once they saw Jerry bend over from a body blow they knew it would only be a matter of time before the fight was over. Actually it took longer than they expected cause John Beechnut was scared of getting hit, but once Go-Hard hit him 'OH GOD' it looked like he was breaking him in half. He hit him with a two piece combination to the body that lifted him off his feet with each impact, a right left right three piece combination then a uppercut to Jerry sent him sprawling on his back. This gave Alan a chance to get up and come back at him.

Alan approached him cautiously and squared up, he caught Go-Hard with two straight overhands a left and right, unfortunately for him they had little to no effect. Lil Go-Hard took'em and rolled with'em then hit him with a right cross, left hook, right uppercut to the body that dropped him to his knees and he finished it off with a right kick to the side of the face. Ike and Artez who had arrived back at the court and watched their nephew put on a fight show started clapping. "Bravo Bravo," Ike yelled. "Now that's what da fuck I'm talking bout, that boy could be Heavyweight Champ of the world one day," shouted Artez. Ike who was thinking of a way to hustle up some money whispered to Artez and they walked off towards Coulter St.

"You still playing Go-Hard?" asked Satch. "Hell naw not right now, I'ma sit over here and smoke this 'L', I might play again after I finish." "Shit nigga you ain't the only one smoking, I'm tryna hit that bitch too," Page another player said. "Aight da rest of ya'll niggas tryna play roughhouse?" Satch asked the rest of the players. "And I won't talking to ya'll three niggas that just got ya'll ass whipped." All three guys got up and walked off with Alan Noble looking back at Lil Go-Hard "cuz I wouldn't think about it if I was you," Satch said.

As they made their way over to their car Ike and Artez suddenly materialized "Ey shawd lemme holla at ya'll niggas right quick," Ike said. When they got up on them at the car Ike and Artez both had guns in their hands, Artez had a black 9 mm Beretta and Ike had a Ruger 9 mm. "Ya'll can make this real sweet and easy or real mothafuckin hard," Artez said. "Shawd I'ont believe this shit," Alan Noble said. "Believe it nigga, now run those pockets," Ike stated emphatically. "Ya'll really think we got some money on us just leaving the basketball court?" asked Alan.

"You think you hard huh nigga? I see you got a lot of muthafuckin mouth" Ike said "alls I know is you betta come with some kinda guap before somebody gets hurt out this bitch." "I gotta get mine out the car," John said. "Me too," said Jerry. "Where at in da car?" Ike asked. "Inside da armrest," answered John. "What about you shawd? Where yo's at?" Artez asked Alan.

"Didn't I say I ain't got no money?" "What? Who da -blop blop blop blop-da fuck you think you talking to?" Artez screamed as he hit Alan upside the head with the gun. "Ya'll niggas betta hurry da fuck up and any funny shit somebody's ass getting shot," Ike said. John opened the car door reached in and got his wallet then stepped back to give Jerry room so he could do the samething. Both guys were scared shitless they had never been robbed before, they both went in their wallets to retrieve their money and handed it to Ike.

Then they looked at Alan who was holding the side of his head and glowering at Artez. Unlike John and Jerry he wasn't scared he had been running the streets since the age of 12 and won't nobody taking shit from him. "Oh you still wanna play tough huh?" asked Artez 'Blaow Blaow' he let loose with the nine 'Blaow Blaow Blaow' he continued to let loose. "Aww shit" Alan yelled as he was hit twice in the leg and once in the foot. "Let's go nigga," Ike yelled.

Ike and Artez ran back down T-St and turned up Mechanicsville as John jumped in the car grabbed his cell phone and called the police and paramedics. Everybody on the basketball court heard the gunshots but nobody saw Ike and Artez running; however Lil Go-Hard who was still sitting on the bench smoking had a funny feeling who was involved. Satch who was on an old head round there thought he also knew who was involved but of course he won't go say nothing. The good thing was Lil Go-Hard was still on the bench and hadn't left or made any phone calls since the altercation earlier, so he couldn't be implicated for anything.

Northside:

After leaving the Sattelite the 'Family;' Fatty, Te-Mundre, Cheeks, Shaun and Sassy went to Waffle House where Shaun met up with Sonya again, Cheeks finally got to holla at Charmaine who told him he better start saying more than just speaking to her. Fatty and Milnet met up there and went thru their usual back and forth bickering while waiting for their food. Te-Mundre had even put his bid in wit Crystal. Sassy and Tajon were standing outside talking when his man Sherrod from school rode up with his cousin Robert. Getting out the car while his cousin was talking on the phone and seeing Tajon talking to Sassy, Sherrod called out to Tajon "Come'ere Ta."

"Aight hold up for a minute," Tajon responded. Sherrod replied by saying "Man that bitch can wait." "Who da fuck you calling a bitch? You bitch ass nigga," Sassy replied angrily.

"You responded didn't it," was Sherrod's reply. He was jealous of the fact that Sassy and Tajon were talking, he wanted Sassy for himself although he had never said anything to indicate this fact to her. "Nigga you got me fucked up, I will fuck yo punk ass up," Sassy said.

"You and who else?" asked Sherrod "Make me beat yo ass like da ho you is, then me and my cousin go run a train on your trifling ass," he finished. Fatty noticing his sister's demeanor thru the window got up and headed out the door with Milnet asking "Where da fuck you going?" Cheeks, Te-Mundre, and Shaun hearing this turned to look after their brother, noticing the way he was walking all three brothers got up to follow him. "Who ass you go beat and run a train on my nigga?" Fatty asked. "I'm talking bout that slut over there my nigga tryna front on me for," Sherrod said smirking.

By now all four brothers were outside and Fatty was walking up on Sherrod; Tajon said "Sherrod why da fuck you gotta call her out her name, I told you I'd be there in a minute, fuck's wrong with you?" "Man fu-" and that was all he said before Fatty dropped him with a one hitter quitter right hand. Soon's he hit the ground Fatty started stomping him "Nigga that's my mafukin sister you disrespecting, you go run a train on who? you pussy bitch, her name's Sassy, that's Ms. Sassy to yo punk ass." While Fatty was stomping Sherrod; Cheeks, Te-Mundre, and Shaun all ran up on the car.

Cheeks went to the driver's side where Robert had gotten out and was attempting to help his cousin shouting "fuck's wrong with you get da fuck off my cousin." 'Wop wop' Cheeks caught him with a two piece which knocked him across the hood, as he tried to roll off the hood Te-Mundre caught him with a left that sent blood flying from his mouth. When he hit the ground Shaun kicked him in the face, Fatty had picked Sherrod up and was open hand smacking him 'splat smack smak.' "What's her name nigga?" "Sassy Sassy," Sherrod pleaded. 'Wop' "Nah mafucka that ain't what I said.

'Wop wop' Fatty hit him again. "What's da fuck's her name?" "Ms. Sassy man, Ms. Sassy." "And don't you fuckin forget it, you hear me?" Fatty emphasized. "Yeah yeah," Sherrod answered. Fatty stood him up and 'Blop' Shaun dropped him. All four brothers walked off and went back in Waffle House where they told the waitress they wanted their food boxed to go. After talking to their prospective women all the brothers left with Sassy except for Fatty who left with Milnet....

Now this afternoon all five siblings were at home sitting out on the porch talking when Ms. Fox came out the house "So how was the club last night?" she asked. Everybody looked around and said "the club was fine." "Really, so what happened after the club?" "Ain't nothing happen Ma," Te-Mundre said. Ms. Fox taking her time lighting her cigarette said "Is that so? Then why did I get a phone call early this morning telling me my kids were up at Waffle House fighting?"

Everybody groaned at the sametime "awww" "Aww ass somebody betta start talking. Now!" Sassy spoke up and told her mama what happened the night before, "Don't blame them them ma, it won't their fault I ain't even know they had come out and heard what that boy said." "Why did that boy call you those names Sassy?" "I'ont know maybe he was jealous cause I was talking to Tajon, I do know I never gave him or anybody else a reason to call me those names tho, I swear ma." "I believe you baby, I'm just glad your brothers were there."

"Ma how you find out anyway?" asked Cheeks. "Don't worry bout all that just know I got my ways," Ms. Fox said as she put her cigarette out and walked in the house. She had gotten a call from Donald Abrams her kids second cousin thru their father, who told her he was at McDonald's across from Waffle House on Hull St. the night before and saw the Family in the parking lot fighting. He said he didn't know what the cause of it was, but whatever the reason they beat the people something terrible. He called so that she could be of aware of what happened in case the police got involved, although hadn't none come by the time he left McDonald's.

After Ms. Fox went in the house, Fatty asked Sassy if she thought she would have any trouble out of Sherrod at school. "Naw, matter fact Tajon called this morning to apologize for the way his boy acted and said not to worry bout him cause he was going to have words with him today. He said Sherrod knew not to fuck with him cause he would beat his motherfucking ass." "Well if that nigga even look at you funny you call one of us. You hear me?" Fatty said to her. "Yeah" "Aight lemme make this phone call," Fatty said as he got up and walked off.

"Ello" "What's up Curser?" "Ey Ese' wha be good wit you?" "Same ole same ole." "Lemme guess Ese you ready?" Curser said. "You know it," replied Fatty. "Come to the store in 20 minutes." "Aight...."

Twenty minutes later Fatty was walking thru the door of the store "Hey amigo I see you remember what I said about being late eh?" "Hell nah, I was at home not doing nothing that could stop me from being here that's all," Fatty said with the hint of a smile on his face. "Yea whatever, come to the back wit me." Fatty followed Curser to the back of the store where Curser opened a door, stepped down into a room and opened another door that led to what looked like a storage room. Curser held the door as Fatty entered among boxes and bottles stacked against each other and two tables running parallel to each other.

"So what is it exactly you want Ese?" Curser asked. "Right now I only want one onion," Fatty said. "Ah lemme guess you want to test the product first." "Something like that." "No problem, that's a smart move on your part, now look in one of those boxes over there against the wall." Fatty went and opened one of the boxes, inside were stacks of smaller boxes, "Go head reach inside and pull out one," Curser told him.

"Now come over here and open that box with the make-up kit on it." Inside was a small black digital scale, Fatty opened the first box and dumped the contents on a plate that Curser had placed on the table. "How much you think all that is?" Curser asked him. "It's more than a onion, I'd say somewhere between 2 to 2 and a quarter which is a half-a-big." "Put it on the scale and find out," Curser told him.

"It's 56 grams which is 2 onions," Fatty said looking at Curser "Good Ese you pay for one, take the other and pay for it when you come back." "Nah uh! I told you before I don't take no fronts, so I'ma only get the one I came here for and when I can afford more I'll pay for more." "Ok Ese, I was just testing you to see if you were a man of your word, how bout this I give it to you and you owe me nothing. Even if you decide not to do business with me." "On one condition, that I'm not binded to do business with you and I won't ever hear about this again, I wanna be able to walk away when I'm ready to."

"No problem Ese, in fact I think maybe I need to meet your brothers in case something happens to you and they have to take over." "That'll work, lemme holla at'em." "Ok amigo, you straight now?" "Yeah here's yo money, $750 count it." "Naw Ese I trust you, how can we do business if there is no trust." "You my type of nigga, now you got any more of that Jamaican ganja you had da other day." "No question Ese, what you want?"

"What da price on a onion?" Fatty asked. "For you amigo, give me $70." "Aight bet , here you go and I'll be in touch with you soon." "Aight amigo, here you go be careful wit that Jamican Ganja it'll put you on your ass if you smoke too much at one time." "You must dont know who I am or something," Fatty told him as they walked out the store. "Aight I'm out," Fatty said.

RCJ-Tier E3:

Darnell from Washington Park, Mason from Jackson Ward, Poo-Lou and Smiley from Mosby Court, Carl and Deshaun from 1st and 5th Ave in Highland Park were all sitting in front the TV watching music videos when Wesley from the Fan district walked up and changed the channel without saying a word to anyone. "Nigga what da fuck you think you doing? asked Poo-lou. "Ya'll know Lt. Horsley said no videos until after 6:00," Wesley replied. "Shawd if you don't get your po-lice ass out front the TV and turn it back where it was, it's go be trouble in dis mafucka," Mason said.

"I ain't turning shit back, ain't nobody tryna to go on restriction," stated Wesley. "Nigga fuck restriction, Lt. Horsley and you too, now turn that shit back," Deshaun said. "Fuck you, ya'll niggas only thinking bout yourselves," Wesley retorted. Darnell got up and walked towards the TV all of a sudden without warning he turned and hit Wesley with a vicious three piece combination, starting and ending with a left.

As Wesley hit the ground Darnell hit him with another right and viciously kicked him in the head, leaving him in a puddle of his own blood. Darnell turned around walked back to the TV and turned it back to videos. As Wesley was trying to pick himself up off the floor Smiley jumped up ran over and hit him so hard that a tooth flew across the floor along with some more blood. Wesley fell sideways leaking and that's where they left him until the deputy came 12 minutes later.

Chapter 15- West End:

Gamal had decided he wasn't going to kill Lil Ray-Ray and his crew, but he was going to teach them a lesson. To make sure Ray-Ray didn't contact his boys Simmy and Black Pete, he went to Ms. Emerson and told her he was keeping Ray Ray with him and taking him to the boxing matches up Fredricksburg the next day. Ms. Emerson didn't mind, anything to keep her grandson off the street, plus she knew Gamal was a good boy and wasn't into anything that would get Ray-Ray into any kind of trouble. Little did she know. Gamal, Chris Stevenson, Dre Jr., and Lil Ray-Ray all went to Wal-Mart where they bought four Co2 high powered assault paint ball gun, then went back around the way and dropped Chris Stevenson and Ray-Ray off.

Gamal and Dre headed around Fairfield hoping to catch Black Pete and Simmy out together. Arriving over Fairfield they first drove down Seldon St, then went around to Rosetta. Not seeing either Black Pete or Simmy they decided to ride thru the whole Fairfield. After riding up and down every street they came back to Seldon, turned on Rosetta then rode down and went up to Phaup St where they saw Simmy walking out his cousins house.

"Ain't that one of them niggas?" asked Gamal. "I think so" Dre said "I think that's da nigga Simmy remember shawdy said that was his cousin's place." "Yeah, slow down and let'im start up the street then I'ma jump out on'im," Gamal said. Simmy was walking towards Seldon not paying attention when Gamal got out the car and started walking towards him. Walking past him, Gamal turned and stuck his gun in Simmy's side.

"Aight this what we go do, you go get yo ass in this car, if you get in peacefully you have my word you won't die, but if you refuse or try to fight, then I'll light you ass up right here and leave you stinking. You make the choice." "How I know your word's good?" Simmy asked. "Cause if I wanted you dead, you woulda been, you ain't even realize who you was walking past, now get in the car." Simmy thought about it, he really was in a no-win situation so he decided to take his chances and get in the car. Once inside Gamal said "Shawdy you already know what this about, so we ain't even go play no fucking games or beat around the bush, where yo nigga Black Pete at?"

"How da fuck I know where he at? I ain't his mafuckin baby sitter," answered Simmy. "For yo sake You betta hope we find him or yo ass go pay for both of ya'll and just so you know we already got Ray-Ray, so you ain't got to wonder bout him. You'll see'im in a minute. Dre circle around dis bitch one more time see if we see this nigga, if not head on back round da way," Gamal said. Dre turned on 23rd St came down made a left on Seldon then went back around and came up Rosetta, still no sign of Black Pete.

"Fuck it this nigga and Ray-Ray just go have to do," Gamal said. As they came back up to 23rd and made a right they rode past Cool Lane apts, walking out the apts lighting a cigarette was Black Pete. "You see that, there go Black Pete," Dre said. "Yeah I see'im, he think his ass safe. Pull down by where he just came from then take the tone, get out call'im to you and make 'im get in the car. It'll work betta if you do it considering he might recognize me," Gamal said.

Dre pulled the car over grabbed the gun, cocked it and called to Black Pete as he was getting out the car. "Pete, Pete nigga I know you hear me." "Who dat?" "It's Mane," Dre lied. "Who?" "Mane nigga, Ray-Ray's cousin. You know who got some smoke?" "Yeah my nigga in these apts," Black Pete said walking back to Dre.

"Fo sho, how da bags is? I ain't tryna get nuttin small for my money." "Naw nigga da bags propa trust me." "How far we gotta go?" Dre asked as they turned and headed back towards the apts. "We just gotta go up in these apts, where da hell Ray-Ray ass at anyway, I ain't seen'im in a couple-a-days?" "I thought he was round here, that's why I came round here."

As they approached the apts Dre slowed down some and let Black Pete get in front then he pulled the gun from behind his back and pointed it at Pete's back. "Ay Pete here go da money shawd." When Pete turned around he saw Dre standing there pointing the straight at his chest. "What da fuck shawdy?" "Ain't no what da fuck nigga, what we go do is walk over to that green Century and get in, you can try to run but I'll kill your ass right there on the spot or you can ride wit me and live."

"Shawd, I ain't got no money," Black Pete said. "Nigga this ain't no mothafuckin robbery, again ride wit me you live, if not you die, plain and simple." Black Pete watched Dre and thought he was standing too far back to buck, but if got in the car he may not come back alive, however he did say he wouldn't kill'im if he went with him. "Aight nigga I'll take my chances and ride wit'chu." "Good now walk to that car like I said."

As they headed to the car Gamal got out "Bring yo punk ass round here and get up front." Now Black Pete was real confused "Man what ya'll nig-" "Shut da fuck up and get in the car before we change our minds and shoot your ass," Gamal said. Black Pete looked in the car and saw Simmy sitting by hisself, so he got in the front seat, Gamal got in the back seat with Simmy while Dre slid under the wheel. "You still don't know what dis about right, well lemme give you a piece of advice, don't stick nobody up if you not go remember who it was you got," Gamal said to Black Pete.

"Don't wonder bout Ra-Ray, he'll be where we going now, ya'll lil niggas got balls but ya'll don't now who to fuck with and who not to fuck wit. then ya'll go brag about what you did, stupid mafuckas, now yo lil asses gotta pay the piper." "I thought you said you won't go kill us," Simmy said. "I ain't go kill you, but that don't mean you ain't go pay," Gamal answered. Dre pulled the car up in the back of the abandoned house. "Get out," Gamal commanded.

Everybody got out and went inside where Dre directed them upstairs to a back room where Chris, Poppi, and Ray-Ray were waiting. "Now that we all here we can get this show on the road, ya'll three niggas disrespected me now I want to know why I shouldn't kill ya'll ass right here right now?" Gamal asked. "Cause you gave us yo word you wouldn't," Ray-Ray said. "Fuck that he gave his word I didn't," Poppi said pulling out his gun and cocking it. Seeing and hearing this all three young men realized this was true.

"I'm waiting for a better answer," Gamal said. "Aight man we apologize to all ya'll niggas," Black Pete said. "That's a start I like that, but here's what we go do, since ya'll wanna disrespect me I'ma give you a chance to beat my ass one on one in front my niggas. If either one of ya'll win I'll give all ya'll $500 a piece, and that's non-negotiable starting with Ray-Ray. Chris had rolled a Dutch and was just lighting it as he passed it to Gamal who took it and inhaled deeply. "Ahh ain't nothing like a lil weed to get you going, you ready Ray-Ray?" "Yeah nigga."

"Oh you sound confident, let me take care of you real quick, here take this blunt," Gamal said handing the blunt back to Chris. Ray-Ray stepped up and got in his stance, Gamal got to bouncing on the balls of his feet and before he knew what hit him Gamal had hit him with a three piece. It wasn't hard enough to drop him but hard enough to stun him, when he came at Gamal swinging he got caught with a barrage of body blows that seemed to pick him up off his feet. With each blow he backed Ray-Ray up onto the wall and using the wall as ropes he pummeled Ray-Ray from head to body, it was so quick Ray-ray never landed a blow.

Gamal wanted to especially make Ray-Ray and Simmy pay; Ray-Ray for coming up with the plan to rob him and

Simmy for bragging bout it. He felt as though they had both disrespected him personally and for that they would pay heavily. When Gamal stepped back to let Ray-Ray stand on his own Ray-ray fell face down, as he was falling gamal kicked him in the stomach causing him to gag and cough up blood. "Where dat mafuckin blunt at?" Gamal asked looking around.

"Nigga you don't need to be smoking while you doing this shit, fuck around one of dem niggas catch yo ass and drop you or stand there and go blow for blow wit yo ass," Poppi said handing Gamal the Dutch. Gamal inhaled and blew out a cloud of smoke, "You ready Pete?" Pete didn't answer he just sat there and kept looking at Gamal. "Pete you hear me talking to you nigga?" Still no answer "Oh you go hard huh? Aight nigga lemme finish this up and we go handle our business."

Gamal handed the blunt to Dre "Aight let's do this," he said walking over to Black Pete and once again bouncing on his toes. He led out with a lazy left, but because it was lazy Pete saw it coming and moved out of the way, "Whooa, you missed by a mile nigga," Poppi said. Gamal then threw a left hook over hand right combination. But Black Pete sidestepped the right caught the left on the shoulder and hit Gamal with a solid right uppercut followed by a solid right cross that rocked Gamal back on his heels."Damn that nigga taking it to yo ass nigga, Pop told you not to hit that blunt, you moving mighty slow my nigga," Chris Stevenson called out.

Gamal trying to get hisself together reached out to grab Pete who rushed in and started hitting him with body blows 'bow bow bow,' he backed Gamal up even further. Instead of trying to finish Gamal off Pete backed away and let him get himself together, this time when Pete rushed in Gamal caught him with two stiff jabs and a left uppercut that sent Pete into the wall.

When he came off the wall Gamal caught him with a right cross, left hook, short straight right that dropped him to his knees. Gamal went to kick him but thought better of it, stepped back and said "get up nigga," Black Pete looked up with blood running out his mouth.

"Get up mafucka I ain't go hit you no more." Black Pete pushed hisself to his feet still wary of Gamal "You stood your ground I respect that, I ain't go hit you no more I underestimated you and paid for it. Now get yo ass back over there with Ray-Ray. Gamal walked back to where Dre, Poppi, and Chris were standing "that nigga almost beat yo ass," Dre said and they all started laughing. I'ont know if you should try that last nigga or not, he might be da one to beat yo ass," Poppi said. "Shid for real that last nigga beat his ass, that's why he told him to get up he won't go fight him no more," Chris said.

"Fuck everyone of ya'll long and hard, how bout that? He ain't beat nobody I just underestimated his young ass that's all," responded Gamal. "Aight you underestimated him, truth is that nigga went to yo ass," Dre said. "You wanna hit da last of this blunt?" Chris asked. "Fuck naw, I don't wanna hit mafuckin blunt, what I'ma do is punish this last mafucka." "Don't fuck around and he be the one to knock yo ass out," Poppi said as Gamal walked off.

"Aight nigga you know what time it is front and center," Gamal said to Simmy who took his time getting up. Simmy was trying to figure out how he was going to fight Gamal, as Gamal walked up bouncing on the balls of his feet again. But instead of standing flat-footed Simmy got to bouncing on the balls of his feet too and instead of jabbing, came in bobbing and weaving as though he was Mike Tyson. In the background you heard Dre, Poppi, and Chris say "uh oh" they knew Simmy was in trouble and Gamal didn't disappoint them as he went in chin to chest. As Gamal came barging in Simmy didn't know what to do, instead of throwing punches he backed up on the wall.

With nowhere to run he was at the mercy of Gamal who came in throwing body shots, first he caught Simmy with a wicked four piece to the body. With each blow you could hear the wind being knocked out of him, then with Simmy leaning over Gamal caught him with two successive vicious uppercuts and a right cross. Gamal stepped back and as Simmy was falling he caught him with a left jab, straight overhand right, left cross that dropped him to the floor where Gamal commenced to kick and stomp on him. By the time he was finished Simmy was bleeding from the nose, mouth, and out the side of his eye, he had Gamal's Timbaland boot print all over his face, body, and clothes.

Nobody knew why Gamal went off on Simmy as bad as he did, they all wrongly thought it was because of what had just transpired between him and Black Pete. Ray-Ray wasn't quite sure, but he thought Simmy was the one that had ran his mouth bragging about what they had done. Black Pete wasn't sure either, all he knew was he was glad it wasn't him. Gamal stepped back up and looked down at Simmy who was coughing and spitting up blood, he looked up at Gamal and tried to stand. As he put his hands on the floor to push himself up, Gamal kicked him in the ribcage area catching him with the toe of his boot.

Then he looked down into Simmy's face again and that's where he aimed his foot catching Simmy squarely in the jaw sending blood spewing everywhere. Gamal stepped back over to his boys "Whip who ass nigga?" he said to no one in particular. Nobody said anything they all just stood around looking down at

Simmy in their own thoughts. "Aight this what we go do now, since ya'll niggas wanna play with guns, we got four high powered paint ball guns in da next room." Poppi left out and came back with the guns and extra balls.

"Now this how we go play this game, ya'll three niggas go stand ya'll lil asses somewhere over there by the wall, we go post up on dis side with the guns and ya'll ain't go have shit. We go shoot at ya'll til all the balls gone and I'ma tell you it's a lotta balls 1,000 to be exact. We ain't tryna hit nobody in the face on purpose, but if it happen oh well at least that's betta than the alternative. Right? Any questions?" Gamal stated.

"What's the alternative?" Ray-Ray asked. "Show 'em what da alternative is Pop." Poppi pulled his .40 cal out again "Only thing this da real deal" Poppi said "Ya'll niggas wanna go for the alternative, I'd be happy to oblige you." "Naw" "Hell naw" "That's aight" they all said in unison. "Aight then, Chris roll up another blunt while we load these mothafuckas, I want the AK looking one," Gamal said referring to the paintball gun that looked like an AK-47 assualt rifle. "I want the one look like the D.E.," said Chris cracking open the Dutch and referring to the Desert Eagle. Poppi and Dre took the twin uzi looking ones.

After he finished loading his gun Gamal pulled the slide back and let loose 'fow,' "Oh shit," Ray-Ray said as he and Black Pete jumped out the way. "Oh shit what? Wait til these mafuckas start firing at ya'll mafuckin ass at da sametime, ain't nowhere to run then. So what ya'll go do? And just so ya'll know and understand if anything and I do mean anything happen to the person ya'll bragged to, you'll rather wish death upon your own ass. Cause I'm coming afta mamas, kids, grandmas, the whole fucking family, understand," Gamal said.

All the youngsters nodded their heads 'yea,' the only one

who hadn't said anything to anybody was Ray-Ray so he wondered which one of his boys Gamal was talking to. Simmy and Black Pete both were hoping to God it won't the people they had told; besides Sassy, Simmy also told Corrine, Pep, and Shu-Shu. Black Pete told Tim, Kathy, and Cito. "Suuuuuu cmm cmm, now that's what I'm talking bout," Dre said inhaling "this some crucial nigga." "Then pass that shit nigga, I'm ready to shoot me some niggas," Poppi said.

"Fuck that ya'll niggas ready?" "You know it." "Hell yea" and head nods answered Gamal's question. "Aight" 'Fow' Gamal fired the first shot then 'Fow pop pop fow pop fow fow pop pop pop fow fow splat bok.' "Ah" "Ah" "Shit" "Damn" "Get da fuck out my way" Ray-Ray, Black Pete, and Simmy said as the firing continued 'Fow pop pop fow fow.' All three guys were dancing, jumping and pushing each other down trying to get out the way of the paint balls; 'Plooww' "Ahh shit," Black Pete hollered as he got hit right under the chin by Chris Stevenson.

"Oh shit Chris got the first head shot," said Poppi, "I'ma get the next one," he yelled excitedly as he started aiming just for the head. "Where da fuck that blunt at?" Gamal asked. "You shoot high and I'ma shoot low," Dre said to Poppi. Gamal was the first one to need more paintballs "Ay yo hand me a box of dem balls Pop." "Here" 'Flak flak splat' "Ahhh," Simmy got hit three times simultaneouslyy by Chris, Poppi, and Dre.

'Click click' "Shit I'm out lemme get some more balls," Poppi said. "Here," Gamal threw him the same box of balls back. Dre and Chris ran out next. 'Fow fow fow fow fow' Gamal swept the fake AK back and forth hitting all three young men. This went on for about another 35 minutes with each of the three young men getting their skin broken and bleeding profusely from their wounds. They had been hit all over their bodies with each one taking their fair share in the face, when it was all over you couldn't tell they hadn't been shot with real guns the way their bodies looked.

"Aight ya'll niggas done, I'ma keep my word and not kill ya'll ya'll mafuckas betta thank god for Ms. Emerson although she don't know nothing bout what's going on between us. Let this be a lesson to ya'll never stick-up a nigga you know especially if he live somewhere you be at all the time or know where you be at. Matter fact we don't condone or endorse nobody sticking up unless ya'll beefing or something, now if ya'll want to get money let me know and I'll see what I can do for you." Gamal said.

They were all nodding their heads 'yea' and checking their bodies at the sametime. "What da hell a head nod mean? Speak up mafuckas," Poppi said. "Yeah we tryna get some money man," Lil Ray-Ray said. "Aight I'ma holla at you sometime this week Ray-Ray, until then ya'll mafuckas stay da fuck out my way. Got that? Gamal said.

Everybody said "Yea" "Good, now ya'll tryna smoke a blunt fore we leave?" "Yea man." "Give me a Dutch and a bag of weed and let'em roll sump'in up," Gamal said....

Ms. Fox had sent Fatty and Sassy over to her sister's Carrie Jo who was also Danielle's mother, they were to pick up the money and drop off the tickets for their upcoming trip to Atlantic City. While Fatty was talking to Carrie Jo and eating a slice of sweet potato pie, Sassy was outside on the porch with Danielle "Girl it's been so much shit going on it's crazy as hell, my brothers caught up in so much bullshit it don't make sense. You know they was already beefing with Poe St, plus that shit you called me about with dem Hilltop niggas. Well how bout we go to the Sattelite last night and this broad Shaun's been talking to was in there wit her sister and cousin and got to fighting with four other bitches.

Then we go to Waffle House I'm kicking it with Tajon from school when this nigga name Sherrod from school roll up and started disrespecting me out the blue for no reason. But he ain't know my brothers were with me. Fatty heard what he said to me and beat his ass, when his nigga tried to jump in my other brothers got in it and they beat both them niggas asses. But the trip part is, we got home late last night early this morning,but first thing this morning mama had us all lined up questioning us bout what happened." 'Whaat? How da fuck she find out so fast?" Danielle asked. "I'ont know she won't say just we can't hide nothing from her."

"Damn, well you know Gamal pulled up on Lil Ray-Ray da other day," said Danielle. "Whud, what happened?" "I ain't quite sure alls I know is they scared da shit outta him, Poppi said he know they put the fear of god in'im and that they were going to get the rest of'em later, that's all he would tell me." "Ya'll go ride wit me down to the market to pickup this 12 pack of Budweiser for Carrie Jo?" Fatty asked. "Hell yeah I need some Dutch's anyway" Danielle said "Hold up let me get my purse," she continued.

Once at the market they all went in to get what they wanted; Sassy got her a Mystic and Reese's Peanut Butter cup, Danielle got a Pepsi, sunflower seeds and a box of Dutch cigarellos. Fatty got the 12 pack for Carrie Jo, a Mystic and a Big Texas cinnamon swirl. After paying for his stuff they were all about to walk out when Fatty said he wanted to play his numbers and put some minutes on his phone. Sassy and Danielle went on out and got in the car, neither one paid any attention to the two guys standing on the corner. Sassy had just put in a

Young Jeezy mix CD and Danielle was in the back rolling a Dutch when Fatty made his way out the store.

Walking with his head down looking at the lottery tickets in his hand he never saw the two guys running towards him with their guns drawn. It was Dorez from Poe St and his cousin Pokey from Carter St in the West End, Dorez had noticed Fatty when he pulled up and got out the car. He knew about Fatty fucking Mitch's girl Reyna and was one of the shooters on back of the pickup that shot up Barton. And because he along with everybody else thought it was Fatty and his brothers that shot up Poe St, he felt like it was his duty to get Fatty when he saw him. As for Pokey, Dorez was his fam, so if he had beef, then Pokey had beef no questions asked.

Dorez and Pokey thought they had the drop on Fatty, underestimated him and because they were shooting wildly, gave him time to pull his gun from his waist and fire back. And though his bullets got close to his intended targets, he too missed. At first Sassy thought she was hearing gunshots on the CD until she looked up and saw Fatty shooting his gun "What the fuck Fatty? she screamed as she turned to see who her brother was shooting at. Danielle looked up and saw her cousin blazing away 'Blaw blaw blaw, Bow bow bow, Bop bop bop; ping zing, crack' were the sounds you heard from guns being fired, hitting their car as well as others.

Danielle rolled out the side of the car with her baby nine and started busting back, she too missed her target but with the threat of getting shot at by two different people Dorez and Pokey took off running up the block. Fatty seeing Sassy at the wheel jumped in the passenger side while Danielle jumped in the back. "Catch them niggas Sass," Fatty said. Sassy hit the gas and sped out the parking lot closing the gap between them and the two shooters, Fatty and Danielle both leaned out the window and started shooting. Dorez and Pokey turned and tried to take a short cut when a bullet grazed Dorez's leg "ahh" he yelled out as he felt a burning sensation on his leg, they made it behind some buildings and Sassy kept on going.

"Shawd, I don't believe these pussy ass niggas just shot at me," Fatty said loudly. "Who da fuck was those niggas anyway?" asked Sassy. "One of'em looked like that nigga Dorez from Poe St but I'ont know who the other one was," Fatty said. "That looked like Pokey from Carter St, L.Gizzle's lil brother," Danielle said. "Well he just fucked up shooting at me and this pussy ass nigga Dorez, I'ont know what the fuck he was thinking I'ma have his ass for dinner," Fatty stated vehemently.

"Why da fuck they shooting at you?" Sassy asked. "I'ont know Sass, unless it got something to do wit that shit with Mitch behind his bitch Reyna. Don't worry I'ma end this shit real mafuckin quick, fuck this niggas ain't go keep gunning for me. And I'ont want ya'll telling mama or Carrie Jo unnerstand?" Fatty stated. "Yeah we unnerstand,"Sassy replied. "Cuz don't worry Pokey done fucked up, he already know we supposed to be beefing wit dem Carter St niggas anyway. Now he want to shoot at my mafuckin family, oh naw his ass go get it and if dem Carter St niggas wanna bring it they can get it too," Danielle stated.

"Naw cuz I want you to fall back right now, alls I want to know is where this nigga rest at and where he hang at, don't ya'll do nothing trust me before this week over they go feel my wrath," Fatty said to Danielle. "Give Carrie Jo the beer and tell her we had to run, but don't tell her what happened, if she asks tell her you don't know cause we was gone when it started." "Fatty I don't lie to my mama cuz, but to keep her and Aunt Fox from worrying theyself sick about you I will. Be careful cuz, love ya'll." "We love you too." "Aight Sass take care girl." "You too cuz," Sassy replied.

When they pulled off Fatty looked at his sister and asked "You alright Sass?" "Yeah I'm cool, just wondering why my brothers stay in so much beef, I mean its like damn, every time I turn around ya'll beefing." "I feel your pain and unnerstand where you coming from, but most of this beef we ain't start but we damn well go finish them. Yeah Shaun beat Rel's ass in da club but Rel also disrespected him and yeah I fucked Mitch's girl, but me and Mitch ain't cool like that, plus she said they don't fuck wit each other no more. And the other night you think we go sit back and let a nigga disrespect our lil sister, you know all of us will kill a nigga behind you. The shit today I guess Dorez wanna take up Mitch's beef, if not it don't matter no way, he and his cousin fucked up.

"I know and unnerstand believe me I do, I'm just scared something's gonna happen to one of ya'll, somebody's gonna get hurt or wind up going to jail and I don't want that to be one of ya'll." "None of us do, hopefully god willing nothing will, now stop worrying and cheer up, shit we ain't worried bout nothing and neither should you." "I'ma cheer up, just give me a chance to get over what happened today," Sassy said. "Aight, but get it together before we get home and mama see you, you know she notice err'thing," Fatty said as he and Sassy shared a laugh.

Chapter 16- Southside:

Billy Blu, Frye, Breedo, Pow-Wow, and Phil were on Rosecrest Ave in Hillside Ct talking about the shooting that happened earlier that week. "Shawd, ya'll niggas still don't know who dat was that came thru here blazing da other day?" Breedo asked. "From what I hear, it was either some niggas from Chicago Ave or them mafuckas from Clopton Terrace," Billy Blu answered. "But da niggas dat got shot was supposed to be some of them LBC niggas from Afton and you know they supposed to be beefing with Chicago Ave and Clopton Terrace," Frye said. "How you know so much?" asked Phil.

"Cause they was leaving my cousin Tish's house" answered Frye. "She said she talked to Lil Ron-Ron from Afton and he told her Lil K.O. said he thought it was da mafuckas from Clopton Terrace, cause it was two bitches hanging out the windows shooting. And ya'll know Snooky Boo from Clopton Terrace da only bitch round here that go hard like that." " I say we hit'em up one night this week or wherever we see one of them mafuckas at," Breedo said. "Ya'll know Snooky Boo is Miguel and Worm's cousin and Jawan from round there is Ms. Selma's over on Columbia nephew," Frye said.

"Ain't that the same place Miguel and Worm hang at?" Phil asked. "Yeah and ya'll know Ms. Selma be having the Diddy's by the bottle, so all we gotta do is lay and wait cause they'll be coming back sooner or later," Pow-Wow said. "We just gotta play Miguel and Worm close," Breedo said. 'Why we go hit they ass up in da first place, they ain't shoot at none of us or nobody from round here," Phil asked. "Damn Stupmo why you think? Cause them niggas shot up our hood, now they got the police thinking niggas from round here shot up them LBC niggas," Breedo said.

"Fuck that I'm ready to get at them Afton niggas too, they ain't have no reason coming round here knowing they beefing, I'ont care who dey peoples is," Frye said. Everybody nodded their heads 'yea' but it was Pow-Wow that spoke up "Naw we might get at'em later, but right now I think we should let'em be, it ain't their fault Snooky Boo and nem shot at'em." "I think so too Pow," Billy Blu said "ain't no need to start a beef for no reason, but Clopton Terrace go feel us." Sounds of "no doubt' and "no questions" sang out.

Meanwhile Juice and Monopoly had counted up the take from the robbery and came up with $125,000 in cash, 4 lbs. of weed, 8 kilos of cocaine, and 4 kilos of heroin. "Damn cuz, I thought you said all dem mafuckas sold was weed" Juice said "this shit right here is the mother lode, for real." "I know right, shit I thought that was all they sold. We shoulda been robbed they ass," replied Monopoly.

"Who you telling nigga? But check this shit out, who we go sling this shit to? You know mafuckas ain't go trust our ass, these niggas subject to think we tryna set they ass up so we can rob'em," Juice said while holding a brick of cocaine in his hand. I'm thinking bout that now nigga, how bout we sell the coc to Big Jack and Monk from up Amelia? Break the weed down into dimes and onions, and sell it to'em at decent prices, you know them niggas go hop on it just to say they got a connect in Richmond. Specially if the connect is us," Monopoly said.

"Ok, but what bout the dope?" Juice asked. I'm thinking bout hollering at Smeech over Northside, you know he slinging the fuck out the dope, this way we don't have to worry bout nobody asking where we got it all from? Monopoly said while rolling a Dutch. "All that sounds good but right now I'm tryna splurge wit some of dis bread, $125,000 that's $62,000 a piece nigga, getting rid of the drugs can wait for awhile. A nigga tryna go shopping and shit, hit Georgetown and some more shit," said Juice. "I know that's right, I'm right along wit'chu," Monopoly replied....

Phlop phlop, 'mmm' phop 'mmm' smak 'ahh shit' 'ungh

ungh' phlow phlow 'mmm'- were all the sounds you heard as P.J. was slamming into Tricey from behind. He looked up and broke into a big grin, standing on the other side trying to choke her to death by shoving his whole dick down her throat was Do-Do. Tricey had called P.J. earlier from her sister Peaches house to see what he was doing. "S'up who dis?" P.J. had answered. "Hey baby how you doing?" Tricey had responded.

"I'll be doing aight soon's I know who da fuck this is," replied P.J. "Oh really, well who else go suck yo dick while they man standing there watching," Tricey quipped. "Oh shit, what's up sexy lady? Yo nigga ain't kill yo ass afta that shit?" "What? Hell naw, I mean he call hisself whipping my ass and putting me out, I just moved to my sista's house over the south, he been calling talking bout he wanna talk and shit." "Say word, that nigga pussy whipped like that? Damn! What'chu do to'em? Lick his ass and swallow his cum at the sametime?" P.J. asked. He couldn't believe that nigga was still trying to make her his girl 'damn that nigga hard up' he thought.

Tricey laughed and said "You should know. Anyway I ain't doing shit so I called to see what you was up to." "Right now me and my nigga Do-Do heading ova da south to take care of something real quick." "Is that right? What ya'll getting into good tonight?" "You if you want us to," replied P.J. "What that supposed to mean?" "You know what it means." "I'ont know bout all that."

"Shid I'ont know why not, we already on our way over da south, once we handle our business we could just swing by, pick you up then go get a room or something." "P.J. let's get one thing straight aight, I ain't no ho or slut or none of that shit alright." "Ain't nobody say nothing bout you being a slut or nothing, I'm just saying we tryna have some fun wit'chu that's all." "How bout you come pick me up and I let you know then." "That's what's up sexy lady. Where you at?" "Over the new Blackwell Townhouse apts on Boston Ave apt#42, four doors down from the corner." "Aight I'll call you when I get on the street, gimme bout 20 minutes." "Aight."

"You get your wish today nigga," P.J. said to Do-Do after hanging up. "That ain't what it sound like to me, sound like she said naw bout me," Do-Do responded. "She talking bout she don't know but come get her anyway. What da fuck you think? It's already out there now, if she won't wit it she would've just said 'hell no' and cursed me out but she didn't so that tells us she wit it." "We'll see nigga, we will see," was all Do-Do could say.

They picked Tricey up and went to the Comfort Inn on Midlothian Tnpk., once in the room they rolled a couple of Dutch's and sparked up when Tricey spoke up " Nigga I ain't say I was wit dis shit."Ay yo, shut da fuck up I ain't tryna hear that shit right now, what I want is for you to come ova here and give my dick a massage. Ain't nobody said nothing else bout that shit, Do-Do just go sit here while we smoke these blunts and wait for this switch to hit us back," P.J. said. Tricey looked over at Do-Do then got up and walked over to the bed where P.J. was sitting, she climbed up on the bed took her left hand and started rubbing P.J.'s dick thru his pants.

"Uh uh that ain't go cut it, you know you gotta let'im out his cage," said P.J. He and Do-Do both were smoking blunts. Tricey unbuttoned and unzipped his P.J's jeans and pulled his dick out, once she had it out she started running her hands up and down the shaft gently squeezing here tugging there. She played with the head and kept swirling her fingers all around it, she kept looking from P.J. to Do-Do. Within the blink of an eye she had stuck the head in her mouth, she licked all around it then went all the way down on it. She put her hand on it and proceeded to start pumping while sucking, all you could hear was 'sslurp sslurp ssslurrp.'

"Turn that ass around so I can play with that pussy," P.J. demanded. Tricey did what she was told all the while keeping P.J.'s dick in her mouth. Because she had on a cheerleader like skirt with a pair of black and red thongs, when she turned around her big round caramel ass was staring him in the face. P.J. flipped the skirt and smacked her on the ass which made her shake it back in his face, he pulled her thong to the side and slid his middle finger in her dripping wet pussy.

Tricey moaned 'mmmm' as he started moving his finger in and out "You like that don't'chu?" he asked her. "Um hmm," she answered. "I know you do, but I know wha'chu really want, you want me to put this muthafuckin dick up-n-ya." "Um hmm," she answered again rocking back and forth on his fingers as he had now stuck his index finger into her along with his middle finger. "That's what I figured, so what we go do is put on a lil show for Do-Do, shit it'll be like he watching a live flick.

"Now I'ma pull this thong down and hit it from da back, I want you to look at Do-Do eye-to-eye the whole time, okay." "Um hmm" "I can't hear you." She pulled his dick out her mouth with a 'sslurrp pop' and said "I said okay." With that she got up in position so she could be looking directly in Do-Do's eyes while licking her lips and smiling lasciviously at him. P.J. stood up got behind her ripped her thong off, smacked her on the ass pulled her to him, spread her ass cheeks and entered her hot wet pussy.

She caught her breath 'umph' then P.J. started stroking her and you could hear her juicy pussy making squishy sounds 'coocup coocup.' Do-Do couldn't help hisself he reached down and started stroking his dick while looking into Tricey's eyes. P.J. seeing what Do-Do was doing started laughing and then really started banging Tricey's back out 'Phow Phow Phow' "ahh ahh ahhh umhh." "Damn nigga, you tryna kill shawdy ain't you?" Do-Do said. "Shawd, what I'm tryna figure out is why you ain't got your dick down her throat yet? Lemme find out yo ass scared," P.J. said.

"Scared ass, shid nigga I thought yo ass was putting on a show, but since you asked shit I ain't got no problem sticking my dick down her throat," Do-Do said already standing up with his dick in his hand. Tricey who was cumming at the sight of Do-Do's dick and being fucked by P.J. at the sametime greedily swallowed Do-Do's dick up as he stuck it in her face. "Got damn shawdy," Do-Do said. "Sslurp slurp" "Damn shawdy got some bum," he said as he put his hand on top of her head and guided her up and down his shaft.

Tricey who knew her head game was nice hearing this really started getting into it while trying to throw her ass back at P.J. who was pounding the shit out her pussy. "Damn nigga you cheesing hard as shit, that pussy must be a smoka, shiit I'm tryna get soma that too," Do-Do said. "Aight nigga, switch then," P.J. responded. Tricey had a hold of Do-Do's dick, sucking like there was no tomorrow, she couldn't help herself she was horny as hell even after P.J. had pulled out she didn't want to release Do-Do.

"Aight baby don't worry he ain't going nowhere you go get to kiss'em again fo we finish here, right now he want to beat the putty cat up," Do-Do said as he pulled his dick out her mouth. Tricey went to chase after it when P.J. stepped up and stuck his dick in her mouth "Where you going? Fuck you chasin that dick for? Here go one for you to suck on." "Unc unc," was her answer. Because he fucked her first P.J. had went raw squirrel, now Tricey was tasting not only his dick but her own juices as well. She didn't care though, she was so caught up in the moment.

Do-Do got behind her reached up and smacked her pussy lips "Damn shawdy you got some fat ass pussy lips," he said. After putting on his condom he spread her ass cheeks and inserted his dick, Tricey immediately stopped sucking P.J.'s dick for a minute to get used to Do-Do's dick. It wasn't that he had the biggest dick in the world, but he had hit a spot that hadn't been hit in quite some time and this was causing her pussy to convulse overtime. "What da fuck, fuck you stop for?" P.J. asked. Tricey started sucking again but Do-Do was putting in work, she didn't know whether she wanted to keep P.J.'s dick in her mouth or take it out so she could moan.

She decided to take it out and jerk on it while smacking it on her face and kissing all over the head. "Unh Unnnh Unnnnhh ssshiit," she moaned. P.J. couldn't help it he was ready to bust all in her face, he took his dick in his hand and stuck it back in her mouth. "Unc unc unc," were the sounds she made as P.J. shoved his dick to the back of her throat. Do-Do pulled out her sopping wet pussy which made her back up chasing after him "um um," she said.

Do-Do spread her legs a little wider, pushed her ass cheeks up and apart, positioned his dick at her asshole and entered. "Unnhhh," she moaned as she tried to pull away, but P.J. held her head on his dick as he continued to fuck her mouth. Do-Do gave one more shove and was all the way in, after staying still for a few seconds he started pulling back then pushing forward again. Pretty soon he had set a steady pace and was fucking the shit outta Tricey in the ass. 'Plow plow smack' "Unhh," she moaned.

Tricey couldn't believe this nigga was in her asshole, but strangely enough she liked it, it felt good, not only was she already cumming but now she thought she was on the verge of having an orgasm. Do-Do feeling good about hisself looked over at P.J. and smiled, then raised both hands in the air as he continued to beat Tricey's asshole up. P.J. seeing this did the samething and the two friends gave each other high fives using both hands clasping them together forming a steeple above Tricey as she continued to do her thang. Tricey started pumping P.J.'s dick furiously as she was cumming and couldn't stop, next thing P.J. knew he was cumming all down her throat. She swallowed some then pulled him out and let him cum on her face as well as in her mouth while wiping and smacking it on her lips.

Do-Do seeing this put his hand in the small of her back and started slamming into her ass 'Pow pow pow pow' "ah ahh," she moaned. P.J. completely drained, backed away from her which allowed her to duck her face on the bed and wipe his cum and her sweat off her face on the sheets. Do-Do pulled back again and told her to turn over on her back which she did, he pulled her to the edge of the bed, put her legs on his shoulders and slammed her onto him, sending all his dick up into her at one time. "Uh-" Tricey couldn't make a sound seeing as how it got stuck in her throat.

'Phlam phlam phlam phlam,' he slammed into her time and time again "Ah Ah Ahhh Ah Ahh Ahhhiieettttt shit shit shiit," Tricey moaned and yelled as she had that big orgasm she had felt building up. Do-Do kept slamming until he was ready to bust, Tricey feeling his dick beginning to swell and knowing he was about to cum jumped off his dick snatched the condom off and started sucking his dick. "Daamn," both Do-Do and P.J. said at the sametime. Tricey was going to work "Sslurrp sslurrp bmmm" then Do-Do bust off "Ah shit girl." "Bm bmpp bm," was all you heard as Tricey completely drained him.

FInishing it off with a kiss on his dickhead "mmpwa" she sat up, turned to look at P.J. and asked "Satisfied now?" "Hell yeah, da fuck you think?" "I think if I was a trick I could charge top dollar for that performance," she said laughing getting off the bed walking towards the bathroom. "You betta believe it shawdy, shit I wish we hada recorded it so we could make some real scrilla," Do-Do said. "I know that's right," Tricey replied.

"Shawd make some room so a nigga can wash off," Do-Do said to her. "P, roll sum'pin nigga, what da fuck? Nigga need sumthin to smoke and drink afta that workout," he continued. "I got 'chu nigga be patient," responded P.J. "Workout, lemme find out yo ass is done afta one nut nigga," Tricey said looking at Do-Do and winking. "Hell nah girl, you crazy? Fo we leave here yo ass go be begging for our ass to stop. Da fuck wrong wit'chu?" Do-Do retorted. "Aight nigga if you say so, we;ll see," Tricey said. "Yeah we'll see," Do-Do replied smacking her on the ass as walked out the bathroom....

Sonya was laying in her bed sleep when Crystal came in "Sonya Sonya wake up, wake da fuck up." "I'm up dammit, what da fuck's wrong wit'chu?" "Dan and nem got hit last night!" Crystal shouted. "Fuck you talking bout Crys? Got hit how?" "They got shot." "What?" Sonya screamed jumping up.

"I just got off the phone wit Janae, she said bout 6 or 7 people got shot over there last night and she knew that Lil Goo, Corey, Slick, and Dan all got hit, but she not sure how bad." "What? What time last night? How come ain't nobody call and tell me?" Sonya questioned putting her clothes on; "Did anybody die?" "I ain't sure but they all went to MCV, she said Marlay tried to call you last night but you ain't answer your phone." "Damn, damn double damn, lemme call Marlay and see what's up," Sonya said dialing Marlay's number.

"Hel-lo?" "Marlay, where's Dan?" "He at da hospital, calm da fuck down he ain't dead, got hit in the back of the ankle a lil above his Achilles whateva that is. And where the fuck was you at last night?" "I was at the Sattelite if you must know. Is Dan coming home or what?" "Yeah he coming home, they said they wanted to keep him 24 hours to make sure ain't no bone fragments move down into his arteries." "Well did anybody die and did he say what happened?"

"Far as we know ain't nobody dead, I heard one of the guys from up the street got hit in the back but he ain't die. Ain't nobody sure what happened, alls we know is that one nigga walked from one way and another from the other way and they both started shooting." "I'm on my way down MCV to see'im," Sonya said. "Do what you do, but I'm going back to sleep, you can bring his black ass home too," Marlay said before hanging up. "Come on" Sonya said to Crystal "we going to the hospital." "What I'm going for? That ain't my nigga, and judging from last night he ain't yo's no more either,"Crystal said. "First of all you going to show support and second of all he's still my man until I say otherwise...."

Unbeknownst to Sonya, Michelle was already at the hospital, her cousin Poochie had called and told her what happened. "Damn, look at you" Michelle said "What happened to my baby?" "Yeah look at me, I be aight tho. I'ont know who them niggas was but somebody's ass is grass, you betta believe it. How da hell you find out anyway?" "My cousin Poochie called me this morning and told me. Yo girl ain't been down here yet?" "Naw I ain't seen nor heard from her, far as I know she don't even know yet."

"I'ont guess so considering da way she was all up in a nigga's face last night in the Sattelite." "Stop playing wit me Michelle, I ain't in the mood for that shit." "Nigga what da fuck I'ma be playing for, matter fact I got to fighting wit the bitch, I threw a drink in her face and me, Trina, Daneisha, and Leslie went to dat ass." "Fuck you throw a drink in her face for and I know damn well ya'll four ain't bank her." "Wha'chu mean what I do it for? You forgot that bitch came over to my house starting shit and no we didn't jump'er, she had Crystal and Charmaine wit'er.

"Damn Chelle you tryna let her know we still fucking around or sum'pin." "Nigga she needs to know, is it my fault the bitch don't know what to do to keep the dick at home and why da fuck she ain't been up here yet? The way she was all up in that nigga's face, it wouldn't surprise me if she didn't stay with him last night. "What nigga you keep talking bout?" "I'ont know his name, alls I know is he came in there with three more niggas and a broad, look like all of'em family or sum'thin.

What I do know is he and yo bitch was sitting at the table for a long ass time talking while Charmaine and Crystal were on the dance floor, then the nigga paid for all their drinks." Sonya and Crystal had gotten to the hospital and talked to Lurch, Slick's uncle; he told them what he knew and told Sonya to tell Dan to get at him when he got out. Walking up to Dan's room they heard him talking, then they heard a female's voice; Sonya got to the door and couldn't believe her eyes "What da fuck? Bitch you got some nerve coming up here,' Sonya said. "Fuck you mean I got some nerve, ain't'chu the one was in the club in a nigga's face last night? That's why yo ass just getting up here to check on your man," Michelle quipped.

"Bitch, I'ma finish beating yo ass from last night," Sonya snapped. "Hold da fuck up, so you were in da Sattelite last night," Dan asked Sonya. "Yeah, and" "Fuck you mean and? Who was the nigga who face you was all up in?" "First off nigga, dude pulled up on me, second off how da hell yo go question me when this bitch threw a drink in my face, then I get up here and she here wit you. How da hell you explain that?"

"I ain't got shit to do with what happened in the club, remember you jumped on her last week, as for her being here at least she got here early, why da fuck you just getting here?" Sonya and Crystal couldn't believe their ears "Know what Dan? I'm tired of this this busllshit, so I'ma go head and step off, let her take you home, matter fact don't even call me when you get home. I'm done." With that Sonya turned around and walked out the room, Crystal looked from her sister to Dan and Michelle "Fuck both of ya'll. Dan you ain't shit, all my sister did was love you and you took her for granted, I hope she mean what she say. As for you bitch, when I see you outside this hospital, I'ma beat dat ass real good," and with that she too turned and walked out.

East End:

Standing in front of Cassidy's apartment. Tre, Ski, Cap,and Turk, aka The New York Boyz; were getting ready to ride over Ayanna's house when Minga from New York came walking down the street. "What's good my up top fam?" "Ain't nothing Ma, what's good wit'chu," Tre replied. "Shit a bitch tryna make some money so she can get her shot on," Minga responded. "Get your shot on, we thought you had gone back up top it's been so long since we saw yo ass," Turk said. "Back up top, naw fam not recently. But why should I come round here when ya'll got them niggas up on Carmine selling ya'lls shit, I can just go right out there and get straight."

All four brothers turned to look at each other when she said this. "Wha'chu mean niggas on Carmine selling our shit? How you know it's the same as ours?" Tre asked. "Nigga please, as much of ya'lls shit I done smoked, you know damn well I know it when I smoke it." "Aight so tell me this, who you cop it from then?" Cap asked. "From this nigga name Reece or one of his niggas, damn why all the questions? Ya'll act like you don't know who you got slingin for you."

"Listen Minga, I'ont know if you heard or not but we got jacked a while ago," Tre said. "What? Stop joking." "Ain't no damn joke," Ski said. "How bout I give you $20 so you can buy some and bring it back so we can see for ourselves," Tre said. "I'm cool wit that, but how but one of ya'll go wit me, so you will know and see who and where I got it from."

"I ain't got no problem with that, I'll be the one to take that walk but I'ma play back while you go cop, that way they won't recognize me," Tre said. Tre and Minga walked off thru the cut, leaving the rest of the brothers standing in front of Cassidy's apt. Coming up to Carmine St., Minga walked a little faster once she saw Maurice and Kalil standing out by the cut. "What's up cutie?" she said walking up to Maurice calling him by the name she always called him.

'What up Mama Minga?" Maurice replied. "Shit, a bitch tryna get 3 for her last $20." "Is that so, Minga you know damn well that ain't yo last twenty dollars, specially with dude standing back there waiting on you," Maurice said. "Who dude is anyway?" Kalil asked looking up the block. "This trick nigga name Jerry that work at Phillip Morris."

"Word and you talking bout yo last twenty, more like da

first twenty, I know that nigga got a pocket full of money," Kalil said. "Just make sure he keep spending," Maurice said."You know I will cutie just make sure it's worth it." "Oh it's worth it trust me, but then again you already know that," Maurice replied. "And you know this," Minga said smiling.

Minga walked back to Tre and they headed back the way they had come, soon as they got out of sight Minga handed Tre the three rocks. Once back in Cassidy's apt Tre dropped two of the rocks on the coffee table while he looked at the other one. "Damn sho look like our shit," Tre said. "Ay yo Minga befroe we started slingng this beige shit, anybody else have it?" Ski asked. "Hell nah, how you think ya'll was able to blow so fast, ya'll came wit that bomb ass N.Y. shit that was different from everybody else.

You know how long it's been since we had some beige around here?" "Ey thanks Minga, you can keep the coc and we go keep this between us aight fam?" Tre said. "No doubt, just cause we in VA don't mean we can't look out for each other, specially since we all from up top in the real city," Minga said before she left out. Then Tre spoke "Aight ya'll, it's like this we know these niggas selling our shit which means they're the ones that jacked us. I'ont even want the shit back but what I do want is these niggas heads."

"Why don't we just go round there now and bust on these niggas," Turk said. "That's what I'm getting at Turk right now they don't know we know they slinging our shit, so what we go do is ride up on'em and let loose on they ass son,"Tre said.. "So what we go hit'em today or what?" asked Ski. "I say we hit'em today just in case that bitch Minga decides to play both sides of the fence," Cap said. "Yo you think she'd try some stupid shit like that?" Turk asked.

"Could be, I don't put nothing past nobody son especially a fiend, just cause she from up top don't mean nothing" Tre said "Let's strap up then ride on these niggas asses, aftawards we go lay low at Ayanna's for the rest of the night, we'll come here tomorrow and see what the word is," he finished. The brothers loaded their guns; Tre had his .44 Desert Eagle with the 12 round clip and one in the chamber, giving him 13 altogether. Cap who was go drive had his .40 cal with the 8 round clip with the one in the chamber 9 altogether. Turk had the choppa with a 30 round clip and Ski had a 9 mm Beretta with a 17 round clip.

"Ya'll niggas ready?" Tre asked. "No doubt son," replied Ski. "Yeah, lets go already, I'm ready to make these niggas feel this red son," Turk said. "Just be calm nigga we go do this quick and be out," Cap said. "Aight let's ride," Tre said. The brothers headed out with Turk giving the "Blllaaat call of the Bloods. Once in the car they headed over to Carmine St., when they got on the street they saw Kalil getting in a white Chrysler New Yorker and pull off.

"Follow'em Cap" Tre said "we may find out where them niggas rest at and catch'em slipping like they did us," he continued. Kalil, Maurice, and Matt were on their way over Kalil's cousin Tawanna's house in Jackson Ward, they never knew they were being followed. Coming off the highway they turned right onto Chamberlayne Ave, then another right on Charity St., they pulled down to park at the stop sign on Charity and St. Peter. While looking for the box of Dutch's that Maurice had dropped between the seats, they never saw the green Chevy Caprice that turned the corner behind and pulled up beside them. Once Cap stopped the car everybody bailed out with guns drawn and blazing; Tre out the front, Turk and Ski out the back.

'Cak cak cak cak cak bok bok bok bok.' Matt being the

driver was the first one hit; the first bullet from Tre's Desert Eagle caught him in the neck, the second one cut his ear in half, then Maurice got caught in the forearm causing him to scream out in pain 'ahhh.' While Tre was shooting Ski was also letting loose with his 9 mm, he hit Kalil in the jaw and caught Reese in the left thigh. Turk had ran around the other side of the New Yorker and when his brothers stopped shooting he let the choppa go ' yop yop yop ya ya ya ya ya ya yop yop yop.' He hit Kalil in the shoulder ripping his arm from his body to the point that it was dangling, he tore thru the back of Maurice's seat and ripped a hole out thru his stomach. He hit Matt on the right hand ripping the pinky finger off, he hit Kalil again in the right thigh and the bullet traveled down and came out thru his calf.

By the time he was finished the New Yorker looked like swiss cheese on both sides. The brothers jumped back in their car and were out.

Chapter 17-HCJ Dayroom 21:

Darrell was sitting on the table talking to Jeff waiting for the deputy to call his name so he could get out "Man don't let that shit wit Chazz and Jakeela stress you out." "I'm good my nigga, afta I thought about it I said on't chase'em replace'em," Jeff responded. "Shawdy go head wit that shit, who da fuck you think you talking to, this me nigga Darrell yo road dawg, your right hand you know I know betta than that shit. You might get another broad but you damn sure ain't leaving Jakeela so stop lying nigga." Jeff laughed "Yeah aight you might be right, notice I said might be cause right now I swear I'm thinking bout firing her ass."

"I know that's right, afta that shit Angie pulled her ass is definitely fired, she don't even know I'm on my way home today but boy-o-boy do I got a surprise for her ass. Kysheema coming to get me this morning, take me to see my mama and from there back to her place to relax, I'll see that bitch afta some sex and then more sex," Darrrell said. "You talking bout me, don't you get your self in no trouble behind that bitch, go see Lil Darrell and then jet, you know she go be sweating yo ass," Jeff replied. "Yeah she go think cause of Lil D., I'ma forgive her ass, but not this time, this time she done fucked up for real. I ain't saying Sheema go take her place but it's damn sure up for grabs, either way she assed out, you betta believe it and when I find out who that nigga was he assed out too.

I hope this nigga got some change cause I damn sho go rob his ass b-fo I murk him. But yo I want you to stay on point, don't let that nigga Chazz rock you to sleep," Darrell said looking at his right hand man. "Nigga you know that ain't go happen so don't even worry bout that, you just stay out til I come home." "No doubt," Darrell replied. "Jenkins Darrell Darrell Jenkins ATW," Deputy Reling called. "Aight," Darrell responded. "Aight my nigga be easy," Jeff said giving his man dap.

"No question and you take yo time don't get caught up in no more bullshit, give me a coupla weeks and I got you my nigga you know that," Darrell said. "Fa sho," Jeff replied. "Jenkins" the deputy called again "Jenkins let's go." "Man I'm coming, hold yo muthafuckin horses. Call me shawdy, mama'll accept the call you know that," Darrell said as he was leaving. "No doubt."

After changing from jail clothes to his street clothes, Darrell was headed outside when he passed Ms. Jasper coming in, she winked her eye and kept going, he just smiled. Once outside Darrell breathed in the fresh air and heard a car horn blowing, looking around he saw Ky-Sheema pulling up in her burgundy 2010 Nissan Maxima. She got out and met him coming to the car, throwing her arms around his neck she stuck her tongue down his throat "Damn" he said pulling back. "Damn what nigga?" You think that's something wait til I get your ass home," she said.

Darrell held Sheema back and looked at her, even this early at 7:00 in the morning she was beautiful, standing 5'1" light red bow legs with hazel eyes, this woman was the epitome of sexy and fly. She had the cutest, sexiest smile he had ever seen, often times when he was locked down he would ask hisself why he kept putting up with Angie's shit when he knew that she was nowhere near the woman Sheema was. "What da hell you looking at Darrrell?" "Nothing just admiring your beauty." "Well let's go so I can admire that dick I ain't seen in a while."

"Damn I ain't been out 60 minutes and you talking bout the dick already." "What da fuck you think, shit I ain't had no sex since your ass been gone and that damn dildo ain't the real fucking thing," she quipped. "I hear you baby, but first I want to stop and see my mama, then we can go to the house." "I ain't got no problem with that, but you musta forgot what I said the other day on the phone," Sheema said as they were getting in the car. "And what's that?"

"That I was going to drain that mothafucka this morning" she said putting the car in drive "so you might as well pull it out right now." "How da fuck you go drain'em and you driving, I'ont need you to play with'em I did enough of that myself." "Nigga if it's one thing you know I don't do, it's play games, now stop talking and pull that mufucka out. Now." "Yo ass crazy," was all Darrell could say as he unbuckled and unzipped his pants, pulling his dick out in the process. "Now that's what the fuck I'm talking bout," Sheema said reaching over grabbing hold of

Darrell's dick.

"Sheema what da fuck I tell you." "Shut da hell up Darrell I got this okay." She pulled into the parking lot of the local high school and cut the car off. "What da fuck we doing here?" Darrell asked. "You talk too much, now let your seat back." "What?" "Damn, let your seat back nigga, what da fuck?" Darrell did as she said.

Sheema took his dick and started running her hand up and down it's length, over and around it's head. She leaned in to kiss Darrell then lowered her head "Aww look at my baby you missed me, come'ere give me kiss," she purred as she gave Darrell's dick a nice deep kiss. "Ahh," Darrell said. Sheema went down lower on the shaft and started working her jaws and tongue at the sametime. "Ssluurp slurrp gulp gulp." "Damn Sheema damn damn damn I missed you baby," Darrell said and he meant it.

Besides being sexy and fly Sheema also had the best head game of anybody he knew. Sheema pulled back kissed the head again, then let her tongue swirl around it again, she stuck her tongue in his pisshole, then she shoved the head in her mouth and yanked it back out again 'rrp ssluurrp slurp.' Darrell put his hand on the back of her head, she knew he was close now. Darrell started pumping her mouth 'bpmmb bpmmb.' "Unh Unh shit Sheema, ahhh ahhhh damn baby. Oh shit aight aight that's it, leave'em alone baby. Sheema what da fuuck damn!" 'Pwwaa' Sheema said giving his dick one last kiss before coming up for good.

"Damn you sho did miss us for real, huh?" Darrell said. "Wha'chu thought nigga, wait til I get yo ass home in bed," she replied. "I hear you baby, lemme go see my mama for a lil while then we can go to the house." "When you going to see your son and his mama?" "I'll see my son later, as for Angie fuck her I ain't go worry bout that bitch at all." "Yeah nigga I heard that before."

"Naw I'm telling you baby, fuck that bitch you'll see, matter fact you probably go be ready to put me out the house by the end of the week." "So you saying you staying wit me til the end of the week?" Sheema asked. "Yeah maybe even longer we'll see." "Oh so that bitch fucked up while you was down and now you out, you want to pay her back then you go run back to her afta ya'll make up." "Fuck naw that chapter in my life is over and done with, believe me when I tell you, the reason I said we'll see is because I plan on staying at my mama's house a coupla days.

But as for fucking wit that bitch that's one thing you ain't gotta worry bout. You see who picked me up this morning don't you, that in itself should tell you something." "Whatever nigga, don't feed me no lies, I'll believe it when I see it," Sheema stated. "You'll see baby trust me you'll see."

Eastend:

Ayanna got home abut 9:00 in the morning from work to find Cassidy knocked out on the sofa beside Cap who was on the other end sleep. "Cassidy Cass wake yo ass up." "Alright already damn, fuck you wake me up for?" Cassidy snapped. "How long you been here?" Ayanna asked her lil sister. "All night why?" "Where Stan at?"

"I'ont know he was supposed to go to the club last night, then back to the house. Why?" "Who he went to the club with?" "I'ont know Kalil and nem I guess." "I hope not," Ayanna said. Cassidy was sitting up now as were the rest of her cousins; Turk was on the floor, Ski was over in the chair and Tre was stretched out on the love seat.

"What da fuck you mean you hope not?" Cassidy asked. "Cass, Kalil and nem got shot last night," Ayanna answered. "What?" "Tawanna called me this morning when I was on my way from work, she said Kalil and nem were on their way to her apartment when they got shot sitting in the car." Hearing this the brothers started looking at each other. Tawanna was Ayanna's best friend and being Kalil's cousin, she knew how tight Kalil and Stan were. "Nooo! Please tell me you lying Yanna," Cassidy pleaded.

"I wish I was Cass, Wana said she know at least one person died, but she ain't sure who and she knew the other two were life threatening." "Nooo! Lemme call Stan," Cassidy said looking for her phone. Tre asked Ayanna "What ya'll know dem niggas or something?" Ayanna studied her cousin "Know'em Tawanna's my best friend and Kalil is her cousin, plus them Stan's niggas the niggas he run with everyday." "Get the fuck outta here," Ski said.

"Man fuck them niggas," Turk said. "What?" Ayanna asked incredulously looking at Turk. Tre, Cap, and Ski just glared at him willing him to shut da fuck up, but as always his mouth just kept on running. "I said fuck them niggas," he said again. "Stan ain't answering his phone, I called his mama and daddy's house and didn't get no answer. Yanna you gotta take me to the hospital,' Cassidy said. "Why don't you call MCV first and see if they got Stan registered there," Ayanna said.

"Even if they don't you taking me to the hospital, I know he'll be coming there to check on his niggas," Cassidy said. "Aight," Ayanna replied as Cassidy walked off down the hall. "Now back to you Turk, why would you say that? It ain't like you know them?" "Them the niggas that jacked us in Cassidy's house! Turk said heatedly. "What?" "Turk shut the fuck up damn son," Tre said. "You talk too damn much," Cap said. "What da fuck ya'll talking bout? Please tell me ya'll ain't have nothing to do with that shooting," Ayanna said. "What da fuck? Them niggas jacked us in your sista's house and you worried bout them, I hope all they asses die," Turk said as Cassidy was walking back in the living room.

Ayanna looking at Cassidy said "Tre please tell me he's lying." "I wish I could," Tre responded. "Ya'll niggas crazy? Do ya'll realize what the fuck ya'll done? If Stan ain't get shot and he find out it was ya'll, he coming for ya'll heads, ours too since we family. Not to mention the rest of the niggas in Whitcomb will be gunning for ya'll too," Ayanna said. "What da fuck ya'll talking bout?" Cassidy asked.

"Them niggas that got shot yesterday, the same niggas that jacked us, so they got what they deserved," Turk said pointing his fingers like a gun. "What the fuck you mean they got what they deserved, nigga that's my man's crew and he may have been one of the ones hit. Ya'll stupid mafuckas done put me and Yanna in the middle of some bullshit," Cassidy snapped. "Cass, calm down what did the hospital say?" Ayanna asked. "They said some shit bout they can't divulge that information right now, that means we gotta go down there like right fucking now.

Ya'll mafuckas betta pray Stan won't in that car or I'ma kill ya'll my damn self," Cassidy said. "Ya'll stay your asses right here til we get back, let's go Cass," Ayanna said. And the sisters left out.

Westend:

FIlmore Dean and Duke were standing on the corner of Grace St. by the police station "You really go give these pigs some info?" Duke asked Filmore. "Man, it's not like I want to, but they talking that 3 year shit. Why you think I sent'em at Gamal and nem over at Chantel's on Grayland, I figured they would find a lil something over there and that would be it. But them stupid mafuckas ain't find shit so now they want something else." "You got anything else?" asked Duke. "Yeah that shit that happened the other day at the market," Filmore said. That won't all he had, but that's all he felt Duke needed to know. "That's crazy cause I got something on that too, plus that shooting that happened over Southside in Hillside," Duke said. "How da hell you know something bout over Southside?" Filmore asked. "Cause one of the niggas that got shot was my lil cousin from Afton." "Damn he aight?" "Yeah lil nigga got hit in the ankle," Duke said. "It's 10:50 let's go and get this over with," Filmore said.

They walked in and asked for Detectives Smithers and Long. The desk Sgt. found Det. Long at his desk but Smithers wasn't in sight, she gave Det. Long the paper with the names on it. "Well I'll be damn," he said to himself. He half expected them not to show up, especially Duke who they barely knew. He found Det. Smithers coming out the bathroom "Smithers guess who's out front?" "I don't feel like guessing right now."

"Alright, here take a look at this," Det. Long said handing Smithers the piece of paper he had just received. "You shitting me Long?" Like Det. Long he too didn't' think the crackheads would show up. "Hell naw, Cooper just bought me that," Det. Long said indicating the paper. "Well let's go get'em and split'em up, you take one in interrogation room one and I'll use a different one," Det. Smithers said. "The two detectives walked out "Well, well, well, what do we have here? We didn't think the two of you would make it down here, so since ya'll here I guess it's safe for us to say you got something for us," Det. Smithers

said.

"Whatever man, can we get this over with?" Filmore stated. "Why Filmore what's the rush? You gotta get your morning fix?" Det. Long goaded Filmore. "Fuck you Long, how bout that," Filmore responded. "Hey now, let's stop with the shenanigans Filmore you coming with me and Duke you're going with Det. Long," Smithers said. As they all headed to the back Capt. Spurlock was coming in the front office and saw them "Ain't this a bitch," he said to himself as he walked over to the desk Sgt and found out it was indeed the two CI's who were supposed to come in, he broke into a wide grin and said "they better have something useful."

Det. Long and Duke went in interrogation room 1, while Smithers and Filmore went in room 3. "Aight, before we get started, can I get you anything to drink?" Det. Long asked as they both took their seats. "Nah I'm good." "You sure cause we don't know how long we could wind up being here," Det. Long inquired. "Yeah, I' m sure." "Aight then, let's get down to business," the detective said while placing a tape recorder on the table between them.

"I need you to start by telling me your name and age." "O'Shea Wright and I'm 42." "Good now Mr. Wright you said you have some information for us this morning? Det. Long asked. "Yeah" "Okay before you start Mr. Wright, do you swear that the information you're about to give is the truth and to the best of your knowledge?" "Yeah" "Okay go ahead."

"Aight first I got something on that shooting up at da Market the other day." "What shooting are you talking about, cause as I can recall nobody's been shot at the market recently? Det. Long asked. "Nah ain't nobody get shot but it was a shootout, I think it was either Saturday or Sunday. Any way it was a shootout and even though I ain't got the exact names of everybody involved, I do know that one of the people was from off Carter St. and the word is he was shooting at some nigga from over Northside." "And you don't have no names?"

"Nah" "Do you know what it was about?" "Nah but I hear it was a female involved too." "Really a female? See now I'm starting to think you're pulling my leg," Det. Long said. "Look man what the fuck I'ma lie for, ya'll said I was going to jail if I ain't have nothing for you and I did come to ya'll this morning." "That's true, alright you got anything else?" "You heard bout that shooting over Hillside the other day?" "You talking bout Hillside Court over Southside?"

"Yeah" "What about it?" "Well one of'em that got shot was my cousin Keith Osborne, he got hit in the ankle or calf, anyway from my understanding they supposed to be beefing wit Chicago Ave and Clopton Terrace." "Wait a minute" Det. Long said "who supposed to be beefing wit Chicago and Clopton Terrace, Hillside?" "Nah man, Afton" "Afton? What Afton got to do with it?" Det. Long asked confused, Duke had his attention now for sure. "I'ont know man, all I know is that Afton got some kind of beef with Chicago Ave and Clopton Terrace going on."

"Let me ask you this, was that Afton that shot up Clopton a couple of weeks ago?" "I'ont know I done told you err'thing I know," Duke said. "Alright sit here for a minute I'll be right back," Det. Long told him. While Det. Long was talking with Duke, Det. Smithers was in the other room talking to Filmore "Alright state your name and age for me," Det. Smithers said "Man you already know my name," Filmore said. "Look stop playing fucking games, you know the damn routine everytime you do this you give your fucking name, now just do what the fuck I say."

"Now again state your name for me." "Filmore Dean 41years old." Do you swear that the information you're about to give is the truth to the best of your knowledge?" Yeah Yeah I do damn." "Alright what do you have for me?" Smithers asked. "You know the shootout at the marketplace the other day?" "Yes" "Well I happen to know one of'em was from Northside."

"And how do you know that?" "Cause I had went up on Carter St earlier that day and this nigga I ain't neva seen before was up there and I heard somebody tell him they had garbage dope over on Poe St. Anyway later on when I was coming down the street I saw him and one of them niggas from Carter St. shooting at this nigga coming out the store. Ol' boy started shooting back and one of them broads that be round by that house ya'll went in jumped out the back of the car and started shooting at the niggas from Poe and Carter St." "Hold up, you telling me a female was involved?"

"Yeah, and it was another female driving the car." "Do you know the name of the guy from Carter St.?" Naw, I just know when I go thru there he be out there from time to time." "What about the guy coming out the store, you ever seen him or the girl shooting before?" Det. Smithers questioned. "Naw, I ain't neva saw the guy before, but da broad she be talking to the people that be in that house ya'll ran up in. You know the one ya'll ain't find nothing in."

"Is it her house?" "Naw man, she just be over there talking to'em all the time." "So let me get this straight, two guys one from Carter St here in the West End and one from Poe St. over Northside were involved in a shooting that took place a few days ago at the marketplace. They were shooting at a guy coming out the store and a female from around here that was in the car he was riding in. Is that correct?" "Yeah" "So what you're saying is that the Poe and Carter St guys started shooting first?" "Yeah" "Alright, anything else you would like to add?" "Nope" "Well stay here and I'll be right back," Det. Smithers said.

Det. Long was in Capt. Spurlock's office when Smithers got there "Aright Smithers what you got for us?" Capt. Spurlock asked him. Det. Smithers gave them the rundown on what Filmore had told him. "Well at least we know one thing for sure," Capt. Spurlock said. "And what's that?" Smithers asked. "That there was a female shooting back at the guy from Carter and Poe Sts and that somebody from round here is beefing with either Poe or Carter St. We need to get the names of everybody involved, call over the 3rd Precinct find out if Poe is beefing with anybody and if so with who.

We also gotta find out who this female was and who she was with. Long you need to call Southside and find out if what this guy said was true, if so let them know what he said and find out if the same female was involved with both shootings. Two females in separate shootings is highly unlikely, Smithers is that all your guy had to say?" "Yeah Capn." "Aright cut'em both loose, but make sure they know we may need to talk with'em both again," Capt. Spurlock said. "Aight Captn," they both said as they were leaving out his office.

After being released Duke and Filmore left out the precinct together, they were coming down the steps when Poppi and Dre rode past and noticed them talking. "What da fuck Filmore doing coming out the police station?" Dre asked. "I'ont know what he got going on, but knowing Filmore ain't no telling," Poppi said. "Yeah, but best believe we'll find out sooner or later," Dre said.

Chapter 18-Eastend:

Cassidy and Ayanna arrived at MCV Hospital and Cassydy found Stan outside smoking a cigarette, talking on the phone and cursing like crazy. When they first got there Tawana, Katrell, Amanda, and Tonio were all in the visitation room, Tawana told them where Stan was. Cassidy immediately went to find Stan while Tawana filled Ayanna in on what she knew, "Maurice and Kalil were both dead and if Matt were lucky he would be paralyzed." "Oh my god!" Ayanna yelled, "Wana I'm so sorry, they know who did it?"

"Nah, all I'm hearing from round the way is it was four niggas but don't nobody know who it was," Tawana said. "Damn. Let me go find Cass and Stan, see how he's doing." "He fucked up girl, that nigga been snapping, we had to calm his ass down. I finally convinced him to go outside, he was crying and some more shit, talking crazy, nigga talking bout going to war." "You know them his niggas, he probably believe he shoulda been wit'em, although I'm glad he won't, Cassidy would've really been all to pieces, she was going crazy coming down here not knowing if he had been shot or not. Let me go, I'll be right outside if you need me," Ayanna said.

When Ayanna got outside she saw Cassidy looking at Stan who was on the phone going off. Looking in her little sister's face, Ayanna could see Cassidy was scared "What's up Cass?" she asked walking up beside Cassidy. "Yanna I ain't never seen'im like this before, the police came out the substation twice already to tell'im to calm down, he talking bout taking out niggas families and some more shit. "He say anything bout what happened?" Ayanna asked. "He said Maurice and Kalil both got killed and he not sure if Matt go make it." "That's what Wana said, but do they know who did it?"

"I'ont know he ain't say yet, he been on the phone damn

near the whole time I been out here." "Man what the fuck!" Stan exclaimed after getting off the phone. "Stan what's going on?" Cassidy asked sincerely. "I'ont know Cass, all I keep hearing is it was three or four niggas in a dark car, whoever it was they just pulled up, got out and started dumping." 'Stan,Wana told me bout Reece and Kalil, I'm so sorry, we go keep Matt in our prayers you know them was our niggas too," Ayanna said. "Thanks Yanna, I can't figure this shit out to save my life, I mean we ain't beefing wit no damn body but somebody had a beef wit us."

"I'm just so happy that for once you won't wit them," Cassidy said walking over hugging Stan. "You may be happy but I'm fucked up Cass, all us would've been together but Kyrell and Tayvon came thru and I rode with them to Benny's over on Leigh St to shoot dice before we hit the club. The projects in a uproar right now, both Whitcomb and Jackson Ward. Niggas round Whitcomb ready to ride on da Ward, but I told'em I ain't think nobody ova there had nothing to do with it. I talked to Frye and Blaine ova da Ward and they both said niggas wanna know who we beefing with cause now it's their beef. Their families round their and you know all them lil kids was outside, luckily none of'em got hit, but still niggas shot without thinking bout the kids."

Ayanna noticing one of the police in the substation watching them out the window and a nurse who had just came outside smoking a cigarette, said to them "let's go inside ya'll too many people watching us. We need to find out how Matt's doing anyway...."

Back at Ayanna's; "Turk you talk too got damn much," Cap said. "Like I said fuck them niggas and if Stan want some he can get it too," Turk responded. "Turk you dumb ass, this ain't even bout them niggas no more, this about family, this bout Cassidy, Ski said. "What about Cass, she ain't got shit to do wit this," Turk said. "She got everything to do wit it Turk, she in a fucked up position, not only was them her man's niggas but they from round there where she live at. When word get out that it was us that hit them niggas up, Cass go have to deal with Stan and them mafuckas over Whitcomb. Shit her life might even be in danger, much as I know she ain't go want to, she might have to move from over there son," Tre said to his youngest brother.

"Cassidy's family, she go side with her family first," Turk replied. "Fuck that, the bigger question is did Stan know it was them niggas that jacked us and if he did know, was he down with it?" Cap asked. "Nah son, I don't think so" Tre said "think about his reaction when we told'im what them niggas said bout him." "But that could've been a play off too Tre just to try and throw us off," Turk countered. "Nah, I'm wit Tre on this one, I don't think he had anything to do with it either son, but just to be sure we need to watch his reaction to us," Ski said. Everybody agreed with this statement. "As for Cass we just go have to wait and see how it affects her as well," Tre said. Again everyone agreed. "Until then fuck it," Cap said.

Westend:

Gamal, Poppi, Dre Jr., and Ma Vick were at the laundromat on Main and Randolph St; Ma Vick was on the phone with the police station "Police, how may I help you?" the desk Sgt. Miller answered and asked. "Yes I was calling to see if Filmore Dean or O'Shea Wright had been released yet?" "One moment please.., you say Filmore Dean?" "That's right." "Well according to our records there's been nobody bought in here by that name, what was the other name?" "O'Shea Wright." "No ma'am there's no record of either one of those names having been brought in here today or yesterday," Sgt. Miller said. She had taken over for Sgt. Adrian who had left for the day due to a family emergency, therefore Sgt. Miller didn't know that Filmore and Duke had in fact been in there not too long ago.

"OK thank you ma'am," Ma Vick said and hung up. Ma Vick was shaking her head "What she say?" Gamal asked. "She said neither one of them mafuckas had been arrested or was even in the computer for yesterday or today, I would say them two mafuckas is ya'lls snitches." Ma Vick was cool, she was Chantel's aunt on her mother's side. She was from the street, her man Wendall had been on of the most paid heroin dealers in the Westend when he fell 20 years ago, instead of her fucking with the next big hat dealer she decided to pick up the sack herself.

At first Wendall had objected when she told him what she was thinking about doing, but when she explained that she was doing it to keep money on his books, the bills paid and not to mention she wouldn't have to fuck with none of them wannabe hustlas,he relented. Her gave her his three different connects numbers and told her to tell Seven and Bushwick he wanted to talk with them on the phone, he gave her weight sizes and costs of certain weight. In short he gave her the hustle game he had. When he called home later that week he told Seven and Bushwick they were to treat her the same as always and that at least one of them should be present at all times when she handled her business. He told them to make sure Toya, Vicki, Tonya, and the rest of the girls they had working the streets understood that Vicki was in charge while he was gone and any insubordination would be dealt with swiftly and accordingly.

Seven and Bushwick stuck with Vicki all the way, they beat niggas ass who tried to short change or con her, they had their own security detail to watch her back to make sure nobody tried to rob her. In return for their loyalty to both her and her man she made sure they were well paid and their families wanted for nothing. By the time Wendall came home 15 years later, Vicki had made so much money there was no need for Wendall to step back in the street, so they opened up a shoe store with Seven and Bushwick as the managers.

"You really think it was them Ma Vick," Dre Jr asked. "Hell yeah, I think it was them, why else would they be coming out the police station if they hadn't been arrested. Ya'll niggas betta handle this shit before I tell Wendall and we handle it, shit got them mafuckas running up in my niece's house," Ma Vick said. "We go take care of it, you got my word on that," Gamal said. " I hope so," Ma Vick responded.

Eastend:

After Stan, Ayanna, and Cassidy left the hospital they went back to Cassidy's apt in Whitcomb Ct. "What I don't fucking get, is who woulda known they was going over Jackson Ward" Stan said "I mean I left'em on the strip, so that means they had to leave off the strip to go round there." "Stan you sure ya'll ain't beefing wit nobody, what about somebody else from Whitcomb beefing wit them niggas from Jackson Ward?" Ayanna asked. "Naw Yanna, I know for a fact we ain't beefing wit nobody, as for da rest of Whitcomb we ain't heard nothing bout no beef although anything's possible." Stan's cellphone rings, looking at it he don't recognizethe number "Who da fuck is this?" he said to himself as he answered.

"Yeah" "Hello is this Stan?" "Who dis?" "This Janel from off Sussex, I was over my aunt Yvonne's house on Carmine yesterday sitting on da porch when that junkie bitch Minga walked up on Kalil and Reece. I'ont know what she said but I do know that bitch had somebody else wit her and it was a guy." "You say Minga?" "Yeah" "How you know dude was wit her?" "Cause I saw all three of'em Minga, Kalil, and Reece turn around to look up the street at him and when she walked off, she walked up to'im and they walked off together."

"But you couldn't see who the nigga was?" "Nah, he was too far away." "Aight, now tell me this, how you get this number?" "My aunt gave it to me afta we heard what happened, I told her about Minga and she told me to call you." "Aight thanks shawdy, and don't tell nobody else what you just told me." "I won't." "Hey lemme ask you this, ain't Minga from New York?" When Stan said this both Cassidy and Ayanna looked at each other but he missed it.

"I'ont know lemme ask my aunt." Janel came back on the phone "she said she from New York, New Jersey somewhere up top but she ain't exactly sure where." "Aight thanks again Janel, I'ma holla at'chu soon." "No Problem." "Damn!" Stan said after getting off the phone, "I gotta find this bitch Minga and find out who this nigga was that was with her." "But I thought I heard her say they walked up on Matt and Kalil, so how would that play out?" Cassidy asked. "I'ont know but I gotta talk to Minga then I'll know more unless Matt gets betta and can talk."

Northside:

Cheeks, Shaun, Lil Q, Hammerhead, and Smoke were riding up Hospital St in Jackson Ward; "Once we drop ya'll off, ya'll go thru the back hit dem niggas up, then run down thru the Old Dodge City to that first street, make your first right we'll meet ya'll niggas up on Roberts St.," Cheeks said. Fatty had decided to give Lil Q the ok to get his revenge on Poe St after the bullshit Dorez had pulled over the Westend. Cheeks dropped Lil Q, Hammerhead, and Smoke off on the corner of Minor St. The three young men walked up the block and turned into the side street that led to the back of the apts. Coming up to the apts they saw an older lady and man carrying groceries in the house.

Walking around the side of the apartment building they saw a group of about five people in front of the apartments three were sitting down; two in lawn chairs, one on a milk crate and the other two were standing. Lil Q said "We go keep on walking as though we go walk past them, then we just go stop and let loose." Walking up they observed that three of the group were older guys in their late 20's or early 30's and that two of the guys were perhaps in their late teens, early 20's although they didn't recognize any of them. Petey who was 20 and played football for Battery Park thought he recognized Hammerhead who used to play for Hotchkiss said "that nigga on the left" and that was as far as he got.

'Blaw blaw blaka blaka baw baw baw blaka blaw blaw blaw blaka blaka blaka blaka baw baw baw.' When the shooting started Petey and the rest of the gang couldn't get out the way fast enough; Petey got hit in the side, left leg, and upper left shoulder. Two of the guys sitting down got caught in the legs as they stood to run; one of them got hit in the lower back and ass. The other guy sitting down got hit in the chest when he tried to stand and got thrown backwards. the other guy that was standing who just so happened to be Dorez got hit in the elbow, grazed across the jawline and twice in the back as he was running trying to get away.

When the shooting finally finished Q, Hammerhead, and Smoke took off running made a left on North Ave, then turned and ran up the side street leading back up into Dodge City just as Cheeks had told them to do. They met Cheeks and Shaun on Roberts St as planned, "How'd everything go?" Shaun asked. "Aight" everyone said. "Yo ya'll niggas alright?" Cheeks asked. "Yeah nigga" Lil Q answered "we just tryna catch our breath, that's a long ass run from ova there to here." "Ya'll niggas hit anybody?" Shaun asked.

"Did we hit anybody, shawdy it was five of them niggas out there and I swear I believe we hit all five of they asses up," Smoke said hyped up. "Cuz, I saw one nigga fly backwards ova his chair after he stood up," Hammerhead said. "So ya'll niggas think ya'll hit all five of'em ?" Shaun asked them. "Think? Nigga I'm 100% we hit all five of'em," Lil Q boasted. "Aight nigga since you so confident ya'll hit all of'em, how many you think ya'll killed?" asked Cheeks.

They all looked at each other "I'ont know if any of'em go die, but I do know they all got hit nigga," Lil Q stated. "One more question, ya'll see any witnesses?" Cheeks asked looking thru the rearview mirror. Again they all looked at one another, but this time Hammerhead spoke up "Nah we ain't see no witnesses, though when we came thru the back it was an older couple carrying bags in the house, they ain't pay us no mind though." "You sure?" Shaun asked. "Yeah I'm sho we hit them niggas out front the apartments, we saw the couple out back, how would they know it was us shooting," Hammerhead said.

"Aight shawdy ya'll niggas did good, leave them guns in here so we can get rid of'em, we go let Fatty know everything went well and we'll holla at ya'll later," Cheeks said. After dropping the guys off on the strip Cheeks and Shaun headed out of town to the river their father used to take them to go fishing when they were kids, so they could get rid of the guns....

Fatty, Marquell, and Big C., were standing around

watching the pickup basketball games at Hotchkiss Field "Shawd, these mafuckas love that shit we got now," Marquell said. "He ain't lying bout that, er'body be coming back asking for his ass they'ont want to fuck wit nobody else, they'll leave if he ain't out there and come back later just so they can get his shit," Big C. said. "Oh I believe him they been running me down up our way too" Fatty said " Now the question is do we holla at'im today for the 'big' or do we wait a coupla days?" he continued. "I think ya'll need to holla today, that way ya'll don't run out and everybody on both strips will basically have the same thing," Big C stated.

"I think you right C., and with everybody having the samething we'll lock it down from here all the way to Chamberlayne. But we proly go have to re-up again this week too and that'll be three times in one week, I'ont know how he'll feel bout that," Fatty said. "So what at least he'll know we moving that shit fast, shit he know good as that shit is how mafuckas go react," Marquell said. "Ya'll got a point, lemme call him now," Fatty said. "Amigo what's good?" Curser said answering the phone.

"Shit, of course you know why I'm calling." "Si amigo, when you tryna see me?" "Today if possible," Fatty answered. "Ok amigo come to the store about 7:30 this evening." "My nigga, I'll be there," Fatty said before hanging up. Fatty told Marquell what Curser said as they watched Big C dribbling and shooting a basketball on the court. "Let's run to my house so I can give you my money," Marquell said. "Na uh nigga, you coming wit me," Fatty said. "Fuck you talking bout, you handle the business and tell'im next time you go bring one of your brothers wit'chu so he'll be expecting it," Marquell stated. "Nigga already said he wanted to meet my brothers anyway, so yeah that'll work," Fatty replied. "Ey C., we go run to my house right quick, we be back," Marquell said. "Aight," Big C replied.

Chapter 19-Southside:

Arthur Gantz was standing on Chicago Ave talking to Lil Goo, Dan Johnson, KenVale and Alberto. "Shawd, I'm telling ya'll it was them LBC niggas from Afton that shot at us, I saw Lil James getting in a Cherokee back in the alley," Arthur was saying to the group. "What da fuck was you doing in da alley?" KenVale asked. "That's where I ran afta we couldn't get in the house." "So you know for sure it was da LBC?" KenVale asked again. "It had to be, you know Lil James wouldn't have done it with nobody else, besides ya'll know they was go try to get some get back from when Goo and Slick shot Blip and nem."

"How da fuck you figure we shot Blip and nem?" asked Lil Goo. "Nigga who don't know ya'll shot them niggas, the crazy thing tho, them dumb mafuckas from round there don't know if it was somebody from ova here or somebody from Clopton Terrace. You know they beefing now too," Alberto said. "Yeah, and you know Lil Dread and Lil K.O. got shot ova Hillside, but I'ont know who did it," Dan Johnson said. I'ont give a fuck who else they beefing wit or who shot them, all I know is they started this shit when Blip and Tyshon disrespected us at the store. If Keon won't so mothafuckin high, he wouldn't have bumped into me and we wouldn't have hit they ass up, but like I said fuck'em they started it so we damn so go finish it. I wanna hit dem niggas this week the sooner the better," Lil Goo said....

Juice and Monopoly were up Amelia County sitting in Big Jack's house with Big Jack and Monk. "Man this some good ass mothatfuckin weed," Monk said. "Got damn right, where da fuck ya'll niggas get this weed from, ya'll niggas stuck up a

Jamaican or sumthing?" Big Jack asked. Big Jack and Monk were brothers they met Monopoly and Juice when they were kids coming up Amelia to visit their aunt Marilyn every summer. Even though they were country boys they swore they had city boy swag.

They knew what Juice and Monopoly did but didn't care, shit they had set up a couple of niggas from Amelia for them to rob, so to them it was like what the fuck. But when Juice and Monopoly caught a big score like this one they never told them where it came from cause Jack and Monk couldn't keep their mouth shut for shit, they was always trying to show off for them country ho's and niggas. "Nigga don't worry bout where it came from, just know we got plenty of it for sale and we got weight in that white shit ya'll niggas call yourself tryna sling," Juice said. "Hard or soft?" Monk asked.

"Nigga its however da fuck you want it, right now it's soft, but if you want us to cook it up for you we can do that too," Monopoly said. "And for ya'll niggas we only go charge a extra $50 more if we gotta cook it up for you," Juice stated. "So what the prices lik?" Monk wanted to know. "225 a quarter, 450 a half, and 900 a onion," Monopoly said. "Ya'll niggas paying 11-1200 a onion and 300 a quarter now, so I know ya'll mafuckas go hop on this," Juice said.

'Ya'll mafuckas ain't tryna sell us no bullshit is it, none of that garbage ass shit or dummy type shit is ya'll?" Big Jack asked. "Fuck naw nigga" Monopoly said "we ran across a sweet lick and decided to look out for ya'll. Now if ya'll don't want it we'll be glad to take it to Chubba and you already know he'll hop on it, bad as he want to do business wit us." "Naw nigga we go take it, but ya'll niggas ain't hit nobody round here did it?" asked Monk. "Nigga who said we jacked somebody, M.P. just said we hit a sweet lick, he ain't say we robbed nobody," Juice responded.

"Ya'll mafuckas know we wouldn't put ya'll under the gun like that," Monopoly said. "Yeah right, anyway we go take it, I want a half of hard," Monk replied. "Me too and if the shit any good I might get half soft and half hard next time and let Uncle Boo Boy cook it up for me," Big Jack said. "Same here, but for now pass that blunt around and let us get a quarter of that green shit," Monk said. "No doubt my nigga," Juice replied.

Henrico-Central Gardens:

Sitting in front of his house Darrrell and Ky-Sheema were discussing whether or not she should go in the house with him. "No Darrell I'm not going in the house wit you, I'll sit here and wait for you no matter how long it takes, just don't you forget I'm out here. You have some personal issues to deal with in there alone," Ky-Sheema said. "Fuck that Sheema ain't no issues to work out, I'm going to see my son, maybe bring him with me and keep him for a couple of days, that's it."

"I understand that Darrell, but I will not be the payback bitch, that bitch you throw in your baby mama's face cause she fucked up while you was locked up. Yes I'm here now and I will be here for as long as you want me to be, I'm here now to support you, but you need to go in there alone and deal with your situation. Me going in there is not going to help, it will only make matters worse." "Yeah whatever you say Sheema, aight this may take at least a hour."

"That's ok, where do I have to go? You go handle your business and I'll sit here listening to music or talking on the phone til you come back. I know you going home with me so why would I leave." "You right baby, aight lemme go in here I'll be back in a minute or two." Darrell opened the door to get out "Darrell don't do nothing stupid, I just got you back, I can't have you going back in there." "Don't worry baby I ain't tryna go back either, now sit tight."

Darrell walked to the front door and stuck his key in and opened the door. Walking thru the door he saw that the living room was empty, he walked thru the dining room into the kitchen and again it was empty, coming back thru he could hear Angie talking to somebody and it sounded like it was coming from their bedroom. Heading that way he stopped by Lil Darrell's room, the door was cracked and he could see Lil Darrell on the bed playing with his wrestling men. He missed his lil man, but he would play with him later, first he wanted to see who Angie was talking to. Walking up to their bedroom door he saw Angie laying across the bed on her stomach facing the television in a burgundy Priscilla's thong with pink hearts on it and the matching bra.

She was talking on the phone and so into her conversation that she didn't realize Darrell was standing at the door. "I was thinking you might want some get back tonight, since you claimed you was go blow my back out the other night, but couldn't handle all this ass. You hit it right and you get my whole bum ass head game tonight instead of a lil tease like the other night," Angie said. "I hope that's the same nigga who dick you was sucking when I was on the phone," Darrell said startling her. Angie jumped and dropped the phone "Darrell wha'chu doing here?"

"I live here bitch remember." "I thought you got out next week," Angie said looking at the phone. "That's what da fuck you get for thinking, I thought you was a good girl, my future wife, I guess I was wrong," Darrell said walking over picking up the phone. "Who dis?" Darrell asked into the phone, Angie lunged at him trying to get her phone. 'Whap' Darrell smacked her on the bed. "Who da fuck is this?"

"This Darrell nigga, her baby daddy and her supposed to be man, now who the fuck is this?" "Oh shit! Darrell what's popping homey this Buster from Harvey Rd." "What's popping, you fucking my bitch now?" "I met her Friday, talked to'er on the phone, came over to smoke some weed and we ended up fucking, I ain't find out she was your girl til aftawards." "Uh huh, didn't I talk to you on the phone one night tho?" Darrell asked. "Hell naw Shawdy, I ain't talked to you since that night me and you beat old man Drake out all that money in the gambling spot. That musta been some other nigga."

Angie finally got up and went to leave the room, Darrell grabbed her by the hair and flung her on the bed "Sit your ass down bitch, where da fuck you think you going?" "I was going to check on Lil Darrell." "No you ain't, he aight I checked on him when I came in. Busta you called her or she called you?" "She called me." "Aight look shawdy I'ma be real wit'chu she my baby mama but other than that I'm thru wit da bitch you can have'er. I came to get my son and take him with me for a few days, that should give ya'll enough time to finish what you started."

"Naw shawdy, that's aight you keep that bitch, she was too easy to fuck, plus she licked my dick, all this on the first night we met. No disrespect fam, but shawdy a straight slut, you can do betta than that for real homey." "No disrespect taken and don't worry I already have done betta, but look I'ma holla at you later maybe see you in tha gambling spot or something," Darrell said. "No doubt," Busta replied.

Darrell hung up the phone "Bitch you ain't shit, I thought I had something, I thought I had the queen of Central Gardens instead I got the ho of Central Gardens." Darrell walked over and closed the bedroom door "But you know what happens to ho's who act up and disrespect their man." Angie didn't know what to do she was scared shitless, she knew Darrell was going to hit her again, but she also knew she wasn't trying to lose him either. "Darrell baby, listen please listen," she said backing up across the bed. "I was lonely baby."

"Shut up bitch, how you go play me like that? Not only did you fuck and suck a nigga that I know in my house, but also let a nigga get on da phone and disrespect me." "Baby I swear I didn't let him get on the phone, he took it." 'Whap' he smacked her. "Bitch is that supposed to make it betta." 'Whap' he hit her again. "Darrell" "I said shut da fuck up. How you go suck another nigga's dick, especially wit me on the phone, you just totally said fuck me." 'Whap whap' Darrell smacked her upside the head again.

"Darrell Ba-, Arr" "Bitch don't baby me, who da fuck was it?" Darrell asked her as he held her by the neck choking and squeezing. "E-Bay" "What?" "E-Bay" "Where he be at?" "I can't breathe," Angie said. "You betta hope I let you live, much less let you breathe, now I'ma ask your ass one more time, where he be at?" "He say he from Fairlawn, but I met him on Bolling Rd when I went to buy some smoke from Double S."

"Double S., Steve Shackleford." "Yeah, he said Double S was his cousin." "You know what? I ain't go worry about it I'ma see shawdy sooner or later, as for you we done ain't shit you can say to change it, so don't try. When I leave here tonight I'm taking Lil Darrell wit me, I'll bring him back in a couple of days and I'm giving you two weeks to be out my shit." "Leave, where you going? Where you taking my baby?" "Bitch don't play that baby shit wit me, you won't thinking bout no baby when you was sucking and fucking err'body, like I said he leaving here wit me and if you call the police you already know what it is."

"Darrell you know I would never call the police on you." "I don't know shit about you no more, other than I hate yo mothafucking ass, now get your ass in there and pack him some clothes while I go see'im." He took Angie and threw her up against the wall, then he went in the room with Lil Darrell who jumped up at the sight of his daddy and ran into his arms. "Daddy" "Hey lil man what's up?" "Nuthing, I missed you daddy." "Daddy missed you too man, but daddy's not go leave you again, okay?" "Kay"

"You been a good boy while daddy was gone?" Darrell asked him while tickling his stomach "Heeeee Heee, yeah." "That's my boy, you wanna stay wit daddy for a coupla days?" "Yeah" "Good, aight let's get your wrestling men and put them in a bag, your mom's packing your clothes." "Okay," Lil Darrell said jumping down going to get the bag Darrell had gotten him to carry the wrestling men in before he got locked up. "Angie you got his clothes ready?"

"Yeah I got'em ready," Angie said coming in the room "Lil Darrell you going with your daddy for a few days, I'll be over Nana's house to see you sometime tomorrow ok." "You betta call before you come, cause we might not be there." "What'chu mean you might not be there?" "Just what the fuck I said, we might not be there, we not go be staying there." "Wha'chu talking bout Darrell? Where da hell you plan on taking my baby?" Angie said raising her voice.

"Like I said don't pull that baby shit on me Angie and have you forgotten he's my baby too, I mean you do remember that don't you? You know I wouldn't take him nowhere dangerous, so just fucking relax." "Relax, how da fuck you expect me to relax and you talking bout taking my baby god knows where." "You shoulda thought about that before you decided to suck and fuck half of Richmond, You ready Lil D?" "Yeah" "Aight give your mama a hug, I sure ain't go tell you to kiss'er, who knows where da fuck her mouth been."

"Darrell I know you hurt and I'm sorry, but we'll work thru this baby." "Nah, you got me fucked up Angie, you lucky your ass still breathing much less working thru something. You played me, you and that pussy ass nigga but don't worry I'm thru I swear, now get the fuck out da way so we can leave." "I need a number so I can call and check on Lil Darrell." "You don't need a muthafucking thing, I got him he alright, he'll call you when he wants to, now move."

"Come'ere Lil Darrell give mama a hug." Lil Darrell went and gave his mama a hug, Angie's face was sore where Darrell had slapped her and she flinched when Lil Darrell's cheek touched hers. "Sorry mama" "That's ok baby, you go have fun with your daddy ok." "Kay" "And mama'll see you soon, now don't forget to call mama and let her know you alright okay?" "Kay, I love you mama." "Mama loves you too." "You ready lil man?" Darrell asked his son. "Yeah" "Aight let's go."

Father and son walked towards the front door. Darrell I know you not driving with no license and think you go take my baby with you." "You think I'm stupid or something Angie, I got a ride, damn." "A ride wit who?" "Don't fucking worry bout it," Darrell said as he and Lil Darrell went out the front door. Darrell grabbed his son's hand and started towards the car, Sheema was sitting on the hood talking on the phone when they came out the house, she got up walked around to the driver's side and got in.

"Who da fuck is that? I know damn well you ain't bring no

bitch to my house to pick up my son and think he staying over her house," Angie said walking behind them. Darrell stopped and turned to face her. "Bitch number one that's not your house, number two at least I didn't fuck her or nobody else for that matter in the house that we shared. Number three don't you ever disrespect her and call her out her name again, she ain't neva did nothing to you, all she did is give me a ride." "Darrell don't give me that shit, I know you fucking that bitch, you disrespecting me by taking my son around another woman."

Darrell got to the car and put Lil Darrell inside. "Lil D this Sheema, we go be staying with her for a few days alright?" "Alright daddy, hi Sheema." "Hey Lil D., make sure you put your seat belt on ok." "Ok" "I'll be right back," Darrell said as he closed the door and started back towards the house. Seeing the look in Darrell's eyes made Sheema cringe, when he started towards the house Sheema fearing the worse for everybody jumped out the car and called his name. "Darrell." But he just ignored her and kept going.

"Darrell Darrell I know you hear me calling you," Sheema called out. Darrell turned around "What?" "Remember what I said, don't do nothing stupid." "I'm not, I forgot something, I'll be right back." Angie turned around and looked at Sheema "Darrell I know you not leaving Lil Darrell outside with that bitch I don't know." "Angie shut da fuck up and come in the house."

Once in the house Darrell made like he was going to the bedroom with Angie following behind when he whirled around and 'whap' smacked her. Angie fell to the floor "Darrell" "Shut da fuck up, who da fuck you think you is huh? Bitch you and nobody else is go disrespect me." Darrell reached down wrapped his hand in her hair pulled her to her feet and 'whap' smacked her again. Angie fell to the floor "Oww!" "Nah bitch it ain't no oww, I told you, you want to act like a ho, I'm go treat you like a ho."

Darrell reached down grabbed her by the hair again, this time he dragged her to the bedroom, where he slammed her head into the door, releasing her he went to the drawer where he kept his belts and other miscellaneous items. He reached in and grabbed a thick leather belt 'Snap snap' the belt sounded as he snapped it together. Angie holding the side of her face looked up when she heard this "Darrell Darrell, baby I'm sorry I swear I'm sorry," she said trying to stand up. 'Oh I know you sorry, you's a sorry bitch, but when I get thru wit'chu, you go be a sore sorry bitch, believe that.'"" Angie went to run out the room, but Darrell caught her by the hair and flung her on the bed while he closed and locked the door.

Angie crawled all the way to the back of the bed like a scared child crying, when Darrell reached out to grab her she tried to get away but wasn't fast enough. He caught her by the bottom of the robe she had put on while packing Lil Darrell's bag, she was so scared that she came right out the robe which was what Darrell wanted anyway. He leaped across the bed and in one motion 'pap' "Ahh," he hit her knocking her into the wall, he placed his hand and forearm across her back pinning her to the wall and 'pap pap pap pap pap.' "Awww awww Darrell" "Darrell ass bitch, you go snap on me when I ask you a question, cause you got a nigga dick in yo mouth. You triphlant bitch."Waaa waaaa," Angie screamed but to no avail, nobody could hear her. Darrell flung her on the bed again, she tried to roll over on her back but was so sore she couldn't turn all the way over.

'Bak' "Oww" Darrell backhanded her; Bitch you

disrespected me and my son, I know you lost your mothafuckin mind." 'Pap pap pap pap pap,' Darrell started hitting her again but this time on the front of her body, and again Angie tried to get away, 'pap pap pap' "Owww" she shouted as Darrell hit her across the back. "Bitch I fucking hate you, you no good ass slut, I wish I never would've had a baby by your cum drinking ass." Darrell went to the closet reached up on the top shelf and grabbed his black .40 cal, not knowing what he had in mind Angie tried to move but couldn't. Darrell stuck the gun in Angie's mouth "since you like sucking dick so much bitch, let's see how much you like sucking my 40's dick, see how you like the taste of his bullet cum when he shoot off in your mouth."

Tears streaming down her face, Angie was trying to shake her head no "Oh you wouldn't like that but I thought you like sucking dick, didn't you say you had a mean ass head game?" Angie was boo-hooing now, "I mean that is what you told Busta ain't it?" Even thru her tears Angie could see the hurt, anger, and hate written all over Darrell's face, she was more scared now than she had ever been in her life. She knew Darrell had shot people before, so she didn't know if he was going to shoot her now or not. 'Clack' Angie jumped at the sound of the gun when Darrell had pulled the trigger, because of her fear she didn't see him eject the bullet or the clip.

She was scared so bad she was trembling, it was a wonder she didn't piss on herself. "Bitch you ain't even worth it," Darrell said grabbing the clip and walking out the room. But he couldn't let that end it, just when Angie thought he was gone, he came back "Nah fuck that, you played me bitch." He grabbed her by the back of the head, pushed her face into the pillow, pulled the gun and placed it to the back of her head. 'Blaw' he pulled the trigger but this time the gun was loaded, and this time Angie did piss on herself.

Just before he pulled the trigger Darrell moved the gun beside Angie's head by her ear, her whole eardrum sounded like an explosion. Her ears were ringing and she was crying even harder now. "Fuck wit me again bitch and next time it'll be your head exploding," Darrell said as he walked out again. When Angie heard the door slam, she let out a loud wailing sound, she knew then just how bad she had fucked up and that E-Bay's days might be numbered. When Darrell got in the car Sheema asked him "Darrell am I go have to worry bout the police coming to my house looking for you?"

"Nah baby, I told you I won't go leave you and that's just what I meant." "So what happened when you went back in there?" I just let her know in no uncertain terms that we were through and that nothing was going to change that?" "I hope that's all you did." "Trust me baby, you think I would jeopardize losing my son for some stupid ass slut, me and my lil man go have us some fun, ain't that right Lil D.?"

But Lil D didn't answer, he was in the backseat knocked out with a wrestling man in each hand, "He's sleep, been like that for bout 10 minutes before you came out," Sheema said. "That's aright we got the next couple of days to get caught up, but tonight me and you got some more reacquainting to do," Darrell said reaching down grabbing his manhood. "Uh huh whatever nigga, you think you go be able to last this time?" "You go find out, don't get in here and start begging for me to let you catch your breath." "Hah! I can't wait to see this," Sheema said laughing. "I bet'chu can't."

Chapter 20-Seven Gables:

Cassidy and Ayanna had left Stan at Cassidy's apt while

they went back to Ayanna's so Cassidy could get her car, they discussed the situation and decided they had to tell their cousisns what was going on. "Yanna I don't know what to do, I mean they're family, but Stan's my man and I love him to death, not only that but I'm pregnant too." "What? Pregnant when you find this out?" "Day before yesterday, I ain't get a chance to tell Stan yet, I was go tell'im today and then this bullshit came up." "Damn Cass, I mean I love our cousins too but at this time I wish they had stayed up New York, let's hope we can convince them to go back before Stan finds that bitch Minga and she tell'im who was wit her."

'You think they'll go back? You know how them niggas is, they go look at it like that's running and one thing we know is they don't believe in running from shit." "I'ont know Cass, if we can convince Tre that's the best thing for'em they might leave, we might have to act like the police down on it. We'll just play it by ear." "Yanna I just hope if and when Stan finds out it was them, he don't hold it against neither on of us, me or you." "I'ont think he will once he calms down and think about it, plus you gotta remember Kalil and nem did start this shit by robbing them."

""Yeah but they ain't shoot nobody, this shit's all fucked up how you think Wana go feel if she finds out it was our cousins who killed her cousin." "If she find out she go have to deal with it, just like we gotta deal wit the fact her cousin jacked our cousins. Shit I love Wana like a sister and I loved Kalil like he was our cousin too, but the bottom line is they robbed our family and they struck back, hard. But while we worried bout er'body else, we better be thinking bout you Cass." "Bout me, what about me?"

"You know mafuckas go say if you hadn't let Tre and nem

grind out your spot, this shit wouldn't have never happened in the first place. So mafuckas over Whitcomb and Jackson Ward might hold you responsible." "Shit they can't blame me, I ain't tell'em niggas to rob nobody and I sure as hell ain't tell nobody to shoot nobody. All I'm guilty of is tryna help my family get paid." "Yeah, but at what cost? Plus your family was from out of town, New York at that, I tried to tell you what would happen but you just wouldn't listen."

"Look Yanna, you and nobody else can tell me who I can let do what out my place." "That may be true, but look at what's happened because of you letting niggas grind out your house. Was it really worth it? Shit it can be the cause of you losing your man one way or the other." "And how da fuck you figure that?"

"Well you may be Stan's woman or even his baby mama, but them was his niggas from forever. Niggas he grew up with, fought with and hung with everyday, they had a lifetime bond of whatever happens I'm here for you when you need me no questions asked. And what happens if he decides to get Tre'nem back and he happens to kill one or a couple or even all of'em? Could you ever forgive'im? Or could I forgive'im for that matter? Then what if the police find out about him getting at them? Your cousins gone and your man gone cause couldn't nobody tell you who could or couldn't grind out your house."

Cassidy was quiet for a few minutes, finally she spoke "Damn, I hadn't thought bout it like that Yanna." "I know you hadn't Cass, not only that what if the niggas and bitches wanna get at you cause they blaming you for what happened. Look Cass you're my lil sister and I love you, you know I'm not going to let nothing happen to you, but you gotta start thinking. You not from the streets, no matter how much you act like it and try to fit in, the streets have lifetime bonds that are made and sealed thru hardship, struggle, and blood. You gotta be more aware of your actions out here." "Don't worry Yanna afta this shit I'm done wit these mothafucking streets." "I hope so, now let's go in here and let these niggas know what's going on."

The sisters entered the apartment to find their cousins still lounging around, Ayanna went to her bedroom to lay her pocketbook down and then to the bathroom; Cassidy went to the refrigerator got a 24 oz can of Steele Reserve and went to sit on the sofa. Nobody said anything for a minute while, Cassidy opened her beer and lit a Newport "Ya'll mafuckas dun fucked up," she eventually says. "Wh'chu mean we dun fucked up" Turk asks. "Turk shut da fuck up and let her talk," Tre said.

"Two of'ems dead Kalil and Reece, but the otha one Matt, he still living for now, they say if he lucky he'll be paralyzed. Stan's going crazy, I ain't neva seen'em like this, this nigga talking bout touching families and some more shit. Families! That would be me and Yanna. And we ain't have shit to do with this shit." "Fuck that I say we take his ass out B," Turk said.

"Turk I told you to shut the fuck up" Tre said "Cass what you mean he talking bout taking out families? He know who did it?" "Nah he don't, he say they won't beefing wit nobody so he can't figure it out. But before we left Whitcomb he got a phone call, whoever it was said something bout a bitch and a nigga buying some drugs from Matt and Kalil before they were killed." "Something bout the guy standing back while she went to buy the drugs," Ayanna said coming into the living room. "They know who the nigga and bitch was?" Cap asked.

"Nah they said they think it was a bitch from up top but they won't sure,' Cassidy answered. "Bottom line ya'll dun put me and Cass in a fucked up position, ya'll our cousins our family by blood, but them's our niggas our family by friendship. Kalil was Tawana's my best friend first cousin, he was like my lil cousin, before ya'll came down them niggas had our backs no matter what," Ayanna said. "Yo I feel what you saying Yanna, but bottom line is they jacked us and disrespected us, so they had to feel us," Ski said. "And if I'm not mistaken Cass, you were the one talking bout somebody's ass was go pay, now you saying we fucked up?" Cap said.

"That's true, but that was before I knew who was involved, I'm not saying they were right cause they won't. What I am saying is ya'll didn't have to shoot'em, they didn't shoot none of ya'll, ya'll coulda just robbed'em and got yo shit back or sumthing. Anything but shoot'em, much less kill'em," Cassidy said. "Cass we hear wha'chu saying and we unnerstand how you feel, but you know that's not how we get down. Naw they ain't shoot one of us, but they did hit Cap and Turk upside the head with their gats and in our eyes that's just as bad," Tre said.

"Mafuckin right," Turk said. "Listen ya'll we unnerstand but look at the predicament we in, that was my best friend's cousin ya'll killed and Cass's man's niggaz, his street family and he's declared war on anybody he thinks had sumthing to do with it. It's go really fuck wit'em if and when he finds out Cass's family did the shooting, not to mention the fact Cass is pregnant by him, now how da hell ya'll think that's go play out?" "Word you pregnant fam?" Cap asked. "Yeah Cap I am, I ain't even tell Stan yet cause of this shit."

"Yo Cass I'm sorry bout all this drama, but your man's peeps started this shit," Ski said. 'What I want to know is, if the nigga had anything to do with us getting jacked?" Turk asked. Everybody looked at each other "Yeah Turk that is the million dollar question ain't it,' Tre said. Ayanna spoke up "I don't think so, if he did then ya'll would've been the first people he thought about. Even when the Jackson Ward niggas described the car, he never said anything bout ya'll."

"You say dem niggas described the car?" Cap asked. "Yeah them niggas was ready to declare war on Whitcomb cause they thought we bought a beef over there and started shooting while their kids were outside. But Stan tol'em Whitcomb ain't have nothing to do with it and that he didn't have a clue who was behind it," Cassidy said. "So you'ont think Stan thinks it was us?" Tre asked. 'Not right now, hopefully whoever this bitch is and I don't want to know who she is, but hopefully Stan don't find out who she is. But if he do, again hopefully she'll keep her mouth shut," Ayanna said.

"Yall think the bitch go run her mouth?" Cassidy asked. "Honestly Cass, we don't know who da fuck ya'll talking bout, what bitch and what nigga?" Tre asked straight faced. "Aight if ya'll say so, but just know that Stan's looking for whoever that bitch is," Ayanna said. "And what's that supposed to mean, fuck Stan and whoever that bitch is, ya'll mafuckas keep worrying bout Stan. What ya'll forgot them faggot ass niggas jacked us first? Cass, Yanna I love ya'll but them mafuckas got what was coming to'em and I don't feel bad. Stan may be your man Cass, but bottom line he ain't shit to me and if he got beef bout what happened to his niggas then he can get it too," Turk said angrily and emphatically.

"Turk I hear and feel you bro and I second that thought son, but we gotta look at the bigger picture and that's Cass and Yanna, they could have beef coming from every which-a-way. We go have to lay low, play it safe and definitely stay out the projects for awhile," Tre said. "Nah big bro, I think it'll be better if we go back, like you said that way we don't look suspicious," Ski said. "I'ont know, what if the police got a description of the car and happen to see all four of ya'll riding in it. That'll be probable cause to fuck wit ya'll, plus ya'll would be the prime suspects, specially if they saw ya'll over Whitcomb," Cassidy said.

"So what you saying we should be ducking and hiding?" Cap asked. "No Cap, what she's tryna say is we think it would be better for everybody if ya'll dipped out and headed back to New York," Ayanna said. "What?" Tre exploded "That sounds like ya'll telling us to run, sorry cuz ain't no rabbit in our blood, we ain't running from nothing." "Listen Tre, we love ya'll we don't wanna see ya'll go to jail or worse, I really think this thing could get uglier with the way the projects is feeling right now. Don't forget Cass still has to live over there, what if they find out it was her cousins that took out three of their soldiers?

How you think they go feel towards her? That's my sister and ain't nobody go do shit to hurt her without getting hurt they damn selves, but yet instill Stan's her man and them was his niggas, so now she gotta try and placate him. Plus ya'll killed my best friend's cousin, so me and her could wind up beefing for some shit we ain't have nothing to do with. Alls we asking is ya'll think about us in this situation," Ayanna said.

""You right fam, we not thinking of ya'll, how bout we hang around here for a coupla days to make sure ya'll safe, afta that we go back to New York for a few months to let shit die down, before we come back," Tre said. "Come back, come back for what? Ya'll mafuckas know you can't set up shop in Whitcomb no more, so where ya'll plan on setting up shop?" Cassidy wanted to know." "We'll deal with that when the time comes," Tre responded.

Northside;

Sassy was at home sitting on the front porch talking to Tajon on the phone when her line beeped "Hello" "Sassy this Sam from Sam's Kitchen." "What's up Sam?" "Hey girl, look I'm over my cousin's Carla house on North Ave and I just saw your brother Cheeks come flying past here in a gray Lincoln being chased by the police." "What? Chased by the police?" "Yeah" "Where at on North Ave?" "Up here by North and Fendall, he was headed back down towards that way." "Aight thanks Sam, lemme see if I can find out what's going on."

Sassy clicked back over to Tajon and told him she would call him back an emergency had come up, she could hear sirens in the background and asked "What's all that noise?" Tajon told her "it was the police chasing a Lincoln, but the Lincoln was smoking they ass." "Which way they headed?" "Why?" "Cause I think that's my brother they chasing." "Your brother? Oh shit, well he turned right on Gladstone off Cliff headed ya'lls way, wait a minute" Tajon said "he just made another right on Barton headed towards Ladies Mile."

"Where you at?" "I'm on my block of Cliff standing on the corner of Gladstone and Cliff." "Aight lemme go tell my mama what's going on, I'll call you back." Sassy hung up and went in the house. "Ma can I use the car to go to Subway?" There was no way she was go tell her mother that Cheeks was being chased by the police, Ms. Fox would've had a fit.

"Subway, why don't you just fix yourself a sandwich downstairs?" Cause I got a taste for Steak and Cheese." "Yeah Sassy go ahead." "Thanks Ma," Sassy grabbed the keys and hurried out the door to the car while calling Cheeks cellphone. "HELLO!" Cheeks answered sounding amped up. "Cheeks boy what the hell is going on? Where you at?" "Da police chasing me, I'm coming down Richmond Henrico Turnpike towards the

Blvd., I'ma turn on Gladstone and head towards Highland Park."
"Well I got mama's car headed that way, where you want me to
meet you at?" "Meet me on Cliff between the 3000 and 3100
block, park by the alley but on da street, I'll find you." "Aight
boy, be careful."

Sassy turned on Woodrow and came down to Cliff, she saw
Tajon standing on his porch, but he didn't see her cause he didn't
know Ms. Fox's car. Sassy parked at the corner beside the alley
hoping and praying that Cheeks made it there safe. Just as he
said Cheeks hooked a hard left on Gladstone, went down to
Wellington where he made a right then when he got to Northside
Ave he made a hard right and rammed into two parked cars. He
jumped out and took off running towards Richmond Henrico
Turnpike, but in the middle of the block he jumped a fence ran
thru a backyard, jumped another fence, ran thru the alley, came
out on the Turnpike, fast walked towards the Blvd and hit the
woods.

He knew these woods like the back of his hands, he stayed
off the path that ran down the middle instead he ran thru the
thickest part with sticker briars and all. He eventually came up
in the alley between Cliff and the turnpike, he stayed close to the
woods edge until he walked thru the curve, seeing his mother's
car he swiftly walked to it and got in. "Hey Sass, boy am I glad
to see you, you're a life saver." "Lifesaver my ass, what da hell
you do for the police to be chasing you and how you get away?"
Sassy said as she pulled off.

"I'ma tell you but first go thru the turnpike so I can see
what da police doing." Sassy turned on the Blvd., then on the
Turnpike. As they rode thru they saw the police sitting in the
middle of Arnold Ave and at the end of Arnold on the Turnpike.
They saw police in the alley Cheeks had ran down moments

earlier, coming up to Northside Ave they saw police everywhere. They were walking with flashlights out, cars parked everywhere and all over crack head Sham Sham's car, they had the whole block surrounded.

"Damn boy, what the hell you do?" 'I ain't do shit, I was down Highland Park on Crenshaw getting ready to leave when Dirty Birk came up to the car with $40, this dumb ass mafucka stood in the middle of the street blocking the car. After I cuss his ass out and serve him I go to pull off and the police pulling up behind me wit their blue lights going. I'ont know if they saw us or not but I assumed so, plus I'm dirty so I hit the gas and shook they ass." "How you get away?" "I ran'em all ova Highland Park and Northside. Afta talking to you I hit Northside Ave, ran into two parked cars, jumped out ran thru Boo Boo yard, hit da alley, came thru the woods and here I am."

"Boo Boo, I thought he had a yard full of pitts." "He do that's why I went that way, cause da way I figured it, I'd hit da backyard and catch the dogs off guard, by the time the the police hit it the dogs would be on full alert. The police wouldn't be able to get thru without shooting one of'em and that would gimme time to get away, which it did." So what you go tell Sham Sham?" "Shid I'ma tell his ass fake like the car was stolen, he took his house keys off the ring, so he can say he left'em in the car door." "Can't they get your fingerprints out the car?"

"I'ont think so and if they do, all he gotta say is I helped him clean out the car earlier today. Where da hell we going?" "To Subway, I had to tell mama I wanted a Steak and Cheese sub so I could get the car and come save your ass." "Save my ass, how da hell you find out anyway?" "Sam from the restaurant called while I was on the phone with Tajon, then he saw you come down Cliff and turn on Barton before we got off the phone."

"Sam, Tajon?" "Yeah said she was over her cousin Carla's house when you came flying by and Tajon is the guy from school that I was talking to that night at the Sattelite when ya'll got to fighting. Remember the boy I kept dancing with that Mundre kept talking bout." "I know who talking bout, so ya'll talking now?" "Nah we just friends for now, but lemme call him and let'im know everything's fine."

Sassy called Tajon while Cheeks called Sham Sham and told him what the deal was. "So how am I supposed to not know that my car was stolen?" Sham Sham asked. "Just tell'em you was at home sleep so you could go to work tonight and that you must've left your keys in the car door." "Yeah mafucka you go look out for this, I mean that." "Don't worry Sham I got you." "I know you do, but let me get back to sleep so I can be ready whenever they show up." "Aight call me tomorrow." "Don't worry I will."

Cheeks had gotten a sub also while they were at Subway and now he and Sassy were at home and halfway thru their sandwiches when Ms. Fox came downstairs got her 24 oz can of Budweiser out the kitchen popped the lid, lit a cigarette and asked Sassy "where you get Cheeks from?" "He was coming down the street when I was leaving here." "Is that so?" Ms. Fox asked looking at Cheeks. "Yeah Ma," Cheeks answered. "So you telling me Cheeks that won't you Tina Lucille saw wreck a car, jump out and run behind a house while the police was chasing you? And you telling me Sassy that wasn't you she saw coming up the street driving with your brother in the car trying to see what the police were doing?"

Sassy and Cheeks looked at each other knowing they both were in trouble. "Yeah Ma, it was me and yeah Sass came to get me but don't blame her, I called and asked her to come and get me and not tell you where she was going, she ain't know nothing bout the police chasing me." "So you say, but the fact remains she lied to me." "Cause I tol'er to Ma, you know she wouldn't have if I hadn't tol'er to." "Sassy I unnerstand you went to get your brother and you did what he asked you to do, but at the sametime I'm your mama and I told ya'll you could come to me wit anything."

'I know Ma, but" "Ain't no buts, we go leave it at that. Now why don't you tell me why the police were chasing you," Ms. Fox said to Cheeks. He shoots her a line about him 'initially running a stop sign and that he didn't think the police were pulling him over at first. But when he realized they were, he decided no to because he had some weed in his pocket and he wasn't trying to go to jail."

"Some weed huh? More like that crackerjack shit ya'll be running round here selling, ya'll must think I'm a damn fool or something, like I don't know what the hell you doing. Keep on and your ass go wind up in jail and don't call me cause I ain't coming to get your ass, I dun told you. Ya'll go keep on til you go have your sister's ass caught up in some shit, then it's go be hell to pay for real." "Naw Ma it ain't like that, ain't nobody go get Sass caught up in nothing."

"I can't tell, what if the police had known she picked you up tonight? Both of you would've been down 17th St., get on my damn nerves." "I'm sorry Ma I apologize it won't happen again and Sass I apologize to you too, you took a big chance tonight I love you sis." "Apology accepted brother dear and Ma I apologize to you too for lying, I promise it won't ever happen again," Sassy said. "Apologies accepted and Sassy I'm happy you're there for your brothers and they can depend on it, but sometimes you gotta think about yourself baby. I guess people think I'm raising a gang of outlaws," Ms. Fox said as she picked up the phone to call Tina Lucille back.

Westend:

While Cheeks was being chased by the police; Fatty, Te-Mundre, Shaun, Gamal, Poppi, and Danielle were riding on Carter St. Danielle had called Fatty while he and Marquell were weighing their coke out he had gotten from Curser earlier. "What up cuz?" Fatty had said answering the phone. "Hey cuz, I called to tell you that Gamal wanna holla at you bout that lil problem from the store." 'What about it?" "C'mon cuz you know betta than that, you gotta come over here and see what he want."

"When he wanna talk cause I'm busy right now." "Tonight I think." "Lemme finish this up and I'll hit you back." "Aight." 'Fuck's going on?" Marquell asked. "That was my cousin Danielle she said da nigga Gamal wanted to holla at me bout what happened da other day at the store." "What about it?" "I'ont know but I'ma see what he gotta say." "Make sho you strapped, want me to come with you?" "Nah I trust dude Danielle called for'im, plus afta we talked the other day I got a good vibe from'im." "Trust yo instincts, but still go strapped shawdy why can't ol'boy come ova here."

""I'ont know but I'm still going ova there." "Suit yourself, just call me afta you see'im so I can know you aright." "You got that, now let's finish up." After finishing with Marquell, Fatty went to take his 2 ½ Oz's home not wanting to ride over the Westend dirty. Shaun and Te-Mundre were outside when he got home, coming back out the house he called Danielle "So what's up cuz?" "Fatty he wanna know if you can come ova here tonight?"

"Yeah why?" "Got damn Fatty, you know damn well I ain't go talk on this phone, just get yo ass ova here asap." 'Aight, I'm on my way, where he want to meet at?" "Come to my house." "Aight." Shaun and Te-Mundre asked where he was going and both said they were riding with him, of course Te-Mundre said he was carrying his gun just in case, so Shaun said he was carrying his too.

The brothers got to Danielle's house and found out their aunt Carrie Jo was at work, Gamal and Poppi were already there. After everybody spoke, Fatty asked Gamal "What's shaking? Cuz said you wanted to talk." "Yeah, she told us what happened the other day at the store, so I wanted to know if you ready to ride on them niggas tonight or what?" "Why tonight?"

"Cause tonight's Monday and Carter St normally jumps on Mondays, I don't know why so don't ask me why. But them niggas won't be looking to get hit on a Monday trust me and the nigga Faulkner supposed to be having a strip show ova there tonight, so you know all them lil niggas go be out on the block tonight tryna make some money to trick on them ho's. I say we ride over there and let'em have it, afta what you and your family did for me, yo beef is my beef, plus we beefing wit them niggas anyway." ""I'm wit that but I ain't strapped." "You can use mine bro and I'll drive," Shaun said. "Aight that'll work." They all loaded up and rode out; Gamal, Poppi, and Danielle were riding together with Danielle driving, while Shaun was driving for the 'Family.'

Turning on Carter St. the block was indeed jumping, there was at least ten people standing around and moving about, three houses down there were a few more people standing around the yard and sitting on the porch. Fatty anticipating nobody paying attention to the cars riding past called and told Danielle to drive on thru the first time, which she did. After riding thru and around the block they pulled over and decided that Danielle and nem being the first car would dump on the people at the house and Fatty'nem would start at the group standing around and finish the party off, then they would head home. So again they pulled off with Danielle driving the lead car and again as they turned on Carter St nobody was paying attention.

Danielle was already doing the speed limit as she approached the house then slowed down, Gamal and Poppi already had their windows down as they let loose 'bblak blak blak bak bak bak.' Gamal let his Glokk21- .45 go and Poppi let his S&W .45-13rd extended clip go. People started running and hollering as behind them Fatty and Te-Mundre let loose 'blaka blaka blaka blaka blaka blaka,' they both let .40 cals go. Fatty thought he recognized Pokey standing in the crowd and that's where he concentrated 'blaka blaka blaka' he saw the person he thought was Pokey get hit in the leg and upper arm.

Te-Mundre meanwhile was sweeping his gun back and forth, he saw at least two people drop and as they passed the house he and Fatty cut loose again 'blaka blaka blaka blaka blaka.' Shaun hit the gas and they headed back to Northside, but not before stopping by the James River to get rid of the guns. When all was said and done a total of nine people had been shot; Gamal and Poppi both had hit two people apiece, one person's knee was shattered, somebody got hit in the chest, one person got hit in the stomach and one person got hit in the arm. The person Fatty thought was Pokey, was indeed him and the two people Te-Mundre had initially shot, both got hit in the back. And as they pulled off they both hit somebody standing in front the house, one person got hit in the upper thigh and the other person just above the elbow. All in all, it was one of the worse drive-by shootings in Richmond history.

Chapter 21-HCJ Dayroom 21:

"Coghill, Jeffrey Coghill" "Yeah" "Visit," Deputy Hantzel said. "Aight, I'm ready," Jeff answered. Before he left out, he looked at Chazz and smirked. Since he and Darrell had beat Chazz's ass, Chazz had tried to apologize, but Jeff wasn't hearing it. Chazz knew it was Jakeela coming to see Jeff and despite himself a wave of jealousy came over him, so he went to the phone and called his baby mama Lanay.

Jeff was seated in the visitation room when Jakeela walked in, she was looking good and sexy as hell in the baby blue velour Juicy Coture outfit he had bought her. But fuck that she had played and disrespected him and was about to find out he knew about it. "What's up?" he said as she took a seat. "Hey baby, why you ain't call this weekend? I was worried about you." "Worried bout me or worried bout Chazz?" Jeff saw the look of surprise and guilt cross her face before she said "Chazz, why would I be worried bout Chazz?"

"You tell me, you do know he's down here and on my tier don'chu?" "How da fuck would I know that and why would I want to know?" "Oh my bad, he won't on my tier last week when you came down to see'im." Again he saw the look of surprise on her face. "Jeff I don't know what da fuck you talking bout," she lied. "Oh you don't huh? Well how bout this? Darrell saw you the other day when ya'll were in the visiting room all lovey dovey and shit."

"Darrell Darrell, Darrell telling a goddamn lie, I can't believe you even believe some shit like that much less brought it up to me." "Yeah, well how bout this one, I just told you Chazz was on the tier wit me, when we confronted him about it he tried to lie at first. Then he wound up coming clean telling er'thing, how you pulled up on him at Chicken Box asking him to buy you a 'Big Chic,' how you scooped him up that night in my car and ya'll went to the Super 8 where he fucked you all night. How ya'll went to Potomac Mills again in my car and you bought him two pair of Jordans, oh and let's not forget this, you go get his name tattooed above the crack of your ass. That's what got his ass beat the fuck up, nigga lucky he still breathing."

Jakeela didn't know what to say she was speechless, she couldn't believe Chazz snitched her out like that and told every fucking thing at that. Sitting there with tears streaming down her face, she knew she had fucked up. "Jeff baby I'm sorry I swear to god I am." "Save that shit Jakeela I ain't tryna hear it, somebody in my family will be at yo house tonight or tomorrow for my car." "What? How da hell am I supposed to get to work?" "I don't know and I don't give a fuck, tell Chazz to find you a way."

"Fuck Chazz, I ain't his woman I'm your woman and baby mama, how DeMarcus and Tomise s'pose to get to the doctor and babysitter?" "Not my problem, somebody in my family will take'em to da doctor's office you just let'em know when, as for the babysitta you on your own, I can't tell you how you go pull that one off." "You can't take the car that ain't right." "Shid why can't I" You shoulda thought about that before you told niggas it was your car, taking 'nem shopping and fucking 'nem and shit. So now buy you a car and you can do whatever it is you want to do."

"Jeff baby please don't do this, I swear it won't happen again I fucked up okay, but baby if you take the car I'll lose my job then how am I supposed to pay the bills and provide for the twins." "If you lose your job it'll serve you right, my mama will gladly take the twins and raise'em while I'm in here. As for you fucking up, you damn right you did, but forgive you, nah never that, cause if I forgive you once you'll neva respect me and will continue to do it." "No I won't baby, I swear on the twins I won't."

"Don't do that, you lying and you know you lying like I know you lying, so don't swear on my kids heads. Matter fact don't even bother bout coming to see me again, my mama can bring the twins up here and if you don't let her get'em I got other ways to make sure you cooperate. Darrell went home yesterday he ain't but a phone call or letter away, he'll know how to handle the situation." "Jeff you know I would neva keep your kids away from you." "I'ont know shit, but you lucky I'm in here cause if I was out there I would fuck you up." Jakeela looked at Jeff and knew he meant every word he said, somehow, someway she had to get back in his good graces. "Coghill visits up." "Good, don't forget Keela my family coming to get my car, I"ll tell Chazz you said hey." "Fuck you Jeff, I love you." "If you say so," Jeff said as he hung up the phone and walked out the visit. When he got back to the dayroom he told Chazz that Jakeela said hi and laughed.

Southside:

Peaches was ecstatic, her supervisor at the post office had let her off work early for the first time in two years, she was going home and maybe get back in bed or maybe change clothes and go out have lunch with her sister Tricey. Pulling up in front her apartment she sees her man Timbo's green Toyota 4 Runner parked in front her door. Getting out the car, she's wondering what the hell Timbo's doing here this time of day. Walking in the door she doesn't see Timbo but his watch, jewelry, and phone are on the table, his jacket and fitted cap were on the sofa. Setting her pocketbook down she thought maybe he's upstairs in the bedroom, walking upstairs she hears someone moaning.

Coming to the top of the stairs she hears the noise coming from Tricey's room, she turns and heads that way. Stepping in the doorway she sees Tricey with a mouthful of dick and her ass turned up in somebody's face. "What the fuck!" Tricey looked up and Timbo froze "I know damn well that betta not be Timbo you 69'ing with in my house."''" Peaches stepped thru the door and went to the bed, when she saw that indeed it was Timbo she hauled off and 'blip' punched the shit out of Tricey knocking her off Timbo and onto the floor. Then she jumped on the bed and started throwing haymakers left and right.

"I can't fucking believe ya'll fucking in my house, motherfucka you crazy or something and my sister at that." Timbo tried to get away but Peaches was like a mad woman, she looked down saw his manhood laying there reached down grabbed it, lifted it up and 'blop blop.' She punched his balls with two vicious uppercuts causing him to scream out in pain "awww," then she went after Tricey who was trying to grab her clothes and run. "Bitch I'm your sister, I let you move in here afta your nigga put yo ass out and this how you repay me. By fucking and sucking my man."

She said all this while punching Tricey in the face, when she was thru she pulled Tricey's head down by the hair smashing her nose and mouth with two quick knees. Blood went everywhere as Tricey tried to scramble away. "I want both of ya'll sorry sacks of shit out my house, now." Timbo couldn't answer all he could do was hold his nuts and moan, Tricey was holding her nose, crying and trying to crawl out the bedroom when Peaches kicked her in the stomach saying 'trifling bitch."

Peaches was beside herself, she knew if she stayed there somebody's ass would get seriously hurt, so she decided to leave first "When I get back both ya'll sorry ass betta be gone."

Tricey was trying to put her clothes on but her body was sore from the pummeling Peaches gave her, she looked over at Timbo who was sitting on side the bed rocking back and forth. "You go let me leave with you?" He just looked at her, finally he said thru clenched teeth "Hell naw you crazy, for your sister to be out front watching to see if we leave together." "I ain't got nowhere to go or no way to leave here." "You shoulda thought of that before you came onto me." "It ain't like you couldn't've said no." "True, but you still go find your own way from here, I'ma wait til your sista calms down before I try to talk to'er."

"Fuck that you could at least drop me off somewhere, damn let me find out you scared of Peaches." Timbo stood up and grabbed his clothes, it felt like his nuts were in his stomach, almost like he had to shit. "Ahh, shit! Hell naw I ain't scared of Peaches but she mad as hell and I ain't chancing her getting madder, so you on your own." "Yeah well don't ask to hit it again when you see me, with your scared ass." "Don't worry I ain't, I ain't have no business fucking wit yo ass in the first place, specially here."

"Fuck you Timbo," Tricey said as she went in the bathroom. Timbo walked downstairs gingerly, when he got there he found his Movado watch face crushed to pieces, his bracelet broke in three places and his glasses broke in half. He picked everthing up dropped them in his pockets and walked out the house. Tricey realizing that she really had nowhere to go tried calling P.J. but he didn't answer, so she put her pride aside and called Teco, but he didn't answer either. Thinking Teco just didn't wanna talk to her, she called from the house phone, but again no answer, so this time she left a voice message telling him to call her. Not wanting to be alone with Peaches when she got back, Tricey left the house walking....

Snooky Boo, Roland, Davey D., and Jaman were at DTLR in Southside Plaza when Frye, Billy Blu and Breedo from Hillside walked in. "Snooky check out these Maya Moore Jumpman's," Davey D called out. "Check'em out for what, I just got a pair last week," Snooky replied. Hearing Snooky's name called all three guys from Hillside looked up and at each other. Breedo being the closest to Snooky walked over to her and asked "Shawd, you got a cousin name Miguel from Hillside?"

"Why?" Snooky answered staring him in the face. "Cause he always talking bout his cousin Snooky, telling er'body how fine and gangsta she is." "Yeah I got a cousin name Miguel, what's yo name?" My name is 'SPLAT' Breedo hauled off and smacked her catching her off guard and knocking her into a clothes rack. Soon as Breedo hit Snooky, Billy Blu who had slid over next to Davey D., took off and 'whop' punched Davey with a baseball punch in which he cocked his leg up and went thru a pitching motion, knocking Davey to the floor. Seeing his sister get hit Roland caught Breedo with a two piece, Frye started to run up and help Billy Blu with Davey when Jaman caught the back of his shirt and 'baow baow baow baow' hit Frye with four straight sidearm haymakers.

Snooky Boo had got herself together and went after Breedo with a vengence; after Roland had hit him Breedo ducked his head and charged Roland pushing him into the wall where the shoes were. Now Roland and Breedo were going toe-to-toe when Snooky ran over and kicked Breedo in the back of the leg causing him to fall to one knee, then she hit him with a vicious elbow to the jaw knocking him to his hands and knees, where

Roland drew back and kicked him square in the face busting his lip and nose. Jaman had slammed Billy Blu to the ground and was stomping him when Roland yelled "Let's go." Snooky Boo, Roland, Jaman and Davey D all left out got in the car and pulled off, leaving the Hillside niggas in the store to deal with security who was just coming back from lunch break.

Walking in the store looking around, the security officer asked the clerk "What happened?" and she told him about the fight. The security guard who grew up in the hood, walked over and told them to "leave the store before the police arrived," they dragged out to their car and left....."Who the fuck was them niggas?" Roland asked inside their car. "I'ont know, dude asked me was I Miguel's cousin, so whoever they was they know Miguel," Snooky said. "I know that otha nigga hit the fuck out my jaw," Davey D said.

"Well we whipped they ass, but soon's we find out who they was we go strike back, fuck that nigga putting his hands on my sister, his ass bout to get hit wit some hot balls," Roland said. "Go to Wendy's lemme get something to eat," Snooky said to Jaman. "Yeah me too," Davey D said. "Shit we might as well go on the inside," Roland said....Leaving DTLR Frye said to Breedo "I can't believe you smacked that bitch." "Why not? Fuck that bitch, I told ya'll niggas it was on when I saw'em. When I see'em again I'ma blaze they ass," Breedo replied.

"Ain't that them over there in Wendy's parking lot by that car," Billy Blu said from the backseat. "It look like that bitch and that nigga that hit me," Frye said. "Go up and come back around by the drive-thru, if it's them we'll catch'em off guard and wet they ass up," Breedo said. But unknown to them Jaman had seen'em looking and not sure who they were he asked Snooky "who da fuck is that in that car looking over here."

"What car?" "That brown '98.'" Snooky noticing them too said "I'ont know, but whoever they is, they got their signal light on like they coming back."

"What kinda car them niggas riding in?" Jaman asked. "I'ont know but lemme get my ratchet just in case its them niggas," Snooky said. "Me too," Jaman said. Seeing Snooky and Jaman reach in the car under the seats Davey called to Roland who was waiting for their orders "Ro what the fuck Snooky nem up to?" "Fuck you talking bout?" "C'mere," Davey told Roland what he'd seen Snooky and Jaman do. "Grab the orders, lemme see what's going on," Roland said walking outside.

"Fuck is ya'll grabbing yo heat for?" Roland asked. Snooky told him what they'd just saw. "If it was them they coulda just turned up in da parking lot don'chu think?" Roland asked. "Fuck that, I ain't taking no chances, if it was them they can get what they looking for," Snooky said. "Right Snook with the police station right across the street," Roland said to his sister. "Fuck that shit Roland, dem niggas was looking hard, plus we'ont know what them other niggas was riding in, I ain't lettin'em catch me slipping no more," Snooky said. "How bout we just leave now?" Roland said as Davey was coming out the door carrying the bags of food.

They all checked their bags to make sure they were right, got in the car and pulled off, but as they were pulling off the Hillside crew was pulling in. As the Hillside crew was coming around to drive-thru they saw the Clopton Terrace crew turn out "That's them right there ain't it?" Breedo asked. "I think so," Frye said. "Follow'em we'll catch'em when they get out the car and light they ass afire," Breedo said. Snooky who was riding up front with Jaman was eating her double stack burger looking thru the mirror, she wasn't sure if that was the same car or not following them so she decided to wait and see before she said anything.

Instead of going back to Clopton Terrace, Jaman turned into Foot Locker's parking lot. "Where da fuck you going?" Snooky asked. "I wanna see if they got da new Forum's that came out day before yesterday," Jaman said. "My nigga me too," Davey D said chewing on some fries. "Well I'm carrying my ratchet wit me," Snooky said. "For what Snook?" asked Roland.

"Cause I think that was them niggas at Wendy's and they might be following us." "You paranoid as shit," Davey said looking around. 'I'ont see nobody that even resemble them niggas following us." He said this as Jaman was parking the car, but what he didn't see was the car coming from the driver's side that had circled around just as Jaman pulled up in front of Foot Locker. When Davey and Roland go to step out the car 'blaw blaw blaw clak clak clakclak, ping boomiling zing ping; Breedo and Billy Blu had jumped out the car blasting away.

"Shit! I told ya'll niggas," Snooky said jumping out the car returning fire. 'Baka baka baka caka caka clak clak clak baka' were all the sounds you heard as the parking lot turned into a shooting range with human targets. The driver's had now got involved as all seven people were now shooting for survival. "Ahhh" Billy Blu hollered as a bullet struck his hand knocking his gun out. "Aww shit," Davey hollered as he got hit in the upper thigh trying to shoot and run behind another car.

Frye and Breedo both take off running since the '98' was shot up, when Frye gets hit in the back by a bullet from Jaman's gun. Roland and Snooky both chased Breedo who was running between cars, you could hear sirens in the background getting louder and louder. Snooky Boo and Roland suddenly stopped chasing Breedo and ran back to the car, where Jaman had helped

Davey get in. They pulled off just as the police hit the parking lot.

Eastend:

Stan was over Yvonne's house talking to her and Janel when Minga comes walking down the street. "There go Minga right there Stan, she proly just left from round the street scoring since ain't nobody out here and them New York Boys ain't been doing shit," Yvonne said. "Ey Minga lemme holler at'chu for a minute," Stan called out. Minga came sashaying over like she ain't have a care in the world "What you want boy?" "Ay you I'm tryna find out who that nigga was you had wit'chu the other day."

'What other day?" "The other day you came thru here and scored from Kalil and Reece, when you left ol'boy up da street." "Why you want to know that?" "Bitch you know muthafuckin well why he wanna know, you know Kalil and Reece got shot that day," Janel said standing up on the porch.
Minga looked from Janel to Stan, she'd heard Kalil and Reece had been shot, but she didn't know how true it was, she just hoped them niggas from up top won't responsible.

"It was a dude that worked at Phillip Morris." "What's his name and how come he ain't come down wit'chu?" Stan asked. "His name is Jerry and he didn't come down cause he was scared to come in the heart of the projects." "Is that so?" Stan said. "I think you're full of shit, that's what I think," Yvonne said.

"Fuck you Yvonne, like I said this nigga from the suburbs out Chesterfield some damn where the nigga scared shitless of the projects, I met him one night over Highland Park and that day I just so happened to run across him at Aamaco on the corner." "I wanna see this nigga, you got his number or sumthing." "Nah baby, I told you I ran across him at the gas station." "Well you better do something to have his ass round here soon." "I'll see what I can do." "Ain't no see bitch. Do," Janel said.

'Like I said I'll see what I can do." "And like Janel said, don't see, do," Stan said. "Aight, I'll let you know something in a couple of days." "Do that," Stan said as his phone rang and he answered walking off. "S'up cuz," it was Fishman his cousin from Jackson Ward. "Shit, wha'chu up to cuz?" "Not a damn thing standing here flapping my gums tryna see what I can find out bout this shooting."

"That's what I'm calling bout, you got a ride?" "You know I do." "Good meet me at McDonald's on Magnolia in ten mnutes." Stan hung up the phone and walked back over to Yvonne and Janel, Minga had walked off. "That was my cousin Fishman from over da Ward, he said he's got something to tell me about what happened to Kalil and nem, I'm go meet'im at McDonald's. Ya'll want me to bring you back anything?" "Damn right, bring me back a Quarter Pounder wit Cheese meal," Yvonne said. "And bring me back a fish sandwich meal," Janel said. "You want tartar sauce?" "Nah but heavy ketchup and a orange drink." "And either a Coke or Pepsi wit mine," Yvonne stated. "Aight be right back."

Stan walked around to Cassidy's where he had parked his two-tone gray shock body Cadillac, he went in the apartment grabbed the Tec-9 he had just bought from D.K. round Brookfield Gardens. Five minutes later he was in McDonald's parking lot, he decided to go inside and order while waiting for Fishman. Fishman arrived a few minutes later, seeing Stan's car and no Stan he went inside as well. "Shid yo treat cuz," he said walking up beside his cousin. "Hell naw it ain't, it's yo treat, I treated last time."

"You right but look like you buying for more than just yourself," Fishman said as the cashier put the bags on the counter. "I am but what that got to do wit anything, you still can pay for mine," Stan countered. "That's aright, I'll catch you on the rebound." "I know it," Stan said as he walked off to the condiments while Fishman ordered. After Fishman got his order the cousins walked outside, where Fishman had parked his money green Cadillac Deville with 30 day tags, beside Stan's Caddy.

"Nigga you just wanted me to see yo new 'Lac that's all," Stan said eyeing the car. "Naw cuz, I really do got some info for you, but first I got this 'Lac for a steal, I paid $2,500 for it and it's a 2007." "Where you get it from?" "This old white lady out Hanover, it was her husband's but he died, she got another one just like it 'cept it's blue, she want the samething for it tho $2,500. I told her my cousin might want it." "Might, nigga you already know I do." "She had this sweet ass white-on-white Benz I was tryna get, but she won't coming up off that for nothing at all."

"Aight we can do that this weekend, but what you got for me?" Stan asked. "The day yo niggas got hit up, I saw a dark colored Chevy Caprice turn off Chamberlayne onto Charity behind'em, I was at the stoplight on the bridge when they came off the highway." "A dark colored Caprice Classic you sure?" "Yeah I'm sure nigga, I think I seen it in Whitcomb round by where Cassidy live." "Them punk mafuckas, them pussy punk mafuckas, that sound like Cass's cousins from New York I told you bout."

"I'ont know cuz,but how you go handle it if it was Cass's cousins?" "Wha'chu mean how I'm go handle it? They ass bout to get hit, like they hit my niggas." "And what about Cassidy?" "What about Cassidy? Fuck her, she can get it too if she don't like it." "Now you talking crazy. Do she even know they the ones shot your niggas or that yo niggas the ones that robbed her cousins?" "That's a good god damn question cuz, a good god damn question. I'ma find out you can believe that."

"You may not have to question Cass, that look like the car that was following yo niggas right there pulling in Citgo." Stan turned around and looked "That's them niggas." "Yeah, well that's the same car that was following them." "I gots to have these niggas right now cuz, fuck talking to Cass." "Hold up, you strapped?" "C'mon cuz you know betta than that, afta what happened you know I am, I got the Tec in the floor, look." Fishman looked in the car "Nigga yo ass crazy riding around with that bitch out in the open like that."

"Fuck that, I rather be caught with it than without it, you strapped?" "You know it, never leave home without it," Fishman said holding up his .40 cal. "Aight, I'ma pull in behind'em and you pull up on the passenger side cutting them off, they know my car but they don't know yours. I'ma hit the ones on the driver's side, be careful cuz them niggas might still be strapped," Stan said. "Shit fuck'em I ain't worried bout'em being strapped, they betta be worried bout me," Fishman said.

"The cousins got in their cars and pulled off. Ski had just finished putting gas in the car and they were pulling over to put air in the tires when Fishman pulled in the parking lot and Stan pulled in from behind. But instead of being on the driver's side Stan ended up on the passenger side. Almost as soon as he pulled up beside the caprice, Fishman let the .40 go 'bak bak bak,' somehow his first shot missed Tre who was driving and hit Cap who was sitting in the passenger side, in the ear killing him instantly. When Fishman started shooting he caused Tre to swerve, hit the air pump and come to a complete stop. Stan had pulled up and started firing 'tat-ta-ta-ta-tat' the brothers never saw him pull up; he hit Ski in the shoulder and chest and Turk got hit in the upper arm.

Tre tried to pull his gun up to shoot back, but Fishman shot him in the hand and grazed his neck and two bullets from Stan's Tec-9 slammed into his back. Turk also got hit in the chest and throat by Fishman. Fishman pulled off in one direction and Stan in another. Fishman hit Rady St. behind McDonald's, then hit Magnolia, Mechanicsville again and finally the highway as he headed back to Jackson Ward. Stan went thru Central Gardens and came thru Fairfield Court, headed back to Whitcomb. Tre tried to pull off but passed out from all the blood he'd lost.

Chapter 22-Channel 6 News at 6'O Clock:

"Good evening my name is Lisa Sommerville, we begin our news this evening with three separate shootings in the Richmond area in less than 24 hours. The latest one taking place about an hour ago at the Citgo gas station on Mechanicsville Turnpike in Henrico County. Our Rachel Palmer is on the scene at this moment. Rachel what can you tell us?" "Well Lisa, about an hour ago this was the scene of a horrific shooting. According to police two Cadillacs pulled in this gas station and started shooting at another car, inside the car were four people all of whom were injured by bullets.

Once the shooting stopped the cars pulled off and the driver of the other car apparently tried to pull off, but passed out from his injuries and drove into this air pump you see behind me. At least one and possibly all four were fatally injured. At this time it's not known whether the people inside the car were the intended targets or just caught in the crossfire, although police say they did recover at least two guns from the car that was shot up. At this time there are no suspects although police know that two Cadillacs were involved, police are talking to the clerks who were working here at the time and people who were at McDonald's across the street to see if they have any information.

As of this time as far as we know they have nothing. Once again to sum it up uhh! Two cars possibly Cadillacs pulled up in the parking lot of this Citgo gas station on Mechanicsville Turnpike in Henrico County and started shooting at another car, injuring all four occupants of that car. At this time there are no suspects although police are checking for leads. Reporting live from Citgo gas station I'm Rachel Palmer, now back to you Lisa."

"Thank you Rachel, now to the second shooting earlier today at Foot Locker in Southside Plaza, our Janice Avant is on the scene, Janice." "Yeah Lisa, I'm standing here in the parking lot of Foot Locker, a sports apparel store in Southside Plaza where earlier according to witnesses this was the scene of a shootout straight out the movies. According to police and witnesses alike, a dark colored car pulled in the parking lot here and parked, when another car pulled in from the other side and started shooting. The first car returned fire and that's when all hell broke loose. In the midst of people running and ducking fearing for their lives, you had the shooters running, ducking, and hiding behind cars as well.

One witness said it was like a modern day shootout at the O.K. Corral. At least two people were injured, possibly more, with one person being shot in the back, we know that one person got away on foot as well as the first car also and at least two people have been taken to the hospital. Again a shootout reminiscent of the O.K.Corral happened here in broad daylight earlier today at the Foot Locker in Southside Plaza, with at least two people being injured. One person from the second car and we think everybody from the first car got away. Whether anyone in the first car was injured or not, police are not sure, although it's believed at least one person was.

The two people injured have been taken to the hospital, reporting from Southside I'm Janice Avant." "Janice, do police say they know why this happened?" "There are reports of a fight in DTLR across the street at the other part of Southside Plaza. According to reports a woman was approached by a male who said something to her and when she responded he slapped her, that's when a free-for-all fight broke out between the group of people the woman was with and the group the guy was with. It is not known whether this incident is related to the shooting that took place here at Foot Locker, but police are checking all leads to try and find out. Again reporting live from Southside Plaza I'm Janice Avant."

"Thanks again Janice, now to the third shooting in our area, a drive-by shooting on Carter St in Richmond's Westend last night. Our Kirk Wallace is standing by with details, Kirk." "Thanks Lisa, I'm standing here on Carter St., where all is quiet now, but last night according to police was a different story. According to police Carter St., was packed last night when two cars rode thru and started shooting. According to preliminary reports at least 9-10 people were shot, although it's not known whether anyone was fatally hit or not.

Now Lisa some reports say two cars rode thru moments earlier matching the description of the two cars that did the shooting, although that hasn't been confirmed yet. So again, at least 9-10 people were shot last night in a drive-by shooting by two cars here on Carter St in Richmond's Westend. At this time there are no suspects and police are asking anyone with information to please call Crimestoppers. Reporting live from the Westend I'm Kirk Wallace, now back to you Lisa." "Kirk do police know why Carter St was so crowded last night?" "Well Lisa, it seems that there was some kind of party going on at the time, although it's not clear if anyone at the party was the intended target." "Thanks Kirk, now moving on to other news..."

Chapter 23-Northside:

Ike and Artez were riding thru Highland Park on their way over Artez's baby mama Kita's house in the 'Ghetto' up Washington Park on North Ave. "Them lil niggas be out on that corner er'time I come thru here, its gotta be jumping, I know they gettin money," Artez said referring to the young hustlas standing on the corner of 4th and Spruce St. "Ain't that the corner Fat Mo, Beanie and them niggas used to be on?" Ike asked his brother. "Yeah they used to be all up and down that block, I bet them niggas got some dough on'em now, wha'chu think?"

"I think you might be right, why you wanna try'em?" "You know it," Artez said as he continued on down the street while Ike checked the 12 gauge pump shotgun they had laying on the floor in the back of the car. They did a five block circle before they pulled up in front of the guys standing on the corner. Before Artez stopped the car Ike already had the door open "What's happening fellas?" he said hopping out the car with the gun pointed at the four young hustlas. "Ya'll niggas know what time it is," he had caught them completely off guard.

"I want ya'll niggas to lay facedown on the ground wit yo arms raised in front of you," Ike said as Artez was coming around the front of the car. "Go head bruh," Ike said to Artez telling him to go thru the young hustlas pockets. Artez went thru the first guy's pockets and pulled out a wad of money, a pack of Newports, a lighter and some keys. "Ain't you too young to be smoking?" he asked the youngster not really expecting an answer. Moving on to the next one he found a smaller wad of money and a .380 handgun "Damn boy, good thing we made ya'll lay down huh? You might've tried us."

He went thru the other two hustlas pockets and got three more wads of money,he got three cause the last guy had two knots on him. "Thanks fellas it's been nice," Ike said as the brothers got back in the car and pulled off. Ike counted the money "Damn Tez, them lil niggas had $990 on'em, damn near a 'stack.' I guess them niggas is getting a lil paper huh?" "I guess so, we go have to keep a watch on'em they prime meat for another jack move," Artez said.

Southside:

Timbo pulled up in front of Peaches apartment and sat there for a minute looking around, he didn't see any other cars but Peaches Chrysler 300. He was leery and kind of skeptical, Peaches had called and said they needed to talk, she told him to be here around 8:30 that night so they could discuss what happened earlier. He got out walked up to the door, stuck his key in, unlocked it and went inside. He smelt weed in the air but didn't see Peaches, walking upstairs he saw her bedroom door closed, so he walked over opened it and got the surprise of his life.

There looking him in his face was Peaches on her hands and knees gripping the sheets with eyes half closed. Standing behind her sending 10" inches of prime beef dick up in her was his best friend and right hand man Keiwan. "Da fuck?" he said. Peaches looked up at him just as Keiwan had pulled back and rammed all his manhood up in her. "AH Ah AH Shit!" she said as Keiwan went to keep going but stopped to look at Timbo. "Oh hey baby, you go stand there and watch or you go wait downstairs til we finished?" Peaches asked him.

"Keiwan why you stop? I know damn well you ain't finished already?" "Do it feel like I'm finished yet?" Keiwan said as he started stroking again. "I'm just tryna see what your man go do." "I'm go-" Timbo said as he started towards Keiwan. "You go what?" Keiwan said as he reached down picked up his .45 S&W off the nightstand beside the bed and pointed it at Timbo, stopping him in his tracks. "You go do me like that shawdy?" Timbo asked him.

"I ain't doing you like shit shawd, I'm doing Peaches like

she asked me too." "Look Timbo either you watching, waiting downstairs or leaving. It don't much matter which one you do, but whatever you do, you need to hurry the fuck up cause you fucking up my groove, shit I was getting ready to have the big one," Peaches panted. "What? Aight aight, I got'chu I'ma see you Keiwan." "Fuck you mean you go see me? See me now mafucka," Keiwan said pulling out of Peaches and walking towards Timbo, dick swinging and all.

"Keiwan if you don't bring that pretty mothafuckin dick back here, you better. Fuck Timbo, matter fact Timbo you can leave now and never come back. You and Tricey just did me a mothafuckin favor, if I had known Keiwan's dick and fuck game was this good, he woulda been got the ass. But fuck that, as of tonight he can get it when, how and wherever he want. Now put my keys on the bed and get the fuck out my house so we can finish getting our freak on, go find Tricey wit her whorish ass."

"Fuck you Peaches, you acting like a ho now." "That may be true, but I'm acting like a ho with your best friend and we go finish what we started, no get the fuck out. Keiwan bring that dick back over here to mama, baby." As Keiwan walked back to her, she reached out grabbed his dick "sslurrrp muah" gave it a kiss before Keiwan went back up in her. Timbo left out the room and 'blam ' slammed the door behind him as he left the house.

Deep in his heart he knew he couldn't fuck with Keiwan, Keiwan was a gangsta and a certified head bussa straight up, Timbo was a working nigga that sold drugs on the side. They were road dawgs that grew up together, they chose different paths in life and now Timbo had to figure out how to pay Keiwan back....When Peaches had left the house earlier she'd gone to Misa's her best friend's house, Misa had called Keiwan for some 'X' pills, when he got there and saw Peaches he started in. "What's up Georgia Peach or should I say Keiwan's Peach; you mean to tell me Timbo let you out the house without him?" "Fuck Timbo, don't mention that mothafucka's name around me."

"He fucked up huh? Well since he fucked up, why don't you stop playing and let me get a taste of Sweet Peaches?" "Keiwan stop playing wit me." "Who playing, I know that nigga ain't hitting it right, keep it funky. You know you want some gangsta lovin in yo life." "Whatever" "Ain't no whatever, you got my number call me when you want that ass busted up right," Keiwan said as he left.

Peaches had called after she left Misa's house and told Keiwan what time to be at her house, from there it was on, she explained that friend or not she didn't like people in her business, that's why she'd said that shit at Misa's. After calling Keiwan she'd made the call to Timbo; she knew secretly Timbo was jealous of Keiwan and always thought she liked him, although this was the farthest thing from the truth. She decided to play into his insecurities tonight and let him see how it felt to be played right in your face. She just didn't count on Keiwan's dick being so good, she was dead ass serious when she said he could get it when, how, and wherever he wanted it. Timbo had fucked himself and from now on she would be fucking his man.

Northside:

Ike and Artez were leaving Kita's to go meet Bennie in Essex Village to buy some dope, then they were going to 7-Eleven to get a couple of movies out the Red Box. Kita's cousin Nee-Nee had come over and Ike was trying to fuck her, they all agreed to watch some movies, smoke some weed and see how the night ended. Coming down the street beside the apartments in a dark blue Buick Roadmaster was Big Fonzi, his brother Lamar and his son Lil Fonzi. "There them niggas go right there Big F.," Lil Fonzi said to his daddy who didn't mind his oldest son calling him by name. "You sure?" asked Lamar.

"Yeah I'm sure, cause dude got on that same Chicago Bulls jersey," Lil Fonzi who was the one with the two stacks on him when Ike and Artez robbed the young niggas in Highland Park answered his uncle. He hustled around both Washington Park where he lived and round 4th Ave where his grandmother lived. "Pull over," Lamar said to his brother as he pulled the hammer back on his German Ruger 9mm. Big Fonzi pulled over by the alley, parked the car, reached under the seat and grabbed his .357 revolver. "Stay here," he said to his son.

The brothers got out and started towards the apartments "Shawdy ya'll niggas know Frankie that sell the coc round here?" Lamar called to Ike and Artez who both turned around and said "Nah" at the sametime; noticing Big Fonzi with his arm behind his leg Artez called to his brother "Watch out Ike." Artez went to reach under his shirt for his gun, but Big Fonzi already had his gun up 'Booom Boom Booom' the .357 roared as two bullets slammed into Artez's shoulder and upper torso. At the same time Lamar let the '9' go 'clak clak clak clak,' at the sight of Lamar's gun Ike went to take off running but bullets hit him in the lower legs, lower back and upper body. Fonzi and Lamar ran back jumped in the car and pulled off.

MCV Hospital:

The emergency room was in an uproar; with the shooting over Southside earlier, the one from Citgo gas station, the recent one from Northside, not to mention the regular sick people; doctors, nurses, and security people alike were stressed to the maximum. Cassidy and Ayanna had been here for 45 minutes and were still waiting on word about their cousins. They had been at the hair store in Highland Springs when Cassidy had gotten a call from Carol, her next door neighbor. "Hello" "Cass" "What's up Carol?" "I called cause I think your cousins got shot up at Citgo." "What!" Cassidy exclaimed "What the hell you talking bout Carol?" Cassidy asked her.

"I was riding past Citgo a few minutes ago and it's a whole lot of police cars out there, I saw a car that look like your cousin's car wit the doors wide open, police all in it and yellow tape around it." "How long ago was that?" "Bout ten minutes ago, when I got round here the word was it was the New York Boyz." "Aight C., thanks lemme call and see if one of'em answer the phone." "Who got shot?" Ayanna asked as Cassidy hit the end button.

"I'ont know, Carol said she think it was Tre and nem but she won't too sure, I'ma call Tre now." "And I'ma call Cap." "Hello" Somebody said on Tre's phone after about four rings. "Who this?" Cassidy asked "Who're you trying to reach?" "My cousin Tre" "Well I'm sorry Miss this is the police, the owner of this phone has been shot, he's on his way to MCV Hospital right now." 'Was anybody else hurt?" "I'm sorry, right now I'm not able to divulge that information, you have to check with the hospital to find that out." "Thank you officer." "May I have your name and contact information ma'am?" Cassidy gave it to him and hung up.

Ayanna who hadn't reached Cap heard the conversation and asked what happened, Cassidy then filled her in. Now here they were standing outside talking to the police and finding out that indeed it was all four or their cousins that got shot and at least one of'em was dead, if not all of them. "I want to know if Stan had anything to do with it? You tried calling him yet?" Ayanna asked. "Not yet. My nerves are all over the place Yanna, I hope like hell Stan ain't have nothing to do with it, I'ont know what I would do if he did."

"Me either Cass, them is our cousins, our family by blood, but Stan's your man and baby daddy, the father of my future niece or nephew, that would be tough to deal with." "Yanna I shoulda listened to you, I'ont know why I let Tre and nem set up shop in my house, damn, now all this bullshit for nothing." "All that's under the bridge now, let's just hope at least one of'em live and that Stan ain't have nothing to do with it," Ayanna said. "I wonder why he ain't call me yet, I know he heard what happened, lemme call'im and see what he gotta say."

"Yeah," Stan answered. "Stan where you at?" "Round Whitcomb why?" "You heard bout my cousins getting shot?" "Yeah I heard bout'em, but fuck'em." "What?' "You heard me, I said fuck'em. Word round here is they the ones shot Kalil'nem and if they is, then fuck'em I hope they ass dead just like my niggas is, if not I ain't got no problem finishing what other niggas started."

"How da fuck you go say you hope my cousins die?" "Easy like I just did, they shot my niggas what da fuck you want me to say." "Stan did you have anything to do with it?" When she asked this Cassidy held her breath, afraid of his answer. Hell naw! If I did it wouldn't be question of is any of'em dead or not. But lemme ask you somehing Cass, did you know yo cousins was the ones that shot my niggas?"

"I won't sure if they did or not, did you know it was Kalil'nem that robbed them?" Cassidy asked as again she held her breath. "Nah I ain't know, be for real, you think they woulda told me some shit like that and if it was them that jacked yo cousins, why would they say fuck my pussy ass and that I would have to pay too. Come on that don't make no mothafuckin sense." "Uh hun,lemme go see the doctor, he calling for somebody in their family and that's me and Yanna, but we need to talk seriously."

"Aight" "Ain't no aight Stan, we need to talk about more than just this, we need to start coming up with baby names." "What?" "You heard me, but we'll talk about all that later, right now I gotta talk to the doctor bout my cousins." "Aight, I'll see you at the house," Stan said hanging up the phone. Stan had went back to Yvonne's, gave them their food and asked Yvonne to hold onto the gun for him.

He knew that Yvonne was an old female 'G' whose baby daddy was a certified trained-to-go head bussa, and he knew for a fact that she had gotten rid of guns he used in the streets. Plus he slid her $200 as an added incentive. Now he was sitting in Cassidy's place smoking a blunt to hisself and thinking bout Cassidy. "Damn" was all he could say. Back at the hospital Cassidy and Ayanna had just learned Cap and Turk both were dead, Ski was in stable condition and Tre was in critical but stable condition. "Oh my god" was all Ayanna could say as Cassidy burst out crying. The sisters walked off hugging each other and crying at the sametime.

While Cassidy and Ayanna were dealing with their family problems, Lil Go- Hard was dealing with his own. "Man what da fuck? Somebody betta tell me sumthing," he said as his mother and grandmother looked at him. "Lupa" his grandmother called to him using his real name, "If you don't quiet down before somebody hears you boy. Your uncles already laid up in there all shot up, we don't need the police watching and harassing you cause they think you go get somebody back.

'You right grandma but them's my uncles in there and even though I know they do some messed up things, they still my family and I love'em, they taught me everything I know. If it was me laid up in there they'd be ready to lay this whole city down." "That may be true, but ain't no need to bring more police attention to this family than necessary," Grandma said. The doctor came out and called for the family "Is there any family here for the Drab brothers?" "Yeah" "Right here," they all called out, Kita and Nee-Nee were there also, they were the ones who found them and called 911.

"How you doing? My name is Dr. Harvey, I have some good news and some bad news. The good news is that Artez is doing as well as can be expected he's going to live, but he's going to be sore for awhile lucky for him the bullets didn't hit anything vital. But we're still going to keep him for a few days anyway. The bad news is Ike looks like he may be paralyzed, right now we don't know for how long. It may be for a short while, then again it may be permanent, it's all up to his body and how it responds to the physical therapy he's going to have to go thru. The bullet that hit him in the back ruptured his spleen, again depending on how his body responds to the physical therapy will determine if he ever walks again or not."

"Thank you doctor," Mayleen, Lil Go-Hard's mother said. "Thank you Lord, Thank you Jesus for sparing my two boys. I know they're not perfect, but again they're mine and I'm not ready to lose them just yet," Grandma said. "When can we see them?" Kita asked. "Tomorrow would be the earliest time I would recommend. They're sedated now and won't even know any of you are in the room, but at 8:00 tomorrow morning all of you will be able to visit." "Thank you again doctor, may god bless you." 'Thank you ma'am and you're all very welcome."

The next morning MCV was again in an uproar as families were being informed that police had placed those that they came to see under arrest. The only ones not under arrest were the people from Carter St. although the police did question Pokey. "What's up Pokey?" Officer Gaither said entering Pokey's hospital room." Fuck you mean what's up? These mafuckin bullets in my ass, that's what's up," Pokey answered, he had recognized the two detectives when they entered his room as police officers and if it's one thing Pokey hated, it was the police.

"Well that's what happens when you go around shooting at people," Det. Sully said. "Shooting at people, man you crazy as shit, in case you ain't noticed I'm the one that got shot. Mafuckas came thru and sprayed us, you dumb ass mafucka." "Is that so, well word is you and your cousin from Northside were in a shootout at the Market Place about a week ago," Det.Gaither said. "Cousin from Northside, what da fuck is wrong wit ya'll? I ain't been in no god-damn shootout and I ain't got no family from Northside." "You don't have any family around Northside?" Det. Gaither asked.

"Fuck nah." "Well why is people from off your strip saying you have a cousin form over there and he was on ya'lls strip the day of the shootout?" Det. Sully asked. "What people? Man them mafuckas lying they ass off, did they give you a mafuckin name?" "Not yet, but they will, someone will in time they always do," Det. Sully said. "I know god-damn well they didn't cause ain't no name for them to give you." "Okay Pokey just to let you know, we're not placing you under arrest, but we are holding you for further questioning. Right now we're going to question some more people from Carter St. and when the doctors release you, we'll be here to pick you up and take you downtown for more questioning," Det. Gaither said. "Man whatever, do what you feel," Pokey said as the detectives left the room.

The families of Frye and Billy Blu from Hillside had already found out that they both were going to be questioned by the police; Billy Blu's 9mm Luger and Frye's S&W .40 cal were both found at the scene where they'd been shot. Although it was not clear whether the guns belonged to them or the people they'd been shooting at, police were going to run them thru ballistics this morning, plus check their hands for traces of gunpowder. They weren't going to be allowed contact with any family until the police were finished with them. Billy Blu having got hit in the leg and hand could be released if ballistics came back negative. But Frye was touch and go since he got hit in the back, first doctors had to determine if he was going to live and if so, whether or not he was going to be paralyzed. Frye's mother, sister, and fiancé' were all hysterical, the doctor informed them they would keep them updated on his condition and if it looked like he wasn't going to make it, they were going to tell the police to let them visit him before it was too late.

Cassidy, Ayanna and their mother Precious were informed that Tre and Ski were both being placed in police custody until they could be questioned and possibly arrested. "Arrested for what?" Precious wanted to know. "My nephews laying in there shot all da fuck up and you talking bout them being arrested." "Ma'am I'm well aware of your nephews being shot, but there were two guns found in their car also, one was found in the driver's lap and the other between the two back passengers. I'm also aware that the car they were in, fit the description of a car involved in another shooting a couple of days ago.

So we have to question them, do ballistics on the guns and

check their hands and clothes for gunpowder residue," Officer Brantley told them. "Are any of you aware of any trouble they might have had with anyone?" All three women shook their heads and responded "no." "Well it's obvious somebody had it out for them, with the way that car look and how many bullets landed, it's a wonder any of them are alive. We're going to do everything we can to find the shooters and bring them to justice, I promise you that. I'll be in touch with you ladies, I believe an officer has already talked with one of you and gotten your information." "Yeah that would be me," Cassidy said. "

"Well I would like to get all three of ya'lls information so I can keep you all informed of what's going on, plus we may have more questions for you to answer." All three women gave him their information, he thanked them again and left. After finding out there was no change in Tre and Ski's condition, they left and went back to Precious house in Tiffany Meadows.

Meanwhile Lil Go-Hard, his mother Mayleen, his grandmother, and Kita had just been told that Artez had been placed in police custody and when he was well enough, he would be arrested for Possession of Firearm by a Convicted Felon. The gun had been found tucked in his waist. Ike would be questioned and possibly released since he didn't have a firearm on him; he had taken the pump shotgun in Kita's house and left it there thinking they were coming right back. Officer Bailey wanted Kita to recount everything that happened leading up to her and Nee-Nee finding Ike and Artez. She told him that "Artez was her man and baby daddy, and that he and Ike had come over to relax and chill. Her cousin Nee-Nee had come over and Ike was trying to holla at her; Ike and Artez left to go to 7-eleven to get some movies out the Red Box so they could watch."

She said that "bout five minutes after they left out the house her and Nee-Nee heard gunshots." Officer Bailey asked her if she knew how many shots she heard and she said "no." Then she said "because it happened right after they left out, she decided to call Artez's phone to make sure they were okay. After Artez didn't answer, she tried twice more before her and Nee-Nee walked out to see if Artez's car was gone and that's when they found them laid out front shot up." "You won't scared to go out there after hearing gunshots?" Officer Bailey asked her.

"We hear shots round there every night with mafuckas shooting up in the air. How was I to know that my man and his brother were going to be the ones that got shot." "I guess you have a point there, do you think it was Nee-Nee's boyfriend or sex partner that shot them?" "Nah, Nee-Nee don't have no boyfriend, as for sex partner she was just saying she hadn't had sex for 8 months and that Ike might get lucky and hit the lottery last night." "I see, well I'm sorry for the tragedy, but we're going to do everything we can to get to the bottom of this.

Here's my card with all my contact information on it, give me a call if any of you find out anything else. In the meantime let me get all of your information, I may need to contact you all. When Lil Go-Hard gave his name, Officer Bailey looked at him "You're the nephew right?" "Yeah" "You got any beef with anybody that might've taken it out on your uncles?" "Fuck naw man, fuck you talking bout!" "Calm down, I'm just asking. Well do your uncles have any beef that you know of?"

"Not that I know of, but I can't be 100% sure I don't be with them 24 hours a day." "I hear you talking, what they call you in the streets?" "They call me by my name Alvin. Why?" "You ain't got no nickname or street name?" "Nope" "Uh huh alright, well Alvin you're close to your uncles right?" "Yeah" "And you're what 15-16 years old?" "16" "16, okay you're still young man, I know you be out and about in the streets, I ain't saying you breaking no laws or none of that shit. I'm just saying you mess with the girls, you play sports and all that right?"

"Yeah and?" "And when you're out there you're going to hear things, especially things about what happened to your uncles. What I want you to do, even if you don't tell the police what you hear, I want you to stay out of it and let the police handle it." "Yeah right, this'll go unsolved like the rest of the shootings and murders in the city." "Listen son, I understand how you feel and what you're going thru, but don't stress your family any more than necessary. Your uncles already shot up and one of them may even be going to prison, don't do something stupid and get yourself hurt or wind up in jail or prison with your uncle."

"Don' t worry officer he's not, not if I have anything to say about it," his grandmother said. "I hope not ma'am. You gotta be strong and be there to protect your family man, you understand me?" "Yeah I understand you." "Good. Now I've got to go but I'll be in touch with ya'll especially you Alvin, I want to make sure you make it out of the streets and do something positive with your life." They all said their goodbyes and parted ways.

Chapter 23-Westend:

Lil Ray-Ray, Black Pete, and Simmy were walking down Grayland Ave., when Black Pete spotted Duke standing across the street from Chantel's house. "Ain't that the nigga Duke standing over there on the corner watching that house," he asked his two companions. Since that night in the abandoned house when Gamal, Dre Jr, Poppi and Chris Stevenson had shot them with paint ball guns and Gamal had beat all three of their asses one-on-one, they had been getting fronted coke by Gamal. First he gave each of them a 16th just to see what they would do with it and predictably they all came back at the sametime for some more. This time he gave them a 8 ball a piece, but told them instead of staying in the Westend they should hustle in Fairfield too, this way when one area got hot they could go over the other area with no problem.

Again he emphasized the importance of keeping their mouths shut and sticking together. When Dre and Poppi first told him about Duke and Filmore coming out the police station and Ma Vick called up there and was told that neither, Filmore or Duke had been arrested, he suspected them of snitching. But when he and Poppi had seen Duke, asked him about coming out the police station and he flat out lied in their face denying he was there, he knew then they were snitching. "Duke I saw you coming out the police station the other day nigga, fuck kinda charge you got, another trespassing charge?" Poppi had said. "I'ont know what you talking bout youngblood, you ain't see me coming out no police station."

Duke figured since Poppi didn't mention nothing about Filmore Dean that he was bluffing, after all he would've seen Poppi if Poppi had really seen him. "You telling me I ain't see you coming out the police station the other day bout 1:30 in the aftanoon?" "That's what the fuck I'm telling you, fuck would I be doing in a mafuckin police station." "That's what the fuck we want to know," Gamal said "What the fuck you lying for?" "Fuck you figure I'm lying? I'm telling you I won't at no damn police station."

"That's crazy cause I know I saw you and Filmore Dean walking out the police station together," Poppi said. Hearing that Duke realized he was stuck, finally he said "You mighta seen Filmore, but you damn sho ain't see me," Duke snapped. Gamal tapped Poppi saying "Aight, Duke if you say so" as he and Poppi continued up the street. "Gamal I'm telling you that was them niggas we saw," Poppi said. "Oh I know it was them, he all but told us Filmore was there and since he denying being there that means he gotta be hiding something. I take it as he's hiding the fact that they ass snitching, but since we ain't never serve Duke at Chantel's house, at least not to my knowledge anyway that means it had to be Filmore that sent them in there."

"You think so?" "Yep and they'll be dealt with in due time, just give me a minute to come up with something." So the last time Ray-Ray and his crew came to re-up from him, Gamal told them "if they see either Filmore or Duke and beat they ass to the point they went to the hospital, he would give all three of them a quarter ounce a piece." He knew they would do it cause that was more coc than either one of them ever had at one time in their life, to them that was a whole lot. Now they had Duke in their sights and were about to cash in "Sho is," responded Lil Ray-Ray. "What da fuck he watching that house for," Black Pete said, it was more of a statement than a question.

"I'ont know but we got his ass," Ray-Ray said. "When we get to'im ya'll just keep walking pass'im and I'ma set it on him," Black Pete said. Continuing up the street they eventually crossed over one-by-one; coming abreast of Duke, Ray-Ray said "Duke, fuck you doing watching that house?" Duke looked at each one of the youngsters, he knew Ray-Ray vaguely but he couldn't say from where. "Ain't nobody watching that house young'un, I'm just standing here minding my own damn business, like ya'll should be doing." In truth Duke was scoping out Chantel's spot to see if they were still selling drugs out of there, after Filmore told him that it was him Filmore that sent the police there in the first place, he decided if they were still hustling out of there he could use that information another day.

"Yo ass proly tryna figure out if you can break in there and steal something or not," Simmy said as the trio was walking pass Duke. "Fuck ya'll, like I said ya'll need to-'bop;' Black Pete turned around and stole (punched) Duke in the jaw, now Ray-Ray and Simmy joined him 'pop wop wop.' Duke was by no means soft he could and did put up a fight, but the youngsters had him outnumbered and were hell bent on whipping his ass. Sensing he had no win Duke took off running, but Simmy kicked him from behind sending him sprawling into somebody's yard and over some lawn furniture.

Black Pete kicked him in the stomach and Simmy hit him with a wide arm haymaker 'splot' that broke his jaw and burst his mouth open. Lil Ray-Ray ran up on the front porch, grabbed a metal stool and came running back over, he told Black Pete and Simmy to "stand back." When Duke tried to get up and was on his knees, Ray-Ray held the stool up by two legs and 'bam' smacked Duke in the face with it, he proceeded to hit him four or five more times, when he finished Duke was a bloody pulp lying there sucking up his own blood. The trio took off running for Rosewood to find Gamal and tell him what they'd done.

Amelia County:

Big Jack, Monk, Monopoly and Juice were sitting outside on top of their cars smoking a blunt and drinking, Monk had called Juice and told him they needed a 'Big 8th' of coc, a quarter pound of weed with an extra ounce thrown in. Monopoly and Juice were suspicious because of the big order at one time, but never the less they decided to take it to them anyway. When they got there Big Jack told them they had to wait cause they had a sale for both the coc and weed. "Wait, nigga didn't we tell ya'll we ain't want nobody to know where ya'll got yo shit from," Monopoly snapped. "They'ont know who it's coming from, all they know is we told'em we'll have it later on," Monk said.

"And who you say it's for again?" Juice asked. "The weed for Caitlyn this white bitch I be fucking," said Monk. "They having a party and she wanted to make sure she had some bomb ass smoke to sell her girls coming down here from ODU. And the coc for Danny her brother, all he wants is a half-a-big, we go get the other one." "Ya'll know Caitlyn the white girl that Juice said looked like she had two watermelons in her pants and Danny the white boy ya'll thought was Spanish," Big Jack said. "I know who you talking bout now, the bitch I said ass was phatter than Buffy's and the white boy with that big ass cable for a chain around his neck that I wanted to get," Monopoly said.

"Exactly," Monk replied. "That still don't change the fact we don't want'em to know it came from us," Juice responded. "Ain't nobody go know shit, afta I talked to Juice I tol'em to come bout 7:30, I ain't know ya'll mafuckas was go take all day and get here bout the same damn time," Monk said. As he said this the headlights came down the long dirt road leading to their house, a pale blue Ford Focus pulled up, Caitlyn and Danny got out and walked up to the them. "What's up fellas?" Caitlyn said. "What's up everybody," they all answered back.

"Damn I see ya'll blowing, smell like its some good shit," Danny said. "It is, here hit this," Big Jack said passing him the blunt. "Sssp sssp sssp ucm ucmm" "This ain't no good weed, this that Oaktree Fireweed, this shit some crucial," he said looking at Caitlyn "here try this" he said passing the blunt to his sister. "I know them college hoes go be fucked up off this shit," he continued. "What the fuck you say? Oaktree Fireweed, da fuck is that?" Monopoly asked. "You know everybody say Oak is the best wood to burn in a woodstove?" "Yeah" "Well we call good weed Oaktree Fireweed," Danny said.

"Uccm uccm, this is some fireweed I hope this what ya'll got for me," Caitlyn said passing the blunt to Monk. "You know it baby, I wouldn't sell you nothing but the best," Monk replied. "Aight then let's take care of business people was already starting to show up before we left," Caitlyn said. "Aight come on," Big Jack said as he let them into the house. "You trust them mafuckas?" Juice asked Monopoly after everybody else had went inside. "I do to a point, I'ont think Jack and Monk got the heart to try nuttin stupid like settin us up or nothing."

"What about the crackas?" "I'ont know, but they doing business with Jack and Monk, so they'll be the ones to take the fall not us." Everybody came back out the house at the sametime, Big Jack walked over to Monopoly and Juice while Monk walked Caitlyn and Danny to their car; Monk grabbed Caitlyn's ass with both hands and palmed it while kissing her at the sametime. As Caitlyn and Danny were leaving out the yard, Monk walked back over to where everybody was "Nigga you can't handle all that ass," Juice said to him. "Shid, you mean she can't handle all this dick," Monk said reaching down grabbing hisself. "You in love with that bitch too, this bout the fourth or fifth time I seen her round you when we came up here," Monopoly said.

"Nigga that's my down for whatever white girl, my own personal snow bunny porn star, tell'em Jack that bitch down to suck and fuck whenever and wherever I want to. Shiid, if I tol'er to suck my dick right here in the yard in front of ya'll, she woulda." "He ain't lying bout that shit, last week at da club she wanted to come home with him, this nigga told'er she had to suck his dick in the club if she wanted him to leave with her.

And the bitch did it, in front of er'body. This nigga pushed the table to the side and the bitch pulled his dick out and went to work, you shoulda heard them other bitches in there calling her trifling and er'thing else." "Get da fuck outta here," Juice said.

"Shid nigga, that bitch even swallowed er'thing and cleaned that nigga up with her mouth. You know them black bitches wanted to beat her ass and fuck him up behind that shit." "Yeah but I dun fucked two of them bitches that was in there that night and both of'em sucked my dick tryna show me I ain't need no white girl. But when I asked'em if they woulda done what she did, both of'em said nah and I tol'em that's why I fuck wit her and not them. Them bitches got mad as hell, but guess what they still tryna give a nigga some pussy," Monk said laughing. 'Aight pimping," Juice said laughing.

"Shiit nigga, you need to tell'er to put yo niggas down wit some of her girlfriends, birds of a feather flock together mafucka," Monopoly said. "I got ya'll," "Yeah right, that shit ain't even sound convincing," Monopoly said. "Nah M.P. for real, shawdy put me down wit one of her girls from college and I swear this bitch was a professional porn star," Big Jack said. "Aight nigga, I'll believe it when I see it" Juice replied "Now c'mon let's take care of this so we can get back to Richmond, I got my own personal freak I'm tryna see tonight."

All four of them went into the house where Big Jack gave them $1,800 for the first half-a-big, then another $1,800 for their half-a-big which Juice handed him. Monk gave Monopoly $400 for the weed; $300 for the q.p. and $80 for the extra ounce plus $20 for delivery. "My niggas, I hate to do business and run, but like I said I got some pussy waiting on me," Juice said. "Nigga you talking bout a nigga in love, sound like you pussy whipped to me," Monk said. 'Nah mafucka, this just my second time fucking shawdy, da last time was a quickie before she went to work." "That's even worse, one time and you whipped god-damn shawdy must got some bomb," Big Jack said laughing.

"Fuck ya'll let's ride M.P." "Aight, don't forget to tell that white bitch to put us down wit a couple of her friends," Monopoly said as the two half-brothers headed out the door. "I told you, I got ya'll damn," Monk said. "We go hit ya'll later this week," Big Jack said. "Do that," Monopoly said as they got in the car and pulled off....

They'd been on the road for about ten minutes when Monopoly looked in the rear view mirror "What da fuck?" "What?" "I see bout four sets of headlights and look like they moving fast as shit." Juice looked back and said "Ain't no look like, they is moving fast nigga, but for some reason they'ont look like cars." "Then what the fuck they look like?" "I'ont know, but we'll find out cause they gaining on our ass like a mafucka."

"Is it the police?" "I'ont know, but I'ont think so" going thru a series of curves Juice said "it look like it might be motorcycles but I ain't sure." "Motorcycles I'ont believe that, wouldn't they be riding in a straight line? One behind the other." "I would think so, but they not too far behind us now, you should be able to see for yourself." Monopoly looked in the rearview and side mirrors "It do look like motorcycles too, don't it.' "I told you nigga."

Juice kept watch as the motorcycles got right behind them "I told you it was motorcycles, them mafuckas splittin down the middle to pass us, some on yo side and some on mine." Since there was no oncoming traffic Monopoly veered to the middle of the road giving the bikes on the passenger side more room to pass. "Fuck they coming on that side for I know damn well they gotta be on the grass," he said. As the first two bikes passed them they both had passengers on the back and both passengers looked down into the car. As the bikes pulled ahead the passenger on the driver's side stuck their right fist out with the thumb extended in the air, the person on the passenger side did the samething.

The next two bikes to pass did the samething, as did the next two, all in all it was a total of eight bikes, with passengers on the back of all of them. When the last two pulled up beside them, both passengers had Mac-11 sub-machine guns pointed at the car. They subsequently let loose at the sametime 'bdddddd bddddd.' "What da?" Juice yelled out as he reached for his gun under the floor mat. But he didn't have a chance to get it as bullets tore thru the windshield and shattered his forearm, pierced his bicep, hit his shoulder and both legs.

Monopoly got caught in the chest, upper torso, both legs and his hand. He tried to ram the bikes but they pulled ahead, he did manage to swerve causing the car to plunge in a field eventually coming to a hissing stop. Juice and Monopoly's heads were thrown against the dashboard, Ah-h-h-h" they both groaned. They could hear the growl of motorcycles again sounding like they were coming back towards them, except this time it didn't sound like as many. Monopoly managed to sit up and lean his head back where he saw two motorcycles pull up and two people get off the back and walk towards them.

"Juice" "Huh" Juice answered leaning back just as the bike riders got to the car, they separated again with one on the passenger side and the other on the driver's side. Standing slightly in front of the front doors they let loose again, but this time with Tec-9 sub-machine guns 'tat-ta-tatat-tat 'tat-tat-ta-ta-tat' "Ahhh" "Ahhh" were the sounds you heard as the bullets tore into the car and hit both occupants inside. When their clips were empty the shooters trotted back to the motorcycles leaving Monopoly and Juice both filled with holes up and down their bodies. With all the bullets flying its a wonder neither one of them got hit in the head although Monopoly's ear did get grazed. The motorcycles pulled off and went to join the others who were waiting for them down the road....

Unbeknownst to Monopoly and Juice the white brother and sister they robbed in Chesterfield were the niece and nephew of Mooney a member of the notorious Pit Bulls motorcycle gang. Their uncle had used their house as a stash spot, but when their older brother Kramer became a prospect all that changed. To prove he knew how to make money for the gang, they had agreed to allow him to sell weed for them, it was Kramer that Juice and Monopoly saw leaving heading to his girlfriends house the night they did the robbery. After Kramer became a prospect and it was decided he would be a moneymaker for the gang, Mooney had moved the other drugs to another place he used as a stash spot. But when that spot got raided by the ATF last month, he decided to move them back to Kramer's place temporarily.

By pure coincidence Caitlyn and Danny happened to be Mooney's niece and nephew too, they had learned about the robbery from their cousins Kim and William who were the brother and sister in the house. So when Danny had hit the blunt and said it was Oakwood Fireweed, Caitlyn knew what he was saying, that's the name Mooney gave it to make it sound exotic. Caitlyn had smoked some the day before with Monk and thought it tasted like and smelled like the weed her uncle be having, but she won't sure. When she asked Monk about it, he said he got it from his niggas Juice and Monopoly in Richmond. Caitlyn told Danny later that night and they decided to see if they could get any weight from Monk, who told her "he would have to call his niggas in Richmond to get it."

When Danny and Caitlyn got to Big Jack's house they spotted Juice and Monopoly by their brown Delta 88. "Ain't that them two guys from Richmond they be fucking with?" Danny asked his sister. "Yeah, I think so." "If I remember right Big Jack told me them two be sticking people up, I wouldn't be surprised if they the ones that robbed Kim and William." After they got what they wanted and left, Danny called Kramer and told him what they suspected, Kramer called Mooney and relayed what Danny had just said.

Mooney told Kramer to meet him at Mildred's, Danny and Caitlyn's mother house. When Mooney got there he had some of his gang with him, they inspected the drugs and determined they were indeed their drugs. This time Danny gave them the rundown on how they come by the drugs, Mooney wanted to go shoot everybody in Jack's house, but thankfully the other gang members talked some sense into him. That's when they decided to ride up the road and park on the other side of the cornfield by Jack's house, Danny was told to ride on the back of one of the first motorcycles.

Kramer was to be on the back of one of the last, since it was his spot that got robbed and he was a prospect, he was to be one of the shooters. The thumbs up signal was to indicate to everybody that they had the right car, each passenger on the back was to give the signal so that the gunners wouldn't have to hesitate, they could just start shooting. When the car ran in the field the shooters bikes continued up the road, at which time the third bikes in line came back down with the passengers getting off and finishing the job off. After that they went back up the road joining the others as they rode off, leaving Juice and

Monopoly shot the fuck up.

Chapter 24-Eastend:

Marquell and Davon were standing in front Davon's baby mama Rhonda's apartment down Hilltop smoking a blunt, even though she smoked weed Rhonda didn't allow it to be smoked in the apartment cause their 5 month old daughter Jamiya had asthma. "Shawd this shit we got now killin'nem," Marquell said "I just hope the connect stay on point and keep it coming that way, between Fatty'nem on the Bul and us on Crenshaw we go have Northside and Highland Park on lock." "Yeah but is ya'll go sell weight to niggas from other strips or just niggas on our strips," Davon asked. "Tell you the truth, I'ont even know, we ain't getting but so much right now maybe after we bubble for a while and blow up then we might branch out. But for now it's just for the 'Family.'"

"While they're standing there smoking Jigaloo and Sifu are sitting in a car talking and watching them at the sametime "Who dem niggas is standing over there?" Jigaloo asked. "It look like Rhonda's baby daddy I'ont know who the other nigga is tho," Sifu answered. 'Where shawdy from?" "Highland Park I think." "Stop playing." "I ain't playing nigga, Sheeba told me he was from round there." "These niggas stupid, I know they know my niggas got shot up round there, oh I gots to have'em!" Jigaloo exclaimed.

"You'ont even know if them niggas know the niggas that did it or not." "So fucking what? They from round that way somewhere and it look like them niggas hustle, you know over there er'body know er'body, so if I can't get the ones that shot my niggas, then I'll get them," Jigaloo said as he reached under the seat and pulled out twin Glokk 21's. "I'm going in the house, you know I don't fuck wit no guns nigga," Sifu who got his name cause he'd been practicing martial arts since the age of seven said. "You'ont fuck wit no guns, but you swing samarui swords, Nung chuks and know how to throw them throwing shits, da fuck is da difference."

"The difference is guns are louder and attract too much attention, plus wit guns innocent people get hurt." "Like you can't hurt innocent people wit them stars." "You can, but it's highly unlikely, 99% of the time you're going to hit whatever it is you're tryna hit." "Yeah, well I'm bout hit what I want to hit in a minute," Jigaloo said cocking both guns. "Lemme get in the house before you start, I don't want no part in this, I know you want them niggas that shot Rel and killed Y.K. to pay. But suppose these niggas innocent?"

"Fuck that, they from round there so far as I'm concerned they just as guilty as the niggas who did it." ""Aight then lemme go," Sifu said getting out the car....Davon had went back inside to tell Rhonda they were leaving and he would be back later, Marquell had parked across the parking lot in front of Tom-Tom's baby mama Shaleeta's place. So when Davon came back out they started across that way when 'baka baka buka buka' Jigaloo started shooting. Both Marquell and Davon pulled their guns as they realized it was them who was being shot at.

'Baow Baow Baow Daow Daow Daow' were the sounds Davon's Colt .44 revolver and Marquell's P-229 9mm made as they returned fire and ducked behind a black BMW. When Rhonda heard the shots she ran and looked out the window, she saw Davon shooting over the hood of the BMW and Marquell leaning across the trunk. She didn't have a gun, but she knew she had to do something for her man, she didn't know who they were shooting at or how many, all she knew was she had to do something. She ran to the front door and opened it hoping that Marquell and Davon could make it back inside. When she opened the door, she saw Jigaloo who she knew only in passing, step from behind a Jeep Cherokee with a gun in each hand shooting at Davon and Marquell.

Seeing Davon and Marquell split up, Jigaloo decided to come from behind the Cherokee so he could shoot at them both at the sametime. 'Baka Baka Baka Baka Baow Baow Baow Daow Daow Daow Daow' 'Ping ping wzzz wzzz' were the sounds that filled the parking lot. "Ahh shit," Jigaloo said as a bullet skipped along the ground and slammed into his foot causing him to hop on one leg. This gave Marquell the opportunity to step out from behind the BMW and try to become more accurate, "Shit" Jigaloo said again as another bullet slammed into his left ass cheek making him fall to the ground. 'Daow' the sound seemed to reverberate as Marquell fired the last shot which happened to hit Jigaloo in the back of his upper right thigh knocking him face first to the ground and the guns out his hands.

'Come on nigga," Marquell said to Davon as they jumped up, ran to the car and pulled off. Sifu like Rhonda was standing in the door and saw his man get hit and fall, when he saw Marquell and Davon pull off he ran grabbed Jigaloo's guns, took them in the house, then called the police as he went back to check on Jigaloo. He was informed that the police had already been informed had already been notified and were on their way. When Rhonda saw Davon and Marquell pull off she closed the door, grabbed the house phone and called Davon. "What Rhonda?" "Davon what da fuck is going on? Why da fuck were you and Marquell just in a mothefuckin shootout in front my house? Ain't neither on of you hurt is it?" Rhonda said in one quick breath.

"What da fuck you mean what's going on?" Davon replied as Marquell stopped the car on the bridge going across the creek headed up to Oakwood Cemetery, they both got out and threw their guns in the water on their prospective sides of the bridge. "How da fuck we know? All we know is when we was leaving this nigga started shooting at us. We alright though, who was that nigga, you know'im Marquell, cause I damn sure don't?" "Fuck naw I'ont know'im, shit Rhonda should know'im she the one live over there." 'What da fuck he tryna say? I don't know that mafucka, I see'im from time to time but I don't know his name or nothing else bout him," Rhonda snapped.

"Lemme call you back in a minute, we gotta talk bout this," Davon said. "Alright, I'll call you when the police leave from round here and Davon be careful baby I love you, but more importantly Jamiya loves you, we can't have nothing happen to you. We need you here with us." "Don't worry baby I'ma be aight, you just watch the police and see who talk to'em" "Alright bye baby."

After hanging up with Rhonda, Davon said "Fuck that nigga start shooting at us for?" "I'ont know, but his ass got laid da fuck out, I hope that mafucka ain't breathing no mafuckin more," Marquell said. "We ain't beefing wit Hilltop is it?" Davon wanted to know. "Not that I know of, but I think Fatty and nem is." Soon as Marquell said that his phone rung "Yo" "Man what da fuck is going on? Ya'll niggas aight?" It was Tom-Tom.

"Yeah nigga we aight, damn Leeta called you soon as the shit was over didn't it?" "I guess, ya'll know who that nigga was?" "Nope" "Leeta said she think his name Jigaboo, Jigaloo some shit like that." Jigaloo, I'ont know nobody by that name, you Davon?" "Hell naw" "Fuck ya'll doing down Hilltop anyway and you know Fatty'nem beefing wit them niggas, ya'll know we only move thru there at night right now." "Fuck Hilltop, if Fatty or any of his brothers beefing, then I'm beefing that's my mafuckin family. That's aight tho, cause that nigga laid da fuck out." "Tell me about it, I'ont think he dead," Davon said. "Me either, but if him or any of them niggas want it they can come get it," Marquell said. "Me and C be on Crenshaw when ya'll niggas get round here," Tom-Tom said. "Aight nigga."

Northside:

Shaun and Sonya had been kicking it on a regular basis for a minute and though neither was looking for one they were moving towards a relationship. Right now they were in Riverside Seafood on Brookland Park Blvd., sitting at a table when Cheeks and Charmaine walked in. Like Shaun and Sonya, they too had been kicking it for awhile, but instead of a relationship theirs was more of a friends with benefits relationship more than anything. Even though they both cared about each other and looked forward to seeing each other, neither was ready to call the other one their girlfriend or boyfriend, but technically that's what they were.

"Kenny gimme a two-piece fish and chips meal with a grapeade, he paying for it," Charmaine said pointing at Cheeks sitting at the table with Shaun and Sonya. "Give me the samething Kenny," Cheeks said. "That's for here or to go?" Kenny asked. "Make it to go, just in case I don't have time to finish it here," Charmaine said. "I'ont see why you won't have time, you still gotta finish my head," Cheeks said holding his hair on the side that won't braided. Boy you know I'ma finish your head, but I'm talking bout if one of my appointments show up before I finish eating."

"Bruh you tryna go bowling tonight?" Shaun asked Cheeks. "Shid why not? I ain't doing shit else." "She tryna say we can't fuck wit her and Charmaine bowling," Shaun said pointing to Sonya. "Tryna say oh I know ya'll can't beat us," Sonya said. "Ya'll ain't tryna bet nothing is ya'll?" that was Charmaine who was always looking for a gamble.

"Bet nothing like what?" asked Cheeks. "I'ont know make it light on yourself, but make it a friendly bet no money involved tho," Charmaine said. "And no sex either, before ya'll even think about it," Sonya put in. "Ain't no damn body go say nutting bout no sex Sonya, see where yo damn mind at," Cheeks said. "So name the bet then," Sonya said. Cheeks had gotten the food and put it on another table so he and Charmaine could eat.

"How bout if ya'll win we gotta wash both of ya'lls cars this Saturday" Shaun said "and if we win ya'll gotta cook us dinner and give us massages." "That's two things to ya'lls one," Sonya answered. "Nah Sonya we go let'em have it that way, Shaun think he got all the sense, but come Saturday they go be some car washing mafuckas, shit I want a wash and shine nigga. Afta you wash it, you wax it, wax on/wax off mafucka," Charmaine said as her and Sonya burst out laughing giving each other high fives and Sonya saying "I know that's right." "Ya'll got it twisted, ya'll go be some cooking mafuckas just don't cook no spaghetti," Cheeks said. "Tell'em again bruh and I want a full body massage, from my head to my toes, same way wax on/wax off," Shaun said as he and Cheeks gave each other dap.

"Nigga picture that," Charmaine countered. "Oh so you backing out da bet?" Shaun asked. "Hell naw, I'm saying picture us losing and me having to give you a full body massage, shiit if anything you go be giving my car a full body massage,"

Charmaine said smiling. "If you really think so," Shaun said. "Think, oh we know boo! Trust and believe that," Sonya said. "We'll see tonight then, ya'll wanna meet us there or ya'll coming thru here first?" Cheeks asked.

"That's on ya'll," replied Sonya. "How bout we meet ya'll at Hanover Lanes bout 9:00?" Shaun asked. "That'll work," Charmaine answered. "Damn this Grapeade is good," Sonya remarked. "Ain't it though, they got Cherryade and Limeade too, here and Sam's next door the only places I ever got all three, I come get one or the other everyday I'm at work," Charmaine said. 'I'ma have to start getting one everytime I come over this way," Sonya said as the foursome had finished eating and were walking out the door.

"Cheeks come on here so I can finish your head before I get any more customers," Charmaine said. "Aight. Bruh you go wait for me or you going back to the house?" "Right now I'ma stand here and kick it with Sonya, so I guess I'll be here when you get thru," Shaun answered. "I'll be in there in a few cuz," Sonya said to Charmaine. "Aight."

As Cheeks and Charmaine started back to the shop, two guys came out the barbershop on the corner. "Charmaine, where the fuck Sonya at?" Dan Johnson asked. He and KenVale had been riding up Brookland Park Blvd. leaving KenVale's aunt Nicole's house, when Dan spotted Sonya's Acura sitting across the street from the shop. "Where da fuck you going?" Kenvale had asked him when Dan turned on Hanes Ave. "I think I just saw Sonya's car back there parked on the Blvd., what da fuck she doing round here and why da fuck I ain't been able to catch up wit her."

"Fuck you mean you ain't been able to catch up with her?" "Just what I said nigga, she ain't been at home, she don't answer my calls and she don't fucking return'em either, she better have a damn good excuse I bet'cha that." "Yeah, like she got another man sound like to me," KenVale said as Dan parked the car and the two got out. "Nigga you tripping, Sonya know not to fuck wit me, she know that pussy mines and betta not nobody touch it but me." They had stopped in the first shop on the corner of Brookland Park and Garland to see if Sonya was in there, after not seeing her and finding out she hadn't been in there they were just leaving out when they saw Charmaine.

"Hol'up mafucka, I ain't Sonya's keepa." "I see her car over there and you right here so she must be-oh I see'er, who da fuck dat nigga is?" Dan asked as he headed towards Sonya and Shaun. "Sonya what da fuck you doing round here? And why the fuck I ain't heard from yo ass?" Dan said raising his voice. "Dan you got some nerve questioning me, didn't I tell yo ass at the hospital it was over, you keep fucking with that bitch Michelle, well you can have'er cause I dun moved on."

"Fuck you mean you dun moved on?" "Just like I said, I got a new man in my life I don't need yo no good trifling ass no more." "What? I know god-damn well you ain't talking bout this rooty-poot ass nigga here," Dan said looking at Shaun who was standing behind and off to the side of Sonya. "I damn sure am and don't be disrespecting him, he ain't done shit to you." "I'ma beat his mothafu-whop" Shaun hit Dan on the chin and dropped him, he wasn't going to get in it but when Dan called him out his name, he put him in it.

'Whop whop Bop bop' that was Cheeks hitting KenVale who was getting ready to help Dan. 'Wop wop wop' Shaun hit Dan three more times when he got up, this time when Dan hit the ground Shaun started stomping him 'bomp bomp bomp.' 'Bop blop,' Cheeks hit KenVale again then grabbed him and 'blam' slammed him on the sidewalk. Shaun grabbed Dan and 'bang' ran his head into the newspaper stand. 'What da hell? Shaun, Cheeks, Shaun," that was Ms. Fox who happened to be on her way home riding with Tina Lucille who had stopped the car in the middle of the street after they noticed the fight.

"Cheeks Cheeks" Ms. Fox said coming on the sidewalk amidst all the commotion, "Don't you hit that boy no more, you hear me?" she said pushing Cheeks back. "Shaun get ya'll god-damn asses in that car," she said pushing both her sons toward the car. A small crowd had gathered to watch the fight, now they were watching a pissed off mother curse her sons out. "I ain't going nowhere," Cheeks said. "You what? Who you talking to?" Ms. Fox said while grabbing Cheeks by the arm and 'blam' smacked him upside the head.

"I said get your god-damn ass in the car, now." "But Ma," Shaun started to protest. "But Ma ass, I don't want to hear it, in the car now." They both got in the car as Tina Lucille pulled off. "Out here fighting in the middle of the street like ya'll crazy or something and everybody standing around looking, I know people saying my kids ain't nothing but a bunch of thugs, a gang of outlaws or something." "Ma that dude Shaun was fighting started it, he called Shaun out his name, then he said he was go beat Shaun's you know what, so Shaun hit'em and his boy tried to help'im so I hit him," Cheeks explained to his mother.

"Why would that boy just disrespect Shaun if he don't know him?" "Cause ma, one of them girls out there I been talking to for a while now. I guess dude was her ex-boyfriend and when he saw her, he wanted to know why she been ignoring him, she told'em cause she had a new man. She didn't say it was me, he just assumed it was cause I was standing there," Shaun said. "Ya'll keep on, if this girl got a man, what you want with her Shaun?"

"She broke up with him cause he had sex with her friend," Shaun answered. The family was now back home, "Well you better make sure she really is done with him before you mess with her again." "I know she is Ma." 'I hope so, I still don't want my kids out here fighting in the street especially behind no women." "It won't behind no woman ma, if he don't disrespect or threaten me it never happens."

After Shaun and Cheeks left with their mother, Sonya told Dan she was thru with him for good and not to contact her anymore. Her and Charmaine then went into the shop, once Dan and KenVale got their composure together they attempted to go in there, but were stopped by Sam's boyfriend Jigga who told them "they betta go bout their business before they get fucked up again." Jigga had the other three barbers standing behind him, ready to help him if need be. "Sonya this ain't over, believe me, you still mine and tell that nigga when I see'im that's his ass, he betta have a vest on." "Fuck you Dan bye," Sonya said fuming as Jigga closed the door in Dan's face.

Highland Springs:

Tricey was standing outside Fairfield Commons Mall having just gotten off work, she was waiting for her mother Elanora to pick her up. She saw a Royal Blue with Silver flakes Lexus 430 with thirty-day tags, sitting on chromed out 24's with the music blasting pull up. "Damn, whoever that nigga is he shitting like a mothefucka, if he's by hisself I'ma holla at'im, riding like that I know the nigga got cake," she thought to herself. She was shocked as hell when she saw the passenger door open and a beautiful caramel complexion female standing between 5'7 and 5'9, fly as hell with her hair done flawlessly, jewelry shining, titties, ass, and hips for days. The perfect picture of an African queen step out.

It was Misa, Peaches best friend and a bitch she couldn't stand, "Da fuck is this bitch doing riding wit a nigga pushing something like that," she said to herself. When the driver's side door opened and the driver stepped out, Tricey's mouth fell open she couldn't believe her eyes. Standing there in his Rocawear baggy jeans, Butta Timbaland construction boots, wife beater white tank top, big chain with a equally big charm with his initials sparkling from the diamonds in it and looking like the epitome of a thug, was Teco. "I know damn well he betta not be fucking with this skank ho," She said to herself again.

Walking in her spiked heel Timbaland boots, with more ass than Lisa Raye and Free from 106 and Park combined, Misa looked sexy as hell, looking at her and Teco together they looked like the perfect couple. This only pissed Tricey off even more, sending a jealous rage thru her, she never liked Misa and always thought she wanted to fuck Teco. 'I knew I was right,' she thought to herself. She barged into the parking lot to confront them "What da fuck you doing with her?" she asked Teco. "Don't worry bout what I'm doing wit her, you ain't got shit to do wit it."

"You probly been fucking wit'er all the time." "Nope, don't worry bout how long, just know that I fuck wit her now, so you can leave me da fuck alone." "Bitch I knew you wanted my man all along," Tricey said looking at Misa. "Your man, if he was your man, you wouldn't have fucked and sucked another man especially in his house, but I gotta thank you cause your being a ho bought me and my soul mate together. Teco I'm going on in, you can stand here and deal with this slut if you want to, but I'm not. She proly waiting on Timbo or some other nigga she just met to come pick her ass up," Misa said walking off.

'Fuck you Misa, you a bigger slut than I'll ever be." Misa stopped, turned around, placed one hand on her hip and said "Well if that's true, guess what I'ma be a even bigger slut for Teco and Teco only, nobody else, call me what you want but the bottom line is you fucked up. You a lil girl tryna do grown woman things, Teco's my man now so you can stop calling him and don't come by our house, cause trust, you may be Peaches sista but I will beat yo ass wit no problem if you show up there." With that Misa went in the mall. Tricey turned around to look at Teco with tears streaming down her face 'How da fuck you go mess with my sister's best friend?"

"How da fuck you go fuck a nigga in my house? How da fuck you go fuck your sister's man in her house? Shid same way you did that, is the same way I'ma fuck her. Except she's my girl now so she gets spoiled, you know all the things you used to get; shopping sprees, treated like a queen, the royal freak treatment in bed. Only thing we got more money to do all that with, cause I hit the lottery for $100,000 the day after you fucked that nigga in my house. So like Misa said thank you, cause you cleared the way for me to find a real woman and stop playing wit lil girls," Teco said as he went in the mall leaving Tricey standing there crying, feeling ashamed and embarrassed at herself....

What Tricey didn't know was Peaches hooked Teco and Misa up in the first place. Before Tricey left the apartment the day Peaches caught her and Timbo fucking she called Teco and left a message for him to call her back. When he called back Tricey was gone and Peaches answered the phone. "Hello" "Peaches where Tricey at?" "I'ont know where da fuck her trifling ass at and personally I don't care, long as she don't come back here."

"You know why da fuck she called me?" "I guess so you could come get her and she could move back in wit'chu." "She know that shit ain't happening, not afta that bullshit she did." "What she do?" "Oh you'ont know? She fucked a nigga in my house and when I came home his boy was sitting there watching a movie with a gun in his lap. This nigga pulled the gun on me and made me sit there and listen while his boy was fucking Tricey, when we walked in the room she was sucking his dick."

"What? That bitch ain't shit I swear, she my sista but she the biggest ho in Richmond. I came home early from work today and caught her and Timbo 69'ing in my house." "Say word" "Word, I tried to beat the shit out both of'em, I hit him in the nuts so hard two times I hope his ass go sterile and I stomped her to the ground, I had to catch myself before I caught a murder charge." "What the fuck wrong wit her Peaches? She act like she just gotta fuck every nigga she meet." "I'ont know, she know betta than that, mama ain't raise us to be no ho's and Pop made sure we knew the games niggas played. So I just don't know, I do know she ain't coming back over my mothafuckin house no fucking more. As of right now I'm done with both of'em, but I'ma get they asses back you watch. Matter fact you remember my friend Misa?"

"Misa, Misa you talking bout that tall fly ass chick right?" "That's the one, Tricey can't stand her cause for one thing she think Misa likes you, which she do and for another she say I act like Misa more my sister than her. Before today I would've never done that, but now fuck that, I know Misa wouldn't have done what Tricey did, that's for damn sure. But look, I know you ain't tryna get back wit Tricey's trifling ass?" "Hell naw" 'Aright let me call Misa for a minute and I'll call you right back." "Do that"

Peaches called Misa and told her she was about to make her dream come true, she told Misa what Tricey had done to both her and Teco. "So" Peaches asked Misa "is it cool to give Teco your number?" "Hell yeah girl! Your sista don't know what to do with that, afta I put my thing down Tricey go be a thing of the past." "Aight lemme call him back and tell'im to call you." "Aight tell'im I'm waiting on his call." Peaches hung up and called Teco back, she gave him the number and told him to call Misa then cause she was waiting. He thanked her, made the call and the rest was history. Misa turned out to be way more woman than Tricey could ever hope to be, there was no way in hell he would ever go back to Tricey.

Chamberlayne Farms:

'Phlow Phlow Phlow' "Ooooh god-dammit" "Phlow Phlow Phlow pow pow' "This wha'chu want?" Darrell asked. "Yes yes yeesss," Mrs. Jasper screamed 'Pow pow' he smacked her on the ass again and said "I can't hear you." 'Phlow baow baow phlow' "Yes baby yes" 'Baow' "Yesssdddd shit" Mrs. Jasper said as Darrell punished her from the back. He'd called her earlier from his mother's house while he and Lil Darrell were over there, she'd wanted to see him and agreed to pick him up at 8:00, but she told him he couldn't spend the night. Nothing against him, she just didn't believe in letting a man spend the night the first time they came over, plus she had to be at work at early tomorrow morning, 6:00 to be exact.

"Turn over," Darrell said to her. "Uh uh, you keep that thing away from me," she said turning over and trying to slide across the bed. Darrell grabbed her by the upper thighs, pulled her to him, threw her right leg over his shoulder, reached across her shoulders grabbed the top part of the mattress and 'Blaow' slammed into her. "Ahh" her voice caught in her throat 'Blaow Blaow Blaow Phlow Phlow' "Ahhh Dooohhh, I'm cuumminn" she said as she squirted nice hot cum all over his dick and balls.

'Blaow Blaow blaow Phlow,' "Ahh Daaamn," she said grabbing onto him, squeezing him and cumming even harder. This time she had the big 'O' and as she came, he came with her "Aaaahhh, damn girl damn damn damn, you tryna fuck around and make a nigga fall in love." "If you fall in love it's cause you want to, not cause I made you," she replied. Darrell rolled off her and Ms. Jasper whose real name was Candice, but everybody called Candy, got up and went in the bathroom to wash up. Darrell grabbed the 'L' off the nightstand and sparked up.

Coming back in the room Candy asked "What time is your cousin picking you up?" "Between 11 and 11:30," he said while puffing the Dutch and watching her clean his dick off with the washcloth and her mouth. "Bmmp Bmmp Plop" "Good she said pulling his dick out her mouth and looking over at the clock, which read 10:40. "Think you can go another round before you leave?" she asked as she licked his balls and ran her hand up and down his dick stroking him back to erection. "Shid wit'chu doing shit like that, hell yeah! All night if I have to."

'Ssluurp Ssslurrp mmmhmm," she said as she reinserted his dick in her mouth and was now slobbing it down and slurping it up. When she had it good and hard, she climbed on top of him, put his dick at the entrance of her pussy and lowered herself down on it. She stopped halfway down, came back up and lowered herself again, this time going the whole length down. She eventually set a pace and before long she was riding frog style 'squish plop squish plop' were the sounds their bodies made from their lovemaking. Darrell reached up under her thighs and started lifting her up and bringing her back down.

"Oh shit! Darrell what you doing? Oh oh uh unh don't do that." "Shut up, you'ont like it?" "Yeah, you crazy ahhh." Darrell then put her legs up on his shoulders while he continued to pick her up and bring her down, now he was sending his dick straight up in her; going all the way into her stomach. "Ah ahh shit, you in my stomach baby" 'Baow Baow Baow' Darrell was now meeting her on the downstroke. All of a sudden Darrell held her in place rolled over, slid to the floor and planted his feet while still inside her 'Blop Blop Blaow Blaow Blaow Blaow Blaow' he started banging.

"No'oh unh don't d- shiit," she said sliding her tongue in his ear, then trying to bite his neck. 'Blaow Blaow Blaow Blaow' "Mmmmm" she said burrowing her head into the crook of his neck alternating between biting and licking both his neck and earlobe. "Umph unnngh," he said as he came all inside her. "Purrrr," was the sound she made as she felt him cumming and their lovemaking came to an end. 'Plop' he pulled his dick out.

"Now that's what I call good loving, enough to make a bitch think about calling out from work." "Sounds good to me," Darrell answered. "I said think about nigga, I just missed a couple of days cause I was sick, I can't afford to miss no more right now," she said. 'Besides it wouldn't matter no way, I still wouldn't let you spend the night, you could leave later but not stay all night," she said from the bathroom. "Yeah right another round and yo ass'll be out cold snoring until tomorrow morning, you wouldn't know if I stayed or not,' Darrell said teasing her.

"You right, that's why your ass leaving when your cousin gets here, besides I know your mother's wondering what time you'll be back to get your son." "Not really I tol'er I might not come home tonight, she'll put him to bed and I'll just go get him early tomorrow." Darrell's phone rang "Yeah" he answers. "I'm outside," his cousin Corey said. "Aight, I be out in a minute."

"Damn nigga you timed that shit just right," she said while again wiping his dick off. "I guess so." "Sslurrp slurp muah; damn take that thing out here before we get started again. Make me feel like it's hypnotizing me or something," she said laughing and standing up. "Nah not hypnotizing, you mean dick-notizing," he said smirking. "Whatever, get it outta here so I can get some sleep." "Aight I'm leaving. When you want me to call you again?" "Friday or Saturday, I'm off this weekend, so whichever day suits you best." "This time when I come I'm staying the night, I'ont care what you say."

"If you say so." "Ain't no if I say so, me and him say so," he said grabbing his dick. "She don't want us to leave tonight for real, but we all agreed the we can wait til the weekend to have some more fun," he continued. "Mm-hmm" "I know mm-hmm" he said as he grabbed and kissed her, then said "I'll call you." "Do that take that blunt with you, I'ont need no more tonight." "Aight see you this weekend my sweet and tasty Candy," he said walking out the door. "We can't wait," she said patting her pussy.

Darrell walked outside and got in Corey's car "Damn nigga who da fuck is dis bitch?" Corey asked. "Shawdy from down the jail I was telling you bout, but fuck that you bring da heaters?" "Yeah I got'em, but what da fuck you need'em for?" "Good lemme see'em go round by Harvey Road apartments," Darrell said as he started telling Corey what was going on. After talking to Candy he had called Sheema and told her, he and Corey was going out-of-town to check on this car Corey wanted to buy.

He asked Sheema to pick up Lil D from his mother's house and she agreed. After Candy picked him up, she asked him if he smoked weed, he said "yeah" and she said "good cause she was going to get some from her cousin." He asked her about smoking and working at the jail, she told him they didn't piss them, it was the belief of the sheriff that what you did on your own time away from work was your business. Even so she still didn't let nobody at work know she smoked, she just didn't trust them like that. When she pulled up in front of an apartment building on Boiling Rd., Darrell asked who she knew around there.

"My cousin Double S., he got some crucial smoke, plus he looks out for cuz, you wanna come in?" "Naw, go head I'm aight." "I be right back." Darrell didn't go in because he didn't want Double-S knowing he was home, he knew Angie wasn't stupid enough to tell neither Double S or E-Bay he was home. While watching Candy go up to the apartment, he saw a dark skin guy about 6' feet standing in the yard say something to her as she approached.

Once Candy was in the house he watched as two guys approached the dark skin guy, who then went behind the building came back around a few minutes later called one of the guys to the side of the building and handed him something. The guy then handed him something that looked like money and walked off with his friend; the dark skin guy folded the money and came back around the front smoking a cigarette. Candy came out the house and the guy walked over talking to her again, this time he reached out for her but she pushed his hand away, came back to the car and got in.

"Stupid mothafucka," she said. "Who dat?" "That mothafuckin E-Bay" "Who?" he wanted to be sure he heard her right. "E-Bay, that black mothafucka that was just standing outside, that's Double S's cousin on his daddy's side, I'm Double

S's cousin on his mother's side. That stupid ass nigga keep tryna holla at me, I keep telling him I rather fuck a dog than to fuck his ugly ass." "I saw'im try to grab you when you came back out the house." "Yeah mafucka go ask me who I got in my car, when I said none of his business, he go say whoever it is, is a lame ass nigga anyway if I'm fucking wit'em. Talking bout I'm scared to fuck wit a real gangsta, I sure hope he ain't talking bout hisself, cause if he is I hate to see what a fake gangsta looks like."

"I saw'im go beside the building and serve somebody," Darrell said. "He was tryna sell weed, but he was also tryna take Double S's clientèle plus giving'em smaller bags, so Double S tol'im if he go sell weed he couldn't do it around here. That's when he started selling crack, but Double S won't let him sell it in the house, so he sells it outside." 'I see his ass tryna hide, but still all out in the open," Darrell stated. "I told you the nigga stupid." So when Candy had stopped by the store to get some Dutch's, Darrell had called Corey and told him where to come pick him up from and to "bring two gats wit'im."

Riding past Double S's apartment they saw E-Bay sitting on the porch. "Go round the block and drop me off, then come back around park, walk up to shawdy and ask'im for a half-a-gram. He go have to go round the back to get it, that's when I'ma stick his ass, you go back to the car and meet me in the same spot you dropped me off. Keep one of the burners in case you need it." "How you know he go serve me?" "That dumb mafucka, he'll serve any fucking body."

"Aight cuz, I hope you know wha'chu doing?" "I do, now lemme out right here." Darrell got out and walked up a sidewalk before cutting across the grass; Corey went around the block and pulled up in front the apartment where E-Bay was still sitting.

After checking his gun and tucking it in his waistband, he got out and walked towards E-Bay who was smoking a blunt.

"Yo stickman Marvin round here?" he asked E-Bay. "Who?" "Marvin" "Nah" shawdy ain't no Marvin round here." "I came round this way earlier and hollered at him a couple of houses down, I ain't see nobody over there, I thought maybe you was him." "You got a 25?" "Marvin gave it to me for 20." "I ain't Marvin you want it or not?"

"Yeah, if it's a proper point five." "It's proper nigga damn, I got da scale right here to weigh it for yo ass," E-Bay said reaching down beside the porch moving a brick and bringing a small black digital scale back up. "Aight that's what it do." 'Stay right here," E-Bay said walking to the side of the building.

He never saw Darrell standing behind the building as he went over to the mulch surrounding a tree, reached down in it and pulled up a sandwich bag with what looked like small blocks of crack in it. He was looking in the bag and trying to get in the light while walking back to the front when 'Blok' Darrell hit him across the bridge of his nose with the butt of the gun. "Da fuck?" E-Bay said as fell to the ground and dropped the bag. "Ain't no what da fuck nigga, this that lame ass nigga that was round here today, who slut of a baby mama you had sucking yo dick on the phone." 'Blok' Darrell said this as he hit E-Bay again.

"Nigga you know what this is, empty them pockets," Darrell said reaching down picking up the bag of crack. For all his bluster E-Bay knew this nigga was bout his business and just might shoot him, although he ain't know what bitch he was talking bout and what he meant calling hisself a lame. He figured if he gave him everything in his pockets the nigga wouldn't shoot him, so he reached in his right pocket and pulled out a stack of folded up money. Then he reached in his left pocket and pulled out another stack of money. "This betta be all nigga," Darrell said picking up the money while keeping the gun trained on E-Bay.

After picking the money up, he said "in case you wondering I was the nigga on the phone when that bitch Angie sucked yo dick and you took the phone from'er." "Shawdy I know-" 'Blok' Darrell hit him again. "Shut da fuck up and this evening when Candy came by here, I was that lame ass nigga in da car and you just got fucked by that lame. E-Bay looked up at Darrell when he said this, Darrell walked closer and 'Baow' shot him in the face. When E-Bay hit the ground Darrell stood over top of him and 'Baow Baow Baow Baow' shot him four more times in the body before taking off running. Corey was sitting where he was supposed to be, Darrell hopped in and Corey pulled off.

Eastend:

"What you got cuz?" Charmaine asked Sonya. "Four," replied Sonya. "We going seven." "Seven, what's up bruh?" Cheeks asked Shaun. "I got three," Shaun answered. "We going seven too." "Seven, Char we betta make ours, I ain't tryna be sitting here naked," Sonya said. "Shiit you damn near naked now," Shaun said. "Shit, ya'll closer to being naked than we is," Sonya replied. "Don't worry cuz, we got this," Charmaine said.

The foursome were over Charmaine's apartment in Bradford Manor. After the brothers left with their mother and Jigga sent Dan Johnson on his way, Sonya called Shaun to apologize for Dan. He'd told her not to worry it wasn't her fault and at least he knew she won't lying about leaving her man. She'd gone around his house to see him and told Cheeks that

Charmaine said she would have to finish his hair before they went bowling because she had gotten busy. But when Sonya and Charmaine showed up, they decided to go back to Charmaine's so she could finish Cheeks hair.

Once the blunts were rolled, drinks were poured and while Charmaine was braiding Cheeks hair they decided not to go bowling, but to play spades instead, strip spades at that. Two-out-of-three, every set you had to take something off. If you lost the game you had to take two things off, the losers of two games had to strip naked, sit there and smoke a blunt in front of the other two. This was game three, they both had won a game a piece, the score was 28-28 whoever made seven won the game.

Sonya and Charmaine both were sitting in their bras and thongs, while the brothers were sitting only in their boxers. Being that they were playing strip spades; no jokers or kitty, Charmaine knew she had the boss two spades, Ace and King, with the King of Hearts. With the lead on her Charmaine's first two plays were the Ace and King of Spades, everybody played so this left five more spades out there. Her next play was a seven of Hearts, which Shaun won by playing the Queen of Hearts, he came right back and played the Ace of Hearts. Next he played the four of Clubs which bought the Ace out of Sonya's hand, who in turn played the King of Clubs right back.

Now Sonya and Charmaine had four books to Cheeks and Shaun's two. Sonya played the five of Hearts, Shaun played the two, Charmaine played the King and Cheeks cut it with the two of Spades. "I hope you ain't count that," Cheeks said to Charmaine who was visibly upset. "Just play," was her reply. 'Okay how bout this?" he said playing the Queen of Spade, thus drawing the 8 from Shaun and the Jack from Charmaine who said "Damn." "Oh my bad, you thought that was go get in,"

Cheeks said. "Fuck you," Charmaine responded.

"Play bruh," Shaun said. That made it 4 books to 4 books. Cheeks came out with the three of Diamonds, which Sonya wound up winning with the Ace, she came back and won the next book with the King of Diamonds. Six books to four, the women way, one more book and they would win. Sonya came back with the Queen of Clubs, that walked around the board until Shaun cut it with the 10 of Spades; six books to five. Shaun played the 9 of Diamonds, which brought the Jack from Sonya, but Cheeks cut it with the 5 of spade. "That's what I'm talking bout bruh," Shaun said. Then Charmaine played the 7 of spade. "Ha, naw you mean that's what I'm talking bout cuz," Sonya said giving Charmaine five across the table.

Cheeks and Shaun sat there stunned looking at each other. "Hold da fuck up, how da fuck you do that?" Cheeks asked. "Do what?" Charmaine asked back. "You know what, how da fuck you got another spade? All the spades were gone, I had the last one." "How you figure you had the last one?" Charmaine asked again. "Cause I counted the cards," responded Cheeks. "You ain't count shit Cheeks, so just pull them boxers off boo," Sonya said.

"Nah hold up, I think you reneged Charmaine," Shaun said. "Prove it Shaun, call the book baby, but if you pull the wrong one back ya'll gotta eat our pussies right here in front the other couple," Charmaine said seriously. "What? Both brothers exclaimed. "Ya'll heard her, so pull the book mothafucka," Sonya said laughing. "Oh hell naw, I ain't eating no pussy," Cheeks said. "Then I guess ya'll lose, so strip nigga," Charmaine said to Cheeks.

"Nah bruh I got this, I know she cheated, gimme a minute I'ma figure out which book she went back in," Shaun said.

"When we find the right one, ya'll both go get on your knees and suck our dicks side-by-side on the sofa," Cheeks said. "Fuck naw nigga! Who da fuck you think you talking to," Sonya said emphatically. "I'm talking to Sonya and Charmaine, you know she cheated that's why you so upset," Cheeks said looking Sonya in the eyes intensely. "I ain't cheat shit nigga, like I said pull the book mothafucka," Charmaine replied.

"So it's a bet then, whoever is wrong then the others go give'em some head?" Cheeks asked. Charmaine looked at Sonya and said "Yeah it's a bet." Everybody looked at Sonya and she responded "Yeah, I guess so." "Aight lemme see," Shaun said looking at the books in front of Charmaine. "I think you pulled it from this one," he said reaching for the fourth book, but all of a sudden he pulled the second book and flipped it over.

"What I tell you," Cheeks said. "Uggh damn Char," Sonya said furiously. There in the second hand that was played was the King, three, and four of spades, but the other card was a six of diamonds. After having won the book with the King, when she scooped the cards up and patted them in place Charmaine had the six of diamonds on the back and let the seven of spades fall in her lap. Sonya knew Charmaine had reneged cause she played the seven, but neither cousin thought Shaun or Cheeks would pick the right book when they agreed to the bet.

"Shid, I'ont know bout you bruh, but I say we roll a blunt, let'em smoke half of it naked while they get they nerves up, then we sit back on the sofa and smoke the other half while we getting our Jimmy's waxed," Shaun said laughing. "Shid, I'm wit that," Cheeks replied laughing also. "Fuck ya'll I ain't doing shit," Sonya said. "Damn Sonya, lemme find out you ain't a woman of your word," Shaun said. "Fuck you Shaun, I am a woman of my word, but what I do wit my man, I do in private for him and him only."

"Come on Sonya, we did agree and besides all us family in here who go find out? I know I ain't go tell nobody, I know you ain't and I think if these two brothers wanna keep fucking wit us they won't either," Charmaine said. "Fo real fo real, fuck we look like telling somebody what we did wit our girls, that'd be some sucka ass shit," Cheeks said. "I'ont know roll da blunt and we'll see," Sonya said. "Well why you waiting to see Sonya, ain't ya'll supposed to be getting naked?" Cheeks asked.

"We go do it just give us a minute, damn nigga what's da rush?" Charmaine said. "Ain't no rush, but while ya'll bullshitting I'ma fix me another drink," Cheeks said. "Fix me one too bruh," Shaun said. As Cheeks pushed back from the table, his hand hit one of the books and knocked it to the floor, by instinct Sonya looked down. "What da hell? Lemme see them cards Cheeks," she said as Cheeks bent down to pick them up.

"What da hell what Sonya?" Shaun asked. "Ain't but three cards in this book," Sonya said holding up the cards and looking at the spot where Cheeks knocked them down from. "Stop tripping it was four cards in that book," Shaun said. "Well, where the other one at then Shaun? Cause it damn sure ain't on the table or the floor," Charmaine said standing up and looking from the table to the floor. "Naw fuck that lemme count them cards in each book," Sonya said.

"Count'em for what?" Cheeks asked. "Cause I think you went back in one of them books that's for what," Sonya said picking up the books one by one counting the cards in them. "Look at this shit Char, these niggas cheating their ass off," Sonya said counting the last book which had five cards in it. Cheeks knowing they didn't have seven books had taken the 5 of spades out of one book, used it a second time and not having time to put a replacement in the book, had dropped the 4 of clubs on top of the first book. Not thinking anyone would count the books, plus he figured that Sonya and Charmaine would be so concerned about making their books that they wouldn't notice that the 5 of spades had already been played.

"Ya'll mafuckas got the nerve to act like ya'll mad and shit, when ya'll ass sitting here doing the same damn thing," Charmaine said. "Man fuck that, all them cards was in that book, I musta pushed one up when my hand hit that first book," Cheeks said. "If that's the case, the whole row would be messed up and outta line, but it ain't, just that first book you knocked down and that last book wit five cards in it," Charmaine said. "And ya'll tryna get somebody to suck ya'll dick, shit not in this lifetime," Sonya said. "Oh hell naw, ya'll lost the game, which means ya'll lost the bet that go wit the game; getting naked, smoking a blunt and ya'll lost the bet about Charmaine reneging," Shaun said.

"Fuck that ya'll mafuckas go pay up too, if I get naked Shaun you getting naked also," said Sonya. "And ain't no sucking going on, if ain't no eating going on," Charmaine quipped. "Wha'chu tryna say Charmaine?" Cheeks asked. "Just what I said, ya'll hollering bout we lost the bets, technically ya'll lost the bets too, so if ya'll want yo dicks sucked ya'll mafuckas go eat some pussy too." "I'ont know bout all that Char," Sonya said.

"Look Sonya we all grown here and we all lost the bets, so we all gotta pay up or shut up. Lemme find out you worried bout Dan finding out," Charmaine said to her cousin. "Fuck Dan, he ain't my man no more, Shaun is! How many times I gotta tell you that." "So what's da problem Sonya?" Charmaine asked. "The problem is I don't want nobody looking at me and Shaun while we're having sexual relations."

"Excuse me sexual relations, but ain't nobody go be looking at ya'll. How bout if we did 69 at the sametime? Me and Cheeks, you and Shaun, that way we all busy getting our freak on at the sametime?" Charmaine asked Sonya. "Wha'cu mean at the sametime? Everybody in the same room?" "Why not?" Charmaine replied. "Cause me and Shaun ain't even had sex together yet and you talking bout 69'ing that's why not." "So! We smoke a blunt, cut the lights off in the living room and go for what we know, you can get a blanket if you want to, me I don't need no cover, how bout you Cheeks?"

"Hell naw I'ont need no cover, Sonya loosen up, stop being a prude," Cheeks said. "Fuck you Cheeks, ain't nobody being a prude, where da hell that blunt at anyway...." And so it happened there that night the two couples did 69 on the living room floor; Sonya and Shaun on one side of the sofa with a blanket throwed over top of them. Cheeks and Charmaine on the other side of the sofa with no cover on them. There was more slurping, sucking, moaning and groaning going on than in a porno flick, until finally Charmaine stood up and said "Fuck this cuz I'm going in my room, I gotta feel all this dick up in me, ya'll can go in the other room if you want to, come on Cheeks," she said reaching out grabbing his dick and leading him to the bedroom.

Shaun and Sonya kept going for another five minutes, as Sonya was in the middle of cumming when Charmaine made her little speech. Finally when she stopped cumming she released Shaun's dick from her mouth and asked him if he wanted to go in the room, he responded with "it don't matter to me." "Come on then," she said getting up. On their way to the room they heard the bed in Charmaine's room 'thump ump ump' and Charmaine "ah oh oh shit Cheeks." "Damn they ain't waste no time did they?" Sonya said. "Neither is we," Shaun said after locking the door, grabbing Sonya giving her a deep tongue kiss and pushing her on the bed so they could do what Cheeks and Charmaine was doing.

Chapter 25-Southside:

After the shootout at Foot Locker; Snooky Boo and Roland dropped Davey D., off at Chippenham Hospital where he told the hospital staff and police who had to be called that he was walking down the street. A car pulled up beside him, two guys jumped out and tried to rob him, when he refused to give them anything one of'em shot him before jumping back in their car and pulling off. A car coming up the street had seen what happened, pulled over, helped him in the car, bought him to the hospital and dropped him off. When the police inquired as to why the people just dropped him off, he said "they didn't want to be involved in no way. But they didn't want to see him bleed to death either, so they didn't give him their name, just dropped him off and kept moving." When asked bout their age, he told them it was a middle age couple.

After dropping Davey off, Snooky had called Miguel to find out what was going on. "Hello" Miguel answered. "Midge who you beefing wit?" Snooky asked. "Beefing, I ain't beefing wit no damn body, what da fuck you talking bout?" "We was just in DTLR at the Plaza, when three niggas came in, one of'em came up to me and asked me was I Snooky and did I have a cousin name Miguel?" "What?"

"Yeah, when I questioned him, he said you be talking bout me all the time, bout how fine I am and how gangsta I am. When I tol'em yeah I was yo cousin, this nigga hauled off and smacked me, so you know we had to wreck shop up in that mothafucka."

"What he look like?" "Bout five-ten, five-eleven slim dark skin wit a chin strap beard and a low hair cut." "I'ont know who the fuck that coulda been."

"It don't matter we left they ass stretched out in there and went to Wendy's, when we left there these niggas followed us to Foot Locker and started dumping on us." "What? Ain't nobody hit is it?" "Me and Roland aight, but Davey got hit in da leg, we dropped him off at Chippenham." "Where ya'll at now?" "On our way back to the Terrace." "Aight gimme a minute lemme see what I can find out, in order for me to talk to the nigga bout you that'd mean he somebody I fuck wit, not beefing wit. Either way he violated. How many niggas was it?" "Three" "Aight, I'ma hit you back in a short." "Do that"

Miguel hung up with Snooky and walked over to Ms. Selma's to see if he could find out anything, as luck would have it Worm was sitting on the porch. "S'up shawd?" Miguel asked Worm walking up. "Shit, you heard bout what happened?" Worm asked. "What?" "Breedo, Frye, and Billy Blu supposedly was in a shootout up Foot Locker, Frye and Blly got hit, Breedo got away that's how er'body round her know about it." "Shawd you betta be lying." "Lying for what? I'm telling you what the word is."

"Them niggas was shooting at Snooky'nem." "Stop playing Midge, how you figure that?" "Snooky just called and said some nigga walked up on her in DTLR asked her name and was she my cousin, then smacked her. They all got to fighting, then the niggas followed them from Wendy's and started dumping on'em in Foot Locker parking lot. Her and Roland aight, but Davey got hit." "Shawd I'ma murk Breedo ass right now," Worm said pulling out and cocking his P-89 9mm. "Hol'up lemme call Snooky back."

"Yeah," Snooky said answering the phone. 'Snook its some niggas name Breedo, Frye, and Billy Blu from round here." 'How you find out?" "Worm just told me Breedo back round here telling mafuckas what happened. Worm ready go blast his ass right now." "Fuck dem niggas get at us for?" 'I'ont know unless it was behind that shit wit them Afton niggas the other week."

""What them niggas got to do wit it?" 'I'ont know, but don't worry we go hit Breedo and the rest of his crew when they hit the block tonight." "Don't do nothing til we get ova there, what time they normally out there?" "All evening til bout 3 or 4 in the morning." "Aight ya'll lay low for now and if we'ont get'em tonight, we'll get'em one day this week, watch yo' selves tho, since they know I'm yo cousin they might try to get at ya'll." "You ain't gotta worry bout that, them niggas know what time it is wit us."

But later on that night Roland unable to let things rest for a day or two, insisted on going to hit Breedo and crew. He called Miguel, told him and Worm to be ready cause they was go blast on Breedo and nem that night. Now riding on Rosecrest in Hillside Court, Lil Twist who was driving and Worm, who was in the passenger seat saw Breedo, Phil, and Pow Wow standing in front of Lady's apartment. There were two more people standing with them and a few people on the porch shooting dice. "There go Breedo punk ass right there," Worm said.

"Let's hope his ass still be there by the time we come back thru," Lil Twist replied. "They ass ain't going nowhere no time soon, they be out there all night damn near; Breedo dumb ass don't know if the police looking for him or not and he got his ass right out there on front street, dumb ass mafucka," Worm said. Breedo and crew won't paying attention, they were focused on watching out for the police and listening to Breedo recount what happened at Foot Locker. "What da fuck you smack da bitch for anyway?" Phil asked. "Cause nigga, I told ya'll when I saw them bitch ass niggas it was on, that dumb bitch fell right into my hands, I couldn't resist."

"You couldn't resist. What da fuck? Da police got Frye and Blu, plus them niggas got hit. Did ya'll mafuckas hit anybody?" Pow Wow asked. "Yeah nigga ole boy that was driving got hit, I'ont know if he dead or not, but I know he got hit." "I know the police go be all over this mafucka, undercovers and all," Phil said. 'Ain't nobody go be able to make no money round this bitch, plus we go have to keep a eye on Miguel and Worm since you used Miguel's name," Pow Wow said.

"They'ont know who I was tho," Breedo said. "Sooner or later they go find out, so ya'll niggas betta be on point," Chubb one of the other guys standing there said. "Shid for all that them niggas betta-dat-dada-dat tat-tata-tat baow baow baow baow splat splat splat,' the night was suddenly lit up with gunfire. 'Tat-ta-tat' one person by the porch fell as they were trying to stand and run. 'Splat splat' "Aghh" another person fell; 'dat-dada-dat' "ughh" Chubb yelled as he got hit in the back of the knee and upper back. 'Baow baow baow' Bezel the other guy standing in the group fell immediately as he got hit in the side and the bullet came out his kidneys, while falling he caught two more bullets in the shoulder.

'Blaow Bla-' Breedo had turned around and started shooting back while trying to get away, but in doing so he left himself wide open. 'Thup thup thup thup,' the bullets slammed into him; one in his chest, two in the stomach and one in the upper thigh. Seeing Breedo fall, the four shooters all took off running back thru the cut to the car that was waiting for them....After doing the drive-thru and seeing Breedo'nem on the strip Lil Twist and Worm went back to Geraldine's, Worm and Miguel's mother house to pick up Snooky, Roland, and Miguel. It was decided that Twist would drive the car, let everybody out, pull off go round the block, then come back thru pick everybody up and head to Darlene's. Roland, Snooky, Miguel, and Worm's aunt house in Danville to lay low for a couple of days and get rid of the guns.

At the same time this was going on Dets. Mashburn and Coleman were out Clopton Terrace questioning people about Snooky and her crew. They had talked to Billy Blu at the lock-up, who having only been shot in the hand, had been released into police custody. Billy Blu knowing he was facing five years or better for being in possession of a firearm after being a convicted felon, discharging a firearm in public after being declared a convicted felon and a violation with at least four years over his head. Told them "that as far as he knew Hillside was beefing with Clopton Terrace, cause they had heard it was the Terrace who supposed to have shot the Afton niggas in Hillside."

"And who supposed to be the shooters?" Det. Mashburn asked. "I'ont know, some bitches from what I hear." 'Really, you telling me that some females shot up Hillside Court?" Det. Coleman asked. "That's what da fuck I said." "And just who da hell these females supposed to be?" Det. Coleman wanted to know. "I'ont know all that either, but I do know they got a bitch over there name Snooky that supposed to go hard as a mafucka," "Snooky you say?" Det. Coleman asked.

'Snooky Boo as a matter of fact." "Snooky and Boo?" Det. Mashburn asked. "Nah mafucka, Snooky Boo, its one name Snooky Boo got it?" "Yeah we got it, was that who ya'll was shooting at today?" Det. Mashburn wanted to know. "I ain't sure I think so." "And who all was with you and Travis Briar aka Frye when all this went down?" Det. Coleman asked. "Man hold up, ya'll keep asking me all these questions and expecting me to answer, ya'll mafuckas must go let me go or sumthin," Billy Blu snapped.

'Let you go, yeah right, what we might do is drop a couple of charges, give you a petty ass charge and put in a word with the prosecutor that you were very cooperative" Det. Coleman said smiling. "That petty charge must go be a misdemeanor or no violation." "The misdemeanor we can handle, as far as the violation that's up to your p.o., but we can put in a good word with them also and try to help you out. But first you gotta help us out," Det. Mashburn said.

"Aight, it was a nigga name Breedo." "Breedo, what's Breedo's real name?" Det. Mashburn asked. "I'ont know man, all I know is Breedo." "Were ya'll the ones fighting in DTLR also?" Det. Coleman asked. "Yeah" "What was that all about?" "I ain't quite sure, but the same thing I guess. Breedo asked a bitch in there what was her name, when she answered he smacked her."

The detectives then left out the room to go talk with their Captain, after that they placed Billy Blu under arrest; charging him with misdemeanor fighting in public and misdemeanor being around a gun after being a convicted felon. The magistrate refused to give him a bond, so he had to be transferred down the Richmond City Jail until arraignment the next morning...."Do you know a young lady by the name of Snooky Boo?" Det. Coleman asked Mrs. Crayton the old lady whose house the bullett went in when the LBC had shot up Clopton Terrace. "Yeah I know a Snooky that be round here, why?" "Is she known to carry guns?" Det. Coleman asked.

"Snooky? Not that I know of, she wouldn't have to, she got two older brothers and a bunch of boy cousins who all protected her and made sure she knew how to fight. Why?" "We have reason to believe she might have something to do with a shooting at Southside Plaza earlier, do you know if she hangs with another female or not?" asked Det. Mashburn. "Again not that I know of, all you see her with is family, her brothers and cousins." "Do you think she could've been involved in the shooting?" Det. Mashburn asked.

"Snooky? As far as I know I would say nah, but then again anything is possible." "Have there been anymore problems around here since the night the bullet hit your sofa?" Det. Coleman asked. "No sir" "Okay ma'am we thank you and we'll be in contact once we catch those shooters. One more thing, do Snooky live around here?" Det. Mashburn asked. "Yeah she live down in the corner apartment building apt. C., with her mother and brothers." "Okay thank you again ma'am," Det. Coleman said.

The detectives left and went to Snooky's apartment, but wasn't nobody home, so they left a card for Snooky to call them ASAP. Leaving Clopton Terrace they heard the call of shots fired, victims down in Hillside Court and headed in that direction. Arriving in Hillside they found pure carnage; with six people down, two of whom were dead, one was barely hanging on and the other three were living but for how long was anybody's guess. The detectives walked up and surveyed the mayhem while being conscious of the crying and screaming going on around them. All of a sudden there was a high pitch shrill scream as someone hollered out "Oh my god Breedo, noooo! Breedo get up."

They turned around to see a young lady trying desperately

to get over to where one of the bodies were laid out. Looking at each other they walked over and looked down at the body that a medical examiner was pulling a sheet up over. They then walked over to the young lady and Det. Coleman asked "Excuse me ma'am, did I hear you say Breedo?" The woman whose name was Lynette and was Breedo's baby mama couldn't answer she was crying so hard.   But a couple of people standing there answered for her "Yeah" "That's what she said." "And how would she know that?" Det. Mashburn asked. "That's her baby daddy, don't you think she would know him," someone answered. "Thank you ma'am, my name is Det. Coleman and this is Det. Mashburn, here is my card, give it to her when she calms down and tell her to call me." 'Fuck you mothafucka, ya'll need to be looking for the mafuckas who did this," Lynette sobbed.

"Ma'am I assure you we are, as a matter of fact we woulda been paying Breedo a visit either tonight or tomorrow we have reason to believe he was involved in a shooting today at Southside Plaza," Det. Coleman said. "We fear this may be retaliation," Det. Mashburn finished for his partner. "I don't care wha'chu believe just catch da mafuckas that shot Breedo," Lynette screamed. "We will ma'am, believe me we will and please take that card and call us as soon as possible. Again we're sorry for your loss," Det. Coleman said as they walked off, heading back to the victims.

After talking to other people at the scene the detectives left heading back to the precinct. "What you think?" Det. Coleman asked his partner. "I think we need to find Snooky Boo and get some answers fast, before this becomes an all out war," Det. Mashburn said lighting a cigarette. "I think you right, but damn Mash, you think this bitch really got that much pull and that bad that she laid these guys down like this. Not to mention what they did at Foot Locker?" 'I'ont know Cole, but right now that's what it look like." "You right, we better find her and see what she has to say."

Westend:

It was 1:30 in the morning Gamal and Poppi were riding down Meadow St. in crackhead Diane's Avolon when they passed Filmore Dean walking down the street. Gamal who was driving, pulled in the car wash's parking lot. "Filmore what's happening?" Poppi said getting out the car. "What's up youngblood?" Filmore responded. "Shit, where you headed to?" Poppi asked him. "My sister's house." "How long you go be over there cause we got some new shit we just cooked up we want you to test." "Who is we?" "You know me and my niggas, tho right now it's just me and Gamal."

"Why ya'll need me to test it?" "Cause we let a couple of otha people test it, but you know them mafuckas just go say what they think we wanna hear." "Aight give it here." "Nigga is you crazy? Get yo dumb ass in the car, you wanna go by yo sister's house first?" "Nah she can wait, she ain't know I was coming over there no way, I was going to borrow some money but this way I ain't gotta bother her," Filmore said getting in the car. "Filmore Dean what da fuck is going on? Where da fuck you going this time of night?" Gamal asked.

"I just told youngblood, I was headed to my sista's house before she left to go to work so I could borrow some money, but ya'll niggas saved me a trip." "Borrow some money for what? You been coming to get a lookout without no money and taking three months just to pay $10 back," Gamal said. "That's why I was tryna get some money, cause I know ya'll niggas tired of looking out." "Nah nigga you was going to borrow some money cause you was going to score from somebody else, we ain't seen you in a minute where da fuck you been?" Poppi asked him.

"Just taking my time youngsta, just taking my time. Yo where the fuck we going?" Filmore asked as Gamal hit the highway. "Nigga just sit back and relax, we going where the otha mafuckas that tried it at, that way you can tell'em how the shit really is," Gamal said. "How many people out here?" "Why nigga you scared?" asked Poppi. "Hell naw youngsta, scared of what? I was just wondering what ya'll would've done if you hadn't seen me?" "We woulda found somebody else, but lucky for us we found you being that we trust your word on shit like this, we know you ain't go cut no corners," Gamal said pulling a cigarette out the box.

"Gimme one of them cigarettes and hell naw I ain't go cut no corners, like that last shit I got from ya'll, that shit taste like ammonia that's why I ain't been back in a while," Filmore said while lighting his cigarette. Gamal cut the music up as all three guys started bobbing their heads to a Yo Gotti, Lil Boosie, and Young Jeezy mix CD that Tyrus, Gamal's younger brother had made for him. Gamal got off the highway in West Point, took some busy rural roads, then took a couple of backroads. "Damn, ya'll niggas travel all over to get that paper don't it?" Filmore asked. "Mafuckas don't just get high in the Westend or Richmond for that matter Filmore," Poppi said.

"I know that, but we way out here in da boonies, got-damn it's woods on both sides nigga." "You act like you ain't never been to the country before mafucka," Gamal said. "I have, but I ain't never gone out there to get high, specially in the middle of the night." Gamal turned onto a path covered by grass and dirt, he went about a quarter mile down and around a curve where he made another turn, then he stopped by a foot path.

"What da fuck?" Filmore exclaimed. "Fuck wrong wit'chu?" Gamal asked. "I'ont see no house, where da fuck they getting high at?" "Nigga just bring yo scared ass on here, we go walk this path that lead to the house. You follow Gamal and I'ma follow you," Poppi said as all three got out the car. Just like Poppi told him to, Filmore followed behind Gamal "God-damn nigga, how da fuck ya'll even know bout dis place?" "Easy mafucka, niggas get high in here and people that get high spend money and you know I know where all the money spots at," Gamal replied.

'Clop' "Wha-" 'Clop Clop;' Poppi had pulled his gun from his waist and hit Filmore in the back of the head. Gamal hearing the noise turned around and kicked him in the side of the head. "Nigga you think we don't know you sent the police up in shawdy house a couple weeks ago," Gamal said. "What, coug coug I don't know what you talking bout," Filmore said trying to pick hisself up off the ground. 'Clop' this time Gamal hit him.

"Did you or that nigga Duke get locked up last week?" Poppi asked. "Locked up, hell naw I ain't get no locked up." "Then what da fuck ya'll doing coming out the police station the o'er day?" Gamal asked. "Coming out da police station, I went wit Duke to report his nephew bike being stolen," Filmore lied. 'Blop Clop,' Poppi kicked and hit him again with the butt of the gun. "Nigga we talked to Duke and he said neither one of ya'll had been to the police station, which means ya'll mafuckas lying to cover something up," Gamal said. "Cause what reason would both of ya'll have to lie, unless you was tryna hide something," Poppi added.

"How da hell would I know why he said that" All I know is we went down there cause somebody stole his nephew Ryan's bike out his front yard," Filmore lied again "Now why he said what he said, I don't know," he finished. "Oh you know why," Gamal said as he pushed the safety button on the trigger with his thumb. 'Baow' he shot Filmore in the back of the knee. "Talk mafucka or die," Gamal said pointing the gun at Filmore's back. "I tol-tol ya'll what happened," Filmore said laboring for breath, he had already decided they were going to kill him, so what was the use in telling them anything.

Poppi held up his hand for Gamal to hold up a minute, then he picked up a stick which he stuck in the hole in Filmore's knee that the bullet had just made. "Aghh aaghh," Filmore yelled as Poppi began twisting the stick. "Aight aight man yeah yeah, we tol'em something, but it won't nuttin bout ya'll, aghh," he yelled. "So it was ya'll that sent the police in Chantel's house?" Gamal asked him. "I did that by myself, but I ain't tell'em where to look, they asked if I buy drugs there and I tol'em yeah," even in pain Filmore lied.

"I think you lying," Poppi said. 'Blaow' "Aghh," Filmore yelled as Poppi shot him in the back of the other knee. "Me too," Gamal said as he too shot Filmore 'Baow Baow Blaow Blaow' they took turns shooting him until he moved no more and they were sure he was dead. "You wanna cover'im up or bury'im or sumthin?" Poppi asked. "Nah, I say we leave'im right here, ain't nobody go find'im, besides if we touch'im we risk leaving our DNA. This way we touch nothing on'im and don't nobody know he was wit us," Gamal said heading back to the car.

Northside:

Fatty pulled up to the Days Inn with Milnet in the car "Be right back," he said as he got out to pay for the room. Walking in the lobby there's a guy leaning over the counter talking to the female clerk behind the counter "You got a suite open for da night?" Fatty asked the clerk. The guy leaning over the counter looked over his shoulder and it was Mitch from Poe St. "Fatty what's up?" "You tell me what's up?" Fatty responded. "Lemme holla at you once you pay for your room." "Aight."

After Fatty got the keycard he went outside and gave it to Milnet so she could go up to the suite. Mitch came outside so the clerk couldn't hear what they were saying. "Fatty look, I heard all the rumors bout I supposed to've sent some niggas to shoot up Barton." "That's what I heard too." "Why you hear it happened, cause you fucked my baby mama right?" "Yeah" "Well it's yeah and nah, yeah it happened because of that, but nah I ain't tell niggas to do it. What happened was somebody tol'me they seen ya'll together and when I asked her about it she lied, then I made up some shit about something somebody said and she came clean about ya'll.

When niggas found out they wanted to come at ya'll, but I tol'em nah cause it won't on you. Number one me and you ain't fuck wit each other like that, we knew each other in speaking only; number two how was you to know that was my baby mama, it ain't like you saw us together or something. What I said was if it was a nigga I fucked wit or was beefing wit, I'd blast his ass, but this all fall back on her ass. Them young niggas tryna get a rep and be down wit a nigga, wanted to show their loyalty so they got together and came at ya'll. Then when our shit got hit niggas said it was ya'll retaliating, but I tol'em I knew it won't ya'll cause I saw you at the basketball game that night."

"I saw you too, but you need to get them lil niggas under control, er'time I turn around they tryna hit us up." "So I heard, I heard da lil nigga Dorez and his cousin over da Westend supposed to got at you." "Fuck yeah, I had my lil sister and my cousin with me. Niggas lucky ain't none of my family get hit, although if I catch they ass, they go pay." "Right now you ain't gotta worry bout that, niggas came thru last week and sprayed, Dorez got hit, now the police got his ass. They say somebody told on'im." "Told what, it won't nobody but him and that other nigga he was with and I know it won't me and my family that told."

"Nah Fatty you ain't hear bout that strip party over the Westend that got shot up." "Fuck naw" "Yeah well anyway, bout nine or ten people got hit and somebody over there supposed to've told on Dorez." 'You think it was his cousin?" "How da fuck I know? I'ont know them niggas like that." "If the police do got'em they ass betta be thanking god, cause if I catch'em I'ma put some mini-missles in'em. What about the rest of yo people down there, what's up wit them?"

"I told er'body to fall back, if I find out a nigga from round there keep pushing this dead issue they go have to deal with me, then I'ma bring'em to you and let you do wha'chu want wit'em. That's my word." "So you saying the beef squashed?" "Shiit for real it won't no beef, them niggas started something they ain't have no business starting in da first place." "Aight Mitch, I'ma take yo word for it." "Do that," Mitch said as they slapped five together and went their separate ways.

Chapter 26-RCJ:

"What's up Tre?" Cassidy asked. "Hey Cass," he answered back. "Hey cuz," Ayanna spoke. "What's up Yanna?" Cassidy and Ayanna were down at the city jail visiting Tre who went to court for arraignment yesterday on gun charges. "Your lawyer go get you a bond hearing?" Ayanna asked. "He betta, shit I ain't tryna sit up in this hot box for no three months, yo call this number and remind his ass, tell'im to schedule one asap," Tre said pulling the lawyer's card out his pocket and calling the number off to them as Ayanna wrote it down.

"I'ont see why that judge ain't give you no bond no way, talking that flight risk shit. They give niggas wit millions of dollars bond and they the ones can leave the country and go wherever da fuck they want," Cassidy said. "I know Cass, but I didn't expect'em to give me one no way, they scared my ass going back to New York and they'll never be able to find me." "How you doing in here, I heard they don't like New York niggas down here?" Ayanna asked. "I'm doing, from my unnerstanding they ain't got me in general population, they got me on what's called the felony unit-D tier, D-2 right, it ain't but twelve single cells so that's good."

"I know yo ass need some money on the books," Cassidy said. "I got bout a yard, but ya'll could leave yo family some if you got it." 'We got you cuz. Any word on Ski? The hospital ain't telling us shit and yo mama going crazy," Ayanna said. "I know she is, tell moms I'm cool, they ain't got shit on me, the gun was in my lap but they'ont know if it fell out Cap's hand or what. As for Ski all I keep getting is it's touch and go, this shit's really fucking wit me fam, Cap and Turk both dead and Ski barely hanging on. I'm all fucked up."

"We are too Big Cuz" Cassidy said "I wanna know if Stan was involved?" 'Me too," Ayanna said. "Stan?" Tre stopped to think and ponder this question before he answered "Cass, I ain't go lie to you, I'm not sure if he was or not. I know the car that pulled up beside me won't him, I ain't never seen this car before, the car on the other side I didn't get a chance to see." 'What kinda car was on your side?" Ayanna asked. "A Cadillac I think, yeah I think it was a green Cadillac."Stan got a blue Cadillac,"

Cassidy said.

"Nah but this won't Stan, I saw this nigga's face, it look like somebody I seen before but it won't Stan." "Well one thing we know, it won't none of Stan's niggas that's for sure," Cassidy said. "How aunt Precious holding up?" "Moms gangsta wit it nigga you know that, but she wanna know why you locked up and you the one got shot," Cassidy said. "Word" "Hell yeah, mama was down the hospital spaszing da fuck out on everybody. Nurses, doctors, police, and us too if we said something she won't tryna hear," Ayanna said.

"Yo tell Aunt Precious I'm straight and not to worry, tell'er I said I love her, thanks for the support, and when I get out this joint I'm coming to give her a big sloppy kiss on the cheek like I used to do when we were kids," Tre said smiling. "Eww," the sisters said in unison cracking smiles. "Times up," Officer Bailey said. "He telling ya'll it's time to go already?" Ayanna asked. "Yeah" "Damn it ain't been twenty minutes yet," said Cassidy. "We ain't been in here twenty minutes CO.," Tre said to Officer Bailey. "It's been thirty-five minutes, I gave ya'll fifteen extra minutes so be happy."

"Aight," Tre turned back to his cousins "he says it's been thirty-five minutes." "Damn that time flew past," Ayanna said. "Yeah it did. But don't forget to call the lawyer and tell moms I said don't worry bout me, I'm good." "We will and we go leave you bout $100 on the books, so you should be straight," Cassidy said. "Your mama's supposed to be down here sometime this week," Ayanna said. 'Aight, love ya'll fam." "N.Y. let's go," Officer Bailey said. "I'm coming, gotta go fam." "You betta call us," Cassidy said. "I will," Tre responded walking out the door. After leaving $50 a piece on Tre's books, the sisters were on their way to their mother's house "How you feel now Cass? You still think Stan had something to do with it?" Ayanna asked her sister. "I'ont know Yanna, I mean Tre said he knew it won't Stan cause he saw the guy's face, but he ain't know who was in the other car." "He also said he thought he'd seen that guy before, he just didn't know where," Ayanna added. "What you think, do you think Stan did it?" Cassidy asked. "I don't think so, but if he didn't then who did?"

"It coulda been anybody from Whitcomb, you know everybody knew their car and Stan did say the word round there was that the New York Boyz shot Kalil'nem." "That's true, but who we know got a green Cadillac?" "I'ont know, but we gotta keep our eyes and ears open, word'll get out soon." "You be careful who you fuck with round there, cause if they think your cousins shot Kalil'nem they could blame you," Ayanna said. "I know that Yanna but I ain't worried, shit you talking bout me, your ass betta be careful too. You talked to Tawanna?" "Not since the hospital, I'ma call'er soon tho. In the meantime let's hope this shit dies down and Ski and Tre come out of it okay," Ayanna said in their mother's driveway.

HCJ-Dayroom 21:

"Jeffrey Coghill," the mailman called "Right here," Jeff answered. After getting his mail Jeff went to his cell, when he looked at the envelope it hadn't been opened yet. "Damn somebody forgot to check this letter," he said to hisself. Opening it up, seven pictures came out "Damn! He said. "God-damn, oh my, okay my nigga, shid dis nigga crazy," he said pulling out two letters which he proceeded to read. "My nigga crazy as shit," he said laughing to hisself and looking at the pictures again as he left the cell.

Coming to the top of the stairs, Vic and Samson two old

heads were standing there talking. "Check dis shit out," he said handing three of the pictures to them. "Damn nigga, that's yo man ain't it?" Vic asked. "Yeah mafucka crazy as shit ain't it?" "How da fuck you get these?" Samson asked. "Thru da mail, my letter hadn't been opened, whoever check the mail ain't never see'im." "Who dat is? Shawdy phatta than a mafucka," Samson said.

"Shid, pussy look like it's betta than a eighth of dope," Vic said. "Ya'll niggas ain't go believe me, so I ain't saying." "Damn nigga, I'm tryna use'em later on to get my thing off wit Mary Palm and her five sistas," Vic said grabbing hisself. "Nigga you go beat yo dick so much you go fuck around and fall in love wit yo hand, old mafucka," Jeff said laughing. "Shit at least I ain't gotta worry bout getting burnt or catching that monkey nigga," Vic responded. "Shid, I'ont know, if you use soap and that shit get down in yo pisshole, that bitch burn like a mafucka my nigga," Samson said.

"Fo real, like you dun fucked five burning bitches," Jeff said. "Ya'll niggas crazy, I ain't using no damn soap, I 'm using lotion and hair grease ya'll don't know nothing bout that shit." "Hair grease and lotion, fuck you tryna do cum back to back mafucka?" Samson asked. "Nah nigga, give it that extra wet feeling, I got a hella imagination mafucka, make me think about my girl cumming," Vic said. "Yo old ass crazy, fuck around have a heart attack," Jeff said. "Call it wha'chu want, but if yo ass been locked up much as I have you'd have a helluva imagination too," Vic replied.

"Yeah yeah, let me run downstairs right fast," Jeff said walking down the steps. "Don't forget me nigga," Vic said. "I got'chu," Jeff replied. Jeff got downstairs, walked over to Chazz who was sitting down watching T.V. and dropped the envelope in his lap. Chazz looked up at Jeff, picked up the envelope and looked inside, there were the same seven pictures Jeff had seen plus one of the letters that was in there with them. Chazz started looking at the pictures "What da fuck! he exclaimed.

The first picture he saw was his girl Lanay naked on hands and knees looking into the camera. The second one, she was holding her legs in the air spread open and had reached around spreading her pussy lips apart. The third picture he jumped up "I'ma kill this bitch," she was in the same position as the first but Darrell was standing behind her, he too was naked and in this picture Lanay was turned slightly on a angle so you could see Darrell's dick inside her. The fourth one she was on her back, just like the second one and again Darrell was in the picture, but standing to the side with his dick in her mouth as they both looked in the camera. The fifth one Darrell was on his back, Lanay was on top of him facing the camera with her legs spread so you could see she was sitting halfway down on his dick.

The sixth one again Darrell was on his back, but this time Lanay was on her knees beside him with her hand around the base of his dick and her mouth covering the head plus about four extra inches with her tongue laying on its underside, damn near touching the top of her hand. And the seventh one had a close-up shot of them, with Darrell still on his back and Lanay still had her hand around his dick, but up a little higher. The only difference was this time Darrell propped up on his elbows looking at the camera as was Lanay, who had her tongue hanging out her mouth with what looked like thick white cum on it, plus all over her face and in her hair. "I'ma kill this nigga Darrell," Chazz exclaimed without thinking. "You go do what? To who?" Jeff asked smirking. Chazz looked at Jeff with both murder and tears in his eyes "Nigga Jakeela ain't his girl, he ain't have shit to do with what down between me and you." "That's my nigga, I woulda did the samething for him, you know that. Go head read the letter....

Dear Chazz,

Let me start by saying you ain't shit nigga, good as I am to you and with all the shit I done put up with you, you had to do some sheisty shit like this. How da fuck you go fuck one of your nigga's girl? Don't say you ain't know that was his girl, cause you did. Much less, how you go tell him all about it. I know by now you saw the pictures and I know you saying I'ma kill this bitch. Well fuck you mafucka, I had your kids and stood by you thru all your cheating and shit, but this is the last straw. How it feel nigga to know a nigga you know got all up in this pussy that used to be yours and for the record nigga, Jeff can get the same treatment when he comes home if he wants it. Damn right I sucked his dick and swallowed his cum, it tastes real good too, I gave him all the good loving and special treatment I used to give you. Remember when I used to do that to you and you would beg me not to touch you anymore, well he did the samething, but instead of stopping he turned me over and fucked me in the ass. Then he pulled out, put it in my pussy and punished me from behind again. Shid, that shit was so good he coming back this weekend and we go have a repeat performance, if not a better one. And just so you know he ain't tell me nothing about you and Jakeela, she did. That's what you get for fucking with a trifling ass, childish ass little girl. I started to beat her ass, but changed my mind. I'm just go fuck her man like she did mine, only thing is I may record it and send it to her, that's if Jeff don't mind. You don't think he'll mind do you? Ask him for me and let me know what he says. Don't even worry about getting no more money from me, tell Jakeela to send you some, but I just sent Jeff $50 today so when you see him go to the store, just know I paid for it. I'm the one feeding him, like I hope he feeds me his dick when he gets out. Don't worry about calling or writing, cause I had the number changed and I'm go send the letter back to you.

Fuck you,

Your ex-girl, Lanay

P.S. My pussy's sore as a mothafucka,
you think Darrell will be able to make
it sore again this weekend? Is it a good
idea to fuck him again while I'm sore or
should I just suck his dick and fuck him
when I ain't sore no more? Damn she
throbbing just thinking bout him punishing
her again.

Chazz looked at Jeff who said "Nah I'on't mind, do you mind? Shit we might get paid, wha'chu think?" Chazz threw everything in Jeff's face and swung at him, Jeff easily sidestepped the punch and hit him with a one hitta-quitta knocking him to the floor. "Nigga don't be mad at me it's yo fault, ain't nobody tell you to fuck my bitch, like I said payback's a bitch. Shit I ain't da one fucking yo woman, that's my man, but I damn sho will fuck'er when I go home, believe that." Jeff picked up the pictures and walked back to his cell passing by Vic and Samson "Well I guess we know whose ol'lady that was," Vic said.

"Ya'll young niggas crazy, don't let that nigga rock yo ass to sleep, ya'll fucking wit his woman like that," Samson said. "Shid, he started it Samson, he shouldn't have fucked wit my baby moms, then none of this shit would've happened."

"Sometimes you need to look at the woman, if she'll fuck a nigga you know and she knows you know him, then she ain't worth having as your woman," Samson said. "Hell naw she ain't, if she do that, then she can't be trusted period, it's plenty of different fish in the sea. All you gotta do is keep casting your rod and be patient, sooner or later the right one go bite," Vic put in.

"I feel what ya'll saying," Jeff said. "Don't just feel, hear youngsta. It's a lot of piranhas and sharks out there, but a real goldfish is hard to find," Samson said. "Aight aight, I hear ya'll," Jeff said walking off. "Don't forget I'm still tryna use that later on," Vic said. "I told you I got you, just holla at me when you want'em," Jeff said as he looked over the railing at Chazz hanging up the phone and redialing again. "That's what his dumb ass get," he said to hisself as he walked in his cell. Sitting on the bed, he picked up the other letter and re-read it, this one was from Darrell to him.

My nigga,

What's up Shawdy? I know yo ass tripping right now. Man I ain't even try to fuck shawdy, I was with my cousin Corey at Chevron on Chambelayne the other night when I ran into her. While Corey was in the store I was pumping the gas when Lanay walks out speaks to me and start pumping her gas. How bout Jakeela pull up in the parking lot and jumps out screaming on me talking bout 'I need to mind my own damn business.' When I asked her what she was talking bout, she said she'd been down there to see you and that you told her I said I saw her up there visiting Chazz. I was like 'I ain't lie did I?' She go say 'who she fucking is her business, I ain't got shit to do wit it.'

I'm like 'Jeff my right hand man, my best friend fuck you mean I ain't got shit to do with it. Bottom line you was fucking Chazz and coming to see him in the same jail my nigga in,' this bitch had the nerve to say 'so fucking what? What you didn't know, wouldn't hurt you.' Cuz, I started to smack the shit out that bitch, but at that moment Lanay walked over and asked her 'Excuse me, did I hear you say you were going to see Chazz and you were fucking him?' Yo dumb ass baby mama go respond with 'And so what?' Lanay snapped 'So what? That's my baby daddy bitch, that's so what.'

Keela came back wit 'baby daddy, not yo man so back da fuck up bitch.' Lanay was like 'No bitch, my man and my baby daddy get it straight, but since you say you were fucking him, you can have his sorry no good ass.' After that shit and then some Jakeela finally left, Lanay asked me what I knew so I told her, shit Keela had already told her anyway. She took my number, called me bout a hour later and that's when we made these pics, we used a digital camera with a automatic timer. Cuz shawdy got some bum too, she said she ain't never cheated on Chazz, but this won't cheating, this was payback. She serious bout giving you some ass too nigga. I know you wondering how we got the pics thru, shawdy's uncle's best friend is the mailman down there and he cool as shit. She got her uncle to holla at him and he agreed to bring this letter to you unopened. Be cool my nigga and watch that snake mafucka, I know once he see them pics he go snap.

One Love
Darrell

P.S. If you call me Sunday
bout 7:30 in the evening, I'll
let you listen to me burn

shawdy up.

Chapter 27-MCV Hospital:

"What you think?" Det. Smithers asked his partner as they were leaving the hospital from seeing Duke. "I think somebody did a number on ole Duke, that's what I think," Det. Long answered. "Yeah, but who and why?" "That's a good question, the way I figure it couldn't be behind him and Filmore coming down the precinct, cause more than likely he would be dead instead of laid up in the hospital." "But geez Long, the guy's damn near dead, he's got a tumor on his brain, a busted blood vessel in his eye that's go require surgery, plus the doctors think he may have nerve damage. They didn't kill him, but they damn sure tried."

"But don't you think they would've shot him or at least stabbed him if they were trying to kill him." "Yeah, I was kinda thinking along those same lines." "What we need to do is find Filmore and see what he's heard and still try to find this female that was shooting at the market. Any word on who Poe St. supposed to be beefing with?" "I talked to Landers from Third Precinct, she said from what they hear Poe and Brookland Park Blvd., is supposed to be caught up in some kind of war, but also Poe had been shot up at least two different times within the past month and a half. They don't know by who, so they're not too sure that Poe and the Blvd are really beefing."

"Well if Poe is beefing with the Blvd., what the hell they doing shooting around the Westend?" "Didn't Filmore say he thought the guy from Poe and this Pokey were shooting at somebody from Northside?" "Yeah, but that don't prove it was nobody from the Blvd." "Nah, but it's a starting point." "How bout we ride by that house we ran up in and see who's out there.

Maybe we'll run across one of them females that was involved in the shooting." "Fine by me."

Downtown:

Ayanna had called Tawanna to see how she was doing, Tawanna had told her she was doing fine, even though the realization that Kalil was gone was hard. They agreed to meet up at 'Over the Top' hair salon to talk; now they were standing outside talking because they didn't want nobody in the salon to hear their conversation. "Wana I know it's been hard on ya'll, how Miss Kate doing?" Ayanna asked referring to Kalil's mother. "She holding up, she know Kalil won't no angel, but still that was her child." "I know that's right, this shit out here is crazy, you know all four of my cousins got shot up right?" Ayanna stated.

"Yeah I heard, but even though I'm sorry for your grief, I can't say that I'm sorry for what happened to your family Yanna. You know I love you like a sister, but let's be real about the situation, my cousin and his crew stuck-up your cousins and your cousins killed'em in retaliation." "So you knew Kalil and nem stuck-up Tre and nem all the time?" "Nah not all the time, I knew they were fed up wit Tre and nem taking all their clientèle and they won't from Whitcomb, not to mention they won't from Richmond period. When you told me about yo cousins getting stuck-up, I ain't know Kalil and nem did it until a couple of days later.

I over heard Matt ask Kalil what he thought me and Cassidy both would do if we found out they'd been the ones who stuck Cassidy's cousins. Kalil's answer was he ain't know, but as long as everybody kept their mouth shut, neither one of us would find out. I came out my bedroom practically begging

Kalil to tell me they weren't the ones who did that. Yanna you know how cocky that nigga was, this nigga looked at me and said 'aight I won't then.' I'm like come on Kalil, you know that's Yanna and Cassidy's family which might as well be our family too, they my sistas from another mother. This nigga had the nerve to say 'I ain't say we did it, I just said I won't tell you we did it.'

So I asked him straight up if they did it and he said the less I knew the betta. Yanna I swear to you, I went off on their ass in that house I tol'em that shit was coming back on'em and they didn't believe it. Talking bout this Richmond they ain't worried bout nobody from New York doing nuthing to'em, besides them niggas ain't know who did it." As Tawanna said all this she had tears running down her face, Ayanna didn't want to but she had to ask "What about Stan?" "When I asked'em how they could rob Stan's girl cousins, Reese was like 'fuck Stan he ain't need to know what happened either.'

But they all had lil sneaky smiles, almost like smirks on their faces, which made me think there was more to it than that. And when I asked if Stan had anything to do with it, Kalil went off 'Hell naw Stan ain't have shit to do with nothing' I wanted to tell you, but I ain't know how you was go take it." "Damn Wana you know you coulda talked to me, I mean yeah Tre and nem's my blood family, my kinfolks and all, but you my family too, I couldn't hold what Kalil'nem did against you. That's street shit, me and you ain't got nothing to do wit no street shit." "I know Yanna, but still."

"But still, how you know Tre and nem killed Kalil'nem?" "Cause after if happened, Maxine from on Charity St., came to get me and tell me what happened. You shoulda seen the car Yanna, holes was everywhere, Maxine described the car that did it and said it was four niggas in it. By the time everybody else finished talking bout what happened and describing the kind of car that did it, I was pretty sure it was Tre and nem, but when somebody came up and said they saw the same car in Whitcomb, I knew it was them." "You knew at the hospital?"

"Not for sure, but when I got back home, and went around where it happened and everybody was telling me the samething, I knew." "How come you ain't let me know?" "For what? I was already stressed behind the shit Yanna, won't need for you to be stressed too, besides would you have believed me if I woulda told you so." "Probaly so, afta you called me that morning when I got to the house and told Cass, everybody was looking all funny in the face. Turk spoke up and was like 'fuck dem niggas,' when Cass asked'im why he said that he said 'they the ones that jacked us.' Wana you talking bout you went off, you shoulda seen and heard Cass, she was ready to kill everybody in the house but me.

We won't sure they was the ones that did it until afta we got back from the hospital. When we found out for sure they did it, we tol'em they had to leave and go back to New York. I asked'em why they had to shoot Kalil and nem, they was just as much my family as Tre and nem was. Cap said 'payback.' Cass was like 'they ain't shoot ya'll, so why ya'll ain't just rob them back' and Cap was like 'they disrespected him by putting a gun in his face.' We tol'em niggas was mad and wanted revenge, we just ain't know it was go happen this fast, shit niggas in both projects wanted'em they lucky they made it long as they did."

"I know, is all of'em dead?" "Nah Tre down the jail on the Felony unit, Ski still in the hospital, but Cap and Turk both dead." "Damn Yanna, all this for what, a lil bit of money, drugs, and cause niggas from out-of-town wanna eat in our city." "I know Wana, I'm sorry bout everything you know that, Kalil won't just your cousin, he was my cousin as well." "I know right, but I'm sorry too Yanna, I love you girl and you know I would never want to see no harm come to you or your family." "Same here." "We still sistas?" "For life girl."

Downtown- Lock-up: Ninth St.

After riding by Chantel's house and not seeing anything or anybody and being unsuccessful locating Filmore Dean, Det. Long and Smithers had returned to their precinct to find a notice for them to contact Det. Landers over at the Third Precint. Det. Long made the call and Det. Landers told him to meet her down at the lock-up. Now just getting there, they had the Sgt. at the front desk call Det. Landers to the front. "What's up Long?" she asked. "Nothing much, trying to figure out why you asked us down here."

"Well I have somebody in custody you may want to talk to." "And who is that?" Det. Smithers asked. "A guy from off Poe St., by the name of Dorez Sanderson," Det. Landers answered as she led the way down the hall to an interrogation room. "And why would we be interested in him?" Det. Long asked. "Because after I talked to you Long, there was a shooting on Poe St., five people were shot and Dorez was one of them.

We questioned the victims, my partner Hunt who's down at the hospital now with his daughter who is sick and myself. Anyway in the process of questioning the victims nobody could tell us who was behind the shooting, but the four other victims all said they thought Dorez had a cousin over the Westend but couldn't remember his name. I remembered you said something about somebody from Poe St. shooting over the Westend, so I called you so you could question him for yourself." "Thanks we appreciate that, but did ya'll get a chance to question him yourselves?" Det. Long asked.

"Yeah we did, but we didn't ask him nothing about the Westend, we asked if he knew who shot him and of course he said no. Then we asked if he was beefing with anybody. Again he said no, at least not him personally, but that Poe St. had so many people hating on them that it was hard to say who they was beefing with. When we asked about the problems with the Blvd., he laughed and said if you want to call it that, then yeah they was beefing with the Blvd. I asked him why they were beefing and he said he didn't know."

"So he did say they were beefing with the Blvd?" Det. Smithers asked. "Yeah" "Thanks again that's a big help, now let's see if he'll tell us about the shooting over our side of town," Det. Long said. The three detectives entered the interrogation room where Dorez was sitting with his wrists handcuffed together on top of the table. "Dorez, this is Det. Long and Det. Smithers they want to ask you some additional questions," Det. Landers said walking up to the other side of the table and remaining standing.

"Dorez what's up my man? I'm Det. Long." "And of course I'm Det. Smithers. First off Dorez, we understand that Poe St. and the Blvd. are supposed to be beefing, is that correct?" "Didn't I already tell ya'll that one time?" Dorez said. "Calm down man damn, we just trying to touch bases that's all. Now can you tell us why ya'll are beefing?" Det. Smithers asked.

"Man I don't know, why da fuck do niggas beef most of the time, proly behind some bitch or sumthin, who da hell knows. Seem like we been beefing forever." "Yeah, but it never really came to no gunplay. This is a whole nother level," Det. Long said. "Tell me something, was that you shooting at the Market

Place over the Westend a couple of weeks ago?" Det. Long asked. "Shooting at da Market Place, wha'chu talking bout."

"Come on Dorez, you know what he's talking bout, your cousin Pokey already told us it was ya'll shooting up there," Det. Smithers said. Dorez looked around at all three detectives, he didn't know whether to believe them or not. On the one hand they could be lying, but on the other, how would they know it was him and Pokey shooting unless Pokey told them. "Man I ain't falling for that playing one against the other bullshit, my cousin ain't tell ya'll nuttin like that." The detectives looked at each other, they knew they had him now.

"How else would we know unless he told us," Det. Long stated. "He said it was some guy and girl from Northside you was beefing with," Det. Smithers put in. Again Dorez took time to think about what they said, finally he spoke up "it won't nobody I was beefing wit, it was somebody Carter St., was beefing with." "But ya'll were the ones shooting, by ya'll I mean you and Pokey, ya'll were the ones shooting up at the Market Place?" Det. Smithers asked. "Yeah man." "Tell us what happened, you help us and we'll help you," said Det. Long.

Dorez took a deep breath, then he started "We was walking towards the store when this car pulled up in the parking lot, a guy and a girl got out and went inside. Pokey says that's this nigga name Fat something or another and the bitch that robbed two of his niggas off Carter St. The girl came back out and got in da car, but when dude came out Pokey started shooting, ole boy started shooting back, so I started shooting too." "What about the girl?" Det. Long asked. "She got back out da car and started dumping back at us too, so Pokey takes off running and I did the samething."

"So the girl did shoot back?" Det. Smithers asked. "Yeah"

"And what did you say their names were?" "Fat something or another and I'ont know da broad's name." "You know where they're from?" Det. Long asked. "Nah all I know is Pokey said they robbed somebody on Carter St., so I figured they were from over the Westend since he knew that." "What kind of car were they in?" Det. Long asked.

"Man I ain't good with different kinds of cars." "Alright let me get this straight, you and your cousin Pokey were walking to a store, namely The Market Place in the Westend. When Pokey sees a guy he says supposedly robbed two people on Carter St., Pokey pulls out his gun and starts shooting at the guy as he's coming out the store. The guy shoots back, so you pull out your gun and start shooting, then the girl that's with him jumps out the car and starts shooting at ya'll also, at which time you and Pokey take off running. Is that correct?" Det. Smithers said.

"Yeah, that's correct." "You got anything else you want to add?" "Nah that's it." "Alright, Det. Landers go take you on back in da lock-up, we'll be contacting you down the jail real soon," Det. Long said. "Down da jail, I'ma make bond ya'll see me on da land." "Make bond, nah not right now, you ain't even go get a bond until you're formally charged." "Formally charged, charged with what, I told ya'll everything you wanted to know."

"So you say, but we still gotta check your story out, cause see Pokey told us he ain't have no family over Northside, so now we go see what he has to say about all this," Det. Smithers said smiling and waving his hand at the tape recorder which was sitting in the middle of the table recording everything Dorez said. Dorez looked at all three officers smiling at him as realization hit; they had played him using that one against the other tactic on him anyway. "Fuck ya'll mafuckas." "No you fucked yourself," Det. Long said as all the detectives got up and left Dorez sitting there by hisself.

Chapter 28-Northside:

Fatty, Cheeks, Te-Mundre, Shaun, Marquell, Big-C, Tom-Tom and Davon were standing on Crenshaw discussing recent events. "Fuck ya'll niggas doing standing outside in da middle of Hilltop anyway knowing we beefing wit dem niggas?" Cheeks asked Marquell and Davon. "Shawd, we was leaving Rhonda's, I'ont even know where dis nigga came from," Davon said. "Fo real nigga came out shooting two guns at the sametime like he was in a movie or some shit," Marquell added. "Ya'll still don't know who da nigga was?" Fatty asked.

"Rhonda said she talked to Leeta who said she'd heard thru the grapevine the nigga's name was Jigaloo, Jigaboo, some shit like that," Davon replied. "Yeah Leeta said the nigga run wit a couple of niggas named Y.K. and Rel, but that Y.K. got killed when him and Rel got shot up Pine Camp," Tom-Tom said. "Rel? Ain't that da nigga ya'll beefing wit?" Marquell asked looking at Shaun and Cheeks. "Yeah, I beat his pussy ass at da afta hours spot, then dem pussy mafuckas got at us at McDonald's, so you know we had to get back at they ass," Shaun answered. "Still that don't say why this nigga got at ya'll," Cheeks said.

"Any of ya'll know this nigga?" Fatty asked. Everybody answered "naw." "Maybe he did it just cause ya'll from over dis side of town, he ain't know who ya'll was and it just so happen that all us run together," Fatty stated. "Maybe, but whatever the reason he got a couple of hot balls in his ass, so the shit backfired on'im. I know they ass mad for real now, that's what? One dead and two hit, one in their own hood. Them niggas go want some get back, ya'll niggas know that," Marquell stated.

"That's for damn sure, so all of us go have to be on point, specially when we hit the clubs," Big-C said. "No shit" "That's for real" were a few of the replies that were heard. "Speaking of being on point, I talked to Mitch from Poe St da other night," Fatty said. "Fuck you mean you talked to'im?" Marquell asked. "Just what I said nigga, other night me and Milnet went to the Days Inn and this nigga was in the lobby talking to the bitch behind the desk.

When he turns around and see me, he says he wants to talk to me, we go outside and I sent Milnet to the room. He tells me he knows of the rumors about him sending niggas to shoot up the Bul cause of me fucking Reyna. I tell'im I heard the samething and he says they lies, that he made the statement if it was a nigga he was beefing with or one of his niggas he would blaze they ass. But me and him won't cool like that and we ain't never had no beef, plus I never saw him and Reyna together so how was I supposed to know she was his girl. Basically he said he didn't feel like I disrespected him, it was more so on her not me. He was like them young niggas always tryna prove theyselves to a nigga, always wanna be in a nigga's good graces and shit."

'So this nigga bitching up?" Te-Mundre said. "Nah Mundre I'ont think he bitching up, I think things mighta got blown out of proportion, shawdy was like he'ont even fuck wit dem lil niggas that came at us. He even told me bout da lil nigga Dorez, said shawdy got shot da other day and last he heard the police had him. I asked'im if he thought shawdy would snitch on who he was shooting at in the Westend or who he thought shot him and he said he didn't know. I'm like you don't know and that's when he said he don't know them lil niggas like that. Long story short, we squashed the beef supposedly?"

Supposedly?" Davon asked. "Yeah supposedly, I agreed to squash it, but I let'im know if anything happens to any of us and I hear it was them, then it's on again. And he said if he hear of anything happening he was go bring da person to me personally and let me handle'em." "You believe'im?" Tom-Tom asked. "To a point I do, I can't say one way or another if he sent them niggas at us, but I do believe he wanna squash the beef. One reason cause he don't wanna deal wit all the heat from da police it could bring. Plus worrying but us, not to mention with dis nigga Dorez in custody he may think da nigga go snitch on'im by saying Mitch tol'em to shoot at us or paid'im to do it or some shit. So yeah I do believe he wanna squash it."

"What about us? He say anything bout us?" Marquell asked. "Nah, he said he heard it was the Bul that came thru and wet that party up. He told niggas it couldn't have been me cause he saw me at da basketball game that night and they'ont know who it was that shot up Carter St., or shot Dorez' nem while they was on Poe. You know I ain't give'em no clue that we had nuttin to do wit it." "Aight nigga fuck all that beefing shit, what's up wit that work?" Big C asked.

"No question, mafuckas been running round here like crazy behind that shit," Tom-Tom said. "Shid, down our end too, but we go strike between tonight and sometime tomorrow," Fatty answered. "I hope ya'll niggas get enough that we don't run out so fast this time," Davon said. "I swear, what ya'll niggas need to do is just sell weight and let us do the flat-footing," stated Tom-Tom. Marquell and Fatty both laughed. "We gettin to that just give us time shawdy," Marquell said. "Just hurry da fuck up," Davon said. "Ey I'm going to Mike's," Cheeks said referring to Michael Simpson's store on the corner. "Me too bro hold up," Shaun said. "Shid I'm going too," Tom-Tom said. "Me too," Big

C. said as they walked off. "Bring back a couple of Dutch's," Marquell said. "Aight," was the response....

Twenty minutes later Munchy, O.J. and Bodie the dope (heroin) dealers were standing on the corner of Barton and Crawford; Lil Q and Smoke were standing in crackhead April's front yard. Hammerhead was walking with crackhead Linda as they passed O.J. and crew on the corner. "Hamma you goin'na get yo trick on ain't it?" O.J. joked. "Fuck naw nigga, I gotta run to my bama right fast." "We know so you can get yo trick on mufucka," Munchy said laughing. "Not that it's any of ya'lls business, but he don't need nuthing to get some of dis pussy, he can get it for free. Ya'll need to stop hating especially you Munchy, didn't you just give me a half-a-gram of coc the otha day to trick wit'chu, as ya'll say," Linda said laughing. "Word, not Mr. I don't pay for no pussy Munchy?" Bodie said still laughing.

While this was going on Drop, Peter Pop, Black Ben, and Dip Dap were standing in front of Lucky's when a dark green '98 pulled in the parking lot. Drop and Dip Dap were in the middle of the parking lot hollering at a couple of females who were pulling off "I'ma call you tonight," Drop yelled when 'Bop Bop Bop Blaow Blaow Blaow Blaow Blaow Blaow.' 'Ping sprack sprack whizzz,' gunshots rang out the windows of the '98. "Aghhh," Drop yelled as he was hit in the right thigh, stomach, and upper sternum; Dip Dap got hit in the chest, shoulder, and upper arm. Black Ben yelled as he got hit in the back of the right upper arm while going thru the door of Lucky's. 'Scrrrrr,' the car sounded as it squealed wheels pulling out the parking lot onto Barton and flying across Brookland Park Blvd while staying on Barton.

Hearing the gunshots and seeing the car pulling out the

parking lot headed their way, Lil Q and Smoke ran to get their guns from their various hiding spots. 'Blaow Blaow Blaow Blaow Blaow Blaow Blaow Blaow Tat-ta-tat-ta-ta-tat-tat.' Both Lil Q and Smoke opened up on the car, 'scrreec boom,' the '98 hit a parked car then slammed into the back of another one. Munchy, O.J. and Bodie seeing what was happening all ran to get their guns, arriving back at the corner they saw that the car had crashed. Next they see the front passenger side door and the back door on the driver's side open, with somebody sliding out both doors.

Seeing the guy in the passenger's side get out with a gun in his hand, Munchy and O.J. cut loose 'baka baka baka caka caka caka caka.' The bullets tore into the young man's upper body, knocking him back on the car. Simultanously Lil Q and Smoke ran down and opened fire on the guy getting out the back 'Blaow blaow blaow Tat-ta-tat-tat,' but the guy pulled his gun up and started shooting back as he tried to run. He never saw Bodie coming towards him 'Baka baka baka baka' Bodie opened up, he caught the guy in the legs, groin and stomach. The bullets from Lil Q and Smoke tore into his back and side leaving holes thru out his body, he dropped in the middle of the street.

Bodie ran up on the car and 'Blak blak blak blak' opened fire on the driver hitting him in the chest, stomach, middle part of his thigh and cheekbone. Everybody took off running in separate directions leaving three bodies laid out on Barton Ave.

Southside:

Club Destiny's was jammed packed, cars were parked everywhere, traffic moving around the club was slow and congested. Destiny's known as a Big Girl club had more than it's share of both big girls or any other size female for that matter here tonight. It seemed as though the whole city was somewhere around or inside tonight, and the Chicago Ave. niggas were out in full force. "Shid, I'ont know bout ya'll but I'm tryna leave up out here wit one of these big girls tonight," Arthur Gantz said to Lil Goo, KenVale, Dan Johnson, and Corey Dillard who all stood surveying the floor and watching Slick and Alberto sandwich a medium sized red-bone who looked as though she was fucking them both right there on the dance floor. "You ain't the only one shawd, I'm tryna find me some wet-wet myself, my nigga," Corey said. "All ya'll niggas fuck wit is big girls, fuck is up wit that?" Dan asked.

"Nigga didn't you just hear me say I'm tryna find me some wet-wet, big girls don't go dry, they stay wet all night long," Corey replied. "Hell yeah, plus you can punish a big girl and not worry bout her saying you in her stomach or she can't take it. And they give that good loving nigga," Arthur Gantz added. "I hear ya'll, but give me my skinny bitches, they all pussy and they take plenty of dick," KenVale said. "Yeah but them skinny bitches don't let'chu get but one nut, then they wanna go to sleep. A big bitch want to fuck and fuck and fuck, shiit she'll have yo ass telling her you wanna go to sleep," Corey said.

"Whatever nigga, me personally I take'em however they come; big, tall, extra small, long as they cute don't make me no difference long as they pussy ain't no garbino. All pussy make you cum," Dan said as he moved off in the direction of a short thick dark skin woman with a nice round ass and the right size titties to match. With all their eyes on Slick, Alberto and the red-bone girl, nobody noticed the guys moving thru the crowd until 'Blop,' Slick got punched in the jaw, then all hell broke loose. There was screaming, shouting, pushing and shoving as the Chicago Ave crew went to help their niggas.

Alberto seeing Slick get hit did a jump punch catching the guy that hit Slick which happened to be Lil Ron-Ron of the LBC, in the eye staggering him. He couldn't follow up because he got pushed from behind by somebody trying to get out the way of Dan and Lil Bighead who were exchanging punches. When he heard a girl scream, Dan had turned just in time to see Lil Bighead throwing a punch at him, he bobbed a little trying to avoid getting hit, but still got caught in the shoulder, now they were trading punches left and right. 'Blop Blop,' Dan got caught from behind by Lil Quincy who was another member of the LBC, Quincy's older brother Big Quincy and Arthur Gantz were rumbling and falling over the tables. Big Quincy hit Arthur causing him to fall onto two plump women who were trying to get out of the way.

Lil Dread, Lil K.O. Corey Dilllard and KenVale were in a free-for-all battle with punches going here, there, everywhere. Next thing you knew everybody had switched up and was fighting a different person. Lil Goo and Lil Ron-Ron were now going at it, when security which was actually off duty Richmond Sheriff's deputies bumrushed the floor. They were grabbing people and slinging them out the way trying to get to the fight, by the time they got to the first fighters they saw the floor had practically cleared, leaving a open space to fight in. Deputies Simpson and Tolliver grabbed Lil Goo and Lil Ron-Ron and dragged them thru the crowd, down the steps and out the front door.

Deputies Turner and Harvey followed with Slick and Lil Bighead, now the rest of the fighters noticing the deputies coming ran trying to get down the stairs and out the door. Once outside the deputies were trying to keep everything peaceful and get the crowd moving, when out of nowhere 'baka baka baka claka claka claka.' "Iiiiiiiii," there was yelling and screaming as gunshots erupted.

Chapter 29-Channel 8 Morning News:

"Good morning, I'm Allison Sweeney, we begin this morning's newscast with two shootouts here in Richmond within the last 24 hours. The latest one occurred around 3'o clock this morning over Southside at Club Destiny's, according to Richmond police and eyewitnesses there was a fight inside the club involving several people. After Security which were off duty sheriff deputies broke it up and put several of the combatants out, shots were fired. Richmond police arrived on the scene and became involved. Our Claire Munsford is on the scene, Claire what can you tell us?"

"Well Allison we know that there was a fight here inside this club, Club Destiny's which is directly behind me. According to eyewitnesses the fight was between two groups of young men from here in the Southside. After security broke up the fight and put several of the participants out, gunshots were fired, Richmond police arrived and got involved by exchanging gunfire with the shooters. A total of five people were hit; four people believed to be involved and an innocent female bystander, no police were wounded although two of the victims are believed to've been hit by the police. Several arrests have been made and Richmond police say they're working on making more soon, I spoke with an officer who was here at the scene and he described it as totally chaotic.

The officer whose name is Officer Bridgeforth said according to witnesses accounts one group of guys were standing in the corner of the club talking, one guy walks off as two more guys walk up, one of whom punches somebody on the dance floor. After that bedlam ensued. Now Allison as you said several off duty Richmond Sheriff's deputies were doing security here, and immediately broke the fight up and threw the fighters out. But once outside a different more violent type of fight broke out; the fighters went to their cars to retrieve their guns, returned and started exchanging gunfire. Richmond Police were in the area and responded to a report of shots fired, when they arrived on the scene the sheriff's deputies were trying to pinpoint the exact location of the shooters. The shooters apparently unaware of the police being on the scene continued shooting, with as many as five different sounding guns being fired simultaneously.

Once police identified the location of the shooters, they ordered the shooters to put down their weapons at which time more gunfire was exchanged. Police say some of the shooters were running and firing at the sametime, while others were hiding behind parked cars or standing out in the open. The officers identified themselves as police officers and still more gunfire was exchanged, a young woman trying to get out of harm's way was fatally shot in the chest. This prompted both the police and sheriff's deputies to open fire, which led to at least two of the shooters being hit, albeit fatally. Those two victims were found with their guns either in their hands or laying beside them. When all was said and done five people were hit and five people were arrested.

The officer went on to say that right now, none of the victims or people arrested were being identified, he also said pending further investigation all officers involved both sheriff's deputies and police would be identified at a later time. Once again fighting broke out here at Club Destiny's on Richmond's Southside, after being broken up and thrown out the club participants of the fight got into a shootout. Richmond police were called in and tried to intervene but instead of resolving the conflict peacefully, the police as well as the off duty Richmond Sheriff's deputies doing security here had to get involved. After exchanging gunfire with several suspects the conflict was eventually calmed down.

Five people were found to be wounded, three fatally one of which was an innocent bystander and five people were arrested with more arrests to come. Reporting live from Southside Richmond I'm Claire Munsford, now back to you Allison." "Claire were any officers hit or were any shots fired at the officers deliberately?" "No Allison none of the officers were hit, as for being fired on, Officer Bridgeforth said that as of right now they don't think no one took deliberate aim at any of the Officers."

"Thank you Claire, now on to our next story, this too a shooting but coming out the Northside, it happened yesterday evening between the hours of 7:30 and 8:30 p.m. Again several people were injured this time three of them fatally, our Gillian Agee is on the scene, Gillian." "Thank you Allison, I'm standing here on the corner of Barton Ave and Brookland Park Boulevard. Where yesterday around 7:30 in the evening gunshots rang out both in the parking lot of this Lucky's Convience store that you see behind me here and farther up the street here on Barton Ave.

According to police a dark colored car pulled into this parking lot here at Lucky's Convience store here on Brookland Park Blvd., and started shooting at several people who were standing either in the parking lot here or in front of the store. Two people in the parking lot were hit and another person was also injured as they tried to run up in the store apparently trying to get away from the shooters. After shooting up the parking lot, the car pulled off headed up Barton Ave., where it was apparently met with gunfire itself causing it to crash. It appears two of the passengers, one in the front and one in the back managed to get out the car where they were met with gunfire. The front passenger was shot right beside the front door, the back passenger managed to make it into the middle of the street where he too was gunned down and he was found with a gun in his hand.

The driver was still in the car, but he too was found fatally shot from where it look like somebody shot down into the car. As of this time police have no suspects and very few clues as to who shot the three guys in the car. However they say this is a known drug area, that's also known for its violence, keep in mind there was another shooting here two months ago. So just to recap, a dark colored car pulled into the parking lot of this Lucky's convience store here on Brookland Park Blvd., and started shooting, hitting three people. Then it pulls off and heads up Barton Ave here, where it was subsequently shot up itself and all three occupants inside were killed.

Richmond police have no suspects at this time, although this is a known drug area, reporting live from Northside, Richmond I'm Gillian Agee back to you Allison." "Gillian do police know the names of the occupants inside the car?" "At this time if they do they're not releasing them pending notification of family members, so that the bodies can be positively identified." "Thank you Gillian, now moving on, Amelia County police have identified the two bodies discovered there two weeks ago. The bodies of Raymond 'Juice' Baur and Josh 'Monopoly' Ogilsby, two half brothers and both of Richmond were discovered by passing motorists who notified police. Our Bruce Harper has the latest on this story."

"It was about two weeks ago, when passing motorists notified the Amelia County Sheriff's Dept., of a car sitting off to the side of the road in a field. When sheriff's deputies arrived they found the bodies of 22 year old Raymond 'Juice' Baur and 21 year old Josh 'Monopoly' Oglisby two half brothers, both of Richmond and both had been shot. According to sheriff's deputies, the car had been shot up pretty bad and it looks like they could have been shot by a passing vehicle, although with bullets on both sides of the car police are trying to figure out how that happened. Based on the evidence so far it looks like as though the car ended up in the field after being forced from the road. No word on whether either one of the yong men are still living or not, just that they have been positively identified.

Police are asking anyone with information to call the Amelia County Sheriff's Department, reporting from Amelia County this is Bruce Harper." "Thank you Bruce, it's been a violent year here in Richmond so far, but the past two months have been extremely violent. There have been 52 people shot and 22 people killed including those from yesterday and early this morning. Richmond police are baffled by the rise in violence, particularly gun violence, they fear that the homicide rate is only going to get worse before it gets better. There is an underlying fear that the homicide rate will escalate back up into the high numbers of the early 1990's.

Yesterday Richmond Police Chief Fred Morrison called a press conference where he announced the formation of the Four Corner Task Force. The task force will consist of four different task forces carrying out coordinated raids and searches at the sametime on the same days in all four corners of the city. That's North and Southsides, East and Westends. The task force will be focusing on known drug dealers, people on probation and parole, people that hang on the corners everyday and whatever other problems people in the neighborhoods report. When we return Darius Jordan will be here with the weather."

Chapter 30-Third Generation Club:

"I'm leaving Ms. Fox's house," Sherry Cumersome said into the phone "We on our way to a birthday party for one of my coworkers. Me and Ms. Fox, at her club Third Generation. I ain't think you woulda wanted to go, I had to talk her into going. She ain't want to go cause it's her birthday and the club had been rented so she couldn't rent it for her birthday. I tol'er I knew the girl having the party and she practically begged me to come, I ain't have nobody to go with so I asked Ms. Fox to go and we could celebrate her birthday together.

You know Fatty in the streets girl, he act like they his woman instead of me. Aright, I'll talk to you tomorrow," Sherry said as she hit the end button on her cell phone. "Yeah Fatty, Te-Mundre, Cheeks, Shaun, and even Sassy with her fast ass all of'em in the streets somewhere tonight, but this shit go change. I ain't raising no damn street runners and who was that asking you all them damn questions on the phone?" Ms. Fox wanted to know. "That was my cousin Shawnette, she wanted to know why I ain't ask her to go." "Well why didn't you?" "I'ont know, I guess I felt like she wouldn't fit in with this crowd, I mean by this being a casual dressing party and all, and you know she don't know how to dress casual.

Everything she wear make her look sluttish, plus she don't know how to drink, she be dun got drunk over here and showed her ass. S'cuse me Ms.Fox, but she woulda embarrassed me and I ain't want that. Especially since this is your club and I be coming over here with you all the time too, they been dun said I can't come back no more because of her, so bump that." "You right about that, sound like Suzy Williams, she get on my damn nerves sometimes, she can be embarrassing as hell, up in every man's face she sees once she gets drunk. She don't realize don't no man want no woman that can't hold her liquor, no self respecting man noway.

Damn it's a lot of cars out here tonight, this woman must be mighty popular," Ms. Fox said as they pulled into the parking lot. "I think she is, everybody at work love her to death," Sherry replied. They checked theirselves in the mirrors, got out and walked to the entrance. Upon entering Ms. Fox spoke to Curtis the club member working the door "What's up Curtis?" "Ain't nothing Fox, how you doing?" "I'm doing well on my birthday." "Happy Birthday." "Thanks I see why I couldn't rent the club tonight, whoever this woman is she seems like she's mighty popular." "Yeah she is, just not as popular as you Fox," Curtis said smiling. "Shut up boy," Ms. Fox said smiling as she led Sherry into the club.

"SURPRISE!" Everyone yelled. Ms. Fox stopped and looked around, then she turned to Sherry who was standing there smiling and said 'surprise' before giving Ms. Fox a hug. "Gurrl," was all Ms. Fox could say before everybody came over to her led by Fatty and the rest of her kids. "Happy birthday Ma, we surprised you for real huh," Fatty said hugging his mother and handing her a cup of Budweiser. "Happy birthday Ma," they all said one by one, with each one hugging her and kissing her on the cheek. Next up came her sisters Maxine, Carrie Jo, Jerleen, Mable, Alicia and Ann followed by her brothers; Lloyd, Edward, Benjamin, Mckinnly, James and Deshields.

Her nieces and nephews, some cousins from Tappahannock

which is where she was originally from. There was Tina Lucille, Fat Red and a host of her other friends from right here in Richmond, not to mention the club members. There were members from her kids father's family, as well as Bushead and his wife Halle who did Ms. Fox's hair, even her godson Cosmo and his wife. To say that she was happy was an understatement, everybody partied and had a good time. Ms. Fox was especially delighted to meet Sonya, Charmaine, and Crystal. Although Te-Mundre made it clear Crystal won't his girlfriend they were just friends, but Cheeks and Shaun introduced Charmaine and Sonya as their girlfriends.

Sassy even introduced Tajon to her, but she too made it clear they were just friends. The highlight of the night was when Ms. Fox led her family out on the dance floor, they got in a circle and one by one they all danced with her. At the end of the night they all sang 'Happy Birthday' to her while she had her arms locked thru Sherry's on one side and Sassy's on the other. When it got to the 'How old are you part' with her, Sassy and Sherry rocking side to side; Ms. Fox answered "I'm 21 years old." And everybody fell out laughing.

The phone call Sherry had received was from Fatty to make sure they were on their way, so he could have the parking lot clear of anybody Ms. Fox would recognize. After telling Fatty they were on their way, Sherry had continued the conversation by herself, to throw Ms. Fox off.

To Be Continued

www.ingramcontent.com/pod-product-compliance
Lightning Source LLC
Chambersburg PA
CBHW080821250626
47160CB00008B/2820